THE 12 BEST SHERLOCK HOLMES STORIES

ARTHUR CONAN DOYLE

SANAGE
PUBLISHING HOUSE

Paperback: 978-936205473-9
Hardback: 978-936205210-0
eBook: 978-936205331-2

Printed by: Manipal Technologies Limited, Manipal

Sanage Publishing House LLP
Mumbai, India

sanagepublishing@gmail.com

Sir Arthur Ignatius Conan Doyle (22 May 1859 – 7 July 1930) was a British writer and medical doctor. Doyle began writing while studying at the University of Edinburgh Medical School, which he joined in 1876. Doyle graduated in 1881 and was employed as a surgeon on the steamer Mayumba on its voyage to the West African coast. He created the character Sherlock Holmes in 1887 for A Study in Scarlet, the first of four novels and fifty-six short stories about Holmes and Dr. Watson.

The Sherlock Holmes stories are generally considered milestones in the field of crime fiction.

Sherlock Holmes, the most well-known fictional detective, has been listed with Guinness World Records as the "most portrayed movie character" in history.

CONTENTS

1. The Adventure Of The Speckled Band 5
2. The Red-Headed League 31
3. A Scandal In Bohemia 56
4. The Five Orange Pips 81
5. The Adventure Of The Dancing Men 101
6. The Adventure Of The Empty House 127
7. The Adventure Of The Priory School 149
8. The Final Problem 182
9. The Musgrave Ritual 201
10. The Reigate Squires 221
11. The Adventure Of The Second Stain 242
12. The Adventure Of The Devil's Foot 269

THE ADVENTURE OF THE SPECKLED BAND

On glancing over my notes of the seventy odd cases in which I have during the last eight years studied the methods of my friend Sherlock Holmes, I find many tragic, some comic, a large number merely strange, but none-commonplace; for, working as he did rather for the love of his art than for the acquirement of wealth, he refused to associate himself with any investigation which did not tend towards the unusual, and even the fantastic. Of all these varied cases, however, I cannot recall any which presented more singular features than that which was associated with the well-known Surrey family of the Roylotts of Stoke Moran. The events in question occurred in the early days of my association with Holmes, when we were sharing rooms as bachelors in Baker Street. It is possible that I might have placed them upon record before, but a promise of secrecy was made at the time, from which I have only been freed during the last month by the untimely death of the lady to whom the pledge was given. It is perhaps as well that the facts should now come to light, for I have reasons to know that there are widespread rumours as to the death of Dr. Grimesby Roylott which tend to make the matter even more terrible than the truth.

It was early in April in the year '83 that I woke one morning to find Sherlock Holmes standing, fully dressed, by the side of my bed. He was a late riser, as a rule, and as the clock on the mantelpiece showed me that it was only a quarter-past seven, I blinked up at him in some surprise, and perhaps just a little resentment, for I was myself regular in my habits.

"Very sorry to knock you up, Watson," said he, "but it's the common lot this morning. Mrs. Hudson has been knocked up, she retorted upon me, and I on you."

"What is it, then—a fire?"

"No; a client. It seems that a young lady has arrived in a considerable state of excitement, who insists upon seeing me. She is waiting now in the sitting-room. Now, when young ladies wander about the metropolis at this hour of the morning, and knock sleepy people up out of their beds, I presume that it is something very pressing which they have to communicate. Should it prove to be an interesting case, you would, I am sure, wish to follow it from the outset. I thought, at any rate, that I should call you and give you the chance."

"My dear fellow, I would not miss it for anything."

I had no keener pleasure than in following Holmes in his professional investigations, and in admiring the rapid deductions, as swift as intuitions, and yet always founded on a logical basis with which he unravelled the problems which were submitted to him. I rapidly threw on my clothes and was ready in a few minutes to accompany my friend down to the sitting-room. A lady dressed in black and heavily veiled, who had been sitting in the window, rose as we entered.

"Good-morning, madam," said Holmes cheerily. "My name is Sherlock Holmes. This is my intimate friend and associate, Dr. Watson, before whom you can speak as freely as before myself. Ha! I am glad to see that Mrs. Hudson has had the good sense to light the fire. Pray draw up to it, and I shall order you a cup of hot coffee, for I observe that you are shivering."

"It is not cold which makes me shiver," said the woman in a low voice, changing her seat as requested.

"What, then?"

"It is fear, Mr. Holmes. It is terror." She raised her veil as she spoke, and we could see that she was indeed in a pitiable state of agitation, her face all drawn and grey, with restless frightened eyes, like those of some hunted animal. Her features and figure were those of a woman of thirty, but her hair was shot with premature grey, and her expression was weary and haggard. Sherlock Holmes ran her over with one of his quick, all-comprehensive glances.

"You must not fear," said he soothingly, bending forward and patting her forearm. "We shall soon set matters right; I have no doubt. You have come in by train this morning, I see."

"You know me, then?"

"No, but I observe the second half of a return ticket in the palm of your left glove. You must have started early, and yet you had a good drive in a dog-cart, along heavy roads, before you reached the station."

The lady gave a violent start and stared in bewilderment at my companion.

"There is no mystery, my dear madam," said he, smiling. "The left arm of your jacket is spattered with mud in no less than seven places. The marks are perfectly fresh. There is no vehicle save a dog-cart which throws up mud in that way, and then only when you sit on the left-hand side of the driver."

"Whatever your reasons may be, you are perfectly correct," said she. "I started from home before six, reached Leatherhead at twenty past, and came in by the first train to Waterloo. Sir, I can stand this strain no longer; I shall go mad if it continues. I have no one to turn to—none, save only one, who cares for me, and he, poor fellow, can be of little aid. I have heard of you, Mr. Holmes; I have heard of you from Mrs. Farintosh, whom you helped in the hour of her sore need. It was from her that I had your address. Oh, sir, do you not think that you could help me, too, and at least throw a little light through the dense darkness which surrounds me? At present it is out of my power to reward you for your services, but in a month or six weeks I shall be married, with the control of my own income, and then at least you shall not find me ungrateful."

Holmes turned to his desk and, unlocking it, drew out a small case-book, which he consulted.

"Farintosh," said he. "Ah yes, I recall the case; it was concerned with an opal tiara. I think it was before your time, Watson. I can only say, madam, that I shall be happy to devote the same care to your case as I did to that of your friend. As to reward, my profession is its own reward; but you are at liberty to defray whatever expenses I may be put to, at the time which suits you best. And now I beg that you will lay before us everything that may help us in forming an opinion upon the matter."

"Alas!" replied our visitor, "the very horror of my situation lies in the fact that my fears are so vague, and my suspicions depend so entirely upon small points, which might seem trivial to another, that even he to whom of all others I have a right to look for help and advice looks upon all that I tell him about it as the fancies of a nervous woman. He does not say so, but I can read it from his soothing answers and averted eyes. But I have heard, Mr. Holmes, that you can see deeply into the manifold wickedness of the human heart. You may advise me how to walk amid the dangers which encompass me."

"I am all attention, madam."

"My name is Helen Stoner, and I am living with my stepfather, who is the last survivor of one of the oldest Saxon families in England, the Roylotts of Stoke Moran, on the western border of Surrey."

Holmes nodded his head. "The name is familiar to me," said he.

"The family was at one time among the richest in England, and the estates extended over the borders into Berkshire in the north, and Hampshire in the west. In the last century, however, four successive heirs were of a dissolute and wasteful disposition, and the family ruin was eventually completed by a gambler in the days of the Regency. Nothing was left save a few acres of ground, and the two-hundred-year-old house, which is itself crushed under a heavy mortgage. The last squire dragged out his existence there, living the horrible life of an aristocratic pauper; but his only son, my stepfather, seeing that he must adapt himself to the new conditions, obtained an advance from a relative, which enabled him to take a medical degree and went out to Calcutta, where, by his professional skill and his force of character, he established a large practice. In a fit of anger, however, caused by some robberies which had been perpetrated in the house, he beat his native butler to death and narrowly escaped a capital sentence. As it was, he suffered a long term of imprisonment and afterwards returned to England a morose and disappointed man.

"When Dr. Roylott was in India he married my mother, Mrs. Stoner, the young widow of Major-General Stoner, of the Bengal Artillery. My sister Julia and I were twins, and we were only two years old at the time of my mother's re-marriage. She had a considerable sum of money—not less than £ 1000 a year—and this she bequeathed to Dr. Roylott entirely while we resided with him, with a provision that a certain annual sum should be allowed to each of us in the event of our marriage. Shortly after our return to England my mother died—she was killed eight years ago in a railway accident near Crewe. Dr. Roylott then abandoned his attempts to establish himself in practice in London and took us to live with him in the old ancestral house at Stoke Moran. The money which my mother had left was enough for all our wants, and there seemed to be no obstacle to our happiness.

"But a terrible change came over our stepfather about this time. Instead of making friends and exchanging visits with our neighbours, who had at first been overjoyed to see a Roylott of Stoke Moran back in the old family seat, he shut himself up in his house and seldom came out save to indulge in ferocious quarrels with whoever might cross his path. Violence of temper approaching to mania has been hereditary in the men of the family, and in my stepfather's case it had, I believe, been intensified by his long residence in the tropics. A series of disgraceful brawls took place, two of which ended in the police-court, until at last he became the terror of the village, and the folks would fly at his approach, for he is a man of immense strength, and absolutely uncontrollable in his anger.

"Last week he hurled the local blacksmith over a parapet into a stream, and it was only by paying over all the money which I could gather together that I was able to avert another public exposure. He had no friends at all save the wandering gipsies and he would give these vagabonds leave to encamp upon the few acres of bramble-covered land which represent the family estate and would accept in return the hospitality of their tents, wandering away with them sometimes for weeks on end. He has a passion also for Indian animals, which are sent over to him by a correspondent, and he has at this moment a cheetah and a baboon, which wander freely over his grounds and are feared by the villagers almost as much as their master.

"You can imagine from what I say that my poor sister Julia and I had no great pleasure in our lives. No servant would stay with us, and for a long time we did all the work of the house. She was but thirty at the time of her death, and yet her hair had already begun to whiten, even as mine has."

"Your sister is dead, then?"

"She died just two years ago, and it is of her death that I wish to speak to you. You can understand that, living the life which I have described, we were little likely to see anyone of our own age and position. We had, however, an aunt, my mother's maiden sister, Miss Honoria Westphail, who lives near Harrow, and we were occasionally allowed to pay short visits at this lady's house. Julia went there at Christmas two years ago, and met there a half-pay major of marines, to whom she became engaged. My stepfather learned of the engagement when my sister returned and offered no objection to the marriage; but within a fortnight of the day which had been fixed for the wedding, the terrible event occurred which has deprived me of my only companion."

Sherlock Holmes had been leaning back in his chair with his eyes closed and his head sunk in a cushion, but he half opened his lids now and glanced across at his visitor.

"Pray be precise as to details," said he.

"It is easy for me to be so, for every event of that dreadful time is seared into my memory. The manor-house is, as I have already said, very old, and only one wing is now inhabited. The bedrooms in this wing are on the ground floor, the sitting-rooms being in the central block of the buildings. Of these bedrooms the first is Dr. Roylott's, the second my sister's, and the third my own. There is no communication between them, but they all open out into the same corridor. Do I make myself plain?"

"Perfectly so."

"The windows of the three rooms open out upon the lawn. That fatal night Dr. Roylott had gone to his room early, though we knew that he had not retired to rest, for my sister was troubled by the smell of the strong Indian cigars which it was his custom to smoke. She left her room, therefore, and came into mine, where she sat for some time, chatting about her approaching wedding. At eleven o'clock she rose to leave me, but she paused at the door and looked back.

"'Tell me, Helen,' said she, 'have you ever heard anyone whistle in the dead of the night?'

"'Never,' said I.

"'I suppose that you could not possibly whistle, yourself, in your sleep?'

"'Certainly not. But why?'

"'Because during the last few nights I have always, about three in the morning, heard a low, clear whistle. I am a light sleeper, and it has awakened me. I cannot tell where it came from—perhaps from the next room, perhaps from the lawn. I thought that I would just ask you whether you had heard it.'

"'No, I have not. It must be those wretched gipsies in the plantation.'

"'Very likely. And yet if it were on the lawn, I wonder that you did not hear it also.'

"'Ah, but I sleep more heavily than you.'

"'Well, it is of no great consequence, at any rate.' She smiled back at me, closed my door, and a few moments later I heard her key turn in the lock."

"Indeed," said Holmes. "Was it your custom always to lock yourselves in at night?"

"Always."

"And why?"

"I think that I mentioned to you that the Doctor kept a cheetah and a baboon. We had no feeling of security unless our doors were locked."

"Quite so. Pray proceed with your statement."

"I could not sleep that night. A vague feeling of impending misfortune impressed me. My sister and I, you will recollect, were twins, and you know how subtle are the links which bind two souls which are so closely allied. It was a wild night. The wind was howling outside, and the rain was beating and splashing against the windows. Suddenly, amid all the hubbub of the gale, there burst forth the wild scream of a terrified woman. I knew that it was my sister's voice. I sprang from my bed, wrapped a shawl round me, and rushed into the corridor. As I opened my door I seemed to hear a low whistle, such as my sister described, and a few moments later a clanging sound, as if a mass of metal had fallen. As I ran down the passage, my sister's door was unlocked and revolved slowly upon its hinges. I stared at it horror-stricken, not knowing what was about to issue from it. By the light of the corridor-lamp I saw my sister appear at the opening, her face blanched with terror, her hands groping for help, her whole figure swaying to and fro like that of a drunkard. I ran to her and threw my arms round her, but at that moment her knees seemed to give way, and she fell to the ground. She writhed as one who is in terrible pain, and her limbs were dreadfully convulsed. At first I thought that she had not recognised me, but as I bent over her she suddenly shrieked out in a voice which I shall never forget, 'Oh, my God! Helen! It was the band! The speckled band!' There was something else which she would fain have said, and she stabbed with her finger into the air in the direction of the Doctor's room, but a fresh convulsion seized her and choked her words. I rushed out, calling loudly for my stepfather, and I met him hastening from his room in his dressing-gown. When he reached my sister's side she was unconscious, and though he poured brandy down her throat and sent for medical aid from the village, all efforts were in vain, for she slowly sank and died without having recovered her consciousness. Such was the dreadful end of my beloved sister."

"One moment," said Holmes, "are you sure about this whistle and metallic sound? Could you swear to it?"

"That was what the county coroner asked me at the inquiry. It is my strong impression that I heard it, and yet, among the crash of the gale and the creaking of an old house, I may possibly have been deceived."

"Was your sister dressed?"

"No, she was in her night-dress. In her right hand was found the charred stump of a match, and in her left a match-box."

"Showing that she had struck a light and looked about her when the alarm took place. That is important. And what conclusions did the coroner come to?"

"He investigated the case with great care, for Dr. Roylott's conduct had long been notorious in the county, but he was unable to find any satisfactory cause of death. My evidence showed that the door had been fastened upon the inner side, and the windows were blocked by old-fashioned shutters with broad iron bars, which were secured every night. The walls were carefully sounded, and were shown to be quite solid all round, and the flooring was also thoroughly examined, with the same result. The chimney is wide but is barred up by four large staples. It is certain, therefore, that my sister was quite alone when she met her end. Besides, there were no marks of any violence upon her."

"How about poison?"

"The doctors examined her for it, but without success."

"What do you think that this unfortunate lady died of, then?"

"It is my belief that she died of pure fear and nervous shock, though what it was that frightened her I cannot imagine."

"Were there gipsies in the plantation at the time?"

"Yes, there are nearly always some there."

"Ah, and what did you gather from this allusion to a band—a speckled band?"

"Sometimes I have thought that it was merely the wild talk of delirium, sometimes that it may have referred to some band of people, perhaps to these very gipsies in the plantation. I do not know whether the spotted handkerchiefs which so many of them wear over their heads might have suggested the strange adjective which she used."

Holmes shook his head like a man who is far from being satisfied.

"These are very deep waters," said he; "pray go on with your narrative."

"Two years have passed since then, and my life has been until lately lonelier than ever. A month ago, however, a dear friend, whom I have known for many years, has done me the honour to ask my hand in marriage. His name is Armitage—Percy Armitage—the second son of Mr. Armitage, of Crane Water, near Reading. My stepfather has offered no opposition to the match, and we are to be married in the course of the spring. Two days ago, some repairs were started in the west wing of the building, and my bedroom wall has been pierced, so that I have had to move into the chamber in which my sister died, and to sleep in the very bed in which she slept. Imagine, then, my thrill of terror when last night, as I lay awake, thinking over her terrible fate, I suddenly heard in the silence of the night the low whistle which had been the herald of her own death. I sprang up and lit the lamp, but nothing was to be seen in the room. I was too shaken to go to bed again, however, so I dressed, and as soon as it was daylight I slipped down, got a dog-cart at the Crown Inn, which is opposite, and drove to Leatherhead, from whence I have come on this morning with the one object of seeing you and asking your advice."

"You have done wisely," said my friend. "But have you told me all?"

"Yes, all."

"Miss Roylott, you have not. You are screening your stepfather."

"Why, what do you mean?"

For answer Holmes pushed back the frill of black lace which fringed the hand that lay upon our visitor's knee. Five little livid spots, the marks of four fingers and a thumb, were printed upon the white wrist.

"You have been cruelly used," said Holmes.

The lady coloured deeply and covered over her injured wrist. "He is a hard man," she said, "and perhaps he hardly knows his own strength."

There was a long silence, during which Holmes leaned his chin upon his hands and stared into the crackling fire.

"This is a very deep business," he said at last. "There are a thousand details which I should desire to know before I decide upon our course of action. Yet we have not a moment to lose. If we were to come to Stoke Moran Today, would it be possible for us to see over these rooms without the knowledge of your stepfather?"

"As it happens, he spoke of coming into town Today upon some most important business. It is probable that he will be away all day, and that there would be nothing to disturb you. We have a housekeeper now, but she is old and foolish, and I could easily get her out of the way."

"Excellent. You are not averse to this trip, Watson?"

"By no means."

"Then we shall both come. What are you going to do yourself?"

"I have one or two things which I would wish to do now that I am in town. But I shall return by the twelve o'clock train, so as to be there in time for your coming."

"And you may expect us early in the afternoon. I have myself some small business matters to attend to. Will you not wait and breakfast?"

"No, I must go. My heart is lightened already since I have confided my trouble to you. I shall look forward to seeing you again this afternoon." She dropped her thick black veil over her face and glided from the room.

"And what do you think of it all, Watson?" asked Sherlock Holmes, leaning back in his chair.

"It seems to me to be a most dark and sinister business."

"Dark enough and sinister enough."

"Yet if the lady is correct in saying that the flooring and walls are sound, and that the door, window, and chimney are impassable, then her sister must have been undoubtedly alone when she met her mysterious end."

"What becomes, then, of these nocturnal whistles, and what of the very peculiar words of the dying woman?"

"I cannot think."

"When you combine the ideas of whistles at night, the presence of a band of gipsies who are on intimate terms with this old doctor, the fact that we have every reason to believe that the doctor has an interest in preventing his stepdaughter's marriage, the dying allusion to a band, and, finally, the fact that Miss Helen Stoner heard a metallic clang, which might have been caused by one of those metal bars that secured the shutters falling back into its place, I think that there is good ground to think that the mystery may be cleared along those lines."

"But what, then, did the gipsies do?"

"I cannot imagine."

"I see many objections to any such theory."

"And so, do I. It is precisely for that reason that we are going to Stoke Moran this day. I want to see whether the objections are fatal, or if they may be explained away. But what in the name of the devil!"

The ejaculation had been drawn from my companion by the fact that our door had been suddenly dashed open, and that a huge man had framed himself in the aperture. His costume was a peculiar mixture of the professional and of the agricultural, having a black top-hat, a long frock-coat, and a pair of high gaiters, with a hunting-crop swinging in his hand. So tall was he that his hat actually brushed the cross bar of the doorway, and his breadth seemed to span it across from side to side. A large face, seared with a thousand wrinkles, burned yellow with the sun, and marked with every evil passion, was turned from one to the other of us, while his deep-set, bile-shot eyes, and his high, thin, fleshless nose, gave him somewhat the resemblance to a fierce old bird of prey.

"Which of you is Holmes?" asked this apparition.

"My name, sir; but you have the advantage of me," said my companion quietly.

"I am Dr. Grimesby Roylott, of Stoke Moran."

"Indeed, Doctor," said Holmes blandly. "Pray take a seat."

"I will do nothing of the kind. My stepdaughter has been here. I have traced her. What has she been saying to you?"

"It is a little cold for the time of the year," said Holmes.

"What has she been saying to you?" screamed the old man furiously.

"But I have heard that the crocuses promise well," continued my companion imperturbably.

"Ha! You put me off, do you?" said our new visitor, taking a step forward and shaking his hunting-crop. "I know you, you scoundrel! I have heard of you before. You are Holmes, the meddler."

My friend smiled.

"Holmes, the busybody!"

His smile broadened.

"Holmes, the Scotland Yard Jack-in-office!"

Holmes chuckled heartily. "Your conversation is most entertaining," said he. "When you go out close the door, for there is a decided draught."

"I will go when I have had my say. Don't you dare to meddle with my affairs. I know that Miss Stoner has been here. I traced her! I am a dangerous man to fall foul of! See here." He stepped swiftly forward, seized the poker, and bent it into a curve with his huge brown hands.

"See that you keep yourself out of my grip," he snarled, and hurling the twisted poker into the fireplace he strode out of the room.

"He seems a very amiable person," said Holmes, laughing. "I am not quite so bulky, but if he had remained I might have shown him that my grip was not much more feeble than his own." As he spoke he picked up the steel poker and, with a sudden effort, straightened it out again.

"Fancy his having the insolence to confound me with the official detective force! This incident gives zest to our investigation, however, and I only trust that our little friend will not suffer from her imprudence in allowing this brute to trace her. And now, Watson, we shall order breakfast, and afterwards I shall walk down to Doctors' Commons, where I hope to get some data which may help us in this matter."

It was nearly one o'clock when Sherlock Holmes returned from his excursion. He held in his hand a sheet of blue paper, scrawled over with notes and figures.

"I have seen the will of the deceased wife," said he. "To determine its exact meaning I have been obliged to work out the present prices of the investments with which it is concerned. The total income, which at the time of the wife's death was little short of £1,100, is now, through the fall in agricultural prices, not more than £750. Each daughter can claim an income of £250, in case of marriage. It is evident, therefore, that if both girls had married, this beauty would have had a mere pittance, while even one of them would cripple him to a very serious extent. My morning's work has not been wasted, since it has proved that he has the very strongest motives for standing in the way of anything of the sort. And now, Watson, this is too serious for dawdling, especially as the old man is aware that we are interesting ourselves in his affairs; so if you are ready, we shall call a cab and drive to Waterloo. I should be very much obliged if you would slip your revolver into your pocket. An Eley's No. 2 is an excellent argument with gentlemen who can twist steel pokers into knots. That and a tooth-brush are, I think, all that we need."

At Waterloo we were fortunate in catching a train for Leatherhead, where we hired a trap at the station inn and drove for four or five miles through the lovely Surrey lanes. It was a perfect day, with a bright sun and a few fleecy clouds in the heavens. The trees and wayside hedges were just throwing out their first green shoots, and the air was full of the pleasant smell of the moist earth. To me at least there was a strange contrast between the sweet promise of the spring and this sinister quest upon which we were engaged. My companion sat in the front of the trap, his arms folded, his hat pulled down over his eyes, and his chin sunk upon his breast, buried in the deepest thought. Suddenly, however, he started, tapped me on the shoulder, and pointed over the meadows.

"Look there!" said he.

A heavily timbered park stretched up in a gentle slope, thickening into a grove at the highest point. From amid the branches there jutted out the grey gables and high roof-tree of a very old mansion.

"Stoke Moran?" said he.

"Yes, sir, that be the house of Dr. Grimesby Roylott," remarked the driver.

"There is some building going on there," said Holmes; "that is where we are going."

"There's the village," said the driver, pointing to a cluster of roofs some distance to the left; "but if you want to get to the house, you'll find it shorter to get over this stile, and so by the footpath over the fields. There it is, where the lady is walking."

"And the lady, I fancy, is Miss Stoner," observed Holmes, shading his eyes. "Yes, I think we had better do as you suggest."

We got off, paid our fare, and the trap rattled back on its way to Leatherhead.

"I thought it as well," said Holmes as we climbed the stile, "that this fellow should think we had come here as architects, or on some definite business. It may stop his gossip. Good-afternoon, Miss Stoner. You see that we have been as good as our word."

Our client of the morning had hurried forward to meet us with a face which spoke her joy. "I have been waiting so eagerly for you," she cried, shaking hands with us warmly. "All has turned out splendidly. Dr. Roylott has gone to town, and it is unlikely that he will be back before evening."

"We have had the pleasure of making the Doctor's acquaintance," said Holmes, and in a few words he sketched out what had occurred. Miss Stoner turned white to the lips as she listened.

"Good heavens!" she cried, "he has followed me, then."

"So, it appears."

"He is so cunning that I never know when I am safe from him. What will he say when he returns?"

"He must guard himself, for he may find that there is someone more cunning than himself upon his track. You must lock yourself up from him tonight. If he is violent, we shall take you away to your aunts at Harrow. Now, we must make the best use of our time, so kindly take us at once to the rooms which we are to examine."

The building was of grey, lichen-blotched stone, with a high central portion and two curving wings, like the claws of a crab, thrown out on each side. In one of these wings the windows were broken and blocked with wooden boards, while the roof was partly caved in, a picture of ruin. The central portion was in little better repair, but the right-hand block was comparatively modern, and the blinds in the windows, with the blue smoke curling up from the chimneys, showed that this was where the family resided. Some scaffolding had been erected against the end wall, and the stone-work had been broken into, but there were no signs of any workmen at the moment of our visit. Holmes walked slowly up and down the ill-trimmed lawn and examined with deep attention the outsides of the windows.

"This, I take it, belongs to the room in which you used to sleep, the Centre one to your sister's, and the one next to the main building to Dr. Roylott's chamber?"

"Exactly so. But I am now sleeping in the middle one."

"Pending the alterations, as I understand. By the way, there does not seem to be any very pressing need for repairs at that end wall."

"There were none. I believe that it was an excuse to move me from my room."

"Ah! that is suggestive. Now, on the other side of this narrow wing runs the corridor from which these three rooms open. There are windows in it, of course?"

"Yes, but very small ones. Too narrow for anyone to pass through."

"As you both locked your doors at night, your rooms were unapproachable from that side. Now, would you have the kindness to go into your room and bar your shutters?"

Miss Stoner did so, and Holmes, after a careful examination through the open window, endeavoured in every way to force the shutter open, but without success. There was no slit through which a knife could be passed to raise the bar. Then with his lens he tested the hinges, but they were of solid iron, built firmly into the massive masonry. "Hum!" said he, scratching his chin in some perplexity, "my theory certainly presents some difficulties. No one could pass these shutters if they were bolted. Well, we shall see if the inside throws any light upon the matter."

A small side door led into the whitewashed corridor from which the three bedrooms opened. Holmes refused to examine the third chamber, so we passed at once to the second, that in which Miss Stoner was now sleeping, and in which her sister had met with her fate. It was a homely little room, with a low ceiling and a gaping fireplace, after the fashion of old country-houses. A brown chest of drawers stood in one corner, a narrow white-counterpaned bed in another, and a dressing-table on the left-hand side of the window. These articles, with two small wicker-work chairs, made up all the furniture in the room save for a square of Wilton carpet in the Centre. The boards round and the panelling of the walls were of brown, worm-eaten oak, so old and discoloured that it may have dated from the original building of the house. Holmes drew one of the chairs into a corner and sat silent, while his eyes travelled round and round and up and down, taking in every detail of the apartment.

"Where does that bell communicate with?" he asked at last pointing to a thick bell-rope which hung down beside the bed, the tassel actually lying upon the pillow.

"It goes to the housekeeper's room."

"It looks newer than the other things?"

"Yes, it was only put there a couple of years ago."

"Your sister asked for it, I suppose?"

"No, I never heard of her using it. We used always to get what we wanted for ourselves."

"Indeed, it seemed unnecessary to put so nice a bell-pull there. You will excuse me for a few minutes while I satisfy myself as to this floor." He threw himself down upon his face with his lens in his hand and crawled swiftly backward and forward, examining minutely the cracks between the boards. Then he did the same with the wood-work with which the chamber was panelled. Finally, he walked over to the bed and spent some time in staring at it and in running his eye up and down the wall. Finally, he took the bell-rope in his hand and gave it a brisk tug.

"Why, it's a dummy," said he.

"Won't it ring?"

"No, it is not even attached to a wire. This is very interesting. You can see now that it is fastened to a hook just above where the little opening for the ventilator is."

"How very absurd! I never noticed that before."

"Very strange!" muttered Holmes, pulling at the rope. "There are one or two very singular points about this room. For example, what a fool a builder must be to open a ventilator into another room, when, with the same trouble, he might have communicated with the outside air!"

"That is also quite modern," said the lady.

"Done about the same time as the bell-rope?" remarked Holmes.

"Yes, there were several little changes carried out about that time."

"They seem to have been of a most interesting character—dummy bell-ropes, and ventilators which do not ventilate. With your permission, Miss Stoner, we shall now carry our researches into the inner apartment."

Dr. Grimesby Roylott's chamber was larger than that of his step-daughter but was as plainly furnished. A camp-bed, a small wooden shelf full of books, mostly of a technical character, an armchair beside the bed, a plain wooden chair against the wall, a round table, and a large iron safe were the principal things which met the eye. Holmes walked slowly round and examined each and all of them with the keenest interest.

"What's in here?" he asked, tapping the safe.

"My stepfather's business papers."

"Oh! you have seen inside, then?"

"Only once, some years ago. I remember that it was full of papers."

"There isn't a cat in it, for example?"

"No. What a strange idea!"

"Well, look at this!" He took up a small saucer of milk which stood on the top of it.

"No; we don't keep a cat. But there is a cheetah and a baboon."

"Ah, yes, of course! Well, a cheetah is just a big cat, and yet a saucer of milk does not go very far in satisfying its wants, I daresay. There is one point which I should wish to determine." He squatted down in front of the wooden chair and examined the seat of it with the greatest attention.

"Thank you. That is quite settled," said he, rising and putting his lens in his pocket. "Hullo! Here is something interesting!"

The object which had caught his eye was a small dog lash hung on one corner of the bed. The lash, however, was curled upon itself and tied so as to make a loop of whipcord.

"What do you make of that, Watson?"

"It's a common enough lash. But I don't know why it should be tied."

"That is not quite so common, is it? Ah, me! it's a wicked world, and when a clever man turns his brains to crime it is the worst of all. I think that I have seen enough now, Miss Stoner, and with your permission we shall walk out upon the lawn."

I had never seen my friend's face so grim or his brow so dark as it was when we turned from the scene of this investigation. We had walked several times up and down the lawn, neither Miss Stoner nor myself liking to break in upon his thoughts before he roused himself from his reverie.

"It is very essential, Miss Stoner," said he, "that you should absolutely follow my advice in every respect."

"I shall most certainly do so."

"The matter is too serious for any hesitation. Your life may depend upon your compliance."

"I assure you that I am in your hands."

"In the first place, both my friend and I must spend the night in your room."

Both Miss Stoner and I gazed at him in astonishment.

"Yes, it must be so. Let me explain. I believe that that is the village inn over there?"

"Yes, that is the Crown."

"Very good. Your windows would be visible from there?"

"Certainly."

"You must confine yourself to your room, on pretence of a headache, when your stepfather comes back. Then when you hear him retire for the night, you must open the shutters of your window, undo the hasp, put your lamp there as a signal to us, and then withdraw quietly with everything which you are likely to want into the room which you used to occupy. I have no doubt that, in spite of the repairs, you could manage there for one night."

"Oh, yes, easily."

"The rest you will leave in our hands."

"But what will you do?"

"We shall spend the night in your room, and we shall investigate the cause of this noise which has disturbed you."

"I believe, Mr. Holmes, that you have already made up your mind," said Miss Stoner, laying her hand upon my companion's sleeve.

"Perhaps I have."

"Then, for pity's sake, tell me what was the cause of my sister's death."

"I should prefer to have clearer proofs before I speak."

"You can at least tell me whether my own thought is correct, and if she died from some sudden fright."

"No, I do not think so. I think that there was probably some more tangible cause. And now, Miss Stoner, we must leave you for if Dr. Roylott returned and saw us our journey would be in vain. Good-bye, and be brave, for if you will do what I have told you, you may rest assured that we shall soon drive away the dangers that threaten you."

Sherlock Holmes and I had no difficulty in engaging a bedroom and sitting-room at the Crown Inn. They were on the upper floor, and from our window we could command a view of the avenue gate, and of the inhabited wing of Stoke Moran Manor House. At dusk we saw Dr. Grimesby Roylott drive past, his huge form looming up beside the little figure of the lad who drove him. The boy had some slight difficulty in undoing the heavy iron gates, and we heard the hoarse roar of the Doctor's voice and saw the fury with which he shook his clinched fists at him. The trap drove on, and a few minutes later we saw a sudden light spring up among the trees as the lamp was lit in one of the sitting-rooms.

"Do you know, Watson," said Holmes as we sat together in the gathering darkness, "I have really some scruples as to taking you tonight. There is a distinct element of danger."

"Can I be of assistance?"

"Your presence might be invaluable."

"Then I shall certainly come."

"It is very kind of you."

"You speak of danger. You have evidently seen more in these rooms than was visible to me."

"No, but I fancy that I may have deduced a little more. I imagine that you saw all that I did."

"I saw nothing remarkable save the bell-rope, and what purpose that could answer I confess is more than I can imagine."

"You saw the ventilator, too?"

"Yes, but I do not think that it is such a very unusual thing to have a small opening between two rooms. It was so small that a rat could hardly pass through."

"I knew that we should find a ventilator before ever we came to Stoke Moran."

"My dear Holmes!"

"Oh, yes, I did. You remember in her statement she said that her sister could smell Dr. Roylott's cigar. Now, of course that suggested at once that there must be a communication between the two rooms. It could only be a small one, or it would have been remarked upon at the coroner's inquiry. I deduced a ventilator."

"But what harm can there be in that?"

"Well, there is at least a curious coincidence of dates. A ventilator is made, a cord is hung, and a lady who sleeps in the bed dies. Does not that strike you?"

"I cannot as yet see any connection."

"Did you observe anything very peculiar about that bed?"

"No."

"It was clamped to the floor. Did you ever see a bed fastened like that before?"

"I cannot say that I have."

"The lady could not move her bed. It must always be in the same relative position to the ventilator and to the rope—or so we may call it, since it was clearly never meant for a bell-pull."

"Holmes," I cried, "I seem to see dimly what you are hinting at. We are only just in time to prevent some subtle and horrible crime."

"Subtle enough and horrible enough. When a doctor does go wrong he is the first of criminals. He has nerve and he has knowledge. Palmer and Pritchard were among the heads of their profession. This man strikes even deeper, but I think, Watson, that we shall be able to strike deeper still. But we shall have horrors enough before the night is over; for goodness' sake let us have a quiet pipe and turn our minds for a few hours to something more cheerful."

About nine o'clock the light among the trees was extinguished, and all was dark in the direction of the Manor House. Two hours passed slowly away, and then, suddenly, just at the stroke of eleven, a single bright light shone out right in front of us.

"That is our signal," said Holmes, springing to his feet; "it comes from the middle window."

As we passed out he exchanged a few words with the landlord, explaining that we were going on a late visit to an acquaintance, and that it was possible that we might spend the night there. A moment later we were out on the dark road, a chill wind blowing in our faces, and one yellow light twinkling in front of us through the gloom to guide us on our sombre errand.

There was little difficulty in entering the grounds, for unrepaired breaches gaped in the old park wall. Making our way among the trees, we reached the lawn, crossed it, and were about to enter through the window when out from a clump of laurel bushes there darted what seemed to be a hideous and distorted child, who threw itself upon the grass with writhing limbs and then ran swiftly across the lawn into the darkness.

"My God!" I whispered; "did you see it?"

Holmes was for the moment as startled as I. His hand closed like a vice upon my wrist in his agitation. Then he broke into a low laugh and put his lips to my ear.

"It is a nice household," he murmured. "That is the baboon."

I had forgotten the strange pets which the Doctor affected. There was a cheetah, too; perhaps we might find it upon our shoulders at any moment. I confess that I felt easier in my mind when, after following Holmes' example and slipping off my shoes, I found myself inside the bedroom. My companion noiselessly closed the shutters, moved the lamp onto the table, and cast his eyes round the room. All was as we had seen it in the daytime. Then creeping up to me and making a trumpet of his hand, he whispered into my ear again so gently that it was all that I could do to distinguish the words:

"The least sound would be fatal to our plans."

I nodded to show that I had heard.

"We must sit without light. He would see it through the ventilator."

I nodded again.

"Do not go asleep; your very life may depend upon it. Have your pistol ready in case we should need it. I will sit on the side of the bed, and you in that chair."

I took out my revolver and laid it on the corner of the table.

Holmes had brought up a long thin cane, and this he placed upon the bed beside him. By it he laid the box of matches and the stump of a candle. Then he turned down the lamp, and we were left in darkness.

How shall I ever forget that dreadful vigil? I could not hear a sound, not even the drawing of a breath, and yet I knew that my companion sat open-eyed, within a few feet of me, in the same state of nervous tension in which I was myself. The shutters cut off the least ray of light, and we waited in absolute darkness.

From outside came the occasional cry of a night-bird, and once at our very window a long drawn catlike whine, which told us that the cheetah was indeed at liberty. Far away we could hear the deep tones of the parish clock, which boomed out every quarter of an hour. How long they seemed, those quarters! Twelve struck, and one and two and three, and still we sat waiting silently for whatever might befall.

Suddenly there was the momentary gleam of a light up in the direction of the ventilator, which vanished immediately, but was succeeded by a strong smell of burning oil and heated metal. Someone in the next room had lit a dark-lantern. I heard a gentle sound of movement, and then all was silent once more, though the smell grew stronger. For half an hour I sat with straining ears. Then suddenly another sound became audible—a very gentle, soothing sound, like that of a small jet of steam escaping continually from a kettle. The instant that we heard it, Holmes sprang from the bed, struck a match, and lashed furiously with his cane at the bell-pull.

"You see it, Watson?" he yelled. "You see it?"

But I saw nothing. At the moment when Holmes struck the light I heard a low, clear whistle, but the sudden glare flashing into my weary eyes made it impossible for me to tell what it was at which my friend lashed so savagely. I could, however, see that his face was deadly pale and filled with horror and loathing. He had ceased to strike and was gazing up at the ventilator when suddenly there broke from the silence of the night the most horrible cry to which I have ever listened. It swelled up louder and louder, a hoarse yell of pain and fear and anger all mingled in the one dreadful shriek. They say that away down in the village, and even in the distant parsonage, that cry raised the sleepers from their beds. It struck cold to our hearts, and I stood gazing at Holmes, and he at me, until the last echoes of it had died away into the silence from which it rose.

"What can it mean?" I gasped.

"It means that it is all over," Holmes answered. "And perhaps, after all, it is for the best. Take your pistol, and we will enter Dr. Roylott's room."

With a grave face he lit the lamp and led the way down the corridor. Twice he struck at the chamber door without any reply from within. Then he turned the handle and entered, I at his heels, with the cocked pistol in my hand.

It was a singular sight which met our eyes. On the table stood a dark-lantern with the shutter half open, throwing a brilliant beam of light upon the iron safe, the door of which was ajar. Beside this table, on the wooden chair, sat Dr. Grimesby Roylott clad in a long grey dressing-gown, his bare ankles protruding beneath, and his feet thrust into red heelless Turkish slippers. Across his lap lay the short stock with the long lash which we had noticed during the day. His chin was cocked upward, and his eyes were fixed in a dreadful, rigid stare at the corner of the ceiling. Round his brow he had a peculiar yellow band, with brownish speckles, which seemed to be bound tightly round his head. As we entered he made neither sound nor motion.

"The band! the speckled band!" whispered Holmes.

I took a step forward. In an instant his strange headgear began to move, and there reared itself from among his hair the squat diamond-shaped head and puffed neck of a loathsome serpent.

"It is a swamp adder!" cried Holmes; "the deadliest snake in India. He has died within ten seconds of being bitten. Violence does, in truth, recoil upon the violent, and the schemer falls into the pit which he digs for another. Let us thrust this creature back into its den, and we can then remove Miss Stoner to some place of shelter and let the county police know what has happened."

As he spoke he drew the dog-whip swiftly from the dead man's lap, and throwing the noose round the reptile's neck he drew it from its horrid perch and, carrying it at arm's length, threw it into the iron safe, which he closed upon it.

Such are the true facts of the death of Dr. Grimesby Roylott, of Stoke Moran. It is not necessary that I should prolong a narrative which has already run to too great a length by telling how we broke the sad news to the terrified girl, how we conveyed her by the morning train to the care of her good aunt at Harrow, of how the slow process of official inquiry came to the conclusion that the doctor met his fate while indiscreetly playing with a dangerous pet. The little which I had yet to learn of the case was told me by Sherlock Holmes as we travelled back next day.

"I had," said he, "come to an entirely erroneous conclusion which shows, my dear Watson, how dangerous it always is to reason from insufficient data. The presence of the gipsies and the use of the word 'band,' which was used by the poor girl, no doubt, to explain the appearance which she had caught a hurried glimpse of by the light of her match, were sufficient to put me upon an entirely wrong scent. I can only claim the merit that I instantly reconsidered my position when, however, it became clear to me that whatever danger threatened an occupant of the room could not come either from the window or the door. My attention was speedily drawn, as I have already remarked to you, to this ventilator, and to the bell-rope which hung down to the bed. The discovery that this was a dummy, and that the bed was clamped to the floor, instantly gave rise to the suspicion that the rope was there as a bridge for something passing through the hole and coming to the bed. The idea of a snake instantly occurred to me, and when I coupled it with my knowledge that the doctor was furnished with a supply of creatures from India, I felt that I was probably on the right track. The idea of using a form of poison which could not possibly be discovered by any chemical test was just such a one as would occur to a clever and ruthless man who had had an Eastern training. The rapidity with which such a poison would take effect would also, from his point of view, be an advantage. It would be a sharp-eyed coroner, indeed, who could distinguish the two little dark punctures which would show where the poison fangs had done their work. Then I thought of the whistle. Of course, he must recall the snake before the morning light revealed it to the victim. He had trained it, probably by the use of the milk which we saw, to return to him when summoned. He would put it through this ventilator at the hour that he thought best, with the certainty that it would crawl down the rope and land on the bed. It might or might not bite the occupant, perhaps she might escape every night for a week, but sooner or later she must fall a victim.

"I had come to these conclusions before ever I had entered his room. An inspection of his chair showed me that he had been in the habit of standing on it, which of course would be necessary in order that he should reach the ventilator. The sight of the safe, the saucer of milk, and the loop of whipcord were enough to finally dispel any doubts which may have remained. The metallic clang heard by Miss Stoner was obviously caused by her stepfather hastily closing the door of his safe upon its terrible occupant. Having once made up my mind, you know the steps which I took in order to put the matter to the proof. I heard the creature hiss as I have no doubt that you did also, and I instantly lit the light and attacked it."

"With the result of driving it through the ventilator."

"And also, with the result of causing it to turn upon its master at the other side. Some of the blows of my cane came home and roused its snakish temper, so that it flew upon the first person it saw. In this way I am no doubt indirectly responsible for Dr. Grimesby Roylott's death, and I cannot say that it is likely to weigh very heavily upon my conscience."

THE RED-HEADED LEAGUE

I had called upon my friend, Mr. Sherlock Holmes, one day in the autumn of last year and found him in deep conversation with a very stout, florid-faced, elderly gentleman with fiery red hair. With an apology for my intrusion, I was about to withdraw when Holmes pulled me abruptly into the room and closed the door behind me.

"You could not possibly have come at a better time, my dear Watson," he said cordially.

"I was afraid that you were engaged."

"So, I am. Very much so."

"Then I can wait in the next room."

"Not at all. This gentleman, Mr. Wilson, has been my partner and helper in many of my most successful cases, and I have no doubt that he will be of the utmost use to me in yours also."

The stout gentleman half rose from his chair and gave a bob of greeting, with a quick little questioning glance from his small fat-encircled eyes.

"Try the settee," said Holmes, relapsing into his armchair and putting his fingertips together, as was his custom when in judicial moods. "I know, my dear Watson, that you share my love of all that is bizarre and outside the conventions and humdrum routine of everyday life. You have shown your relish for it by the enthusiasm which has prompted you to chronicle, and, if you will excuse my saying so, somewhat to embellish so many of my own little adventures."

"Your cases have indeed been of the greatest interest to me," I observed.

"You will remember that I remarked the other day, just before we went into the very simple problem presented by Miss Mary Sutherland, that for strange effects and extraordinary combinations we must go to life itself, which is always far more daring than any effort of the imagination."

"A proposition which I took the liberty of doubting."

"You did, Doctor, but none the less you must come round to my view, for otherwise I shall keep on piling fact upon fact on you until your reason breaks down under them and acknowledges me to be right. Now, Mr. Jabez Wilson here has been good enough to call upon me this morning, and to begin a narrative which promises to be one of the most singular which I have listened to for some time. You have heard me remark that the strangest and most unique things are very often connected not with the larger but with the smaller crimes, and occasionally, indeed, where there is room for doubt whether any positive crime has been committed. As far as I have heard, it is impossible for me to say whether the present case is an instance of crime or not, but the course of events is certainly among the most singular that I have ever listened to. Perhaps, Mr. Wilson, you would have the great kindness to recommence your narrative. I ask you not merely because my friend Dr. Watson has not heard the opening part but also because the peculiar nature of the story makes me anxious to have every possible detail from your lips. As a rule, when I have heard some slight indication of the course of events, I am able to guide myself by the thousands of other similar cases which occur to my memory. In the present instance I am forced to admit that the facts are, to the best of my belief, unique."

The portly client puffed out his chest with an appearance of some little pride and pulled a dirty and wrinkled newspaper from the inside pocket of his greatcoat. As he glanced down the advertisement column, with his head thrust forward and the paper flattened out upon his knee, I took a good look at the man and endeavoured, after the fashion of my companion, to read the indications which might be presented by his dress or appearance.

I did not gain very much, however, by my inspection. Our visitor bore every mark of being an average commonplace British tradesman, obese, pompous, and slow. He wore rather baggy grey shepherd's check trousers, a not over-clean black frock-coat, unbuttoned in the front, and a drab waistcoat with a heavy brassy Albert chain, and a square pierced bit of metal dangling down as an ornament. A frayed top-hat and a faded brown overcoat with a wrinkled velvet collar lay upon a chair beside him. Altogether, look as I would, there was nothing remarkable about the man save his blazing red head, and the expression of extreme chagrin and discontent upon his features.

Sherlock Holmes' quick eye took in my occupation, and he shook his head with a smile as he noticed my questioning glances. "Beyond the obvious facts that he has at some time done manual labour, that he takes snuff, that he is a Freemason, that he has been in China, and that he has done a considerable amount of writing lately, I can deduce nothing else."

Mr. Jabez Wilson started up in his chair, with his forefinger upon the paper, but his eyes upon my companion.

"How, in the name of good-fortune, did you know all that, Mr. Holmes?" he asked. "How did you know, for example, that I did manual labour. It's as true as gospel, for I began as a ship's carpenter."

"Your hands, my dear sir. Your right hand is quite a size larger than your left. You have worked with it, and the muscles are more developed."

"Well, the snuff, then, and the Freemasonry?"

"I won't insult your intelligence by telling you how I read that, especially as, rather against the strict rules of your order, you use an arc-and-compass breastpin."

"Ah, of course, I forgot that. But the writing?"

"What else can be indicated by that right cuff so very shiny for five inches, and the left one with the smooth patch near the elbow where you rest it upon the desk?"

"Well, but China?"

"The fish that you have tattooed immediately above your right wrist could only have been done in China. I have made a small study of tattoo marks and have even contributed to the literature of the subject. That trick of staining the fishes' scales of a delicate pink is quite peculiar to China. When, in addition, I see a Chinese coin hanging from your watch-chain, the matter becomes even more simple."

Mr. Jabez Wilson laughed heavily. "Well, I never!" said he. "I thought at first that you had done something clever, but I see that there was nothing in it after all."

"I begin to think, Watson," said Holmes, "that I make a mistake in explaining. '*Omne ignotum pro magnifico*,' you know, and my poor little reputation, such as it is, will suffer shipwreck if I am so candid. Can you not find the advertisement, Mr. Wilson?"

"Yes, I have got it now," he answered with his thick red finger planted halfway down the column. "Here it is. This is what began it all. You just read it for yourself, sir."

I took the paper from him and read as follows:

"TO THE RED-HEADED LEAGUE: On account of the bequest of the late Ezekiah Hopkins, of Lebanon, Pennsylvania, U.S.A., there is now another vacancy open which entitles a member of the League to a salary of £ 4 a week for purely nominal services. All red-headed men who are sound in body and mind and above the age of twenty-one years, are eligible. Apply in person on Monday, at eleven o'clock, to Duncan Ross, at the offices of the League, 7 Pope's Court, Fleet Street."

"What on earth does this mean?" I ejaculated after I had twice read over the extraordinary announcement.

Holmes chuckled and wriggled in his chair, as was his habit when in high spirits. "It is a little off the beaten track, isn't it?" said he. "And now, Mr. Wilson, off you go at scratch and tell us all about yourself, your household, and the effect which this advertisement had upon your fortunes. You will first make a note, Doctor, of the paper and the date."

"It is *The Morning Chronicle* of April 27, 1890. Just two months ago."

"Very good. Now, Mr. Wilson?"

"Well, it is just as I have been telling you, Mr. Sherlock Holmes," said Jabez Wilson, mopping his forehead; "I have a small pawnbroker's business at Coburg Square, near the City. It's not a very large affair, and of late years it has not done more than just give me a living. I used to be able to keep two assistants, but now I only keep one; and I would have a job to pay him but that he is willing to come for half wages so as to learn the business."

"What is the name of this obliging youth?" asked Sherlock Holmes.

"His name is Vincent Spaulding, and he's not such a youth, either. It's hard to say his age. I should not wish a smarter assistant, Mr. Holmes; and I know very well that he could better himself and earn twice what I am able to give him. But, after all, if he is satisfied, why should I put ideas in his head?"

"Why, indeed? You seem most fortunate in having an *employé* who comes under the full market price. It is not a common experience among employers in this age. I don't know that your assistant is not as remarkable as your advertisement."

"Oh, he has his faults, too," said Mr. Wilson. "Never was such a fellow for photography. Snapping away with a camera when he ought to be improving his mind, and then diving down into the cellar like a rabbit into its hole to develop his pictures. That is his main fault, but on the whole he's a good worker. There's no vice in him."

"He is still with you, I presume?"

"Yes, sir. He and a girl of fourteen, who does a bit of simple cooking and keeps the place clean—that's all I have in the house, for I am a widower and never had any family. We live very quietly, sir, the three of us; and we keep a roof over our heads and pay our debts, if we do nothing more.

"The first thing that put us out was that advertisement. Spaulding, he came down into the office just this day eight weeks, with this very paper in his hand, and he says:

"'I wish to the Lord, Mr. Wilson, that I was a red-headed man.'

"'Why that?' I asks.

"'Why,' says he, 'here's another vacancy on the League of the Red-headed Men. It's worth quite a little fortune to any man who gets it, and I understand that there are more vacancies than there are men, so that the trustees are at their wits' end what to do with the money. If my hair would only change colour, here's a nice little crib already for me to step into.'

"'Why, what is it, then?' I asked. You see, Mr. Holmes, I am a very stay-at-home man, and as my business came to me instead of my having to go to it, I was often weeks on end without putting my foot over the door-mat. In that way I didn't know much of what was going on outside, and I was always glad of a bit of news.

"'Have you never heard of the League of the Red-headed Men?' he asked with his eyes open.

"'Never.'

"'Why, I wonder at that, for you are eligible yourself for one of the vacancies.'

"'And what are they worth?' I asked.

"'Oh, merely a couple of hundred a year, but the work is slight, and it need not interfere very much with one's other occupations.'

"Well, you can easily think that that made me prick up my ears, for the business has not been over good for some years, and an extra couple of hundred would have been very handy.

"'Tell me all about it,' said I.

"'Well,' said he, showing me the advertisement, 'you can see for yourself that the League has a vacancy, and there is the address where you should apply for particulars. As far as I can make out, the League was founded by an American millionaire, Ezekiah Hopkins, who was very peculiar in his ways. He was himself red-headed, and he had a great sympathy for all red-headed men; so, when he died, it was found that he had left his enormous fortune in the hands of trustees, with instructions to apply the interest to the providing of easy berths to men whose hair is of that colour. From all I hear it is splendid pay and very little to do.'

"'But' said I, 'there would be millions of red-headed men who would apply.'

"'Not so many as you might think,' he answered. 'You see it is really confined to Londoners, and to grown men. This American had started from London when he was young, and he wanted to do the old town a good turn. Then, again, I have heard it is no use your applying if your hair is light red, or dark red, or anything but real bright, blazing, fiery red. Now, if you cared to apply, Mr. Wilson, you would just walk in;

but perhaps it would hardly be worth your while to put yourself out of the way for the sake of a few hundred pounds.'

"Now, it is a fact, gentlemen, as you may see for yourselves, that my hair is of a very full and rich tint, so that it seemed to me that if there was to be any competition in the matter I stood as good a chance as any man that I had ever met. Vincent Spaulding seemed to know so much about it that I thought he might prove useful, so I just ordered him to put up the shutters for the day and to come right away with me. He was very willing to have a holiday, so we shut the business up and started off for the address that was given us in the advertisement.

"I never hope to see such a sight as that again, Mr. Holmes. From north, south, east, and west every man who had a shade of red in his hair had tramped into the city to answer the advertisement. Fleet Street was choked with red-headed folk, and Pope's Court looked like a coster's orange barrow. I should not have thought there were so many in the whole country as were brought together by that single advertisement. Every shade of colour they were—straw, lemon, orange, brick, Irish-setter, liver, clay; but, as Spaulding said, there were not many who had the real vivid flame-coloured tint. When I saw how many were waiting, I would have given it up in despair; but Spaulding would not hear of it. How he did it I could not imagine, but he pushed and pulled and butted until he got me through the crowd, and right up to the steps which led to the office. There was a double stream upon the stair, some going up in hope, and some coming back dejected; but we wedged in as well as we could and soon found ourselves in the office."

"Your experience has been a most entertaining one," remarked Holmes as his client paused and refreshed his memory with a huge pinch of snuff. "Pray continue your very interesting statement."

"There was nothing in the office but a couple of wooden chairs and a deal table, behind which sat a small man with a head that was even redder than mine. He said a few words to each candidate as he came up, and then he always managed to find some fault in them which would disqualify them. Getting a vacancy did not seem to be such a very easy matter, after all. However, when our turn came the little man was much more favourable to me than to any of the others and he closed the door as we entered, so that he might have a private word with us.

"'This is Mr. Jabez Wilson,' said my assistant, 'and he is willing to fill a vacancy in the League.'

"'And he is admirably suited for it,' the other answered. 'He has every requirement. I cannot recall when I have seen anything so fine.' He took a step backward, cocked his head on one side, and gazed at my hair until I felt quite bashful. Then suddenly he plunged forward, wrung my hand, and congratulated me warmly on my success.

"'It would be injustice to hesitate,' said he. 'You will, however, I am sure, excuse me for taking an obvious precaution.' With that he seized my hair in both his hands and tugged until I yelled with the pain. 'There is water in your eyes,' said he as he released me. 'I perceive that all is as it should be. But we have to be careful, for we have twice been deceived by wigs and once by paint. I could tell you tales of cobbler's wax which would disgust you with human nature.' He stepped over to the window and shouted through it at the top of his voice that the vacancy was filled. A groan of disappointment came up from below, and the folk all trooped away in different directions until there was not a red-head to be seen except my own and that of the manager.

"'My name,' said he, 'is Mr. Duncan Ross, and I am myself one of the pensioners upon the fund left by our noble benefactor. Are you a married man, Mr. Wilson? Have you a family?'

"I answered that I had not.

"His face fell immediately.

"'Dear me!' he said gravely, 'that is very serious indeed! I am sorry to hear you say that. The fund was, of course, for the propagation and spread of the red-heads as well as for their maintenance. It is exceedingly unfortunate that you should be a bachelor.'

"My face lengthened at this, Mr. Holmes, for I thought that I was not to have the vacancy after all; but after thinking it over for a few minutes he said that it would be all right.

"'In the case of another,' said he, 'the objection might be fatal, but we must stretch a point in favour of a man with such a head of hair as yours. When shall you be able to enter upon your new duties?'

"'Well, it is a little awkward, for I have a business already,' said I.

"'Oh, never mind about that, Mr. Wilson!' said Vincent Spaulding. 'I should be able to look after that for you.'

"'What would be the hours?' I asked.

"'Ten to two.'

"Now a pawnbroker's business is mostly done of an evening, Mr. Holmes, especially Thursday and Friday evening, which is just before pay-day; so, it would suit me very well to earn a little in the mornings. Besides, I knew that my assistant was a good man, and that he would see to anything that turned up.

"'That would suit me very well,' said I. 'And the pay?'

"'Is £ 4 a week.'

"'And the work?'

"'Is purely nominal.'

"'What do you call purely nominal?'

"'Well, you have to be in the office, or at least in the building, the whole time. If you leave, you forfeit your whole position forever. The will is very clear upon that point. You don't comply with the conditions if you budge from the office during that time.'

"'It's only four hours a day, and I should not think of leaving,' said I.

"'No excuse will avail,' said Mr. Duncan Ross; 'neither sickness nor business nor anything else. There you must stay, or you lose your billet.'

"'And the work?'

"'Is to copy out the *Encyclopædia Britannica*. There is the first volume of it in that press. You must find your own ink, pens, and blotting-paper, but we provide this table and chair. Will you be ready tomorrow?'

"'Certainly,' I answered.

"'Then, good-bye, Mr. Jabez Wilson, and let me congratulate you once more on the important position which you have been fortunate enough to gain.' He bowed me out of the room, and I went home with my assistant, hardly knowing what to say or do, I was so pleased at my own good fortune.

"Well, I thought over the matter all day, and by evening I was in low spirits again; for I had quite persuaded myself that the whole affair must be some great hoax or fraud, though what its object might be I could not imagine. It seemed altogether past belief that anyone could make such a will, or that they would pay such a sum for doing anything so simple as copying out the *Encyclopædia Britannica*. Vincent Spaulding did what he could to cheer me up, but by bedtime I had reasoned myself out of the whole thing. However, in the morning I determined to have a look at it anyhow, so I bought a penny bottle of ink, and with a quill-pen, and seven sheets of foolscap paper, I started off for Pope's Court.

"Well, to my surprise and delight, everything was as right as possible. The table was set out ready for me, and Mr. Duncan Ross was there to see that I got fairly to work. He started me off upon the letter A, and then he left me; but he would drop in from time to time to see that all was right with me. At two o'clock he bade me good-day, complimented me upon the amount that I had written, and locked the door of the office after me.

"This went on day after day, Mr. Holmes, and on Saturday the manager came in and planked down four golden sovereigns for my week's work. It was the same next week, and the same the week after. Every morning, I was there at ten and every afternoon I left at two. By degrees Mr. Duncan Ross took to coming in only once of a morning, and then, after a time, he did not come in at all. Still, of course, I never dared to leave the room for an instant, for I was not sure when he might come, and the billet was such a good one, and suited me so well, that I would not risk the loss of it.

"Eight weeks passed away like this, and I had written about Abbots and Archery and Armour and Architecture and Attica and hoped with diligence that I might get on to the B's before very long. It cost me something in foolscap, and I had pretty nearly filled a shelf with my writings. And then suddenly the whole business came to an end."

"To an end?"

"Yes, sir. And no later than this morning. I went to my work as usual at ten o'clock, but the door was shut and locked, with a little square of cardboard hammered on to the middle of the panel with a tack. Here it is, and you can read for yourself."

He held up a piece of white cardboard about the size of a sheet of notepaper. It read in this fashion:

"THE RED-HEADED LEAGUE IS DISSOLVED. October 9, 1890."

Sherlock Holmes and I surveyed this curt announcement and the rueful face behind it, until the comical side of the affair so completely overtopped every other consideration that we both burst out into a roar of laughter.

"I cannot see that there is anything very funny," cried our client, flushing up to the roots of his flaming head. "If you can do nothing better than laugh at me, I can go elsewhere."

"No, no," cried Holmes, shoving him back into the chair from which he had half risen. "I really wouldn't miss your case for the world. It is most refreshingly unusual. But there is, if you will excuse my saying so, something just a little funny about it. Pray what steps did you take when you found the card upon the door?"

"I was staggered, sir. I did not know what to do. Then I called at the offices round, but none of them seemed to know anything about it. Finally, I went to the landlord, who is an accountant living on the ground floor, and I asked him if he could tell me what had become of the Red-headed League. He said that he had never heard of any such body. Then I asked him who Mr. Duncan Ross was. He answered that the name was new to him.

"'Well,' said I, 'the gentleman at No. 4.'

"'What, the red-headed man?'

"'Yes.'

"'Oh,' said he, 'his name was William Morris. He was a solicitor and was using my room as a temporary convenience until his new premises were ready. He moved out yesterday.'

"'Where could I find him?'

"'Oh, at his new offices. He did tell me the address. Yes, 17 King Edward Street, near St. Paul's.'

"I started off, Mr. Holmes, but when I got to that address it was a manufactory of artificial knee-caps, and no one in it had ever heard of either Mr. William Morris or Mr. Duncan Ross."

"And what did you do then?" asked Holmes.

"I went home to Saxe-Coburg Square, and I took the advice of my assistant. But he could not help me in any way. He could only say that if I waited I should hear by post. But that was not quite good enough, Mr. Holmes. I did not wish to lose such a place without a struggle, so, as I had heard that you were good enough to give advice to poor folk who were in need of it, I came right away to you."

"And you did very wisely," said Holmes. "Your case is an exceedingly remarkable one, and I shall be happy to look into it. From what you have told me I think that it is possible that graver issues hang from it than might at first sight appear."

"Grave enough!" said Mr. Jabez Wilson. "Why, I have lost four pound a week."

"As far as you are personally concerned," remarked Holmes, "I do not see that you have any grievance against this extraordinary league. On the contrary, you are, as I understand, richer by some £ 30, to say nothing of the minute knowledge which you have gained on every subject which comes under the letter A. You have lost nothing by them."

"No, sir. But I want to find out about them, and who they are, and what their object was in playing this prank—if it was a prank—upon me. It was a pretty expensive joke for them, for it cost them two and thirty pounds."

"We shall endeavour to clear up these points for you. And, first, one or two questions, Mr. Wilson. This assistant of yours who first called your attention to the advertisement—how long had he been with you?"

"About a month then."

"How did he come?"

"In answer to an advertisement."

"Was he the only applicant?"

"No, I had a dozen."

"Why did you pick him?"

"Because he was handy and would come cheap."

"At half wages, in fact."

"Yes."

"What is he like, this Vincent Spaulding?"

"Small, stout-built, very quick in his ways, no hair on his face, though he's not short of thirty. Has a white splash of acid upon his forehead."

Holmes sat up in his chair in considerable excitement. "I thought as much," said he. "Have you ever observed that his ears are pierced for earrings?"

"Yes, sir. He told me that a gipsy had done it for him when he was a lad."

"Hum!" said Holmes, sinking back in deep thought. "He is still with you?"

"Oh, yes, sir; I have only just left him."

"And has your business been attended to in your absence?"

"Nothing to complain of Sir. There's never very much to do of a morning."

"That will do, Mr. Wilson. I shall be happy to give you an opinion upon the subject in the course of a day or two. Today is Saturday, and I hope that by Monday we may come to a conclusion."

"Well, Watson," said Holmes when our visitor had left us, "what do you make of it all?"

"I make nothing of it," I answered frankly. "It is a most mysterious business."

"As a rule," said Holmes, "the more bizarre a thing is the less mysterious it proves to be. It is your commonplace, featureless crimes which are really puzzling, just as a commonplace face is the most difficult to identify. But I must be prompt over this matter."

"What are you going to do, then?" I asked.

"To smoke," he answered. "It is quite a three-pipe problem, and I beg that you won't speak to me for fifty minutes." He curled himself up in his chair, with his thin knees drawn up to his hawk-like nose, and there he sat with his eyes closed and his black clay pipe thrusting out like the bill of some strange bird. I had come to the conclusion that he had dropped asleep, and indeed was nodding myself, when he suddenly sprang out of his chair with the gesture of a man who has made up his mind and put his pipe down upon the mantelpiece.

"Sarasate plays at the St. James's Hall this afternoon," he remarked. "What do you think, Watson? Could your patients spare you for a few hours?"

"I have nothing to do Today. My practice is never very absorbing."

"Then put on your hat and come. I am going through the City first, and we can have some lunch on the way. I observe that there is a good deal of German music on the programme, which is rather more to my taste than Italian or French. It is introspective, and I want to introspect. Come along!"

We travelled by the Underground as far as Aldersgate; and a short walk took us to Saxe-Coburg Square, the scene of the singular story which we had listened to in the morning. It was a poky, little, shabby-genteel place, where four lines of dingy two-storied brick houses looked out into a small railed-in enclosure, where a lawn of weedy grass and a few clumps of faded laurel bushes made a hard fight against a smoke-laden and uncongenial atmosphere. Three gilt balls and a brown board with "JABEZ WILSON" in white letters, upon a corner house, announced the place where our red-headed client carried on his business. Sherlock Holmes stopped in front of it with his head on one side and looked it all over, with his eyes shining brightly between puckered lids. Then he walked slowly up the street, and then down again to the corner, still looking keenly at the houses. Finally, he returned to the pawnbroker's and having thumped vigorously upon the pavement with his stick two or three times, he went up to the door and knocked. It was instantly opened by a bright-looking, clean-shaven young fellow, who asked him to step in.

"Thank you," said Holmes, "I only wished to ask you how you would go from here to the Strand."

"Third right, fourth left," answered the assistant promptly, closing the door.

"Smart fellow, that," observed Holmes as we walked away. "He is, in my judgment, the fourth smartest man in London, and for daring I am not sure that he has not a claim to be third. I have known something of him before."

"Evidently," said I, "Mr. Wilson's assistant counts for a good deal in this mystery of the Red-headed League. I am sure that you inquired your way merely in order that you might see him."

"Not him."

"What then?"

"The knees of his trousers."

"And what did you see?"

"What I expected to see."

"Why did you beat the pavement?"

"My dear doctor, this is a time for observation, not for talk. We are spies in an enemy's country. We know something of Saxe-Coburg Square. Let us now explore the parts which lie behind it."

The road in which we found ourselves as we turned round the corner from the retired Saxe-Coburg Square presented as great a contrast to it as the front of a picture does to the back. It was one of the main arteries which conveyed the traffic of the City to the north and west. The roadway was blocked with the immense stream of commerce flowing in a double tide inward and outward, while the footpaths were black with the hurrying swarm of pedestrians. It was difficult to realise as we looked at the line of fine shops and stately business premises that they really abutted on the other side upon the faded and stagnant square which we had just quitted.

"Let me see," said Holmes, standing at the corner and glancing along the line, "I should like just to remember the order of the houses here. It is a hobby of mine to have an exact knowledge of London. There is Mortimer's, the tobacconist, the little newspaper shop, the Coburg branch of the City and Suburban Bank, the Vegetarian Restaurant, and McFarlane's carriage-building depot. That carries us right on to the other block. And now, Doctor, we've done our work, so it's time we had some play. A sandwich and a cup of coffee, and then off to violin-land, where all is sweetness and delicacy and harmony, and there are no red-headed clients to vex us with their conundrums."

My friend was an enthusiastic musician, being himself not only a very capable performer but a composer of no ordinary merit. All the afternoon he sat in the stalls wrapped in the most perfect happiness, gently waving his long, thin fingers in time to the music, while his gently smiling face and his languid, dreamy eyes were as unlike those of Holmes the sleuth-hound, Holmes the relentless, keen-witted, ready-handed criminal agent, as it was possible to conceive. In his singular character the dual nature alternately asserted itself, and his extreme exactness and astuteness represented, as I have often thought, the reaction against the poetic and contemplative mood which occasionally predominated in him. The swing of his nature took him from extreme languor to devouring energy; and, as I knew well, he was never so truly formidable as when, for days on end, he had been lounging in his armchair amid his improvisations and his black-letter editions. Then it was that the lust of the chase would suddenly come upon him, and that his brilliant reasoning power would rise to the level of intuition, until those who were unacquainted with his methods would look askance at him as on a man whose knowledge was not that of other mortals. When I saw him that afternoon so enwrapped in the music at St. James's Hall I felt that an evil time might be coming upon those whom he had set himself to hunt down.

"You want to go home, no doubt, Doctor," he remarked as we emerged.

"Yes, it would be as well."

"And I have some business to do which will take some hours. This business at Coburg Square is serious."

"Why serious?"

"A considerable crime is in contemplation. I have every reason to believe that we shall be in time to stop it. But Today being Saturday rather complicates matters. I shall want your help tonight."

"At what time?"

"Ten will be early enough."

"I shall be at Baker Street at ten."

"Very well. And, I say, Doctor, there may be some little danger, so kindly put your army revolver in your pocket." He waved his hand, turned on his heel, and disappeared in an instant among the crowd.

I trust that I am not more dense than my neighbours, but I was always oppressed with a sense of my own stupidity in my dealings with Sherlock Holmes. Here I had heard what he had heard, I had seen what he had seen, and yet from his words it was evident that he saw clearly not only what had happened but what was about to happen, while to me the whole business was still confused and grotesque. As I drove home to my house in Kensington I thought over it all, from the extraordinary story of the red-headed copier of the *Encyclopædia* down to the visit to Saxe-Coburg Square, and the ominous words with which he had parted from me. What was this nocturnal expedition, and why should I go armed? Where were we going, and what were we to do? I had the hint from Holmes that this smooth-faced pawnbroker's assistant was a formidable man—a man who might play a deep game. I tried to puzzle it out but gave it up in despair and set the matter aside until night should bring an explanation.

It was a quarter-past nine when I started from home and made my way across the Park, and so through Oxford Street to Baker Street. Two hansoms were standing at the door, and as I entered the passage I heard the sound of voices from above. On entering his room, I found Holmes in animated conversation with two men, one of whom I recognised as Peter Jones, the official police agent, while the other was a long, thin, sad-faced man, with a very shiny hat and oppressively respectable frock-coat.

"Ha! Our party is complete," said Holmes, buttoning up his pea-jacket and taking his heavy hunting crop from the rack. "Watson, I think you know Mr. Jones, of Scotland Yard? Let me introduce you to Mr. Merryweather, who is to be our companion in tonight's adventure."

"We're hunting in couples again, Doctor, you see," said Jones in his consequential way. "Our friend here is a wonderful man for starting a chase. All he wants is an old dog to help him to do the running down."

"I hope a wild goose may not prove to be the end of our chase," observed Mr. Merryweather gloomily.

"You may place considerable confidence in Mr. Holmes, sir," said the police agent loftily. "He has his own little methods, which are, if he won't mind my saying so, just a little too theoretical and fantastic, but he has the makings of a detective in him. It is not too much to say that once or twice, as in that business of the Sholto murder and the Agra treasure, he has been more nearly correct than the official force."

"Oh, if you say so, Mr. Jones, it is all right," said the stranger with deference. "Still, I confess that I miss my rubber. It is the first Saturday night for seven-and-twenty years that I have not had my rubber."

"I think you will find," said Sherlock Holmes, "that you will play for a higher stake tonight than you have ever done yet, and that the play will be more exciting. For you, Mr. Merryweather, the stake will be some £ 30,000; and for you, Jones, it will be the man upon whom you wish to lay your hands."

"John Clay, the murderer, thief, smasher, and forger. He's a young man, Mr. Merryweather, but he is at the head of his profession, and I would rather have my bracelets on him than on any criminal in London. He's a remarkable man, is young John Clay. His grandfather was a royal duke, and he himself has been to Eton and Oxford. His brain is as cunning as his fingers, and though we meet signs of him at every turn, we never know where to find the man himself. He'll crack a crib in Scotland one week and be raising money to build an orphanage in Cornwall the next. I've been on his track for years and have never set eyes on him yet."

"I hope that I may have the pleasure of introducing you tonight. I've had one or two little turns also with Mr. John Clay, and I agree with you that he is at the head of his profession. It is past ten, however, and quite time that we started. If you two will take the first hansom, Watson and I will follow in the second."

Sherlock Holmes was not very communicative during the long drive and lay back in the cab humming the tunes which he had heard in the afternoon. We rattled through an endless labyrinth of gas-lit streets until we emerged into Farrington Street.

"We are close there now," my friend remarked. "This fellow Merryweather is a bank director, and personally interested in the matter. I thought it as well to have Jones with us also. He is not a bad fellow, though an absolute imbecile in his profession. He has one positive virtue. He is as brave as a bulldog and as tenacious as a lobster if he gets his claws upon anyone. Here we are, and they are waiting for us."

We had reached the same crowded thoroughfare in which we had found ourselves in the morning. Our cabs were dismissed, and, following the guidance of Mr. Merryweather, we passed down a narrow passage and through a side door, which he opened for us. Within there was a small corridor, which ended in a very massive iron gate. This also was opened, and led down a flight of winding stone steps, which terminated at another formidable gate. Mr. Merryweather stopped to light a lantern, and then conducted us down a dark, earth-smelling passage, and so, after opening a third door, into a huge vault or cellar, which was piled all round with crates and massive boxes.

"You are not very vulnerable from above," Holmes remarked as he held up the lantern and gazed about him.

"Nor from below," said Mr. Merryweather, striking his stick upon the flags which lined the floor. "Why, dear me, it sounds quite hollow!" he remarked, looking up in surprise.

"I must really ask you to be a little more quiet!" said Holmes severely. "You have already imperilled the whole success of our expedition. Might I beg that you would have the goodness to sit down upon one of those boxes, and not to interfere?"

The solemn Mr. Merryweather perched himself upon a crate, with a very injured expression upon his face, while Holmes fell upon his knees upon the floor and, with the lantern and a magnifying lens, began to examine minutely the cracks between the stones. A few seconds sufficed to satisfy him, for he sprang to his feet again and put his glass in his pocket.

"We have at least an hour before us," he remarked, "for they can hardly take any steps until the good pawnbroker is safely in bed. Then they will not lose a minute, for the sooner they do their work the longer time they will have for their escape. We are at present, Doctor—as no doubt you have divined—in the cellar of the City branch of one of the principal London banks. Mr. Merryweather is the chairman of directors, and he will explain to you that there are reasons why the more daring criminals of London should take a considerable interest in this cellar at present."

"It is our French gold," whispered the director. "We have had several warnings that an attempt might be made upon it."

"Your French gold?"

"Yes. We had occasion some months ago to strengthen our resources and borrowed for that purpose 30,000 napoleons from the Bank of France. It has become known that we have never had occasion to unpack the money, and that it is still lying in our cellar. The crate upon which I sit contains 2,000 napoleons packed between layers of lead foil. Our reserve of bullion is much larger at present than is usually kept in a single branch office, and the directors have had misgivings upon the subject."

"Which were very well justified," observed Holmes. "And now it is time that we arranged our little plans. I expect that within an hour matters will come to a head. In the meantime, Mr. Merryweather, we must put the screen over that dark lantern."

"And sit in the dark?"

"I am afraid so. I had brought a pack of cards in my pocket, and I thought that, as we were a *partie carrée*, you might have your rubber after all. But I see that the enemy's preparations have gone so far that we cannot risk the presence of a light. And first of all, we must choose our positions. These are daring men, and though we shall take them at a disadvantage, they may do us some harm unless we are careful. I shall stand behind this crate and do you conceal yourselves behind those. Then, when I flash a light upon them, close in swiftly. If they fire, Watson, have no compunction about shooting them down."

I placed my revolver, cocked, upon the top of the wooden case behind which I crouched. Holmes shot the slide across the front of his lantern and left us in pitch darkness—such an absolute darkness as I have never before experienced. The smell of hot metal remained to assure us that the light was still there, ready to flash out at a moment's notice. To me, with my nerves worked up to a pitch of expectancy, there was something depressing and subduing in the sudden gloom, and in the cold dank air of the vault.

"They have but one retreat," whispered Holmes. "That is back through the house into Saxe-Coburg Square. I hope that you have done what I asked you, Jones?"

"I have an inspector and two officers waiting at the front door."

"Then we have stopped all the holes. And now we must be silent and wait."

What a time it seemed! From comparing notes afterwards, it was but an hour and a quarter, yet it appeared to me that the night must have almost gone, and the dawn be breaking above us. My limbs were weary and stiff, for I feared to change my position; yet my nerves were worked up to the highest pitch of tension, and my hearing was so acute that I could not only hear the gentle breathing of my companions, but I could distinguish the deeper, heavier in-breath of the bulky Jones from the thin, sighing note of the bank director. From my position I could look over the case in the direction of the floor. Suddenly my eyes caught the glint of a light.

At first it was but a lurid spark upon the stone pavement. Then it lengthened out until it became a yellow line, and then, without any warning or sound, a gash seemed to open, and a hand appeared, a white, almost womanly hand, which felt about in the Centre of the little area of light. For a minute or more the hand, with its writhing fingers, protruded out of the floor. Then it was withdrawn as suddenly as it appeared, and all was dark again save the single lurid spark which marked a chink between the stones.

Its disappearance, however, was but momentary. With a rending, tearing sound, one of the broad, white stones turned over upon its side and left a square, gaping hole, through which streamed the light of a lantern. Over the edge there peeped a clean-cut, boyish face, which looked keenly about it, and then, with a hand on either side of the aperture, drew itself shoulder-high and waist-high, until one knee rested upon the edge. In another instant he stood at the side of the hole and was hauling after him a companion, lithe and small like himself, with a pale face and a shock of very red hair.

"It's all clear," he whispered. "Have you the chisel and the bags? Great Scott! Jump, Archie, jump, and I'll swing for it!"

Sherlock Holmes had sprung out and seized the intruder by the collar. The other dived down the hole, and I heard the sound of rending cloth as Jones clutched at his skirts. The light flashed upon the barrel of a revolver, but Holmes' hunting crop came down on the man's wrist, and the pistol clinked upon the stone floor.

"It's no use, John Clay," said Holmes blandly. "You have no chance at all."

"So I see," the other answered with the utmost coolness. "I fancy that my pal is all right, though I see you have got his coat-tails."

"There are three men waiting for him at the door," said Holmes.

"Oh, indeed! You seem to have done the thing very completely. I must compliment you."

"And I you," Holmes answered. "Your red-headed idea was very new and effective."

"You'll see your pal again presently," said Jones. "He's quicker at climbing down holes than I am. Just hold out while I fix the derbies."

"I beg that you will not touch me with your filthy hands," remarked our prisoner as the handcuffs clattered upon his wrists. "You may not be aware that I have royal blood in my veins. Have the goodness, also, when you address me always to say 'sir' and 'please.'"

"All right," said Jones with a stare and a snigger. "Well, would you please, sir, march upstairs, where we can get a cab to carry your Highness to the police-station?"

"That is better," said John Clay serenely. He made a sweeping bow to the three of us and walked quietly off in the custody of the detective.

"Really, Mr. Holmes," said Mr. Merryweather as we followed them from the cellar, "I do not know how the bank can thank you or repay you. There is no doubt that you have detected and defeated in the most complete manner one of the most determined attempts at bank robbery that have ever come within my experience."

"I have had one or two little scores of my own to settle with Mr. John Clay," said Holmes. "I have been at some small expense over this matter, which I shall expect the bank to refund, but beyond that I am amply repaid by having had an experience which is in many ways unique, and by hearing the very remarkable narrative of the Red-headed League."

"You see, Watson," he explained in the early hours of the morning as we sat over a glass of whisky and soda in Baker Street, "it was perfectly obvious from the first that the only possible object of this rather fantastic business of the advertisement of the League, and the copying of the *Encyclopædia*, must be to get this not over-bright pawnbroker out of the way for a number of hours every day. It was a curious way of managing it, but, really, it would be difficult to suggest a better. The method was no doubt suggested to Clay's ingenious mind by the colour of his accomplice's hair. The £4 a week was a lure which must draw him, and what was it to them, who were playing for thousands? They put in the advertisement, one rogue has the temporary office, the other rogue incites the man to apply for it, and together they manage to secure his absence every morning in the week. From the time that I heard of the assistant having come for half wages, it was obvious to me that he had some strong motive for securing the situation."

"But how could you guess what the motive was?"

"Had there been women in the house, I should have suspected a mere vulgar intrigue. That, however, was out of the question. The man's business was a small one, and there was nothing in his house which could account for such elaborate preparations, and such an expenditure as they were at. It must, then, be something out of the house. What could it be? I thought of the assistant's fondness for photography, and his trick of vanishing into the cellar. The cellar! There was the end of this tangled clue. Then I made inquiries as to this mysterious assistant and found that I had to deal with one of the coolest and most daring criminals in London. He was doing something in the cellar—something which took many hours a day for months on end. What could it be, once more? I could think of nothing save that he was running a tunnel to some other building.

"So far I had got when we went to visit the scene of action. I surprised you by beating upon the pavement with my stick. I was ascertaining whether the cellar stretched out in front or behind. It was not in front. Then I rang the bell, and, as I hoped, the assistant answered it. We have had some skirmishes, but we had never set eyes upon each other before. I hardly looked at his face. His knees were what I wished to see. You must yourself have remarked how worn, wrinkled, and stained they were. They spoke of those hours of burrowing. The only remaining point was what they were burrowing for. I walked round the corner, saw the City and Suburban Bank abutted on our friend's premises, and felt that I had solved my problem. When you drove home after the concert I called upon Scotland Yard and upon the chairman of the bank directors, with the result that you have seen."

"And how could you tell that they would make their attempt tonight?" I asked.

"Well, when they closed their League offices that was a sign that they cared no longer about Mr. Jabez Wilson's presence—in other words, that they had completed their tunnel. But it was essential that they should use it soon, as it might be discovered, or the bullion might be removed. Saturday would suit them better than any other day, as it would give them two days for their escape. For all these reasons I expected them to come tonight."

"You reasoned it out beautifully," I exclaimed in unfeigned admiration. "It is so long a chain, and yet every link rings true."

"It saved me from ennui," he answered, yawning. "Alas! I already feel it closing in upon me. My life is spent in one long effort to escape from the commonplaces of existence. These little problems help me to do so."

"And you are a benefactor of the race," said I.

He shrugged his shoulders. “Well, perhaps, after all, it is of some little use,” he remarked. “‘*L’homme c’est rien—l’œuvre c’est tout*,’ as Gustave Flaubert wrote to George Sand.”

A SCANDAL IN BOHEMIA

I.

To Sherlock Holmes she is always *the* woman. I have seldom heard him mention her under any other name. In his eyes she eclipses and predominates the whole of her sex. It was not that he felt any emotion akin to love for Irene Adler. All emotions, and that one particularly, were abhorrent to his cold, precise but admirably balanced mind. He was, I take it, the most perfect reasoning and observing machine that the world has seen, but as a lover he would have placed himself in a false position. He never spoke of the softer passions, save with a gibe and a sneer. They were admirable things for the observer—excellent for drawing the veil from men's motives and actions. But for the trained reasoner to admit such intrusions into his own delicate and finely adjusted temperament was to introduce a distracting factor which might throw a doubt upon all his mental results. Grit in a sensitive instrument, or a crack in one of his own high-power lenses, would not be more disturbing than a strong emotion in a nature such as his. And yet there was but one woman to him, and that woman was the late Irene Adler, of dubious and questionable memory.

I had seen little of Holmes lately. My marriage had drifted us away from each other. My own complete happiness, and the home-centred interests which rise up around the man who first finds himself master of his own establishment, were sufficient to absorb all my attention, while Holmes, who loathed every form of society with his whole Bohemian soul, remained in our lodgings in Baker Street, buried among his old books, and alternating from week to week between cocaine and ambition, the drowsiness of the drug, and the fierce energy of his own keen nature. He was still, as ever, deeply attracted by the study of crime, and occupied his immense faculties and extraordinary powers of observation in following out those clues and clearing up those mysteries which had been abandoned as hopeless by the official police. From time to time, I heard some vague account of his doings: of his summons to Odessa in the case of the Trepoff murder, of his clearing up of the singular tragedy of the Atkinson brothers at Trincomalee, and finally of the mission which he had accomplished so delicately and successfully for the reigning family of Holland. Beyond these signs of his activity, however, which I merely shared with all the readers of the daily press, I knew little of my former friend and companion.

One night—it was on the twentieth of March 1888—I was returning from a journey to a patient (for I had now returned to civil practice), when my way led me through Baker Street. As I passed the well-remembered door, which must always be associated in my mind with my wooing, and with the dark incidents of the Study in Scarlet, I was seized with a keen desire to see Holmes again, and to know how he was employing his extraordinary powers. His rooms were brilliantly lit, and, even as I looked up, I saw his tall, spare figure pass twice in a dark silhouette against the blind. He was pacing the room swiftly, eagerly, with his head sunk upon his chest and his hands clasped behind him. To me, who knew his every mood and habit, his attitude and manner told their own story. He was at work again. He had risen out of his drug-created dreams and was hot upon the scent of some new problem. I rang the bell and was shown up to the chamber which had formerly been in part my own.

His manner was not effusive. It seldom was but he was glad, I think, to see me. With hardly a word spoken, but with a kindly eye, he waved me to an armchair, threw across his case of cigars, and indicated a spirit case and a gasogene in the corner. Then he stood before the fire and looked me over in his singular introspective fashion.

"Wedlock suits you," he remarked. "I think, Watson, that you have put on seven and a half pounds since I saw you."

"Seven!" I answered.

"Indeed, I should have thought a little more. Just a trifle more, I fancy, Watson. And in practice again, I observe. You did not tell me that you intended to go into harness."

"Then, how do you know?"

"I see it, I deduce it. How do I know that you have been getting yourself very wet lately, and that you have a most clumsy and careless servant girl?"

"My dear Holmes," said I, "this is too much. You would certainly have been burned, had you lived a few centuries ago. It is true that I had a country walk on Thursday and came home in a dreadful mess, but as I have changed my clothes I can't imagine how you deduce it. As to Mary Jane, she is incorrigible, and my wife has given her notice, but there, again, I fail to see how you work it out."

He chuckled to himself and rubbed his long, nervous hands together.

"It is simplicity itself," said he; "my eyes tell me that on the inside of your left shoe, just where the firelight strikes it, the leather is scored by six almost parallel cuts. Obviously they have been caused by someone who has very carelessly scraped round the edges of the sole in order to remove crusted mud from it. Hence, you see, my double deduction that you had been out in vile weather, and that you had a particularly malignant boot-slitting specimen of the London slavey. As to your practice, if a gentleman walks into my rooms smelling of iodoform, with a black mark of nitrate of silver upon his right forefinger, and a bulge on the right side of his top-hat to show where he has secreted his stethoscope, I must be dull, indeed, if I do not pronounce him to be an active member of the medical profession."

I could not help laughing at the ease with which he explained his process of deduction. "When I hear you give your reasons," I remarked, "the thing always appears to me to be so ridiculously simple that I could easily do it myself, though at each successive instance of your reasoning I am baffled until you explain your process. And yet I believe that my eyes are as good as yours."

"Quite so," he answered, lighting a cigarette, and throwing himself down into an armchair. "You see, but you do not observe. The distinction is clear. For example, you have frequently seen the steps which lead up from the hall to this room."

"Frequently."

"How often?"

"Well, some hundreds of times."

"Then how many are there?"

"How many? I don't know."

"Quite so! You have not observed. And yet you have seen. That is just my point. Now, I know that there are seventeen steps, because I have both seen and observed. By the way, since you are interested in these little problems, and since you are good enough to chronicle one or two of my trifling experiences, you may be interested in this." He threw over a sheet of thick, pink-tinted notepaper which had been lying open upon the table. "It came by the last post," said he. "Read it aloud."

The note was undated, and without either signature or address.

"There will call upon you tonight, at a quarter to eight o'clock," it said, "a gentleman who desires to consult you upon a matter of the very deepest moment. Your recent services to one of the royal houses of Europe have shown that you are one who may safely be trusted with matters which are of an importance which can hardly be exaggerated. This account of you we have from all quarters received. Be in your chamber then at that hour, and do not take it amiss if your visitor wear a mask."

"This is indeed a mystery," I remarked. "What do you imagine that it means?"

"I have no data yet. It is a capital mistake to theorise before one has data. Insensibly one begins to twist facts to suit theories, instead of theories to suit facts. But the note itself. What do you deduce from it?"

I carefully examined the writing, and the paper upon which it was written.

"The man who wrote it was presumably well to do," I remarked, endeavouring to imitate my companion's processes. "Such paper could not be bought under half a crown a packet. It is peculiarly strong and stiff."

"Peculiar—that is the very word," said Holmes. "It is not an English paper at all. Hold it up to the light."

I did so and saw a large "E" with a small "g," a "P," and a large "G" with a small "t" woven into the texture of the paper.

"What do you make of that?" asked Holmes.

"The name of the maker, no doubt; or his monogram, rather."

"Not at all. The 'G' with the small 't' stands for 'Gesellschaft,' which is the German for 'Company.' It is a customary contraction like our 'Co.' 'P,' of course, stands for 'Papier.' Now for the 'Eg.' Let us glance at our Continental Gazetteer." He took down a heavy brown volume from his shelves. "Eglow, Eglonitz—here we are, Egria. It is in a German-speaking country—in Bohemia, not far from Carlsbad. 'Remarkable as being the scene of the death of Wallenstein, and for its numerous glass-factories and paper-mills.' Ha, ha, my boy, what do you make of that?" His eyes sparkled, and he sent up a great blue triumphant cloud from his cigarette.

"The paper was made in Bohemia," I said.

"Precisely. And the man who wrote the note is a German. Do you note the peculiar construction of the sentence—'This account of you we have from all quarters received.' A Frenchman or Russian could not have written that. It is the German who is so uncourteous to his verbs. It only remains, therefore, to discover what is wanted by this German who writes upon Bohemian paper and prefers wearing a mask to showing his face. And here he comes, if I am not mistaken, to resolve all our doubts."

As he spoke there was the sharp sound of horses' hoofs and grating wheels against the curb, followed by a sharp pull at the bell. Holmes whistled.

"A pair, by the sound," said he. "Yes," he continued, glancing out of the window. "A nice little brougham and a pair of beauties. A hundred and fifty guineas apiece. There's money in this case, Watson, if there is nothing else."

"I think that I had better go, Holmes."

"Not a bit, Doctor. Stay where you are. I am lost without my Boswell. And this promises to be interesting. It would be a pity to miss it."

"But your client—"

"Never mind him. I may want your help, and so may he. Here he comes. Sit down in that armchair, Doctor, and give us your best attention."

A slow and heavy step, which had been heard upon the stairs and in the passage, paused immediately outside the door. Then there was a loud and authoritative tap.

"Come in!" said Holmes.

A man entered who could hardly have been less than six feet six inches in height, with the chest and limbs of a Hercules. His dress was rich with a richness which would, in England, be looked upon as akin to bad taste. Heavy bands of astrakhan were slashed across the sleeves and fronts of his double-breasted coat, while the deep blue cloak which was thrown over his shoulders was lined with flame-coloured silk and secured at the neck with a brooch which consisted of a single flaming beryl. Boots which extended halfway up his calves, and which were trimmed at the tops with rich brown fur, completed the impression of barbaric opulence which was suggested by his whole appearance. He carried a broad-brimmed hat in his hand, while he wore across the upper part of his face, extending down past the cheekbones, a black vizard mask, which he had apparently adjusted that very moment, for his hand was still raised to it as he entered. From the lower part of the face, he appeared to be a man of strong character, with a thick, hanging lip, and a long, straight chin suggestive of resolution pushed to the length of obstinacy.

"You had my note?" he asked with a deep harsh voice and a strongly marked German accent. "I told you that I would call." He looked from one to the other of us, as if uncertain which to address.

"Pray take a seat," said Holmes. "This is my friend and colleague, Dr. Watson, who is occasionally good enough to help me in my cases. Whom have I the honour to address?"

"You may address me as the Count Von Kramm, a Bohemian nobleman. I understand that this gentleman, your friend, is a man of honour and discretion, whom I may trust with a matter of the most extreme importance. If not, I should much prefer to communicate with you alone."

I rose to go, but Holmes caught me by the wrist and pushed me back into my chair. "It is both, or none," said he. "You may say before this gentleman anything which you may say to me."

The Count shrugged his broad shoulders. "Then I must begin," said he, "by binding you both to absolute secrecy for two years; at the end of that time the matter will be of no importance. At present it is not too much to say that it is of such weight it may have an influence upon European history."

"I promise," said Holmes.

"And I."

"You will excuse this mask," continued our strange visitor. "The august person who employs me wishes his agent to be unknown to you, and I may confess at once that the title by which I have just called myself is not exactly my own."

"I was aware of it," said Holmes dryly.

"The circumstances are of great delicacy, and every precaution has to be taken to quench what might grow to be an immense scandal and seriously compromise one of the reigning families of Europe. To speak plainly, the matter implicates the great House of Ormstein, hereditary kings of Bohemia."

"I was also aware of that," murmured Holmes, settling himself down in his armchair and closing his eyes.

Our visitor glanced with some apparent surprise at the languid, lounging figure of the man who had been no doubt depicted to him as the most incisive reasoner and most energetic agent in Europe. Holmes slowly reopened his eyes and looked impatiently at his gigantic client.

"If your Majesty would condescend to state your case," he remarked, "I should be better able to advise you."

The man sprang from his chair and paced up and down the room in uncontrollable agitation. Then, with a gesture of desperation, he tore the mask from his face and hurled it upon the ground. "You are right," he cried; "I am the King. Why should I attempt to conceal it?"

"Why, indeed?" murmured Holmes. "Your Majesty had not spoken before I was aware that I was addressing Wilhelm Gottsreich Sigismond von Ormstein, Grand Duke of Cassel-Felstein, and hereditary King of Bohemia."

"But you can understand," said our strange visitor, sitting down once more and passing his hand over his high white forehead, "you can understand that I am not accustomed to doing such business in my own person. Yet the matter was so delicate that I could not confide it to an agent without putting myself in his power. I have come *incognito* from Prague for the purpose of consulting you."

"Then, pray consult," said Holmes, shutting his eyes once more.

"The facts are briefly these: Some five years ago, during a lengthy visit to Warsaw, I made the acquaintance of the well-known adventuress, Irene Adler. The name is no doubt familiar to you."

"Kindly look her up in my index, Doctor," murmured Holmes without opening his eyes. For many years he had adopted a system of docketing all paragraphs concerning men and things, so that it was difficult to name a subject or a person on which he could not at once furnish information. In this case I found her biography sandwiched in between that of a Hebrew rabbi and that of a staff-commander who had written a monograph upon the deep-sea fishes.

"Let me see!" said Holmes. "Hum! Born in New Jersey in the year 1858. Contralto—hum! La Scala, hum! Prima donna Imperial Opera of Warsaw—yes! Retired from operatic stage—ha! Living in London—quite so! Your Majesty, as I understand, became entangled with this young person, wrote her some compromising letters, and is now desirous of getting those letters back."

"Precisely so. But how—"

"Was there a secret marriage?"

"None."

"No legal papers or certificates?"

"None."

"Then I fail to follow your Majesty. If this young person should produce her letters for blackmailing or other purposes, how is she to prove their authenticity?"

"There is the writing."

"Pooh, pooh! Forgery."

"My private note-paper."

"Stolen."

"My own seal."

"Imitated."

"My photograph."

"Bought."

"We were both in the photograph."

"Oh, dear! That is very bad! Your Majesty has indeed committed an indiscretion."

"I was mad—insane."

"You have compromised yourself seriously."

"I was only Crown Prince then. I was young. I am but thirty now."

"It must be recovered."

"We have tried and failed."

"Your Majesty must pay. It must be bought."

"She will not sell."

"Stolen, then."

"Five attempts have been made. Twice burglars in my pay ransacked her house. Once we diverted her luggage when she travelled. Twice she has been waylaid. There has been no result."

"No sign of it?"

"Absolutely none."

Holmes laughed. "It is quite a pretty little problem," said he.

"But a very serious one to me," returned the King reproachfully.

"Very, indeed. And what does she propose to do with the photograph?"

"To ruin me."

"But how?"

"I am about to be married."

"So, I have heard."

"To Clotilde Lothman von Saxe-Meningen, second daughter of the King of Scandinavia. You may know the strict principles of her family. She is herself the very soul of delicacy. A shadow of a doubt as to my conduct would bring the matter to an end."

"And Irene Adler?"

"Threatens to send them the photograph. And she will do it. I know that she will do it. You do not know her, but she has a soul of steel. She has the face of the most beautiful of women, and the mind of the most resolute of men. Rather than I should marry another woman, there are no lengths to which she would not go—none."

"You are sure that she has not sent it yet?"

"I am sure."

"And why?"

"Because she has said that she would send it on the day when the betrothal was publicly proclaimed. That will be next Monday."

"Oh, then we have three days yet," said Holmes with a yawn. "That is very fortunate, as I have one or two matters of importance to look into just at present. Your Majesty will, of course, stay in London for the present?"

"Certainly. You will find me at the Langham under the name of the Count Von Kramm."

"Then I shall drop you a line to let you know how we progress."

"Pray do so. I shall be all anxiety."

"Then, as to money?"

"You have *carte blanche*."

"Absolutely?"

"I tell you that I would give one of the provinces of my kingdom to have that photograph."

"And for present expenses?"

The King took a heavy chamois leather bag from under his cloak and laid it on the table.

"There are three hundred pounds in gold and seven hundred in notes," he said.

Holmes scribbled a receipt upon a sheet of his note-book and handed it to him.

"And Mademoiselle's address?" he asked.

"Is Briony Lodge, Serpentine Avenue, St. John's Wood."

Holmes took a note of it. "One other question," said he. "Was the photograph a cabinet?"

"It was."

"Then, good-night, your Majesty, and I trust that we shall soon have some good news for you. And good-night, Watson," he added, as the wheels of the royal brougham rolled down the street. "If you will be good enough to call tomorrow afternoon at three o'clock I should like to chat this little matter over with you."

II.

At three o'clock precisely I was at Baker Street, but Holmes had not yet returned. The landlady informed me that he had left the house shortly after eight o'clock in the morning. I sat down beside the fire, however, with the intention of awaiting him, however long he might be. I was already deeply interested in his inquiry, for, though it was surrounded by none of the grim and strange features which were associated with the two crimes which I have already recorded, still, the nature of the case and the exalted station of his client gave it a character of its own. Indeed, apart from the nature of the investigation which my friend had on hand, there was something in his masterly grasp of a situation, and his keen, incisive reasoning, which made it a pleasure to me to study his system of work, and to follow the quick, subtle methods by which he disentangled the most inextricable mysteries. So accustomed was I to his invariable success that the very possibility of his failing had ceased to enter into my head.

It was close upon four before the door opened, and a drunken-looking groom, ill-kempt and side-whiskered, with an inflamed face and disreputable clothes, walked into the room. Accustomed as I was to my friend's amazing powers in the use of disguises, I had to look three times before I was certain that it was indeed he. With a nod he vanished into the bedroom, whence he emerged in five minutes tweed-suited and respectable, as of old. Putting his hands into his pockets, he stretched out his legs in front of the fire and laughed heartily for some minutes.

"Well, really!" he cried, and then he choked and laughed again until he was obliged to lie back, limp and helpless, in the chair.

"What is it?"

"It's quite too funny. I am sure you could never guess how I employed my morning, or what I ended by doing."

"I can't imagine. I suppose that you have been watching the habits, and perhaps the house, of Miss Irene Adler."

"Quite so; but the sequel was rather unusual. I will tell you, however. I left the house a little after eight o'clock this morning in the character of a groom out of work. There is a wonderful sympathy and freemasonry among horsey men. Be one of them, and you will know all that there is to know. I soon found Briony Lodge. It is a *bijou* villa, with a garden at the back, but built out in front right up to the road, two stories. Chubb lock to the door. Large sitting-room on the right side, well furnished, with long windows almost to the floor, and those preposterous English window fasteners which a child could open. Behind there was nothing remarkable, save that the passage window could be reached from the top of the coach-house. I walked round it and examined it closely from every point of view, but without noting anything else of interest.

"I then lounged down the street and found, as I expected, that there was a mews in a lane which runs down by one wall of the garden. I lent the ostlers a hand in rubbing down their horses, and received in exchange two pence, a glass of half-and-half, two fills of shag tobacco, and as much information as I could desire about Miss Adler, to say nothing of half a dozen other people in the neighbourhood in whom I was not in the least interested, but whose biographies I was compelled to listen to."

"And what of Irene Adler?" I asked.

"Oh, she has turned all the men's heads down in that part. She is the daintiest thing under a bonnet on this planet. So, say the Serpentine-mews, to a man. She lives quietly, sings at concerts, drives out at five every day, and returns at seven sharp for dinner. Seldom goes out at other times, except when she sings. Has only one male visitor, but a good deal of him. He is dark, handsome, and dashing, never calls less than once a day, and often twice. He is a Mr. Godfrey Norton, of the Inner Temple. See the advantages of a cabman as a confidant. They had driven him home a dozen times from Serpentine-mews and knew all about him. When I had listened to all they had to tell, I began to walk up and down near Briony Lodge once more, and to think over my plan of campaign.

"This Godfrey Norton was evidently an important factor in the matter. He was a lawyer. That sounded ominous. What was the relation between them, and what the object of his repeated visits? Was she his client, his friend, or his mistress? If the former, she had probably transferred the photograph to his keeping. If the latter, it was less likely. On the issue of this question depended whether I should continue my work at Briony Lodge or turn my attention to the gentleman's chambers in the Temple. It was a delicate point, and it widened the field of my inquiry. I fear that I bore you with these details, but I have to let you see my little difficulties, if you are to understand the situation."

"I am following you closely," I answered.

"I was still balancing the matter in my mind when a hansom cab drove up to Briony Lodge, and a gentleman sprang out. He was a remarkably handsome man, dark, aquiline, and moustached—evidently the man of whom I had heard. He appeared to be in a great hurry, shouted to the cabman to wait, and brushed past the maid who opened the door with the air of a man who was thoroughly at home.

"He was in the house about half an hour, and I could catch glimpses of him in the windows of the sitting-room, pacing up and down, talking excitedly, and waving his arms. Of her I could see nothing. Presently he emerged, looking even more flurried than before. As he stepped up to the cab, he pulled a gold watch from his pocket and looked at it earnestly, 'Drive like the devil,' he shouted, 'first to Gross & Hankey's in Regent Street, and then to the Church of St. Monica in the Edgeware Road. Half a guinea if you do it in twenty minutes!'

"Away they went, and I was just wondering whether I should not do well to follow them when up the lane came a neat little landau, the coachman with his coat only half-buttoned, and his tie under his ear, while all the tags of his harness were sticking out of the buckles. It hadn't pulled up before she shot out of the hall door and into it. I only caught a glimpse of her at the moment, but she was a lovely woman, with a face that a man might die for.

"'The Church of St. Monica, John,' she cried, 'and half a sovereign if you reach it in twenty minutes.'

"This was quite too good to lose, Watson. I was just balancing whether I should run for it, or whether I should perch behind her landau when a cab came through the street. The driver looked twice at such a shabby fare, but I jumped in before he could object. 'The Church of St. Monica,' said I, 'and half a sovereign if you reach it in twenty minutes.' It was twenty-five minutes to twelve, and of course it was clear enough what was in the wind.

"My cabby drove fast. I don't think I ever drove faster, but the others were there before us. The cab and the landau with their steaming horses were in front of the door when I arrived. I paid the man and hurried into the church. There was not a soul there save the two whom I had followed and a surpliced clergyman, who seemed to be expostulating with them. They were all three standing in a knot in front of the altar. I lounged up the side aisle like any other idler who has dropped into a church. Suddenly, to my surprise, the three at the altar faced round to me, and Godfrey Norton came running as hard as he could towards me.

"'Thank God,' he cried. 'You'll do. Come! Come!'

"'What then?' I asked.

"'Come, man, come, only three minutes, or it won't be legal.'

"I was half-dragged up to the altar, and before I knew where I was I found myself mumbling responses which were whispered in my ear, and vouching for things of which I knew nothing, and generally assisting in the secure tying up of Irene Adler, spinster, to Godfrey Norton, bachelor. It was all done in an instant, and there was the gentleman thanking me on the one side and the lady on the other, while the clergyman beamed on me in front. It was the most preposterous position in which I ever found myself in my life, and it was the thought of it that started me laughing just now. It seems that there had been some informality about their license, that the clergyman absolutely refused to marry them without a witness of some sort, and that my lucky appearance saved the bridegroom from having to sally out into the streets in search of a best man. The bride gave me a sovereign, and I mean to wear it on my watch chain in memory of the occasion."

"This is a very unexpected turn of affairs," said I; "and what then?"

"Well, I found my plans very seriously menaced. It looked as if the pair might take an immediate departure, and so necessitate very prompt and energetic measures on my part. At the church door, however, they separated, he driving back to the Temple, and she to her own house. 'I shall drive out in the park at five as usual,' she said as she left him. I heard no more. They drove away in different directions, and I went off to make my own arrangements."

"Which are?"

"Some cold beef and a glass of beer," he answered, ringing the bell. "I have been too busy to think of food, and I am likely to be busier still this evening. By the way, Doctor, I shall want your co-operation."

"I shall be delighted."

"You don't mind breaking the law?"

"Not in the least."

"Nor running a chance of arrest?"

"Not in a good cause."

"Oh, the cause is excellent!"

"Then I am your man."

"I was sure that I might rely on you."

"But what is it you wish?"

"When Mrs. Turner has brought in the tray I will make it clear to you. Now," he said as he turned hungrily on the simple fare that our landlady had provided, "I must discuss it while I eat, for I have not much time. It is nearly five now. In two hours, we must be on the scene of action. Miss Irene, or Madame, rather, returns from her drive at seven. We must be at Briony Lodge to meet her."

"And what then?"

"You must leave that to me. I have already arranged what is to occur. There is only one point on which I must insist. You must not interfere, come what may. You understand?"

"I am to be neutral?"

"To do nothing whatever. There will probably be some small unpleasantness. Do not join in it. It will end in my being conveyed into the house. Four or five minutes afterwards the sitting-room window will open. You are to station yourself close to that open window."

"Yes."

"You are to watch me, for I will be visible to you."

"Yes."

"And when I raise my hand—so—you will throw into the room what I give you to throw, and will, at the same time, raise the cry of fire. You quite follow me?"

"Entirely."

"It is nothing very formidable," he said, taking a long cigar-shaped roll from his pocket. "It is an ordinary plumber's smoke-rocket, fitted with a cap at either end to make it self-lighting. Your task is confined to that. When you raise your cry of fire, it will be taken up by quite a number of people. You may then walk to the end of the street, and I will rejoin you in ten minutes. I hope that I have made myself clear?"

"I am to remain neutral, to get near the window, to watch you, and at the signal to throw in this object, then to raise the cry of fire, and to wait you at the corner of the street."

"Precisely."

"Then you may entirely rely on me."

"That is excellent. I think, perhaps, it is almost time that I prepare for the new role I have to play."

He disappeared into his bedroom and returned in a few minutes in the character of an amiable and simple-minded Nonconformist clergyman. His broad black hat, his baggy trousers, his white tie, his sympathetic smile, and general look of peering and benevolent curiosity were such as Mr. John Hare alone could have equalled. It was not merely that Holmes changed his costume. His expression, his manner, his very soul seemed to vary with every fresh part that he assumed. The stage lost a fine actor, even as science lost an acute reasoner, when he became a specialist in crime.

It was a quarter past six when we left Baker Street, and it still wanted ten minutes to the hour when we found ourselves in Serpentine Avenue. It was already dusk, and the lamps were just being lighted as we paced up and down in front of Briony Lodge, waiting for the coming of its occupant. The house was just such as I had pictured it from Sherlock Holmes' succinct description, but the locality appeared to be less private than I expected. On the contrary, for a small street in a quiet neighbourhood, it was remarkably animated. There was a group of shabbily dressed men smoking and laughing in a corner, a scissors-grinder with his wheel, two guardsmen who were flirting with a nurse-girl, and several well-dressed young men who were lounging up and down with cigars in their mouths.

"You see," remarked Holmes, as we paced to and fro in front of the house, "this marriage rather simplifies matters. The photograph becomes a double-edged weapon now. The chances are that she would be as averse to its being seen by Mr. Godfrey Norton, as our client is to its coming to the eyes of his princess. Now the question is, Where are we to find the photograph?"

"Where, indeed?"

"It is most unlikely that she carries it about with her. It is cabinet size. Too large for easy concealment about a woman's dress. She knows that the King is capable of having her waylaid and searched. Two attempts of the sort have already been made. We may take it, then, that she does not carry it about with her."

"Where, then?"

"Her banker or her lawyer. There is that double possibility. But I am inclined to think neither. Women are naturally secretive, and they like to do their own secreting. Why should she hand it over to anyone else? She could trust her own guardianship, but she could not tell what indirect or political influence might be brought to bear upon a businessman. Besides, remember that she had resolved to use it within a few days. It must be where she can lay her hands upon it. It must be in her own house."

"But it has twice been burgled."

"Pshaw! They did not know how to look."

"But how will you look?"

"I will not look."

"What then?"

"I will get her to show me."

"But she will refuse."

"She will not be able to. But I hear the rumble of wheels. It is her carriage. Now carry out my orders to the letter."

As he spoke the gleam of the sidelights of a carriage came round the curve of the avenue. It was a smart little landau which rattled up to the door of Briony Lodge. As it pulled up, one of the loafing men at the corner dashed forward to open the door in the hope of earning a copper, but was elbowed away by another loafer, who had rushed up with the same intention. A fierce quarrel broke out, which was increased by the two guardsmen, who took sides with one of the loungers, and by the scissors-grinder, who was equally hot upon the other side. A blow was struck, and in an instant the lady, who had stepped from her carriage, was the Centre of a little knot of flushed and struggling men, who struck savagely at each other with their fists and sticks. Holmes dashed into the crowd to protect the lady; but, just as he reached her, he gave a cry and dropped to the ground, with the blood running freely down his face. At his fall the guardsmen took to their heels in one direction and the loungers in the other, while a number of better dressed people, who had watched the scuffle without taking part in it, crowded in to help the lady and to attend to the injured man. Irene Adler, as I will still call her, had hurried up the steps; but she stood at the top with her superb figure outlined against the lights of the hall, looking back into the street.

"Is the poor gentleman much hurt?" she asked.

"He is dead," cried several voices.

"No, no, there's life in him!" shouted another. "But he'll be gone before you can get him to hospital."

"He's a brave fellow," said a woman. "They would have had the lady's purse and watch if it hadn't been for him. They were a gang, and a rough one, too. Ah, he's breathing now."

"He can't lie in the street. May we bring him in, marm?"

"Surely. Bring him into the sitting-room. There is a comfortable sofa. This way, please!"

Slowly and solemnly, he was borne into Briony Lodge and laid out in the principal room, while I still observed the proceedings from my post by the window. The lamps had been lit, but the blinds had not been drawn, so that I could see Holmes as he lay upon the couch. I do not know whether he was seized with compunction at that moment for the part he was playing, but I know that I never felt more heartily ashamed of myself in my life than when I saw the beautiful creature against whom I was conspiring, or the grace and kindliness with which she waited upon the injured man. And yet it would be the blackest treachery to Holmes to draw back now from the part which he had in trusted to me. I hardened my heart and took the smoke-rocket from under my ulster. After all, I thought, we are not injuring her. We are but preventing her from injuring another.

Holmes had sat up upon the couch, and I saw him motion like a man who is in need of air. A maid rushed across and threw open the window. At the same instant I saw him raise his hand and at the signal I tossed my rocket into the room with a cry of "Fire!" The word was no sooner out of my mouth than the whole crowd of spectators, well dressed and ill—gentlemen, ostlers, and servant maids—joined in a general shriek of "Fire!" Thick clouds of smoke curled through the room and out at the open window. I caught a glimpse of rushing figures, and a moment later the voice of Holmes from within assuring them that it was a false alarm. Slipping through the shouting crowd I made my way to the corner of the street, and in ten minutes was rejoiced to find my friend's arm in mine, and to get away from the scene of uproar. He walked swiftly and in silence for some few minutes until we had turned down one of the quiet streets which lead towards the Edgeware Road.

"You did it very nicely, Doctor," he remarked. "Nothing could have been better. It is all right."

"You have the photograph?"

"I know where it is."

"And how did you find out?"

"She showed me, as I told you she would."

"I am still in the dark."

"I do not wish to make a mystery," said he, laughing. "The matter was perfectly simple. You, of course, saw that everyone in the street was an accomplice. They were all engaged for the evening."

"I guessed as much."

"Then, when the row broke out, I had a little moist red paint in the palm of my hand. I rushed forward, fell down, clapped my hand to my face, and became a piteous spectacle. It is an old trick."

"That also I could fathom."

"Then they carried me in. She was bound to have me in. What else could she do? And into her sitting-room, which was the very room which I suspected. It lay between that and her bedroom, and I was determined to see which. They laid me on a couch, I motioned for air, they were compelled to open the window, and you had your chance."

"How did that help you?"

"It was all-important. When a woman thinks that her house is on fire, her instinct is at once to rush to the thing which she values most. It is a perfectly overpowering impulse, and I have more than once taken advantage of it. In the case of the Darlington Substitution Scandal, it was of use to me, and also in the Arnsworth Castle business. A married woman grabs at her baby; an unmarried one reaches for her jewel-box. Now it was clear to me that our lady of Today had nothing in the house more precious to her than what we are in quest of. She would rush to secure it. The alarm of fire was admirably done. The smoke and shouting were enough to shake nerves of steel. She responded beautifully. The photograph is in a recess behind a sliding panel just above the right bell-pull. She was there in an instant, and I caught a glimpse of it as she half drew it out. When I cried out that it was a false alarm, she replaced it, glanced at the rocket, rushed from the room, and I have not seen her since. I rose, and, making my excuses, escaped from the house. I hesitated whether to attempt to secure the photograph at once; but the coachman had come in, and as he was watching me narrowly, it seemed safer to wait. A little over-precipitance may ruin all."

"And now?" I asked.

"Our quest is practically finished. I shall call with the King tomorrow, and with you, if you care to come with us. We will be shown into the sitting-room to wait for the lady, but it is probable that when she comes she may find neither us nor the photograph. It might be a satisfaction to his Majesty to regain it with his own hands."

"And when will you call?"

"At eight in the morning. She will not be up, so that we shall have a clear field. Besides, we must be prompt, for this marriage may mean a complete change in her life and habits. I must wire to the King without delay."

We had reached Baker Street and had stopped at the door. He was searching his pockets for the key when someone passing said:

"Good-night, Mister Sherlock Holmes."

There were several people on the pavement at the time, but the greeting appeared to come from a slim youth in an ulster who had hurried by.

"I've heard that voice before," said Holmes, staring down the dimly lit street. "Now, I wonder who the deuce that could have been."

III.

I slept at Baker Street that night, and we were engaged upon our toast and coffee in the morning when the King of Bohemia rushed into the room.

"You have really got it!" he cried, grasping Sherlock Holmes by either shoulder and looking eagerly into his face.

"Not yet."

"But you have hopes?"

"I have hopes."

"Then, come. I am all impatience to be gone."

"We must have a cab."

"No, my brougham is waiting."

"Then that will simplify matters." We descended and started off once more for Briony Lodge.

"Irene Adler is married," remarked Holmes.

"Married! When?"

"Yesterday."

"But to whom?"

"To an English lawyer named Norton."

"But she could not love him."

"I am in hopes that she does."

"And why in hopes?"

"Because it would spare your Majesty all fear of future annoyance. If the lady loves her husband, she does not love your Majesty. If she does not love your Majesty, there is no reason why she should interfere with your Majesty's plan."

"It is true. And yet—! Well! I wish she had been of my own station! What a queen she would have made!" He relapsed into a moody silence, which was not broken until we drew up in Serpentine Avenue.

The door of Briony Lodge was open, and an elderly woman stood upon the steps. She watched us with a sardonic eye as we stepped from the brougham.

"Mr. Sherlock Holmes, I believe?" said she.

"I am Mr. Holmes," answered my companion, looking at her with a questioning and rather startled gaze.

"Indeed! My mistress told me that you were likely to call. She left this morning with her husband by the 5:15 train from Charing Cross for the Continent."

"What!" Sherlock Holmes staggered back, white with chagrin and surprise. "Do you mean that she has left England?"

"Never to return."

"And the papers?" asked the King hoarsely. "All is lost."

"We shall see." He pushed past the servant and rushed into the drawing-room, followed by the King and myself. The furniture was scattered about in every direction, with dismantled shelves and open drawers, as if the lady had hurriedly ransacked them before her flight. Holmes rushed at the bell-pull, tore back a small sliding shutter, and, plunging in his hand, pulled out a photograph and a letter. The photograph was of Irene Adler herself in evening dress, the letter was superscribed to "Sherlock Holmes, Esq. To be left till called for." My friend tore it open, and we all three read it together. It was dated at midnight of the preceding night and ran in this way:

"MY DEAR MR. SHERLOCK HOLMES,—You really did it very well. You took me in completely. Until after the alarm of fire, I had not a suspicion. But then, when I found how I had betrayed myself, I began to think. I had been warned against you months ago. I had been told that, if the King employed an agent, it would certainly be you. And your address had been given me. Yet, with all this, you made me reveal what you wanted to know. Even after I became suspicious, I found it hard to think evil of such a dear, kind old clergyman. But, you know, I have been trained as an actress myself. Male costume is nothing new to me. I often take advantage of the freedom which it gives. I sent John, the coachman, to watch you, ran upstairs, got into my walking clothes, as I call them, and came down just as you departed.

"Well, I followed you to your door, and so made sure that I was really an object of interest to the celebrated Mr. Sherlock Holmes. Then I, rather imprudently, wished you good-night, and started for the Temple to see my husband.

"We both thought the best resource was flight, when pursued by so formidable an antagonist; so you will find the nest empty when you call tomorrow. As to the photograph, your client may rest in peace. I love and am loved by a better man than he. The King may do what he will without hindrance from one whom he has cruelly wronged. I keep it only to safeguard myself, and to preserve a weapon which will always secure me from any steps which he might take in the future. I leave a photograph which he might care to possess; and I remain, dear Mr. Sherlock Holmes,

"Very truly yours,
"IRENE NORTON, née ADLER."

"What a woman—oh, what a woman!" cried the King of Bohemia, when we had all three read this epistle. "Did I not tell you how quick and resolute she was? Would she not have made an admirable queen? Is it not a pity that she was not on my level?"

"From what I have seen of the lady, she seems, indeed, to be on a very different level to your Majesty," said Holmes coldly. "I am sorry that I have not been able to bring your Majesty's business to a more successful conclusion."

"On the contrary, my dear sir," cried the King; "nothing could be more successful. I know that her word is inviolate. The photograph is now as safe as if it were in the fire."

"I am glad to hear your Majesty say so."

"I am immensely indebted to you. Pray tell me in what way I can reward you. This ring—" He slipped an emerald snake ring from his finger and held it out upon the palm of his hand.

"Your Majesty has something which I should value even more highly," said Holmes.

"You have but to name it."

"This photograph!"

The King stared at him in amazement.

"Irene's photograph!" he cried. "Certainly, if you wish it."

"I thank your Majesty. Then there is no more to be done in the matter. I have the honour to wish you a very good morning." He bowed, and, turning away without observing the hand which the King had stretched out to him, he set off in my company for his chambers.

And that was how a great scandal threatened to affect the kingdom of Bohemia, and how the best plans of Mr. Sherlock Holmes were beaten by a woman's wit. He used to make merry over the cleverness of women, but I have not heard him do it of late. And when he speaks of Irene Adler, or when he refers to her photograph, it is always under the honourable title of the woman.

THE FIVE ORANGE PIPS

When I glance over my notes and records of the Sherlock Holmes cases between the years '82 and '90, I am faced by so many which present strange and interesting features that it is no easy matter to know which to choose and which to leave. Some, however, have already gained publicity through the papers, and others have not offered a field for those peculiar qualities which my friend possessed in so high a degree, and which it is the object of these papers to illustrate. Some, too, have baffled his analytical skill, and would be, as narratives, beginnings without an ending, while others have been but partially cleared up, and have their explanations founded rather upon conjecture and surmise than on that absolute logical proof which was so dear to him. There is, however, one of these last which was so remarkable in its details and so startling in its results that I am tempted to give some account of it in spite of the fact that there are points in connection with it which never have been and probably never will be, entirely cleared up.

The year '87 furnished us with a long series of cases of greater or less interest, of which I retain the records. Among my headings under this one twelve months, I find an account of the adventure of the Paradol Chamber, of the Amateur Mendicant Society, who held a luxurious club in the lower vault of a furniture warehouse, of the facts connected with the loss of the British barque *Sophy Anderson*, of the singular adventures of the Grice Patersons in the island of Uffa and finally of the Camberwell poisoning case. In the latter, as may be remembered, Sherlock Holmes was able, by winding up the dead man's watch, to prove that it had been wound up two hours before, and that therefore the deceased had gone to bed within that time—a deduction which was of the greatest importance in clearing up the case. All these I may sketch out at some future date, but none of them present such singular features as the strange train of circumstances which I have now taken up my pen to describe.

It was in the latter days of September, and the equinoctial gales had set in with exceptional violence. All day the wind had screamed, and the rain had beaten against the windows, so that even here in the heart of great, hand-made London we were forced to raise our minds for the instant from the routine of life and to recognise the presence of those great elemental forces which shriek at mankind through the bars of his civilisation, like untamed beasts in a cage. As evening drew in, the storm grew higher and louder, and the wind cried and sobbed like a child in the chimney. Sherlock Holmes sat moodily at one side of the fireplace cross-indexing his records of crime, while I at the other was deep in one of Clark Russell's fine sea-stories until the howl of the gale from without seemed to blend with the text, and the splash of the rain to lengthen out into the long swash of the sea waves. My wife was on a visit to her mother's, and for a few days I was a dweller once more in my old quarters at Baker Street.

"Why," said I, glancing up at my companion, "that was surely the bell. Who could come tonight? Some friend of yours, perhaps?"

"Except yourself I have none," he answered. "I do not encourage visitors."

"A client, then?"

"If so, it is a serious case. Nothing less would bring a man out on such a day and at such an hour. But I take it that it is more likely to be some crony of the landlady's."

Sherlock Holmes was wrong in his conjecture, however, for there came a step in the passage and a tapping at the door. He stretched out his long arm to turn the lamp away from himself and towards the vacant chair upon which a newcomer must sit.

"Come in!" said he.

The man who entered was young, some two-and-twenty at the outside, well-groomed and trimly clad, with something of refinement and delicacy in his bearing. The streaming umbrella which he held in his hand, and his long shining waterproof told of the fierce weather through which he had come. He looked about him anxiously in the glare of the lamp, and I could see that his face was pale and his eyes heavy, like those of a man who is weighed down with some great anxiety.

"I owe you an apology," he said, raising his golden pince-nez to his eyes. "I trust that I am not intruding. I fear that I have brought some traces of the storm and rain into your snug chamber."

"Give me your coat and umbrella," said Holmes. "They may rest here on the hook and will be dry presently. You have come up from the south-west, I see."

"Yes, from Horsham."

"That clay and chalk mixture which I see upon your toe caps is quite distinctive."

"I have come for advice."

"That is easily got."

"And help."

"That is not always so easy."

"I have heard of you, Mr. Holmes. I heard from Major Prendergast how you saved him in the Tankerville Club scandal."

"Ah, of course. He was wrongfully accused of cheating at cards."

"He said that you could solve anything."

"He said too much."

"That you are never beaten."

"I have been beaten four times—three times by men, and once by a woman."

"But what is that compared with the number of your successes?"

"It is true that I have been generally successful."

"Then you may be so with me."

"I beg that you will draw your chair up to the fire and favour me with some details as to your case."

"It is no ordinary one."

"None of those which come to me are. I am the last court of appeal."

"And yet I question, sir, whether, in all your experience, you have ever listened to a more mysterious and inexplicable chain of events than those which have happened in my own family."

"You fill me with interest," said Holmes. "Pray give us the essential facts from the commencement, and I can afterwards question you as to those details which seem to me to be most important."

The young man pulled his chair up and pushed his wet feet out towards the blaze.

"My name," said he, "is John Openshaw, but my own affairs have, as far as I can understand, little to do with this awful business. It is a hereditary matter; so in order to give you an idea of the facts, I must go back to the commencement of the affair.

"You must know that my grandfather had two sons—my uncle Elias and my father Joseph. My father had a small factory at Coventry, which he enlarged at the time of the invention of bicycling. He was a patentee of the Openshaw unbreakable tire, and his business met with such success that he was able to sell it and to retire upon a handsome competence.

"My uncle Elias emigrated to America when he was a young man and became a planter in Florida, where he was reported to have done very well. At the time of the war, he fought in Jackson's army, and afterwards under Hood, where he rose to be a colonel. When Lee laid down his arms my uncle returned to his plantation, where he remained for three or four years. About 1869 or 1870 he came back to Europe and took a small estate in Sussex, near Horsham. He had made a very considerable fortune in the States, and his reason for leaving them was his aversion to the negroes, and his dislike of the Republican policy in extending the franchise to them. He was a singular man, fierce and quick-tempered, very foul-mouthed when he was angry, and of a most retiring disposition. During all the years that he lived at Horsham, I doubt if ever he set foot in the town. He had a garden and two or three fields round his house, and there he would take his exercise, though very often for weeks on end he would never leave his room. He drank a great deal of brandy and smoked very heavily, but he would see no society and did not want any friends, not even his own brother.

"He didn't mind me; in fact, he took a fancy to me, for at the time when he saw me first I was a youngster of twelve or so. This would be in the year 1878, after he had been eight or nine years in England. He begged my father to let me live with him and he was very kind to me in his way. When he was sober he used to be fond of playing backgammon and draughts with me, and he would make me his representative both with the servants and with the tradespeople, so that by the time that I was sixteen I was quite master of the house. I kept all the keys and could go where I liked and do what I liked, so long as I did not disturb him in his privacy. There was one singular exception, however, for he had a single room, a lumber-room up among the attics, which was invariably locked, and which he would never permit either me or anyone else to enter. With a boy's curiosity I have peeped through the keyhole, but I was never able to see more than such a collection of old trunks and bundles as would be expected in such a room.

"One day—it was in March 1883—a letter with a foreign stamp lay upon the table in front of the colonel's plate. It was not a common thing for him to receive letters, for his bills were all paid in ready money, and he had no friends of any sort. 'From India!' said he as he took it up, 'Pondicherry postmark! What can this be?' Opening it hurriedly, out there jumped five little dried orange pips, which pattered down upon his plate. I began to laugh at this, but the laugh was struck from my lips at the sight of his face. His lip had fallen, his eyes were protruding, his skin the colour of putty, and he glared at the envelope which he still held in his trembling hand, 'K. K. K.!' he shrieked, and then, 'My God, my God, my sins have overtaken me!'

"'What is it, uncle?' I cried.

"'Death,' said he, and rising from the table he retired to his room, leaving me palpitating with horror. I took up the envelope and saw scrawled in red ink upon the inner flap, just above the gum, the letter K three times repeated. There was nothing else save the five dried pips. What could be the reason of his overpowering terror? I left the breakfast-table, and as I ascended the stair I met him coming down with an old rusty key, which must have belonged to the attic, in one hand, and a small brass box, like a cashbox, in the other.

"'They may do what they like, but I'll checkmate them still,' said he with an oath. 'Tell Mary that I shall want a fire in my room Today, and send down to Fordham, the Horsham lawyer.'

"I did as he ordered, and when the lawyer arrived I was asked to step up to the room. The fire was burning brightly, and in the grate there was a mass of black, fluffy ashes, as of burned paper, while the brass box stood open and empty beside it. As I glanced at the box I noticed, with a start, that upon the lid was printed the treble K which I had read in the morning upon the envelope.

"'I wish you, John,' said my uncle, 'to witness my will. I leave my estate, with all its advantages and all its disadvantages, to my brother, your father, whence it will, no doubt, descend to you. If you can enjoy it in peace, well and good! If you find you cannot, take my advice, my boy, and leave it to your deadliest enemy. I am sorry to give you such a two-edged thing, but I can't say what turn things are going to take. Kindly sign the paper where Mr. Fordham shows you.'

"I signed the paper as directed, and the lawyer took it away with him. The singular incident made, as you may think, the deepest impression upon me, and I pondered over it and turned it every way in my mind without being able to make anything of it. Yet I could not shake off the vague feeling of dread which it left behind, though the sensation grew less keen as the weeks passed and nothing happened to disturb the usual routine of our lives. I could see a change in my uncle, however. He drank more than ever, and he was less inclined for any sort of society. Most of his time he would spend in his room, with the door locked upon the inside, but sometimes he would emerge in a sort of drunken frenzy and would burst out of the house and tear about the garden with a revolver in his hand, screaming out that he was afraid of no man, and that he was not to be cooped up, like a sheep in a pen, by man or devil. When these hot fits were over, however, he would rush tumultuously in at the door and lock and bar it behind him, like a man who can brazen it out no longer against the terror which lies at the roots of his soul. At such times I have seen his face, even on a cold day, glisten with moisture, as though it were new raised from a basin.

"Well, to come to an end of the matter, Mr. Holmes, and not to abuse your patience, there came a night when he made one of those drunken sallies from which he never came back. We found him, when we went to search for him, face downward in a little, green-scummed pool, which lay at the foot of the garden. There was no sign of any violence, and the water was but two feet deep, so that the jury, having regard to his known eccentricity, brought in a verdict of 'suicide.' But I, who knew how he winced from the very thought of death, had much ado to persuade myself that he had gone out of his way to meet it. The matter passed, however, and my father entered into possession of the estate, and of some £ 14,000, which lay to his credit at the bank."

"One moment," Holmes interposed, "your statement is, I foresee, one of the most remarkable to which I have ever listened. Let me have the date of the reception by your uncle of the letter, and the date of his supposed suicide."

"The letter arrived on March 10, 1883. His death was seven weeks later, upon the night of May 2nd."

"Thank you. Pray proceed."

"When my father took over the Horsham property, he, at my request, made a careful examination of the attic, which had been always locked up. We found the brass box there, although its contents had been destroyed. On the inside of the cover was a paper label, with the initials of K. K. K. repeated upon it, and 'Letters, memoranda, receipts, and a register' written beneath. These, we presume, indicated the nature of the papers which had been destroyed by Colonel Openshaw. For the rest, there was nothing of much importance in the attic save a great many scattered papers and note-books bearing upon my uncle's life in America. Some of them were of the war time and showed that he had done his duty well and had borne the repute of a brave soldier. Others were of a date during the reconstruction of the Southern states, and were mostly concerned with politics, for he had evidently taken a strong part in opposing the carpet-bag politicians who had been sent down from the North.

"Well, it was the beginning of '84 when my father came to live at Horsham, and all went as well as possible with us until the January of '85. On the fourth day after the new year, I heard my father give a sharp cry of surprise as we sat together at the breakfast-table. There he was, sitting with a newly opened envelope in one hand and five dried orange pips in the outstretched palm of the other one. He had always laughed at what he called my cock-and-bull story about the colonel, but he looked very scared and puzzled now that the same thing had come upon himself.

"'Why, what on earth does this mean, John?' he stammered.

"My heart had turned to lead. 'It is K. K. K.,' said I.

"He looked inside the envelope. 'So it is,' he cried. 'Here are the very letters. But what is this written above them?'

"'Put the papers on the sundial,' I read, peeping over his shoulder.

"'What papers? What sundial?' he asked.

"'The sundial in the garden. There is no other,' said I; 'but the papers must be those that are destroyed.'

"'Pooh!' said he, gripping hard at his courage. 'We are in a civilised land here, and we can't have tomfoolery of this kind. Where does the thing come from?'

"'From Dundee,' I answered, glancing at the postmark.

"'Some preposterous practical joke,' said he. 'What have I to do with sundials and papers? I shall take no notice of such nonsense.'

"'I should certainly speak to the police,' I said.

"'And be laughed at for my pains. Nothing of the sort.'

"'Then let me do so?'

"'No, I forbid you. I won't have a fuss made about such nonsense.'

"It was in vain to argue with him, for he was a very obstinate man. I went about, however, with a heart which was full of forebodings.

"On the third day after the coming of the letter my father went from home to visit an old friend of his, Major Freebody, who is in command of one of the forts upon Portsdown Hill. I was glad that he should go, for it seemed to me that he was farther from danger when he was away from home. In that, however, I was in error. Upon the second day of his absence, I received a telegram from the major, imploring me to come at once. My father had fallen over one of the deep chalk-pits which abound in the neighbourhood, and was lying senseless, with a shattered skull. I hurried to him, but he passed away without having ever recovered his consciousness. He had, as it appears, been returning from Fareham in the twilight, and as the country was unknown to him, and the chalk-pit unfenced, the jury had no hesitation in bringing in a verdict of 'death from accidental causes.' Carefully as I examined every fact connected with his death, I was unable to find anything which could suggest the idea of murder. There were no signs of violence, no footmarks, no robbery, no record of strangers having been seen upon the roads. And yet I need not tell you that my mind was far from at ease, and that I was well-nigh certain that some foul plot had been woven round him.

"In this sinister way I came into my inheritance. You will ask me why I did not dispose of it? I answer, because I was well convinced that our troubles were in some way dependent upon an incident in my uncle's life, and that the danger would be as pressing in one house as in another.

"It was in January, '85, that my poor father met his end, and two years and eight months have elapsed since then. During that time, I have lived happily at Horsham, and I had begun to hope that this curse had passed away from the family, and that it had ended with the last generation. I had begun to take comfort too soon, however; yesterday morning the blow fell in the very shape in which it had come upon my father."

The young man took from his waistcoat a crumpled envelope, and turning to the table he shook out upon it five little dried orange pips.

"This is the envelope," he continued. "The postmark is London—eastern division. Within are the very words which were upon my father's last message: 'K. K. K.'; and then 'Put the papers on the sundial.'"

"What have you done?" asked Holmes.

"Nothing."

"Nothing?"

"To tell the truth"—he sank his face into his thin, white hands—"I have felt helpless. I have felt like one of those poor rabbits when the snake is writhing towards it. I seem to be in the grasp of some resistless, inexorable evil, which no foresight and no precautions can guard against."

"Tut! tut!" cried Sherlock Holmes. "You must act, man, or you are lost. Nothing but energy can save you. This is no time for despair."

"I have seen the police."

"Ah!"

"But they listened to my story with a smile. I am convinced that the inspector has formed the opinion that the letters are all practical jokes, and that the deaths of my relations were really accidents, as the jury stated, and were not to be connected with the warnings."

Holmes shook his clenched hands in the air. "Incredible imbecility!" he cried.

"They have, however, allowed me a policeman, who may remain in the house with me."

"Has he come with you tonight?"

"No. His orders were to stay in the house."

Again, Holmes raved in the air.

"Why did you come to me?" he said, "and, above all, why did you not come at once?"

"I did not know. It was only Today that I spoke to Major Prendergast about my troubles and was advised by him to come to you."

"It is really two days since you had the letter. We should have acted before this. You have no further evidence, I suppose, than that which you have placed before us—no suggestive detail which might help us?"

"There is one thing," said John Openshaw. He rummaged in his coat pocket, and, drawing out a piece of discoloured, blue-tinted paper, he laid it out upon the table. "I have some remembrance," said he, "that on the day when my uncle burned the papers I observed that the small, unburned margins which lay amid the ashes were of this particular colour. I found this single sheet upon the floor of his room, and I am inclined to think that it may be one of the papers which has, perhaps, fluttered out from among the others, and in that way has escaped destruction. Beyond the mention of pips, I do not see that it helps us much. I think myself that it is a page from some private diary. The writing is undoubtedly my uncle's."

Holmes moved the lamp, and we both bent over the sheet of paper, which showed by its ragged edge that it had indeed been torn from a book. It was headed, "March 1869," and beneath were the following enigmatical notices:

"4th. Hudson came. Same old platform.

"7th. Set the pips on McCauley, Paramore, and John Swain of St. Augustine.

"9th. McCauley cleared.

"10th. John Swain cleared.

"12th. Visited Paramore. All well."

"Thank you!" said Holmes, folding up the paper and returning it to our visitor. "And now you must on no account lose another instant. We cannot spare time even to discuss what you have told me. You must get home instantly and act."

"What shall I do?"

"There is but one thing to do. It must be done at once. You must put this piece of paper which you have shown us into the brass box which you have described. You must also put in a note to say that all the other papers were burned by your uncle, and that this is the only one which remains. You must assert that in such words as will carry conviction with them. Having done this, you must at once put the box out upon the sundial, as directed. Do you understand?"

"Entirely."

"Do not think of revenge, or anything of the sort, at present. I think that we may gain that by means of the law; but we have our web to weave, while theirs is already woven. The first consideration is to remove the pressing danger which threatens you. The second is to clear up the mystery and to punish the guilty parties."

"I thank you," said the young man, rising and pulling on his overcoat. "You have given me fresh life and hope. I shall certainly do as you advise."

"Do not lose an instant. And, above all, take care of yourself in the meanwhile, for I do not think that there can be a doubt that you are threatened by a very real and imminent danger. How do you go back?"

"By train from Waterloo."

"It is not yet nine. The streets will be crowded, so I trust that you may be in safety. And yet you cannot guard yourself too closely."

"I am armed."

"That is well. Tomorrow I shall set to work upon your case."

"I shall see you at Horsham, then?"

"No, your secret lies in London. It is there that I shall seek it."

"Then I shall call upon you in a day, or in two days, with news as to the box and the papers. I shall take your advice in every particular."

He shook hands with us and took his leave. Outside the wind still screamed and the rain splashed and pattered against the windows. This strange, wild story seemed to have come to us from amid the mad elements—blown in upon us like a sheet of sea-weed in a gale—and now to have been reabsorbed by them once more.

Sherlock Holmes sat for some time in silence, with his head sunk forward and his eyes bent upon the red glow of the fire. Then he lit his pipe, and leaning back in his chair he watched the blue smoke-rings as they chased each other up to the ceiling.

"I think, Watson," he remarked at last, "that of all our cases we have had none more fantastic than this."

"Save, perhaps, the Sign of Four."

"Well, yes. Save, perhaps, that. And yet this John Openshaw seems to me to be walking amid even greater perils than did the Sholtos."

"But have you," I asked, "formed any definite conception as to what these perils are?"

"There can be no question as to their nature," he answered.

"Then what are they? Who is this K. K. K., and why does he pursue this unhappy family?"

Sherlock Holmes closed his eyes and placed his elbows upon the arms of his chair, with his finger-tips together. "The ideal reasoner," he remarked, "would, when he had once been shown a single fact in all its bearings, deduce from it not only all the chain of events which led up to it but also all the results which would follow from it. As Cuvier could correctly describe a whole animal by the contemplation of a single bone, so the observer who has thoroughly understood one link in a series of incidents should be able to accurately state all the other ones, both before and after. We have not yet grasped the results which the reason alone can attain to. Problems may be solved in the study which have baffled all those who have sought a solution by the aid of their senses. To carry the art, however, to its highest pitch, it is necessary that the reasoner should be able to utilise all the facts which have come to his knowledge; and this in itself implies, as you will readily see, a possession of all knowledge, which, even in these days of free education and encyclopædias, is a somewhat rare accomplishment. It is not so impossible, however, that a man should possess all knowledge which is likely to be useful to him in his work, and this I have endeavoured in my case to do. If I remember rightly, you on one occasion, in the early days of our friendship, defined my limits in a very precise fashion."

"Yes," I answered, laughing. "It was a singular document. Philosophy, astronomy, and politics were marked at zero, I remember. Botany variable, geology profound as regards the mud-stains from any region within fifty miles of town, chemistry eccentric, anatomy unsystematic, sensational literature and crime records unique, violin-player, boxer, swordsman, lawyer, and self-poisoner by cocaine and tobacco. Those, I think, were the main points of my analysis."

Holmes grinned at the last item. "Well," he said, "I say now, as I said then, that a man should keep his little brain-attic stocked with all the furniture that he is likely to use, and the rest he can put away in the lumber-room of his library, where he can get it if he wants it. Now, for such a case as the one which has been submitted to us tonight, we need certainly to muster all our resources. Kindly hand me down the letter K of the *American Encyclopædia* which stands upon the shelf beside you. Thank you. Now let us consider the situation and see what may be deduced from it. In the first place, we may start with a strong presumption that Colonel Openshaw had some very strong reason for leaving America. Men at his time of life do not change all their habits and exchange willingly the charming climate of Florida for the lonely life of an English provincial town. His extreme love of solitude in England suggests the idea that he was in fear of someone or something, so we may assume as a working hypothesis that it was fear of someone or something which drove him from America. As to what it was he feared, we can only deduce that by considering the formidable letters which were received by himself and his successors. Did you remark the postmarks of those letters?"

"The first was from Pondicherry, the second from Dundee, and the third from London."

"From East London. What do you deduce from that?"

"They are all seaports. That the writer was on board of a ship."

"Excellent. We have already a clue. There can be no doubt that the probability—the strong probability—is that the writer was on board of a ship. And now let us consider another point. In the case of Pondicherry, seven weeks elapsed between the threat and its fulfilment, in Dundee it was only some three or four days. Does that suggest anything?"

"A greater distance to travel."

"But the letter had also a greater distance to come."

"Then I do not see the point."

"There is at least a presumption that the vessel in which the man or men are a sailing-ship. It looks as if they always send their singular warning or token before them when starting upon their mission. You see how quickly the deed followed the sign when it came from Dundee. If they had come from Pondicherry in a steamer they would have arrived almost as soon as their letter. But, as a matter of fact, seven weeks elapsed. I think that those seven weeks represented the difference between the mail-boat which brought the letter and the sailing vessel which brought the writer."

"It is possible."

"More than that. It is probable. And now you see the deadly urgency of this new case, and why I urged young Openshaw to caution. The blow has always fallen at the end of the time which it would take the senders to travel the distance. But this one comes from London, and therefore we cannot count upon delay."

"Good God!" I cried. "What can it mean, this relentless persecution?"

"The papers which Openshaw carried are obviously of vital importance to the person or persons in the sailing-ship. I think that it is quite clear that there must be more than one of them. A single man could not have carried out two deaths in such a way as to deceive a coroner's jury. There must have been several in it, and they must have been men of resource and determination. Their papers they mean to have, be the holder of them who it may. In this way you see K. K. K. ceases to be the initials of an individual and becomes the badge of a society."

"But of what society?"

"Have you never—" said Sherlock Holmes, bending forward and sinking his voice—"have you never heard of the Ku Klux Klan?"

"I never have."

Holmes turned over the leaves of the book upon his knee. "Here it is," said he presently:

"'Ku Klux Klan. A name derived from the fanciful resemblance to the sound produced by cocking a rifle. This terrible secret society was formed by some ex-Confederate soldiers in the Southern states after the Civil War, and it rapidly formed local branches in different parts of the country, notably in Tennessee, Louisiana, the Carolinas, Georgia, and Florida. Its power was used for political purposes, principally for the terrorising of the negro voters and the murdering and driving from the country of those who were opposed to its views. Its outrages were usually preceded by a warning sent to the marked man in some fantastic but generally recognised shape—a sprig of oak-leaves in some parts, melon seeds or orange pips in others. On receiving this the victim might either openly abjure his former ways or might fly from the country. If he braved the matter out, death would unfailingly come upon him, and usually in some strange and unforeseen manner. So perfect was the organisation of the society, and so systematic its methods, that there is hardly a case upon record where any man succeeded in braving it with impunity, or in which any of its outrages were traced home to the perpetrators. For some years the organisation flourished in spite of the efforts of the United States government and of the better classes of the community in the South. Eventually, in the year 1869, the movement rather suddenly collapsed, although there have been sporadic outbreaks of the same sort since that date.'

"You will observe," said Holmes, laying down the volume, "that the sudden breaking up of the society was coincident with the disappearance of Openshaw from America with their papers. It may well have been cause and effect. It is no wonder that he and his family have some of the more implacable spirits upon their track. You can understand that this register and diary may implicate some of the first men in the South, and that there may be many who will not sleep easy at night until it is recovered."

"Then the page we have seen—"

"Is such as we might expect. It ran, if I remember right, 'sent the pips to A, B, and C'—that is, sent the society's warning to them. Then there are successive entries that A and B cleared, or left the country, and finally that C was visited, with, I fear, a sinister result for C. Well, I think, Doctor, that we may let some light into this dark place, and I believe that the only chance young Openshaw has in the meantime is to do what I have told him. There is nothing more to be said or to be done tonight, so hand me over my violin and let us try to forget for half an hour the miserable weather and the still more miserable ways of our fellow men."

It had cleared in the morning, and the sun was shining with a subdued brightness through the dim veil which hangs over the great city. Sherlock Holmes was already at breakfast when I came down.

"You will excuse me for not waiting for you," said he; "I have, I foresee, a very busy day before me in looking into this case of young Openshaw's."

"What steps will you take?" I asked.

"It will very much depend upon the results of my first inquiries. I may have to go down to Horsham, after all."

"You will not go there first?"

"No, I shall commence with the City. Just ring the bell and the maid will bring up your coffee."

As I waited, I lifted the unopened newspaper from the table and glanced my eye over it. It rested upon a heading which sent a chill to my heart.

"Holmes," I cried, "you are too late."

"Ah!" said he, laying down his cup, "I feared as much. How was it done?" He spoke calmly, but I could see that he was deeply moved.

"My eye caught the name of Openshaw, and the heading 'Tragedy Near Waterloo Bridge.' Here is the account:

"'Between nine and ten last night Police-Constable Cook, of the H Division, on duty near Waterloo Bridge, heard a cry for help and a splash in the water. The night, however, was extremely dark and stormy, so that, in spite of the help of several passers-by, it was quite impossible to effect a rescue. The alarm, however, was given, and, by the aid of the water-police, the body was eventually recovered. It proved to be that of a young gentleman whose name, as it appears from an envelope which was found in his pocket, was John Openshaw, and whose residence is near Horsham. It is conjectured that he may have been hurrying down to catch the last train from Waterloo Station, and that in his haste and the extreme darkness he missed his path and walked over the edge of one of the small landing-places for river steamboats. The body exhibited no traces of violence, and there can be no doubt that the deceased had been the victim of an unfortunate accident, which should have the effect of calling the attention of the authorities to the condition of the riverside landing-stages.'"

We sat in silence for some minutes, Holmes more depressed and shaken than I had ever seen him.

"That hurts my pride, Watson," he said at last. "It is a petty feeling, no doubt, but it hurts my pride. It becomes a personal matter with me now, and, if God sends me health, I shall set my hand upon this gang. That he should come to me for help, and that I should send him away to his death—!" He sprang from his chair and paced about the room in uncontrollable agitation, with a flush upon his sallow cheeks and a nervous clasping and unclasping of his long thin hands.

"They must be cunning devils," he exclaimed at last. "How could they have decoyed him down there? The Embankment is not on the direct line to the station. The bridge, no doubt, was too crowded, even on such a night, for their purpose. Well, Watson, we shall see who will win in the long run. I am going out now!"

"To the police?"

"No; I shall be my own police. When I have spun the web they may take the flies, but not before."

All day I was engaged in my professional work, and it was late in the evening before I returned to Baker Street. Sherlock Holmes had not come back yet. It was nearly ten o'clock before he entered, looking pale and worn. He walked up to the sideboard, and tearing a piece from the loaf he devoured it voraciously, washing it down with a long draught of water.

"You are hungry," I remarked.

"Starving. It had escaped my memory. I have had nothing since breakfast."

"Nothing?"

"Not a bite. I had no time to think of it."

"And how have you succeeded?"

"Well."

"You have a clue?"

"I have them in the hollow of my hand. Young Openshaw shall not long remain unavenged. Why, Watson, let us put their own devilish trade-mark upon them. It is well thought of!"

"What do you mean?"

He took an orange from the cupboard and tearing it to pieces he squeezed out the pips upon the table. Of these he took five and thrust them into an envelope. On the inside of the flap, he wrote "S. H. for J. O." Then he sealed it and addressed it to "Captain James Calhoun, Barque *Lone Star*, Savannah, Georgia."

“That will await him when he enters port,” said he, chuckling. “It may give him a sleepless night. He will find it as sure a precursor of his fate as Openshaw did before him.”

“And who is this Captain Calhoun?”

“The leader of the gang. I shall have the others, but he first.”

“How did you trace it, then?”

He took a large sheet of paper from his pocket, all covered with dates and names.

“I have spent the whole day,” said he, “over Lloyd’s registers and files of the old papers, following the future career of every vessel which touched at Pondicherry in January and February in ’83. There were thirty-six ships of fair tonnage which were reported there during those months. Of these, one, the *Lone Star*, instantly attracted my attention, since, although it was reported as having cleared from London, the name is that which is given to one of the states of the Union.”

“Texas, I think.”

“I was not and am not sure which; but I knew that the ship must have an American origin.”

“What then?”

“I searched the Dundee records, and when I found that the barque *Lone Star* was there in January, ’85, my suspicion became a certainty. I then inquired as to the vessels which lay at present in the port of London.”

“Yes?”

“The *Lone Star* had arrived here last week. I went down to the Albert Dock and found that she had been taken down the river by the early tide this morning, homeward bound to Savannah. I wired to Gravesend and learned that she had passed some time ago, and as the wind is easterly I have no doubt that she is now past the Goodwins and not very far from the Isle of Wight.”

“What will you do, then?”

“Oh, I have my hand upon him. He and the two mates are as I learn, the only native-born Americans in the ship. The others are Finns and Germans. I know, also, that they were all three away from the ship last night. I had it from the stevedore who has been loading their cargo.

By the time that their sailing-ship reaches Savannah the mail-boat will have carried this letter, and the cable will have informed the police of Savannah that these three gentlemen are badly wanted here upon a charge of murder."

There is ever a flaw, however, in the best laid of human plans, and the murderers of John Openshaw were never to receive the orange pips which would show them that another, as cunning and as resolute as themselves, was upon their track. Very long and very severe were the equinoctial gales that year. We waited long for news of the *Lone Star* of Savannah, but none ever reached us. We did at last hear that somewhere far out in the Atlantic a shattered stern-post of a boat was seen swinging in the trough of a wave, with the letters "L. S." carved upon it, and that is all which we shall ever know of the fate of the *Lone Star*.

THE ADVENTURE OF THE DANCING MEN

Holmes had been seated for some hours in silence with his long, thin back curved over a chemical vessel in which he was brewing a particularly malodorous product. His head was sunk upon his breast, and he looked from my point of view like a strange, lank bird, with dull grey plumage and a black top-knot.

"So, Watson," said he, suddenly, "you do not propose to invest in South African securities?"

I gave a start of astonishment. Accustomed as I was to Holmes's curious faculties, this sudden intrusion into my most intimate thoughts was utterly inexplicable.

"How on earth do you know that?" I asked.

He wheeled round upon his stool, with a steaming test-tube in his hand, and a gleam of amusement in his deep-set eyes.

"Now, Watson, confess yourself utterly taken aback," said he.

"I am."

"I ought to make you sign a paper to that effect."

"Why?"

"Because in five minutes you will say that it is all so absurdly simple."

"I am sure that I shall say nothing of the kind."

"You see, my dear Watson,"—he propped his test-tube in the rack, and began to lecture with the air of a professor addressing his class—"it is not really difficult to construct a series of inferences, each dependent upon its predecessor and each simple in itself. If, after doing so, one simply knocks out all the central inferences and presents one's audience with the starting-point and the conclusion, one may produce a startling, though possibly a meretricious, effect. Now, it was not really difficult, by an inspection of the groove between your left forefinger and thumb, to feel sure that you did *not* propose to invest your small capital in the gold fields."

"I see no connection."

"Very likely not; but I can quickly show you a close connection. Here are the missing links of the very simple chain:

1. You had chalk between your left finger and thumb when you returned from the club last night.

2. You put chalk there when you play billiards, to steady the cue.

3. You never play billiards except with Thurston.

4. You told me, four weeks ago, that Thurston had an option on some South African property which would expire in a month, and which he desired you to share with him.

5. Your check book is locked in my drawer, and you have not asked for the key. 6. You do not propose to invest your money in this manner."

"How absurdly simple!" I cried.

"Quite so!" said he, a little nettled. "Every problem becomes very childish when once it is explained to you. Here is an unexplained one. See what you can make of that, friend Watson." He tossed a sheet of paper upon the table and turned once more to his chemical analysis.

I looked with amazement at the absurd hieroglyphics upon the paper.

"Why, Holmes, it is a child's drawing," I cried.

"Oh, that's your idea!"

"What else should it be?"

"That is what Mr. Hilton Cubitt, of Riding Thorpe Manor, Norfolk, is very anxious to know. This little conundrum came by the first post, and he was to follow by the next train. There's a ring at the bell, Watson. I should not be very much surprised if this were he."

A heavy step was heard upon the stairs, and an instant later there entered a tall, ruddy, clean-shaven gentleman, whose clear eyes and florid cheeks told of a life led far from the fogs of Baker Street. He seemed to bring a whiff of his strong, fresh, bracing, east-coast air with him as he entered. Having shaken hands with each of us, he was about to sit down, when his eye rested upon the paper with the curious markings, which I had just examined and left upon the table.

"Well, Mr. Holmes, what do you make of these?" he cried. "They told me that you were fond of queer mysteries, and I don't think you can find a queerer one than that. I sent the paper on ahead, so that you might have time to study it before I came."

"It is certainly rather a curious production," said Holmes. "At first sight it would appear to be some childish prank. It consists of a number of absurd little figures dancing across the paper upon which they are drawn. Why should you attribute any importance to so grotesque an object?"

"I never should, Mr. Holmes. But my wife does. It is frightening her to death. She says nothing, but I can see terror in her eyes. That's why I want to sift the matter to the bottom."

Holmes held up the paper so that the sunlight shone full upon it. It was a page torn from a notebook. The markings were done in pencil, and ran in this way:

Holmes examined it for some time, and then, folding it carefully up, he placed it in his pocketbook.

"This promises to be a most interesting and unusual case," said he. "You gave me a few particulars in your letter, Mr. Hilton Cubitt, but I should be very much obliged if you would kindly go over it all again for the benefit of my friend, Dr. Watson."

"I'm not much of a story-teller," said our visitor, nervously clasping and unclasping his great, strong hands. "You'll just ask me anything that I don't make clear. I'll begin at the time of my marriage last year, but I want to say first of all that, though I'm not a rich man, my people have been at Riding Thorpe for a matter of five centuries, and there is no better-known family in the County of Norfolk. Last year I came up to London for the Jubilee, and I stopped at a boarding-house in Russell Square, because Parker, the vicar of our parish, was staying in it. There was an American young lady there—Patrick was the name—Elsie Patrick. In some way we became friends, until before my month was up I was as much in love as a man could be. We were quietly married at a registry office, and we returned to Norfolk a wedded couple. You'll think it very mad, Mr. Holmes, that a man of a good old family should marry a wife in this fashion, knowing nothing of her past or of her people, but if you saw her and knew her, it would help you to understand.

"She was very straight about it, was Elsie. I can't say that she did not give me every chance of getting out of it if I wished to do so. 'I have had some very disagreeable associations in my life,' said she, 'I wish to forget all about them. I would rather never allude to the past, for it is very painful to me. If you take me, Hilton, you will take a woman who has nothing that she need be personally ashamed of, but you will have to be content with my word for it, and to allow me to be silent as to all that passed up to the time when I became yours. If these conditions are too hard, then go back to Norfolk, and leave me to the lonely life in which you found me.' It was only the day before our wedding that she said those very words to me. I told her that I was content to take her on her own terms, and I have been as good as my word.

"Well, we have been married now for a year, and very happy we have been. But about a month ago, at the end of June, I saw for the first time signs of trouble. One day my wife received a letter from America. I saw the American stamp. She turned deadly white, read the letter, and threw it into the fire. She made no allusion to it afterwards, and I made none, for a promise is a promise, but she has never known an easy hour from that moment. There is always a look of fear upon her face—a look as if she were waiting and expecting. She would do better to trust me. She would find that I was her best friend. But until she speaks, I can say nothing. Mind you, she is a truthful woman, Mr. Holmes, and whatever trouble there may have been in her past life it has been no fault of hers. I am only a simple Norfolk squire, but there is not a man in England who ranks his family honour more highly than I do. She knows it well, and she knew it well before she married me. She would never bring any stain upon it—of that I am sure.

"Well, now I come to the queer part of my story. About a week ago—it was the Tuesday of last week—I found on one of the window-sills a number of absurd little dancing figures like these upon the paper. They were scrawled with chalk. I thought that it was the stable-boy who had drawn them, but the lad swore he knew nothing about it. Anyhow, they had come there during the night. I had them washed out, and I only mentioned the matter to my wife afterwards. To my surprise, she took it very seriously and begged me if any more came to let her see them. None did come for a week, and then yesterday morning I found this paper lying on the sundial in the garden. I showed it to Elsie, and down she dropped in a dead faint. Since then, she has looked like a woman in a dream, half dazed and with terror always lurking in her eyes. It was then that I wrote and sent the paper to you, Mr. Holmes. It was not a thing that I could take to the police, for they would have laughed at me, but you will tell me what to do. I am not a rich man, but if there is any danger threatening my little woman, I would spend my last copper to shield her."

He was a fine creature, this man of the old English soil—simple, straight, and gentle, with his great, earnest blue eyes and broad, comely face. His love for his wife and his trust in her shone in his features. Holmes had listened to his story with the utmost attention, and now he sat for some time in silent thought.

"Don't you think, Mr. Cubitt," said he, at last, "that your best plan would be to make a direct appeal to your wife, and to ask her to share her secret with you?"

Hilton Cubitt shook his massive head.

"A promise is a promise, Mr. Holmes. If Elsie wished to tell me she would. If not, it is not for me to force her confidence. But I am justified in taking my own line—and I will."

"Then I will help you with all my heart. In the first place, have you heard of any strangers being seen in your neighbourhood?"

"No."

"I presume that it is a very quiet place. Any fresh face would cause comment?"

"In the immediate neighbourhood, yes. But we have several small watering-places not very far away. And the farmers take in lodgers."

"These hieroglyphics have evidently a meaning. If it is a purely arbitrary one, it may be impossible for us to solve it. If, on the other hand, it is systematic, I have no doubt that we shall get to the bottom of it. But this particular sample is so short that I can do nothing, and the facts which you have brought me are so indefinite that we have no basis for an investigation. I would suggest that you return to Norfolk, that you keep a keen lookout, and that you take an exact copy of any fresh dancing men which may appear. It is a thousand pities that we have not a reproduction of those which were done in chalk upon the window-sill. Make a discreet inquiry also as to any strangers in the neighbourhood. When you have collected some fresh evidence, come to me again. That is the best advice which I can give you, Mr. Hilton Cubitt. If there are any pressing fresh developments, I shall be always ready to run down and see you in your Norfolk home."

The interview left Sherlock Holmes very thoughtful, and several times in the next few days I saw him take his slip of paper from his notebook and look long and earnestly at the curious figures inscribed upon it. He made no allusion to the affair, however, until one afternoon a fortnight or so later. I was going out when he called me back.

"You had better stay here, Watson."

"Why?"

"Because I had a wire from Hilton Cubitt this morning. You remember Hilton Cubitt, of the dancing men? He was to reach Liverpool Street at one-twenty. He may be here at any moment. I gather from his wire that there have been some new incidents of importance."

We had not long to wait, for our Norfolk squire came straight from the station as fast as a hansom could bring him. He was looking worried and depressed, with tired eyes and a lined forehead.

"It's getting on my nerves, this business, Mr. Holmes," said he, as he sank, like a wearied man, into an armchair. "It's bad enough to feel that you are surrounded by unseen, unknown folk, who have some kind of design upon you, but when, in addition to that, you know that it is just killing your wife by inches, then it becomes as much as flesh and blood can endure. She's wearing away under it—just wearing away before my eyes."

"Has she said anything yet?"

"No, Mr. Holmes, she has not. And yet there have been times when the poor girl has wanted to speak, and yet could not quite bring herself to take the plunge. I have tried to help her, but I daresay I did it clumsily, and scared her from it. She has spoken about my old family, and our reputation in the county, and our pride in our unsullied honour, and I always felt it was leading to the point, but somehow it turned off before we got there."

"But you have found out something for yourself?"

"A good deal, Mr. Holmes. I have several fresh dancing-men pictures for you to examine and what is more important, I have seen the fellow."

"What, the man who draws them?"

"Yes, I saw him at his work. But I will tell you everything in order. When I got back after my visit to you, the very first thing I saw next morning was a fresh crop of dancing men. They had been drawn in chalk upon the black wooden door of the tool-house, which stands beside the lawn in full view of the front windows. I took an exact copy, and here it is." He unfolded a paper and laid it upon the table. Here is a copy of the hieroglyphics:

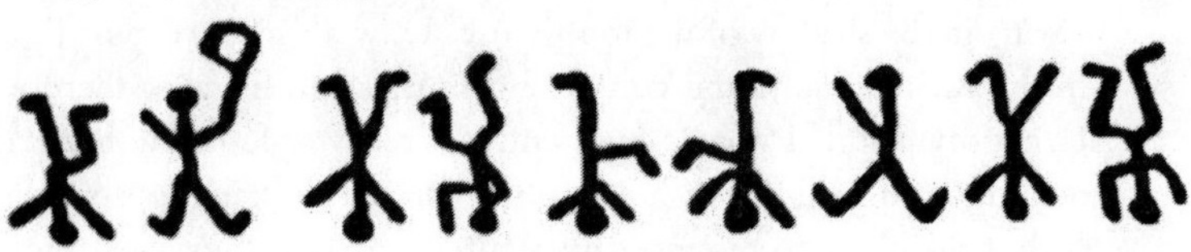

"Excellent!" said Holmes. "Excellent! Pray continue."

"When I had taken the copy, I rubbed out the marks, but, two mornings later, a fresh inscription had appeared. I have a copy of it here:"

Holmes rubbed his hands and chuckled with delight.

"Our material is rapidly accumulating," said he.

"Three days later a message was left scrawled upon paper and placed under a pebble upon the sundial. Here it is. The characters are, as you see, exactly the same as the last one. After that I determined to lie in wait, so I got out my revolver and I sat up in my study, which overlooks the lawn and garden. About two in the morning I was seated by the window, all being dark save for the moonlight outside, when I heard steps behind me, and there was my wife in her dressing-gown. She implored me to come to bed. I told her frankly that I wished to see who it was who played such absurd tricks upon us. She answered that it was some senseless practical joke, and that I should not take any notice of it.

"'If it really annoys you, Hilton, we might go and travel, you and I, and so avoid this nuisance.'

"'What, be driven out of our own house by a practical joker?' said I. 'Why, we should have the whole county laughing at us.'

"'Well, come to bed,' said she, 'and we can discuss it in the morning.'

"Suddenly, as she spoke, I saw her white face grow whiter yet in the moonlight, and her hand tightened upon my shoulder. Something was moving in the shadow of the tool-house. I saw a dark, creeping figure which crawled round the corner and squatted in front of the door. Seizing my pistol, I was rushing out, when my wife threw her arms round me and held me with convulsive strength. I tried to throw her off, but she clung to me most desperately. At last, I got clear but by the time I had opened the door and reached the house the creature was gone. He had left a trace of his presence, however, for there on the door was the very same arrangement of dancing men which had already twice appeared, and which I have copied on that paper. There was no other sign of the fellow anywhere, though I ran all over the grounds. And yet the amazing thing is that he must have been there all the time, for when I examined the door again in the morning, he had scrawled some more of his pictures under the line which I had already seen."

"Have you that fresh drawing?"

"Yes, it is very short, but I made a copy of it, and here it is."

Again, he produced a paper. The new dance was in this form:

"Tell me," said Holmes—and I could see by his eyes that he was much excited—"was this a mere addition to the first or did it appear to be entirely separate?"

"It was on a different panel of the door."

"Excellent! This is far the most important of all for our purpose. It fills me with hopes. Now, Mr. Hilton Cubitt, please continue your most interesting statement."

"I have nothing more to say, Mr. Holmes, except that I was angry with my wife that night for having held me back when I might have caught the skulking rascal. She said that she feared that I might come to harm. For an instant it had crossed my mind that perhaps what she really feared was that *he* might come to harm, for I could not doubt that she knew who this man was, and what he meant by these strange signals. But there is a tone in my wife's voice, Mr. Holmes, and a look in her eyes which forbid doubt, and I am sure that it was indeed my own safety that was in her mind. There's the whole case, and now I want your advice as to what I ought to do. My own inclination is to put half a dozen of my farmlands in the shrubbery and when this fellow comes again to give him such a hiding that he will leave us in peace for the future."

"I fear it is too deep a case for such simple remedies," said Holmes. "How long can you stay in London?"

"I must go back Today. I would not leave my wife alone all night for anything. She is very nervous and begged me to come back."

"I daresay you are right. But if you could have stopped, I might possibly have been able to return with you in a day or two. Meanwhile you will leave me these papers, and I think that it is very likely that I shall be able to pay you a visit shortly and to throw some light upon your case."

Sherlock Holmes preserved his calm professional manner until our visitor had left us, although it was easy for me, who knew him so well, to see that he was profoundly excited. The moment that Hilton Cubitt's broad back had disappeared through the door my comrade rushed to the table, laid out all the slips of paper containing dancing men in front of him, and threw himself into an intricate and elaborate calculation. For two hours I watched him as he covered sheet after sheet of paper with figures and letters, so completely absorbed in his task that he had evidently forgotten my presence. Sometimes he was making progress and whistled and sang at his work; sometimes he was puzzled and would sit for long spells with a furrowed brow and a vacant eye. Finally, he sprang from his chair with a cry of satisfaction and walked up and down the room rubbing his hands together. Then he wrote a long telegram upon a cable form. "If my answer to this is as I hope, you will have a very pretty case to add to your collection, Watson," said he. "I expect that we shall be able to go down to Norfolk tomorrow, and to take our friend some very definite news as to the secret of his annoyance."

I confess that I was filled with curiosity, but I was aware that Holmes liked to make his disclosures at his own time and in his own way, so I waited until it should suit him to take me into his confidence.

But there was a delay in that answering telegram, and two days of impatience followed, during which Holmes pricked up his ears at every ring of the bell. On the evening of the second there came a letter from Hilton Cubitt. All was quiet with him, save that a long inscription had appeared that morning upon the pedestal of the sundial. He inclosed a copy of it, which is here reproduced:

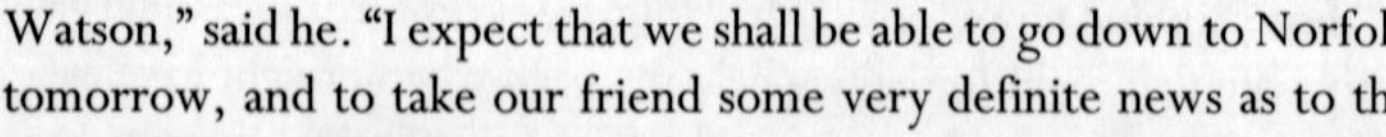

Holmes bent over this grotesque frieze for some minutes, and then suddenly sprang to his feet with an exclamation of surprise and dismay. His face was haggard with anxiety.

"We have let this affair go far enough," said he. "Is there a train to North Walsham tonight?"

I turned up the time-table. The last had just gone.

"Then we shall breakfast early and take the very first in the morning," said Holmes. "Our presence is most urgently needed. Ah! here is our expected cablegram. One moment, Mrs. Hudson, there may be an answer. No, that is quite as I expected. This message makes it even more essential that we should not lose an hour in letting Hilton Cubitt know how matters stand, for it is a singular and a dangerous web in which our simple Norfolk squire is entangled."

So, indeed, it proved, and as I come to the dark conclusion of a story which had seemed to me to be only childish and bizarre, I experience once again the dismay and horror with which I was filled. Would that I had some brighter ending to communicate to my readers, but these are the chronicles of fact, and I must follow to their dark crisis the strange chain of events which for some days made Riding Thorpe Manor a household word through the length and breadth of England.

We had hardly alighted at North Walsham, and mentioned the name of our destination, when the station-master hurried towards us. "I suppose that you are the detectives from London?" said he.

A look of annoyance passed over Holmes's face.

"What makes you think such a thing?"

"Because Inspector Martin from Norwich has just passed through. But maybe you are the surgeons. She's not dead—or wasn't by last accounts. You may be in time to save her yet—though it be for the gallows."

Holmes's brow was dark with anxiety.

"We are going to Riding Thorpe Manor," said he, "but we have heard nothing of what has passed there."

"It's a terrible business," said the stationmaster. "They are shot, both Mr. Hilton Cubitt and his wife. She shot him and then herself—so the servants say. He's dead and her life is despaired of. Dear, dear, one of the oldest families in the county of Norfolk, and one of the most honoured."

Without a word Holmes hurried to a carriage, and during the long seven miles' drive he never opened his mouth. Seldom have I seen him so utterly despondent. He had been uneasy during all our journey from town, and I had observed that he had turned over the morning papers with anxious attention, but now this sudden realization of his worst fears left him in a blank melancholy. He leaned back in his seat, lost in gloomy speculation. Yet there was much around to interest us, for we were passing through as singular a countryside as any in England, where a few scattered cottages represented the population of Today, while on every hand enormous square-towered churches bristled up from the flat green landscape and told of the glory and prosperity of old East Anglia. At last, the violet rim of the German Ocean appeared over the green edge of the Norfolk coast, and the driver pointed with his whip to two old brick and timber gables which projected from a grove of trees. "That's Riding Thorpe Manor," said he.

As we drove up to the porticoed front door, I observed in front of it, beside the tennis lawn, the black tool-house and the pedestalled sundial with which we had such strange associations. A dapper little man, with a quick, alert manner and a waxed moustache, had just descended from a high dog-cart. He introduced himself as Inspector Martin, of the Norfolk Constabulary, and he was considerably astonished when he heard the name of my companion.

"Why, Mr. Holmes, the crime was only committed at three this morning. How could you hear of it in London and get to the spot as soon as I?"

"I anticipated it. I came in the hope of preventing it."

"Then you must have important evidence, of which we are ignorant, for they were said to be a most united couple."

"I have only the evidence of the dancing men," said Holmes. "I will explain the matter to you later. Meanwhile, since it is too late to prevent this tragedy, I am very anxious that I should use the knowledge which I possess in order to insure that justice be done. Will you associate me in your investigation, or will you prefer that I should act independently?"

"I should be proud to feel that we were acting together, Mr. Holmes," said the inspector, earnestly.

"In that case I should be glad to hear the evidence and to examine the premises without an instant of unnecessary delay."

Inspector Martin had the good sense to allow my friend to do things in his own fashion and contented himself with carefully noting the results. The local surgeon, an old, white-haired man, had just come down from Mrs. Hilton Cubitt's room, and he reported that her injuries were serious, but not necessarily fatal. The bullet had passed through the front of her brain, and it would probably be some time before she could regain consciousness. On the question of whether she had been shot or had shot herself, he would not venture to express any decided opinion. Certainly, the bullet had been discharged at very close quarters. There was only the one pistol found in the room, two barrels of which had been emptied. Mr. Hilton Cubitt had been shot through the heart. It was equally conceivable that he had shot her and then himself, or that she had been the criminal, for the revolver lay upon the floor midway between them.

"Has he been moved?" asked Holmes.

"We have moved nothing except the lady. We could not leave her lying wounded upon the floor."

"How long have you been here, Doctor?"

"Since four o'clock."

"Anyone else?"

"Yes, the constable here."

"And you have touched nothing?"

"Nothing."

"You have acted with great discretion. Who sent for you?"

"The housemaid, Saunders."

"Was it she who gave the alarm?"

"She and Mrs. King, the cook."

"Where are they now?"

"In the kitchen, I believe."

"Then I think we had better hear their story at once."

The old hall, oak-panelled and high-windowed, had been turned into a court of investigation. Holmes sat in a great, old-fashioned chair, his inexorable eyes gleaming out of his haggard face. I could read in them a set purpose to devote his life to this quest until the client whom he had failed to save should at last be avenged. The trim Inspector Martin, the old, grey-headed country doctor, myself, and a stolid village policeman made up the rest of that strange company.

The two women told their story clearly enough. They had been aroused from their sleep by the sound of an explosion, which had been followed a minute later by a second one. They slept in adjoining rooms, and Mrs. King had rushed into Saunders. Together they had descended the stairs. The door of the study was open, and a candle was burning upon the table. Their master lay upon his face in the Centre of the room. He was quite dead. Near the window his wife was crouching, her head leaning against the wall. She was horribly wounded, and the side of her face was red with blood. She breathed heavily but was incapable of saying anything. The passage, as well as the room, was full of smoke and the smell of powder. The window was certainly shut and fastened upon the inside. Both women were positive upon the point. They had at once sent for the doctor and for the constable. Then, with the aid of the groom and the stable-boy, they had conveyed their injured mistress to her room. Both she and her husband had occupied the bed. She was clad in her dress—he in his dressing-gown, over his night-clothes. Nothing had been moved in the study. So far as they knew, there had never been any quarrel between husband and wife. They had always looked upon them as a very united couple.

These were the main points of the servants' evidence. In answer to Inspector Martin, they were clear that every door was fastened upon the inside, and that no one could have escaped from the house. In answer to Holmes, they both remembered that they were conscious of the smell of powder from the moment that they ran out of their rooms upon the top floor. "I commend that fact very carefully to your attention," said Holmes to his professional colleague. "And now I think that we are in a position to undertake a thorough examination of the room."

The study proved to be a small chamber, lined on three sides with books, and with a writing-table facing an ordinary window, which looked out upon the garden. Our first attention was given to the body of the unfortunate squire, whose huge frame lay stretched across the room. His disordered dress showed that he had been hastily aroused from sleep. The bullet had been fired at him from the front, and had remained in his body, after penetrating the heart. His death had certainly been instantaneous and painless. There was no powder-marking either upon his dressing-gown or on his hands. According to the country surgeon, the lady had stains upon her face, but none upon her hand.

"The absence of the latter means nothing, though its presence may mean everything," said Holmes. "Unless the powder from a badly fitting cartridge happens to spurt backward, one may fire many shots without leaving a sign. I would suggest that Mr. Cubitt's body may now be removed. I suppose, Doctor, you have not recovered the bullet which wounded the lady?"

"A serious operation will be necessary before that can be done. But there are still four cartridges in the revolver. Two have been fired and two wounds inflicted, so that each bullet can be accounted for."

"So, it would seem," said Holmes. "Perhaps you can account also for the bullet which has so obviously struck the edge of the window?"

He had turned suddenly, and his long, thin finger was pointing to a hole which had been drilled right through the lower window-sash, about an inch above the bottom.

"By George!" cried the inspector. "How ever did you see that?"

"Because I looked for it."

"Wonderful!" said the country doctor. "You are certainly right, sir. Then a third shot has been fired, and therefore a third person must have been present. But who could that have been, and how could he have got away?"

"That is the problem which we are now about to solve," said Sherlock Holmes. "You remember, Inspector Martin, when the servants said that on leaving their room they were at once conscious of a smell of powder, I remarked that the point was an extremely important one?"

"Yes, sir; but I confess I did not quite follow you."

"It suggested that at the time of the firing, the window as well as the door of the room had been open. Otherwise, the fumes of powder could not have been blown so rapidly through the house. A draught in the room was necessary for that. Both door and window were only open for a very short time, however."

"How do you prove that?"

"Because the candle was not guttered."

"Capital!" cried the inspector. "Capital!

"Feeling sure that the window had been open at the time of the tragedy, I conceived that there might have been a third person in the affair, who stood outside this opening and fired through it. Any shot directed at this person might hit the sash. I looked, and there, sure enough, was the bullet mark!"

"But how came the window to be shut and fastened?"

"The woman's first instinct would be to shut and fasten the window. But halloa! What is this?"

It was a lady's hand-bag which stood upon the study table—a trim little handbag of crocodile-skin and silver. Holmes opened it and turned the contents out. There were twenty fifty-pound notes of the Bank of England, held together by an India-rubber band—nothing else.

"This must be preserved, for it will figure in the trial," said Holmes, as he handed the bag with its contents to the inspector. "It is now necessary that we should try to throw some light upon this third bullet, which has clearly, from the splintering of the wood, been fired from inside the room. I should like to see Mrs. King, the cook, again. You said, Mrs. King, that you were awakened by a *loud* explosion. When you said that, did you mean that it seemed to you to be louder than the second one?"

"Well, sir, it wakened me from my sleep, so it is hard to judge. But it did seem very loud."

"You don't think that it might have been two shots fired almost at the same instant?"

"I am sure I couldn't say, sir."

"I believe that it was undoubtedly so. I rather think, Inspector Martin, that we have now exhausted all that this room can teach us. If you will kindly step round with me, we shall see what fresh evidence the garden has to offer."

A flower-bed extended up to the study window, and we all broke into an exclamation as we approached it. The flowers were trampled down, and the soft soil was imprinted all over with footmarks. Large, masculine feet they were, with peculiarly long, sharp toes. Holmes hunted about among the grass and leaves like a retriever after a wounded bird. Then, with a cry of satisfaction, he bent forward and picked up a little brazen cylinder.

"I thought so," said he, "the revolver had an ejector, and here is the third cartridge. I really think, Inspector Martin, that our case is almost complete."

The country inspector's face had shown his intense amazement at the rapid and masterful progress of Holmes's investigation. At first he had shown some disposition to assert his own position, but now he was overcome with admiration, and ready to follow without question wherever Holmes led.

"Whom do you suspect?" he asked.

"I'll go into that later. There are several points in this problem which I have not been able to explain to you yet. Now that I have got so far, I had best proceed on my own lines, and then clear the whole matter up once and for all."

"Just as you wish, Mr. Holmes, so long as we get our man."

"I have no desire to make mysteries, but it is impossible at the moment of action to enter into long and complex explanations. I have the threads of this affair all in my hand. Even if this lady should never recover consciousness, we can still reconstruct the events of last night and insure that justice be done. First of all, I wish to know whether there is any inn in this neighbourhood known as 'Elrige's'?"

The servants were cross-questioned, but none of them had heard of such a place. The stable-boy threw a light upon the matter by remembering that a farmer of that name lived some miles off, in the direction of East Ruston.

"Is it a lonely farm?"

"Very lonely, sir."

"Perhaps they have not heard yet of all that happened here during the night?"

"Maybe not, sir."

Holmes thought for a little, and then a curious smile played over his face.

"Saddle a horse, my lad," said he. "I shall wish you to take a note to Elrige's Farm."

He took from his pocket the various slips of the dancing men. With these in front of him, he worked for some time at the study-table. Finally, he handed a note to the boy, with directions to put it into the hands of the person to whom it was addressed, and especially to answer no questions of any sort which might be put to him. I saw the outside of the note, addressed in straggling, irregular characters, very unlike Holmes's usual precise hand. It was consigned to Mr. Abe Slaney, Elriges Farm, East Ruston, Norfolk.

"I think, Inspector," Holmes remarked, "that you would do well to telegraph for an escort, as, if my calculations prove to be correct, you may have a particularly dangerous prisoner to convey to the county jail. The boy who takes this note could no doubt forward your telegram. If there is an afternoon train to town, Watson, I think we should do well to take it, as I have a chemical analysis of some interest to finish, and this investigation draws rapidly to a close."

When the youth had been dispatched with the note, Sherlock Holmes gave his instructions to the servants. If any visitor were to call asking for Mrs. Hilton Cubitt, no information should be given as to her condition, but he was to be shown at once into the drawing-room. He impressed these points upon them with the utmost earnestness. Finally, he led the way into the drawing-room, with the remark that the business was now out of our hands, and that we must while away the time as best we might until we could see what was in store for us. The doctor had departed to his patients and only the inspector and myself remained.

"I think that I can help you to pass an hour in an interesting and profitable manner," said Holmes, drawing his chair up to the table, and spreading out in front of him the various papers upon which were recorded the antics of the dancing men. "As to you, friend Watson, I owe you every atonement for having allowed your natural curiosity to remain so long unsatisfied. To you, Inspector, the whole incident may appeal as a remarkable professional study. I must tell you, first of all, the interesting circumstances connected with the previous consultations which Mr. Hilton Cubitt has had with me in Baker Street." He then shortly recapitulated the facts which have already been recorded. "I have here in front of me these singular productions, at which one might smile, had they not proved themselves to be the forerunners of so terrible a tragedy. I am fairly familiar with all forms of secret writings and am myself the author of a trifling monograph upon the subject, in which I analyze one hundred and sixty separate ciphers, but I confess that this is entirely new to me. The object of those who invented the system has apparently been to conceal that these characters convey a message, and to give the idea that they are the mere random sketches of children.

"Having once recognized, however, that the symbols stood for letters, and having applied the rules which guide us in all forms of secret writings, the solution was easy enough. The first message submitted to me was so short that it was impossible for me to do more than to say, with some confidence, that the symbol XXX stood for E. As you are aware, E is the most common letter in the English alphabet, and it predominates to so marked an extent that even in a short sentence one would expect to find it most often. Out of fifteen symbols in the first message, four were the same, so it was reasonable to set this down as E. It is true that in some cases the figure was bearing a flag, and in some cases not, but it was probable, from the way in which the flags were distributed, that they were used to break the sentence up into words. I accepted this as a hypothesis, and noted that E was represented by

"But now came the real difficulty of the inquiry. The order of the English letters after E is by no means well marked, and any preponderance which may be shown in an average of a printed sheet may be reversed in a single short sentence. Speaking roughly, T, A, O, I, N, S, H, R, D, and L are the numerical order in which letters occur, but T, A, O, and I are very nearly abreast of each other, and it would be an endless task to try each combination until a meaning was arrived at. I therefore waited for fresh material. In my second interview with Mr. Hilton Cubitt he was able to give me two other short sentences and one message, which appeared—since there was no flag—to be a single word. Here are the symbols. Now, in the single word I have already got the two E's coming second and fourth in a word of five letters. It might be 'sever,' or 'lever,' or 'never.' There can be no question that the latter as a reply to an appeal is far the most probable, and the circumstances pointed to its being a reply written by the lady. Accepting it as correct, we are now able to say that the symbols stand respectively for N, V, and R.

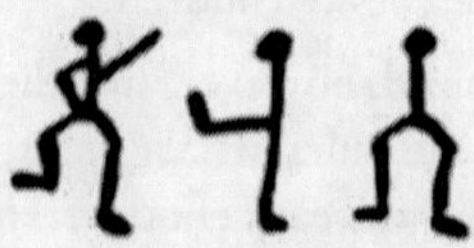

"Even now I was in considerable difficulty, but a happy thought put me in possession of several other letters. It occurred to me that if these appeals came, as I expected, from someone who had been intimate with the lady in her early life, a combination which contained two E's with three letters between might very well stand for the name 'ELSIE.' On examination I found that such a combination formed the termination of the message which was three times repeated. It was certainly some appeal to 'Elsie.' In this way I had got my L, S, and I. But what appeal could it be? There were only four letters in the word which preceded 'Elsie,' and it ended in E. Surely the word must be 'COME.' I tried all other four letters ending in E but could find none to fit the case. So now I was in possession of C, O, and M, and I was in a position to attack the first message once more, dividing it into words and putting dots for each symbol which was still unknown. So treated, it worked out in this fashion:

.M .ERE ..E SL.NE.

"Now the first letter *can* only be A, which is a most useful discovery, since it occurs no fewer than three times in this short sentence, and the H is also apparent in the second word. Now it becomes:

AM HERE A.E SLANE.

Or, filling in the obvious vacancies in the name:

AM HERE ABE SLANEY.

I had so many letters now that I could proceed with considerable confidence to the second message, which worked out in this fashion:

A. ELRI. ES.

Here I could only make sense by putting T and G for the missing letters, and supposing that the name was that of some house or inn at which the writer was staying."

Inspector Martin and I had listened with the utmost interest to the full and clear account of how my friend had produced results which had led to so complete a command over our difficulties.

"What did you do then, sir?" asked the inspector.

"I had every reason to suppose that this Abe Slaney was an American, since Abe is an American contraction, and since a letter from America had been the starting-point of all the trouble. I had also every cause to think that there was some criminal secret in the matter. The lady's allusions to her past, and her refusal to take her husband into her confidence, both pointed in that direction. I therefore cabled to my friend, Wilson Hargreave, of the New York Police Bureau, who has more than once made use of my knowledge of London crime. I asked him whether the name of Abe Slaney was known to him. Here is his reply: 'The most dangerous crook in Chicago.' On the very evening upon which I had his answer, Hilton Cubitt sent me the last message from Slaney. Working with known letters, it took this form:

ELSIE .RE.ARE TO MEET THY GO.

The addition of a P and a D completed a message which showed me that the rascal was proceeding from persuasion to threats, and my knowledge of the crooks of Chicago prepared me to find that he might very rapidly put his words into action. I at once came to Norfolk with my friend and colleague, Dr. Watson, but, unhappily, only in time to find that the worst had already occurred."

"It is a privilege to be associated with you in the handling of a case," said the inspector, warmly. "You will excuse me, however, if I speak frankly to you. You are only answerable to yourself, but I have to answer to my superiors. If this Abe Slaney, living at Elrige's, is indeed the murderer, and if he has made his escape while I am seated here, I should certainly get into serious trouble."

"You need not be uneasy. He will not try to escape."

"How do you know?"

"To fly would be a confession of guilt."

"Then let us go arrest him."

"I expect him here every instant."

"But why should he come?"

"Because I have written and asked him."

"But this is incredible, Mr. Holmes! Why should he come because you have asked him? Would not such a request rather rouse his suspicions and cause him to fly?"

"I think I have known how to frame the letter," said Sherlock Holmes. "In fact, if I am not very much mistaken, here is the gentleman himself coming up the drive."

A man was striding up the path which led to the door. He was a tall, handsome, swarthy fellow, clad in a suit of grey flannel, with a Panama hat, a bristling black beard, and a great, aggressive hooked nose, and flourishing a cane as he walked. He swaggered up a path as if the place belonged to him, and we heard his loud, confident peal at the bell.

"I think, gentlemen," said Holmes, quietly, "that we had best take up our position behind the door. Every precaution is necessary when dealing with such a fellow. You will need your handcuffs, Inspector. You can leave the talking to me."

We waited in silence for a minute—one of those minutes which one can never forget. Then the door opened, and the man stepped in. In an instant Holmes clapped a pistol to his head, and Martin slipped the handcuffs over his wrists. It was all done so swiftly and deftly that the fellow was helpless before he knew that he was attacked. He glared from one to the other of us with a pair of blazing black eyes. Then he burst into a bitter laugh.

"Well, gentlemen, you have the drop on me this time. I seem to have knocked up against something hard. But I came here in answer to a letter from Mrs. Hilton Cubitt. Don't tell me that she is in this? Don't tell me that she helped to set a trap for me?"

"Mrs. Hilton Cubitt was seriously injured and is at death's door."

The man gave a hoarse cry of grief, which rang through the house.

"You're crazy!" he cried, fiercely. "It was he that was hurt, not she. Who would have hurt little Elsie? I may have threatened her—God forgive me!—but I would not have touched a hair of her pretty head. Take it back—you! Say that she is not hurt!"

"She was found badly wounded, by the side of her dead husband."

He sank with a deep groan on the settee and buried his face in his manacled hands. For five minutes he was silent. Then he raised his face once more and spoke with the cold composure of despair.

"I have nothing to hide from you, gentlemen," said he. "If I shot the man he had his shot at me, and there's no murder in that. But if you think I could have hurt that woman, then you don't know either me or her. I tell you, there was never a man in this world loved a woman more than I loved her. I had a right to her. She was pledged to me years ago. Who was this Englishman that he should come between us? I tell you that I had the first right to her, and that I was only claiming my own."

"She broke away from your influence when she found the man that you are," said Holmes, sternly. "She fled from America to avoid you, and she married an honourable gentleman in England. You dogged her and followed her and made her life a misery to her, in order to induce her to abandon the husband whom she loved and respected in order to fly with you, whom she feared and hated. You have ended by bringing about the death of a noble man and driving his wife to suicide. That is your record in this business, Mr. Abe Slaney, and you will answer for it to the law."

"If Elsie dies, I care nothing what becomes of me," said the American. He opened one of his hands and looked at a note crumpled up in his palm. "See here, mister! he cried, with a gleam of suspicion in his eyes, "you're not trying to scare me over this, are you? If the lady is hurt as bad as you say, who was it that wrote this note?" He tossed it forward on to the table.

"I wrote it, to bring you here."

"You wrote it? There was no one on earth outside the Joint who knew the secret of the dancing men. How came you to write it?"

"What one man can invent another can discover," said Holmes. "There is a cab coming to convey you to Norwich, Mr. Slaney. But meanwhile, you have time to make some small reparation for the injury you have wrought. Are you aware that Mrs. Hilton Cubitt has herself lain under grave suspicion of the murder of her husband, and that it was only my presence here, and the knowledge which I happened to possess, which has saved her from the accusation? The least that you owe her is to make it clear to the whole world that she was in no way, directly or indirectly, responsible for his tragic end."

"I ask nothing better," said the American. "I guess the very best case I can make for myself is the absolute naked truth."

"It is my duty to warn you that it will be used against you," cried the inspector, with the magnificent fair play of the British criminal law.

Slaney shrugged his shoulders.

"I'll chance that," said he. "First of all, I want you gentlemen to understand that I have known this lady since she was a child. There were seven of us in a gang in Chicago, and Elsie's father was the boss of the Joint. He was a clever man, was old Patrick. It was he who invented that writing, which would pass as a child's scrawl unless you just happened to have the key to it. Well, Elsie learned some of our ways, but she couldn't stand the business, and she had a bit of honest money of her own, so she gave us all the slip and got away to London. She had been engaged to me, and she would have married me, I believe, if I had taken over another profession, but she would have nothing to do with anything on the cross. It was only after her marriage to this Englishman that I was able to find out where she was. I wrote to her but got no answer. After that I came over, and, as letters were no use, I put my messages where she could read them.

"Well, I have been here a month now. I lived in that farm, where I had a room down below, and could get in and out every night, and no one the wiser. I tried all I could to coax Elsie away. I knew that she read the messages, for once she wrote an answer under one of them. Then my temper got the better of me, and I began to threaten her. She sent me a letter then, imploring me to go away, and saying that it would break her heart if any scandal should come upon her husband. She said that she would come down when her husband was asleep at three in the morning, and speak with me through the end window, if I would go away afterwards and leave her in peace. She came down and brought money with her, trying to bribe me to go. This made me mad, and I caught her arm and tried to pull her through the window. At that moment in rushed the husband with his revolver in his hand. Elsie had sunk down upon the floor, and we were face to face. I was heeled also, and I held up my gun to scare him off and let me get away. He fired and missed me. I pulled off almost at the same instant, and down he dropped. I made away across the garden, and as I went I heard the window shut behind me. That's God's truth, gentlemen, every word of it, and I heard no more about it until that lad came riding up with a note which made me walk in here, like a jay, and give myself into your hands."

A cab had driven up whilst the American had been talking. Two uniformed policemen sat inside. Inspector Martin rose and touched his prisoner on the shoulder.

"It is time for us to go."

"Can I see her first?"

"No, she is not conscious. Mr. Sherlock Holmes, I only hope that if ever again I have an important case, I shall have the good fortune to have you by my side."

We stood at the window and watched the cab drive away. As I turned back, my eye caught the pellet of paper which the prisoner had tossed upon the table. It was the note with which Holmes had decoyed him.

"See if you can read it, Watson," said he, with a smile.

It contained no word, but this little line of dancing men:

"If you use the code which I have explained," said Holmes, "you will find that it simply means 'Come here at once.' I was convinced that it was an invitation which he would not refuse, since he could never imagine that it could come from anyone but the lady. And so, my dear Watson, we have ended by turning the dancing men to good when they have so often been the agents of evil, and I think that I have fulfilled my promise of giving you something unusual for your notebook. Three-forty is our train, and I fancy we should be back in Baker Street for dinner."

Only one word of epilogue. The American, Abe Slaney, was condemned to death at the winter assizes at Norwich, but his penalty was changed to penal servitude in consideration of mitigating circumstances, and the certainty that Hilton Cubitt had fired the first shot. Of Mrs. Hilton Cubitt I only know that I have heard she recovered entirely, and that she still remains a widow, devoting her whole life to the care of the poor and to the administration of her husband's estate.

THE ADVENTURE OF THE EMPTY HOUSE

It was in the spring of the year 1894 that all London was interested, and the fashionable world dismayed, by the murder of the Honourable Ronald Adair under most unusual and inexplicable circumstances. The public has already learned those particulars of the crime which came out in the police investigation, but a good deal was suppressed upon that occasion, since the case for the prosecution was so overwhelmingly strong that it was not necessary to bring forward all the facts. Only now, at the end of nearly ten years, am I allowed to supply those missing links which make up the whole of that remarkable chain. The crime was of interest in itself, but that interest was as nothing to me compared to the inconceivable sequel, which afforded me the greatest shock and surprise of any event in my adventurous life. Even now, after this long interval, I find myself thrilling as I think of it, and feeling once more that sudden flood of joy, amazement, and incredulity which utterly submerged my mind. Let me say to that public, which has shown some interest in those glimpses which I have occasionally given them of the thoughts and actions of a very remarkable man, that they are not to blame me if I have not shared my knowledge with them, for I should have considered it my first duty to do so, had I not been barred by a positive prohibition from his own lips, which was only withdrawn upon the third of last month.

It can be imagined that my close intimacy with Sherlock Holmes had interested me deeply in crime, and that after his disappearance I never failed to read with care the various problems which came before the public. And I even attempted, more than once, for my own private satisfaction, to employ his methods in their solution, though with indifferent success. There was none, however, which appealed to me like this tragedy of Ronald Adair. As I read the evidence at the inquest, which led up to a verdict of willful murder against some person or persons unknown, I realized more clearly than I had ever done the loss which the community had sustained by the death of Sherlock Holmes. There were points about this strange business which would, I was sure, have specially appealed to him, and the efforts of the police would have been supplemented, or more probably anticipated, by the trained observation and the alert mind of the first criminal agent in Europe. All day, as I drove upon my round, I turned over the case in my mind and found no explanation which appeared to me to be adequate. At the risk of telling a twice-told tale, I will recapitulate the facts as they were known to the public at the conclusion of the inquest.

The Honourable Ronald Adair was the second son of the Earl of Maynooth, at that time governor of one of the Australian colonies. Adair's mother had returned from Australia to undergo the operation for cataract, and she, her son Ronald, and her daughter Hilda were living together at 427, Park Lane. The youth moved in the best society—had, so far as was known, no enemies and no particular vices. He had been engaged to Miss Edith Woodley, of Carstairs, but the engagement had been broken off by mutual consent some months before, and there was no sign that it had left any very profound feeling behind it. For the rest, the man's life moved in a narrow and conventional circle, for his habits were quiet and his nature unemotional. Yet it was upon this easy-going young aristocrat that death came, in most strange and unexpected form, between the hours of ten and eleven-twenty on the night of March 30, 1894.

Ronald Adair was fond of cards—playing continually, but never for such stakes as would hurt him. He was a member of the Baldwin, the Cavendish, and the Bagatelle card clubs. It was shown that, after dinner on the day of his death, he had played a rubber of whist at the latter club. He had also played there in the afternoon. The evidence of those who had played with him—Mr. Murray, Sir John Hardy, and Colonel Moran—showed that the game was whist, and that there was a fairly equal fall of the cards. Adair might have lost five pounds, but not more. His fortune was a considerable one, and such a loss could not in any way affect him. He had played nearly every day at one club or other, but he was a cautious player, and usually rose a winner. It came out in evidence that, in partnership with Colonel Moran, he had actually won as much as four hundred and twenty pounds in a sitting, some weeks before, from Godfrey Milner and Lord Balmoral. So much for his recent history as it came out at the inquest.

On the evening of the crime, he returned from the club exactly at ten. His mother and sister were out spending the evening with a relation. The servant deposed that she heard him enter the front room on the second floor, generally used as his sitting-room. She had lit a fire there, and as it smoked she had opened the window. No sound was heard from the room until eleven-twenty, the hour of the return of Lady Maynooth and her daughter. Desiring to say good-night, she attempted to enter her son's room. The door was locked on the inside, and no answer could be got to their cries and knocking. Help was obtained, and the door forced. The unfortunate young man was found lying near the table. His head had been horribly mutilated by an expanding revolver bullet, but no weapon of any sort was to be found in the room. On the table lay two banknotes for ten pounds each and seventeen pounds ten in silver and gold, the money arranged in little piles of varying amount. There were some figures also upon a sheet of paper, with the names of some club friend's opposite to them, from which it was conjectured that before his death he was endeavouring to make out his losses or winnings at cards.

A minute examination of the circumstances served only to make the case more complex. In the first place, no reason could be given why the young man should have fastened the door upon the inside. There was the possibility that the murderer had done this and had afterwards escaped by the window. The drop was at least twenty feet, however, and a bed of crocuses in full bloom lay beneath. Neither the flowers nor the earth showed any sign of having been disturbed, nor were there any marks upon the narrow strip of grass which separated the house from the road. Apparently, therefore, it was the young man himself who had fastened the door. But how did he come by his death? No one could have climbed up to the window without leaving traces. Suppose a man had fired through the window, he would indeed be a remarkable shot who could with a revolver inflict so deadly a wound. Again, Park Lane is a frequented thoroughfare; there is a cab stand within a hundred yards of the house. No one had heard a shot. And yet there was the dead man and there the revolver bullet, which had mushroomed out, as soft-nosed bullets will, and so inflicted a wound which must have caused instantaneous death. Such were the circumstances of the Park Lane Mystery, which were further complicated by entire absence of motive, since, as I have said, young Adair was not known to have any enemy, and no attempt had been made to remove the money or valuables in the room.

All day I turned these facts over in my mind, endeavouring to hit upon some theory which could reconcile them all, and to find that line of least resistance which my poor friend had declared to be the starting-point of every investigation. I confess that I made little progress. In the evening, I strolled across the Park and found myself about six o'clock at the Oxford Street end of Park Lane. A group of loafers upon the pavements, all staring up at a particular window, directed me to the house which I had come to see. A tall, thin man with coloured glasses, whom I strongly suspected of being a plain-clothes detective, was pointing out some theory of his own, while the others crowded round to listen to what he said. I got as near him as I could, but his observations seemed to me to be absurd, so I withdrew again in some disgust. As I did so I struck against an elderly, deformed man, who had been behind me, and I knocked down several books which he was carrying. I remember that as I picked them up, I observed the title of one of them, *The Origin of Tree Worship*, and it struck me that the fellow must be some poor bibliophile, who, either as a trade or as a hobby, was a collector of obscure volumes. I endeavoured to apologize for the accident, but it was evident that these books which I had so unfortunately maltreated were very precious objects in the eyes of their owner. With a snarl of contempt, he turned upon his heel, and I saw his curved back and white side-whiskers disappear among the throng.

My observations of No. 427, Park Lane did little to clear up the problem in which I was interested. The house was separated from the street by a low wall and railing, the whole not more than five feet high. It was perfectly easy, therefore, for anyone to get into the garden, but the window was entirely inaccessible, since there was no waterpipe or anything which could help the most active man to climb it. More puzzled than ever, I retraced my steps to Kensington. I had not been in my study five minutes when the maid entered to say that a person desired to see me. To my astonishment it was none other than my strange old book collector, his sharp, wizened face peering out from a frame of white hair, and his precious volumes, a dozen of them at least, wedged under his right arm.

"You're surprised to see me, sir," said he, in a strange, croaking voice.

I acknowledged that I was.

"Well, I've a conscience, sir, and when I chanced to see you go into this house, as I came hobbling after you, I thought to myself, I'll just step in and see that kind gentleman and tell him that if I was a bit gruff in my manner there was not any harm meant, and that I am much obliged to him for picking up my books."

"You make too much of a trifle," said I. "May I ask how you knew who I was?"

"Well, sir, if it isn't too great a liberty, I am a neighbour of yours, for you'll find my little bookshop at the corner of Church Street, and very happy to see you, I am sure. Maybe you collect yourself, sir. Here's *British Birds*, and *Catullus*, and *The Holy War*—a bargain, every one of them. With five volumes you could just fill that gap on that second shelf. It looks untidy, does it not, sir?"

I moved my head to look at the cabinet behind me. When I turned again, Sherlock Holmes was standing smiling at me across my study table. I rose to my feet, stared at him for some seconds in utter amazement, and then it appears that I must have fainted for the first and the last time in my life. Certainly, a grey mist swirled before my eyes, and when it cleared I found my collar-ends undone and the tingling after-taste of brandy upon my lips. Holmes was bending over my chair, his flask in his hand.

"My dear Watson," said the well-remembered voice, "I owe you a thousand apologies. I had no idea that you would be so affected."

I gripped him by the arms.

"Holmes!" I cried. "Is it really you? Can it indeed be that you are alive? Is it possible that you succeeded in climbing out of that awful abyss?"

"Wait a moment," said he. "Are you sure that you are really fit to discuss things? I have given you a serious shock by my unnecessarily dramatic reappearance."

"I am all right, but indeed, Holmes, I can hardly believe my eyes. Good heavens! to think that you—you of all men—should be standing in my study." Again, I gripped him by the sleeve, and felt the thin, sinewy arm beneath it. "Well, you're not a spirit anyhow," said I. "My dear chap, I'm overjoyed to see you. Sit down and tell me how you came alive out of that dreadful chasm."

He sat opposite to me, and lit a cigarette in his old, nonchalant manner. He was dressed in the seedy frockcoat of the book merchant, but the rest of that individual lay in a pile of white hair and old books upon the table. Holmes looked even thinner and keener than of old, but there was a dead-white tinge in his aquiline face which told me that his life recently had not been a healthy one.

"I am glad to stretch myself, Watson," said he. "It is no joke when a tall man has to take a foot off his stature for several hours on end. Now, my dear fellow, in the matter of these explanations, we have, if I may ask for your cooperation, a hard and dangerous night's work in front of us. Perhaps it would be better if I gave you an account of the whole situation when that work is finished."

"I am full of curiosity. I should much prefer to hear now."

"You'll come with me tonight?"

"When you like and where you like."

"This is, indeed, like the old days. We shall have time for a mouthful of dinner before we need go. Well, then, about that chasm. I had no serious difficulty in getting out of it, for the very simple reason that I never was in it."

"You never were in it?"

"No, Watson, I never was in it. My note to you was absolutely genuine. I had little doubt that I had come to the end of my career when I perceived the somewhat sinister figure of the late Professor Moriarty standing upon the narrow pathway which led to safety. I read an inexorable purpose in his grey eyes. I exchanged some remarks with him, therefore, and obtained his courteous permission to write the short note which you afterwards received. I left it with my cigarette-box and my stick, and I walked along the pathway, Moriarty still at my heels. When I reached the end I stood at bay. He drew no weapon, but he rushed at me and threw his long arms around me. He knew that his own game was up and was only anxious to revenge himself upon me. We tottered together upon the brink of the fall. I have some knowledge, however, of baritsu or the Japanese system of wrestling, which has more than once been very useful to me. I slipped through his grip, and he with a horrible scream kicked madly for a few seconds and clawed the air with both his hands. But for all his efforts he could not get his balance, and over he went. With my face over the brink, I saw him fall for a long way. Then he struck a rock, bounded off, and splashed into the water."

I listened with amazement to this explanation, which Holmes delivered between the puffs of his cigarette.

"But the tracks!" I cried. "I saw, with my own eyes, that two went down the path and none returned."

"It came about in this way. The instant that the Professor had disappeared, it struck me what a really extraordinarily lucky chance Fate had placed in my way. I knew that Moriarty was not the only man who had sworn my death. There were at least three others whose desire for vengeance upon me would only be increased by the death of their leader. They were all most dangerous men. One or other would certainly get me. On the other hand, if all the world was convinced that I was dead they would take liberties, these men, they would soon lay themselves open, and sooner or later I could destroy them. Then it would be time for me to announce that I was still in the land of the living. So rapidly does the brain act that I believe I had thought this all out before Professor Moriarty had reached the bottom of the Reichenbach Fall.

"I stood up and examined the rocky wall behind me. In your picturesque account of the matter, which I read with great interest some months later, you assert that the wall was sheer. That was not literally true. A few small footholds presented themselves, and there was some indication of a ledge. The cliff is so high that to climb it all was an obvious impossibility, and it was equally impossible to make my way along the wet path without leaving some tracks. I might, it is true, have reversed my boots, as I have done on similar occasions, but the sight of three sets of tracks in one direction would certainly have suggested a deception. On the whole, then, it was best that I should risk the climb. It was not a pleasant business, Watson. The fall roared beneath me. I am not a fanciful person, but I give you my word that I seemed to hear Moriarty's voice screaming at me out of the abyss. A mistake would have been fatal. More than once, as tufts of grass came out in my hand or my foot slipped in the wet notches of the rock, I thought that I was gone. But I struggled upward, and at last I reached a ledge several feet deep and covered with soft green moss, where I could lie unseen, in the most perfect comfort. There I was stretched, when you, my dear Watson, and all your following were investigating in the most sympathetic and inefficient manner the circumstances of my death.

"At last, when you had all formed your inevitable and totally erroneous conclusions, you departed for the hotel, and I was left alone. I had imagined that I had reached the end of my adventures, but a very unexpected occurrence showed me that there were surprises still in store for me. A huge rock, falling from above, boomed past me, struck the path, and bounded over into the chasm. For an instant I thought that it was an accident, but a moment later, looking up, I saw a man's head against the darkening sky, and another stone struck the very ledge upon which I was stretched, within a foot of my head. Of course, the meaning of this was obvious. Moriarty had not been alone. A confederate—and even that one glance had told me how dangerous a man that confederate was—had kept guard while the Professor had attacked me. From a distance, unseen by me, he had been a witness of his friend's death and of my escape. He had waited, and then making his way round to the top of the cliff, he had endeavoured to succeed where his comrade had failed.

"I did not take long to think about it, Watson. Again, I saw that grim face look over the cliff, and I knew that it was the precursor of another stone. I scrambled down on to the path. I don't think I could have done it in cold blood. It was a hundred times more difficult than getting up. But I had no time to think of the danger, for another stone sang past me as I hung by my hands from the edge of the ledge.

Halfway down I slipped, but, by the blessing of God, I landed, torn and bleeding, upon the path. I took to my heels, did ten miles over the mountains in the darkness, and a week later I found myself in Florence, with the certainty that no one in the world knew what had become of me.

"I had only one confidant—my brother Mycroft. I owe you many apologies, my dear Watson, but it was all-important that it should be thought I was dead, and it is quite certain that you would not have written so convincing an account of my unhappy end had you not yourself thought that it was true. Several times during the last three years I have taken up my pen to write to you, but always I feared lest your affectionate regard for me should tempt you to some indiscretion which would betray my secret. For that reason, I turned away from you this evening when you upset my books, for I was in danger at the time, and any show of surprise and emotion upon your part might have drawn attention to my identity and led to the most deplorable and irreparable results. As to Mycroft, I had to confide in him in order to obtain the money which I needed. The course of events in London did not run so well as I had hoped, for the trial of the Moriarty gang left two of its most dangerous members, my own most vindictive enemies, at liberty. I travelled for two years in Tibet, therefore, and amused myself by visiting Lhassa and spending some days with the head lama. You may have read of the remarkable explorations of a Norwegian named Sigerson, but I am sure that it never occurred to you that you were receiving news of your friend. I then passed through Persia, looked in at Mecca, and paid a short but interesting visit to the Khalifa at Khartoum the results of which I have communicated to the Foreign Office. Returning to France, I spent some months in a research into the coal-tar derivatives, which I conducted in a laboratory at Montpellier, in the south of France. Having concluded this to my satisfaction and learning that only one of my enemies was now left in London, I was about to return when my movements were hastened by the news of this very remarkable Park Lane Mystery, which not only appealed to me by its own merits, but which seemed to offer some most peculiar personal opportunities. I came over at once to London, called in my own person at Baker Street, threw Mrs. Hudson into violent hysterics, and found that Mycroft had preserved my rooms and my papers exactly as they had always been. So it was, my dear Watson, that at two o'clock Today I found myself in my old armchair in my own old room, and only wishing that I could have seen my old friend Watson in the other chair which he has so often adorned."

Such was the remarkable narrative to which I listened on that April evening—a narrative which would have been utterly incredible to me had it not been confirmed by the actual sight of the tall, spare figure and the keen, eager face, which I had never thought to see again. In some manner he had learned of my own sad bereavement, and his sympathy was shown in his manner rather than in his words. "Work is the best antidote to sorrow, my dear Watson," said he; "and I have a piece of work for us both tonight which, if we can bring it to a successful conclusion, will in itself justify a man's life on this planet." In vain I begged him to tell me more. "You will hear and see enough before morning," he answered. "We have three years of the past to discuss. Let that suffice until half-past nine, when we start upon the notable adventure of the empty house."

It was indeed like old times when, at that hour, I found myself seated beside him in a hansom, my revolver in my pocket, and the thrill of adventure in my heart. Holmes was cold and stern and silent. As the gleam of the street-lamps flashed upon his austere features, I saw that his brows were drawn down in thought and his thin lips compressed. I knew not what wild beast we were about to hunt down in the dark jungle of criminal London, but I was well assured, from the bearing of this master huntsman, that the adventure was a most grave one—while the sardonic smile which occasionally broke through his ascetic gloom boded little good for the object of our quest.

I had imagined that we were bound for Baker Street, but Holmes stopped the cab at the corner of Cavendish Square. I observed that as he stepped out he gave a most searching glance to right and left, and at every subsequent street corner he took the utmost pains to assure that he was not followed. Our route was certainly a singular one. Holmes's knowledge of the byways of London was extraordinary, and on this occasion he passed rapidly and with an assured step through a network of mews and stables, the very existence of which I had never known. We emerged at last into a small road, lined with old, gloomy houses, which led us into Manchester Street, and so to Blandford Street. Here he turned swiftly down a narrow passage, passed through a wooden gate into a deserted yard, and then opened with a key the back door of a house. We entered together, and he closed it behind us.

The place was pitch dark, but it was evident to me that it was an empty house. Our feet creaked and crackled over the bare planking, and my outstretched hand touched a wall from which the paper was hanging in ribbons. Holmes's cold, thin fingers closed round my wrist and led me forward down a long hall, until I dimly saw the murky fanlight over the door. Here Holmes turned suddenly to the right and we found ourselves in a large, square, empty room, heavily shadowed in the corners, but faintly lit in the Centre from the lights of the street beyond. There was no lamp near, and the window was thick with dust, so that we could only just discern each other's figures within. My companion put his hand upon my shoulder and his lips close to my ear.

"Do you know where we are?" he whispered.

"Surely that is Baker Street," I answered, staring through the dim window.

"Exactly. We are in Camden House, which stands opposite to our own old quarters."

"But why are we here?"

"Because it commands so excellent a view of that picturesque pile. Might I trouble you, my dear Watson, to draw a little nearer to the window, taking every precaution not to show yourself, and then to look up at our old rooms—the starting-point of so many of your little fairy-tales? We will see if my three years of absence have entirely taken away my power to surprise you."

I crept forward and looked across at the familiar window. As my eyes fell upon it, I gave a gasp and a cry of amazement. The blind was down, and a strong light was burning in the room. The shadow of a man who was seated in a chair within was thrown in hard, black outline upon the luminous screen of the window. There was no mistaking the poise of the head, the squareness of the shoulders, the sharpness of the features. The face was turned half-round, and the effect was that of one of those black silhouettes which our grandparents loved to frame. It was a perfect reproduction of Holmes. So amazed was I that I threw out my hand to make sure that the man himself was standing beside me. He was quivering with silent laughter.

"Well?" said he.

"Good heavens!" I cried. "It is marvellous."

"I trust that age doth not wither nor custom stale my infinite variety," said he, and I recognized in his voice the joy and pride which the artist takes in his own creation. "It really is rather like me, is it not?"

"I should be prepared to swear that it was you."

"The credit of the execution is due to Monsieur Oscar Meunier, of Grenoble, who spent some days in doing the moulding. It is a bust in wax. The rest I arranged myself during my visit to Baker Street this afternoon."

"But why?"

"Because, my dear Watson, I had the strongest possible reason for wishing certain people to think that I was there when I was really elsewhere."

"And you thought the rooms were watched?"

"I knew that they were watched."

"By whom?"

"By my old enemies, Watson. By the charming society whose leader lies in the Reichenbach Fall. You must remember that they knew, and only they knew, that I was still alive. Sooner or later, they believed that I should come back to my rooms. They watched them continuously, and this morning they saw me arrive."

"How do you know?"

"Because I recognized their sentinel when I glanced out of my window. He is a harmless enough fellow, Parker by name, a garroter by trade, and a remarkable performer upon the jew's-harp. I cared nothing for him. But I cared a great deal for the much more formidable person who was behind him, the bosom friend of Moriarty, the man who dropped the rocks over the cliff, the most cunning and dangerous criminal in London. That is the man who is after me tonight Watson, and that is the man who is quite unaware that we are after him."

My friend's plans were gradually revealing themselves. From this convenient retreat, the watchers were being watched and the trackers tracked. That angular shadow up yonder was the bait, and we were the hunters. In silence we stood together in the darkness and watched the hurrying figures who passed and repassed in front of us. Holmes was silent and motionless; but I could tell that he was keenly alert, and that his eyes were fixed intently upon the stream of passers-by. It was a bleak and boisterous night, and the wind whistled shrilly down the long street. Many people were moving to and fro, most of them muffled in their coats and cravats. Once or twice, it seemed to me that I had seen the same figure before, and I especially noticed two men who appeared to be sheltering themselves from the wind in the doorway of a house some distance up the street. I tried to draw my companion's attention to them; but he gave a little ejaculation of impatience and continued to stare into the street. More than once, he fidgeted with his feet and tapped rapidly with his fingers upon the wall. It was evident to me that he was becoming uneasy, and that his plans were not working out altogether as he had hoped. At last, as midnight approached and the street gradually cleared, he paced up and down the room in uncontrollable agitation. I was about to make some remark to him, when I raised my eyes to the lighted window, and again experienced almost as great a surprise as before. I clutched Holmes's arm and pointed upward.

"The shadow has moved!" I cried.

It was indeed no longer the profile, but the back, which was turned towards us.

Three years had certainly not smoothed the asperities of his temper or his impatience with a less active intelligence than his own.

"Of course it has moved," said he. "Am I such a farcical bungler, Watson, that I should erect an obvious dummy, and expect that some of the sharpest men in Europe would be deceived by it? We have been in this room two hours, and Mrs. Hudson has made some change in that figure eight times, or once in every quarter of an hour. She works it from the front, so that her shadow may never be seen. Ah!" He drew in his breath with a shrill, excited intake. In the dim light I saw his head thrown forward, his whole attitude rigid with attention. Outside the street was absolutely deserted. Those two men might still be crouching in the doorway, but I could no longer see them. All was still and dark, save only that brilliant yellow screen in front of us with the black figure outlined upon its Centre. Again, in the utter silence I heard that thin, sibilant note which spoke of intense suppressed excitement. An instant later he pulled me back into the blackest corner of the room, and I felt his warning hand upon my lips. The fingers which clutched me were quivering. Never had I known my friend more moved, and yet the dark street still stretched lonely and motionless before us.

But suddenly I was aware of that which his keener senses had already distinguished. A low, stealthy sound came to my ears, not from the direction of Baker Street, but from the back of the very house in which we lay concealed. A door opened and shut. An instant later steps crept down the passage—steps which were meant to be silent, but which reverberated harshly through the empty house. Holmes crouched back against the wall, and I did the same, my hand closing upon the handle of my revolver. Peering through the gloom, I saw the vague outline of a man, a shade blacker than the blackness of the open door. He stood for an instant, and then he crept forward, crouching, menacing, into the room. He was within three yards of us, this sinister figure, and I had braced myself to meet his spring, before I realized that he had no idea of our presence. He passed close beside us, stole over to the window, and very softly and noiselessly raised it for half a foot. As he sank to the level of this opening, the light of the street, no longer dimmed by the dusty glass, fell full upon his face. The man seemed to be beside himself with excitement. His two eyes shone like stars, and his features were working convulsively. He was an elderly man, with a thin, projecting nose, a high, bald forehead, and a huge, grizzled moustache. An opera hat was pushed to the back of his head, and an evening dress shirt-front gleamed out through his open overcoat. His face was gaunt and swarthy, scored with deep, savage lines. In his hand he carried what appeared to be a stick, but as he laid it down upon the floor it gave a metallic clang. Then from the pocket of his overcoat he drew a bulky object, and he busied himself in some task which ended with a loud, sharp click, as if a spring or bolt had fallen into its place. Still kneeling upon the floor, he bent forward and threw all his weight and strength upon some lever, with the result that there came a long, whirling, grinding noise, ending once more in a powerful click. He straightened himself then, and I saw that what he held in his hand was a sort of gun, with a curiously misshapen butt. He opened it at the breech, put something in, and snapped the breech-lock. Then, crouching down, he rested the end of the barrel upon the ledge of the open window, and I saw his long moustache droop over the stock and his eye gleam as it peered along the sights. I heard a little sigh of satisfaction as he cuddled the butt into his shoulder; and saw that amazing target, the black man on the yellow ground, standing clear at the end of his foresight. For an instant he was rigid and motionless. Then his finger tightened on the trigger. There was a strange, loud whiz and a long, silvery tinkle of broken glass. At that instant Holmes sprang like a tiger on to the marksman's back and hurled him flat upon his face. He was up again in a moment, and with convulsive strength he seized Holmes by the throat, but I struck him on the head with the butt of my revolver, and he dropped again upon the floor. I fell upon him, and as I held him my comrade blew a shrill call upon a whistle. There was the clatter of running feet upon the pavement, and two policemen in uniform, with one plain-clothes detective, rushed through the front entrance and into the room.

"That you, Lestrade?" said Holmes.

"Yes, Mr. Holmes. I took the job myself. It's good to see you back in London, sir."

"I think you want a little unofficial help. Three undetected murders in one year won't do, Lestrade. But you handled the Molesey Mystery with less than your usual—that's to say, you handled it fairly well."

We had all risen to our feet, our prisoner breathing hard, with a stalwart constable on each side of him. Already a few loiterers had begun to collect in the street. Holmes stepped up to the window, closed it, and dropped the blinds. Lestrade had produced two candles, and the policemen had uncovered their lanterns. I was able at last to have a good look at our prisoner.

It was a tremendously virile and yet sinister face which was turned towards us. With the brow of a philosopher above and the jaw of a sensualist below, the man must have started with great capacities for good or for evil. But one could not look upon his cruel blue eyes, with their drooping, cynical lids, or upon the fierce, aggressive nose and the threatening, deep-lined brow, without reading Nature's plainest danger-signals. He took no heed of any of us, but his eyes were fixed upon Holmes's face with an expression in which hatred and amazement were equally blended. "You fiend!" he kept on muttering. "You clever, clever fiend!"

"Ah, Colonel!" said Holmes, arranging his rumpled collar. "'Journeys end in lovers' meetings,' as the old play says. I don't think I have had the pleasure of seeing you since you favoured me with those attentions as I lay on the ledge above the Reichenbach Fall."

The colonel still stared at my friend like a man in a trance. "You cunning, cunning fiend!" was all that he could say.

"I have not introduced you yet," said Holmes. "This, gentlemen, is Colonel Sebastian Moran, once of Her Majesty's Indian Army, and the best heavy-game shot that our Eastern Empire has ever produced. I believe I am correct Colonel, in saying that your bag of tigers still remains unrivalled?"

The fierce old man said nothing, but still glared at my companion. With his savage eyes and bristling moustache, he was wonderfully like a tiger himself.

"I wonder that my very simple stratagem could deceive so old a *shikari*," said Holmes. "It must be very familiar to you. Have you not tethered a young kid under a tree, lain above it with your rifle, and waited for the bait to bring up your tiger? This empty house is my tree, and you are my tiger. You have possibly had other guns in reserve in case there should be several tigers, or in the unlikely supposition of your own aim failing you. These," he pointed around, "are my other guns. The parallel is exact."

Colonel Moran sprang forward with a snarl of rage, but the constables dragged him back. The fury upon his face was terrible to look at.

"I confess that you had one small surprise for me," said Holmes. "I did. not anticipate that you would yourself make use of this empty house and this convenient front window. I had imagined you as operating from the street, where my friend, Lestrade and his merry men were awaiting you. With that exception, all has gone as I expected."

Colonel Moran turned to the official detective.

"You may or may not have just cause for arresting me," said he, "but at least there can be no reason why I should submit to the gibes of this person. If I am in the hands of the law, let things be done in a legal way."

"Well, that's reasonable enough," said Lestrade. "Nothing further you have to say, Mr. Holmes, before we go?"

Holmes had picked up the powerful air-gun from the floor and was examining its mechanism.

"An admirable and unique weapon," said he, "noiseless and of tremendous power: I knew Von Herder, the blind German mechanic, who constructed it to the order of the late Professor Moriarty. For years I have been aware of its existence though I have never before had the opportunity of handling it. I commend it very specially to your attention, Lestrade and also the bullets which fit it."

"You can trust us to look after that, Mr. Holmes," said Lestrade, as the whole party moved towards the door. "Anything further to say?"

"Only to ask what charge you intend to prefer?"

"What charge, sir? Why, of course, the attempted murder of Mr. Sherlock Holmes."

"Not so, Lestrade. I do not propose to appear in the matter at all. To you, and to you only, belongs the credit of the remarkable arrest which you have effected. Yes, Lestrade, I congratulate you! With your usual happy mixture of cunning and audacity, you have got him."

"Got him! Got whom, Mr. Holmes?"

"The man that the whole force has been seeking in vain—Colonel Sebastian Moran, who shot the Honourable Ronald Adair with an expanding bullet from an air-gun through the open window of the second-floor front of No. 427, Park Lane, upon the thirtieth of last month. That's the charge, Lestrade. And now, Watson, if you can endure the draught from a broken window, I think that half an hour in my study over a cigar may afford you some profitable amusement."

Our old chambers had been left unchanged through the supervision of Mycroft Holmes and the immediate care of Mrs. Hudson. As I entered I saw, it is true, an unwonted tidiness, but the old landmarks were all in their place. There were the chemical corner and the acid-stained, deal-topped table. There upon a shelf was the row of formidable scrap-books and books of reference which many of our fellow-citizens would have been so glad to burn. The diagrams, the violin-case, and the pipe-rack—even the Persian slipper which contained the tobacco—all met my eyes as I glanced round me. There were two occupants of the room—one, Mrs. Hudson, who beamed upon us both as we entered—the other, the strange dummy which had played so important a part in the evening's adventures. It was a wax-coloured model of my friend, so admirably done that it was a perfect facsimile. It stood on a small pedestal table with an old dressing-gown of Holmes's so draped round it that the illusion from the street was absolutely perfect.

"I hope you observed all precautions, Mrs. Hudson?" said Holmes.

"I went to it on my knees, sir, just as you told me."

"Excellent. You carried the thing out very well. Did you observe where the bullet went?"

"Yes, sir. I'm afraid it has spoilt your beautiful bust, for it passed right through the head and flattened itself on the wall. I picked it up from the carpet. Here it is!"

Holmes held it out to me. "A soft revolver bullet, as you perceive, Watson. There's genius in that, for who would expect to find such a thing fired from an airgun? All right, Mrs. Hudson. I am much obliged for your assistance. And now, Watson, let me see you in your old seat once more, for there are several points which I should like to discuss with you."

He had thrown off the seedy frockcoat, and now he was the Holmes of old in the mouse-coloured dressing-gown which he took from his effigy.

"The old *shikari's* nerves have not lost their steadiness, nor his eyes their keenness," said he, with a laugh, as he inspected the shattered forehead of his bust.

"Plumb in the middle of the back of the head and smack through the brain. He was the best shot in India, and I expect that there are few better in London. Have you heard the name?"

"No, I have not."

"Well, well, such is fame! But then, if I remember right, you had not heard the name of Professor James Moriarty, who had one of the great brains of the century. Just give me down my index of biographies from the shelf."

He turned over the pages lazily, leaning back in his chair and blowing great clouds from his cigar.

"My collection of M's is a fine one," said he. "Moriarty himself is enough to make any letter illustrious, and here is Morgan the poisoner, and Merridew of abominable memory, and Mathews, who knocked out my left canine in the waiting-room at Charing Cross, and, finally, here is our friend of tonight."

He handed over the book, and I read:

Moran, Sebastian, Colonel. Unemployed. Formerly 1st Bangalore Pioneers. Born London, 1840. Son of Sir Augustus Moran, C.B., once British Minister to Persia. Educated Eton and Oxford. Served in Jowaki Campaign, Afghan Campaign, Charasiab (despatches), Sherpur and Cabul. Author of *Heavy Game of the Western Himalayas* (1881); *Three Months in the Jungle* (1884). Address: Conduit Street. Clubs: The Anglo-Indian, the Tankerville, the Bagatelle Card Club.

On the margin was written, in Holmes's precise hand:

The second most dangerous man in London.

"This is astonishing," said I, as I handed back the volume. "The man's career is that of an honourable soldier."

"It is true," Holmes answered. "Up to a certain point he did well. He was always a man of iron nerve, and the story is still told in India how he crawled down a drain after a wounded man-eating tiger. There are some trees, Watson, which grow to a certain height, and then suddenly develop some unsightly eccentricity. You will see it often in humans. I have a theory that the individual represents in his development the whole procession of his ancestors, and that such a sudden turn to good or evil stands for some strong influence which came into the line of his pedigree. The person becomes, as it were, the epitome of the history of his own family."

"It is surely rather fanciful."

"Well, I don't insist upon it. Whatever the cause, Colonel Moran began to go wrong. Without any open scandal, he still made India too hot to hold him. He retired, came to London, and again acquired an evil name. It was at this time that he was sought out by Professor Moriarty, to whom for a time he was chief of the staff. Moriarty supplied him liberally with money and used him only in one or two very high-class jobs, which no ordinary criminal could have undertaken. You may have some recollection of the death of Mrs. Stewart, of Lauder, in 1887. Not? Well, I am sure Moran was at the bottom of it, but nothing could be proved. So cleverly was the colonel concealed that, even when the Moriarty gang was broken up, we could not incriminate him. You remember at that date, when I called upon you in your rooms, how I put up the shutters for fear of air-guns? No doubt you thought me fanciful. I knew exactly what I was doing, for I knew of the existence of this remarkable gun, and I knew also that one of the best shots in the world would be behind it. When we were in Switzerland he followed us with Moriarty, and it was undoubtedly he who gave me that evil five minutes on the Reichenbach ledge.

"You may think that I read the papers with some attention during my sojourn in France, on the look-out for any chance of laying him by the heels. So long as he was free in London, my life would really not have been worth living. Night and day the shadow would have been over me, and sooner or later his chance must have come. What could I do? I could not shoot him at sight, or I should myself be in the dock. There was no use appealing to a magistrate. They cannot interfere on the strength of what would appear to them to be a wild suspicion. So, I could do nothing. But I watched the criminal news, knowing that sooner or later I should get him. Then came the death of this Ronald

Adair. My chance had come at last. Knowing what I did, was it not certain that Colonel Moran had done it? He had played cards with the lad, he had followed him home from the club, he had shot him through the open window. There was not a doubt of it. The bullets alone are enough to put his head in a noose. I came over at once. I was seen by the sentinel, who would, I knew, direct the colonel's attention to my presence. He could not fail to connect my sudden return with his crime, and to be terribly alarmed. I was sure that he would make an attempt to get me out of the way *at once* and would bring round his murderous weapon for that purpose. I left him an excellent mark in the window, and, having warned the police that they might be needed—by the way, Watson, you spotted their presence in that doorway with unerring accuracy—I took up what seemed to me to be a judicious post for observation, never dreaming that he would choose the same spot for his attack. Now, my dear Watson, does anything remain for me to explain?"

"Yes," said I. "You have not made it clear what was Colonel Moran's motive in murdering the Honourable Ronald Adair?"

"Ah! my dear Watson, there we come into those realms of conjecture, where the most logical mind may be at fault. Each may form his own hypothesis upon the present evidence, and yours is as likely to be correct as mine."

"You have formed one, then?"

"I think that it is not difficult to explain the facts. It came out in evidence that Colonel Moran and young Adair had, between them, won a considerable amount of money. Now, Moran undoubtedly played foul—of that I have long been aware. I believe that on the day of the murder Adair had discovered that Moran was cheating. Very likely he had spoken to him privately and had threatened to expose him unless he voluntarily resigned his membership of the club and promised not to play cards again. It is unlikely that a youngster like Adair would at once make a hideous scandal by exposing a well-known man so much older than himself. Probably he acted as I suggest. The exclusion from his clubs would mean ruin to Moran, who lived by his ill-gotten card-gains. He therefore murdered Adair, who at the time was endeavouring to work out how much money he should himself return, since he could not profit by his partner's foul play. He locked the door lest the ladies should surprise him and insist upon knowing what he was doing with these names and coins. Will it pass?"

"I have no doubt that you have hit upon the truth."

"It will be verified or disproved at the trial. Meanwhile, come what may, Colonel Moran will trouble us no more. The famous air-gun of Von Herder will embellish the Scotland Yard Museum, and once again Mr. Sherlock Holmes is free to devote his life to examining those interesting little problems which the complex life of London so plentifully presents."

THE ADVENTURE OF THE PRIORY SCHOOL

We have had some dramatic entrances and exits upon our small stage at Baker Street, but I cannot recollect anything more sudden and startling than the first appearance of Thorneycroft Huxtable, M.A., Ph.D., etc. His card, which seemed too small to carry the weight of his academic distinctions, preceded him by a few seconds, and then he entered himself—so large, so pompous, and so dignified that he was the very embodiment of self-possession and solidity. And yet his first action, when the door had closed behind him, was to stagger against the table, whence he slipped down upon the floor, and there was that majestic figure prostrate and insensible upon our bearskin hearth-rug.

We had sprung to our feet, and for a few moments we stared in silent amazement at this ponderous piece of wreckage, which told of some sudden and fatal storm far out on the ocean of life. Then Holmes hurried with a cushion for his head, and I with brandy for his lips. The heavy, white face was seamed with lines of trouble, the hanging pouches under the closed eyes were leaden in colour, the loose mouth drooped dolorously at the corners, the rolling chins were unshaven. Collar and shirt bore the grime of a long journey, and the hair bristled unkempt from the well-shaped head. It was a sorely stricken man who lay before us.

"What is it, Watson?" asked Holmes.

"Absolute exhaustion—possibly mere hunger and fatigue," said I, with my finger on the thready pulse, where the stream of life trickled thin and small.

"Return ticket from Mackleton, in the north of England," said Holmes, drawing it from the watch-pocket. "It is not twelve o'clock yet. He has certainly been an early starter."

The puckered eyelids had begun to quiver, and now a pair of vacant grey eyes looked up at us. An instant later the man had scrambled on to his feet, his face crimson with shame.

"Forgive this weakness, Mr. Holmes, I have been a little overwrought. Thank you, if I might have a glass of milk and a biscuit, I have no doubt that I should be better. I came personally, Mr. Holmes, in order to insure that you would return with me. I feared that no telegram would convince you of the absolute urgency of the case."

"When you are quite restored——"

"I am quite well again. I cannot imagine how I came to be so weak. I wish you, Mr. Holmes, to come to Mackleton with me by the next train."

My friend shook his head.

"My colleague, Dr. Watson, could tell you that we are very busy at present. I am retained in this case of the Ferrers Documents, and the Abergavenny murder is coming up for trial. Only a very important issue could call me from London at present."

"Important!" Our visitor threw up his hands. "Have you heard nothing of the abduction of the only son of the Duke of Holdernesse?"

"What! the late Cabinet Minister?"

"Exactly. We had tried to keep it out of the papers, but there was some rumour in the *Globe* last night. I thought it might have reached your ears."

Holmes shot out his long, thin arm and picked out Volume "H" in his encyclopædia of reference.

"'Holdernesse, 6th Duke, K.G., P.C.'—half the alphabet! 'Baron Beverley, Earl of Carston'—dear me, what a list! 'Lord Lieutenant of Hallamshire since 1900. Married Edith, daughter of Sir Charles Appledore, 1888. Heir and only child, Lord Saltire. Owns about two hundred and fifty thousand acres. Minerals in Lancashire and Wales. Address: Carlton House Terrace; Holdernesse Hall, Hallamshire;

Carston Castle, Bangor, Wales. Lord of the Admiralty, 1872; Chief Secretary of State for——' Well, well, this man is certainly one of the greatest subjects of the Crown!"

"The greatest and perhaps the wealthiest. I am aware, Mr. Holmes, that you take a very high line in professional matters, and that you are prepared to work for the work's sake. I may tell you, however, that his Grace has already intimated that a check for five thousand pounds will be handed over to the person who can tell him where his son is, and another thousand to him who can name the man or men who have taken him."

"It is a princely offer," said Holmes. "Watson, I think that we shall accompany Dr. Huxtable back to the north of England. And now, Dr. Huxtable, when you have consumed that milk, you will kindly tell me what has happened, when it happened, how it happened, and, finally, what Dr. Thorneycroft Huxtable, of the Priory School, near Mackleton, has to do with the matter, and why he comes three days after an event—the state of your chin gives the date—to ask for my humble services."

Our visitor had consumed his milk and biscuits. The light had come back to his eyes and the colour to his cheeks, as he set himself with great vigour and lucidity to explain the situation.

"I must inform you, gentlemen, that the Priory is a preparatory school, of which I am the founder and principal. *Huxtable's Sidelights on Horace* may possibly recall my name to your memories. The Priory is, without exception, the best and most select preparatory school in England. Lord Leverstoke, the Earl of Blackwater, Sir Cathcart Soames—they all have intrusted their sons to me. But I felt that my school had reached its zenith when, weeks ago, the Duke of Holdernesse sent Mr. James Wilder, his secretary, with intimation that young Lord Saltire, ten years old, his only son and heir, was about to be committed to my charge. Little did I think that this would be the prelude to the most crushing misfortune of my life.

"On May 1st the boy arrived, that being the beginning of the summer term. He was a charming youth, and he soon fell into our ways. I may tell you—I trust that I am not indiscreet, but half-confidences are absurd in such a case—that he was not entirely happy at home. It is an open secret that the Duke's married life had not been a peaceful one, and the matter had ended in a separation by mutual consent, the Duchess taking up her residence in the south of France. This had occurred very shortly before, and the boy's sympathies are known to have been strongly with his mother. He moped after her departure from Holdernesse Hall, and it was for this reason that the Duke desired to send him to my establishment. In a fortnight the boy was quite at home with us and was apparently absolutely happy.

"He was last seen on the night of May 13th—that is, the night of last Monday. His room was on the second floor and was approached through another larger room, in which two boys were sleeping. These boys saw and heard nothing, so that it is certain that young Saltire did not pass out that way. His window was open, and there is a stout ivy plant leading to the ground. We could trace no footmarks below, but it is sure that this is the only possible exit.

"His absence was discovered at seven o'clock on Tuesday morning. His bed had been slept in. He had dressed himself fully, before going off, in his usual school suit of black Eton jacket and dark grey trousers. There were no signs that anyone had entered the room, and it is quite certain that anything in the nature of cries or a struggle would have been heard, since Caunter, the elder boy in the inner room, is a very light sleeper.

"When Lord Saltire's disappearance was discovered, I at once called a roll of the whole establishment—boys, masters, and servants. It was then that we ascertained that Lord Saltire had not been alone in his flight. Heidegger, the German master, was missing. His room was on the second floor, at the farther end of the building, facing the same way as Lord Saltire's. His bed had also been slept in, but he had apparently gone away partly dressed, since his shirt and socks were lying on the floor. He had undoubtedly let himself down by the ivy, for we could see the marks of his feet where he had landed on the lawn. His bicycle was kept in a small shed beside this lawn, and it also was gone.

"He had been with me for two years, and came with the best references, but he was a silent, morose man, not very popular either with masters or boys. No trace could be found of the fugitives, and now, on Thursday morning, we are as ignorant as we were on Tuesday. Inquiry was, of course, made at once at Holdernesse Hall. It is only a few miles away, and we imagined that, in some sudden attack of homesickness, he had gone back to his father, but nothing had been heard of him. The Duke is greatly agitated, and, as to me, you have seen yourselves the state of nervous prostration to which the suspense and the responsibility have reduced me. Mr. Holmes, if ever you put forward your full powers, I implore you to do so now, for never in your life could you have a case which is more worthy of them."

Sherlock Holmes had listened with the utmost intentness to the statement of the unhappy schoolmaster. His drawn brows and the deep furrow between them showed that he needed no exhortation to concentrate all his attention upon a problem which, apart from the tremendous interests involved must appeal so directly to his love of the complex and the unusual. He now drew out his notebook and jotted down one or two memoranda.

"You have been very remiss in not coming to me sooner," said he, severely. "You start me on my investigation with a very serious handicap. It is inconceivable, for example, that this ivy and this lawn would have yielded nothing to an expert observer."

"I am not to blame, Mr. Holmes. His Grace was extremely desirous to avoid all public scandal. He was afraid of his family unhappiness being dragged before the world. He has a deep horror of anything of the kind."

"But there has been some official investigation?"

"Yes, sir, and it has proved most disappointing. An apparent clue was at once obtained, since a boy and a young man were reported to have been seen leaving a neighbouring station by an early train. Only last night we had news that the couple had been hunted down in Liverpool, and they prove to have no connection whatever with the matter in hand. Then it was that in my despair and disappointment, after a sleepless night, I came straight to you by the early train."

"I suppose the local investigation was relaxed while this false clue was being followed up?"

"It was entirely dropped."

"So that three days have been wasted. The affair has been most deplorably handled."

"I feel it and admit it."

"And yet the problem should be capable of ultimate solution. I shall be very happy to look into it. Have you been able to trace any connection between the missing boy and this German master?"

"None at all."

"Was he in the master's class?"

"No, he never exchanged a word with him, so far as I know."

"That is certainly very singular. Had the boy a bicycle?"

"No."

"Was any other bicycle missing?"

"No."

"Is that certain?"

"Quite."

"Well, now, you do not mean to seriously suggest that this German rode off upon a bicycle in the dead of the night, bearing the boy in his arms?"

"Certainly not."

"Then what is the theory in your mind?"

"The bicycle may have been a blind. It may have been hidden somewhere, and the pair gone off on foot."

"Quite so, but it seems rather an absurd blind, does it not? Were there other bicycles in this shed?"

"Several."

"Would he not have hidden *a couple*, had he desired to give the idea that they had gone off upon them?"

"I suppose he would."

"Of course he would. The blind theory won't do. But the incident is an admirable starting-point for an investigation. After all, a bicycle is not an easy thing to conceal or to destroy. One other question. Did anyone call to see the boy on the day before he disappeared?"

"No."

"Did he get any letters?"

"Yes, one letter."

"From whom?"

"From his father."

"Do you open the boys' letters?"

"No."

"How do you know it was from the father?"

"The coat of arms was on the envelope, and it was addressed in the Duke's peculiar stiff hand. Besides, the Duke remembers having written."

"When had he a letter before that?"

"Not for several days."

"Had he ever one from France?"

"No, never.

"You see the point of my questions, of course. Either the boy was carried off by force or he went of his own free will. In the latter case, you would expect that some prompting from outside would be needed to make so young a lad do such a thing. If he has had no visitors, that prompting must have come in letters; hence I try to find out who were his correspondents."

"I fear I cannot help you much. His only correspondent, so far as I know, was his own father."

"Who wrote to him on the very day of his disappearance. Were the relations between father and son very friendly?"

"His Grace is never very friendly with anyone. He is completely immersed in large public questions and is rather inaccessible to all ordinary emotions. But he was always kind to the boy in his own way."

"But the sympathies of the latter were with the mother?"

"Yes."

"Did he say so?"

"No."

"The Duke, then?"

"Good Heavens, no!"

"Then how could you know?"

"I have had some confidential talks with Mr. James Wilder, his Grace's secretary. It was he who gave me the information about Lord Saltire's feelings."

"I see. By the way, that last letter of the Duke's—was it found in the boy's room after he was gone?"

"No, he had taken it with him. I think, Mr. Holmes, it is time that we were leaving for Euston."

"I will order a four-wheeler. In a quarter of an hour, we shall be at your service. If you are telegraphing home, Mr. Huxtable, it would be well to allow the people in your neighbourhood to imagine that the inquiry is still going on in Liverpool, or wherever else that red herring led your pack. In the meantime, I will do a little quiet work at your own doors, and perhaps the scent is not so cold but that two old hounds like Watson and myself may get a sniff of it."

That evening found us in the cold, bracing atmosphere of the Peak country, in which Dr. Huxtable's famous school is situated. It was already dark when we reached it. A card was lying on the hall table, and the butler whispered something to his master, who turned to us with agitation in every heavy feature.

"The Duke is here," said he. "The Duke and Mr. Wilder are in the study. Come, gentlemen, and I will introduce you."

I was, of course, familiar with the pictures of the famous statesman, but the man himself was very different from his representation. He was a tall and stately person, scrupulously dressed, with a drawn, thin face, and a nose which was grotesquely curved and long. His complexion was of a dead pallor, which was more startling by contrast with a long, dwindling beard of vivid red, which flowed down over his white waistcoat with his watch-chain gleaming through its fringe. Such was the stately presence who looked stonily at us from the Centre of Dr. Huxtable's hearthrug. Beside him stood a very young man, whom I understood to be Wilder, the private secretary. He was small, nervous, alert with intelligent light-blue eyes and mobile features. It was he who at once, in an incisive and positive tone, opened the conversation.

"I called this morning, Dr. Huxtable, too late to prevent you from starting for London. I learned that your object was to invite Mr. Sherlock Holmes to undertake the conduct of this case. His Grace is surprised, Dr. Huxtable, that you should have taken such a step without consulting him."

"When I learned that the police had failed——"

"His Grace is by no means convinced that the police have failed."

"But surely, Mr. Wilder——"

"You are well aware, Dr. Huxtable, that his Grace is particularly anxious to avoid all public scandal. He prefers to take as few people as possible into his confidence."

"The matter can be easily remedied," said the brow-beaten doctor; "Mr. Sherlock Holmes can return to London by the morning train."

"Hardly that, Doctor, hardly that," said Holmes, in his blandest voice. "This northern air is invigorating and pleasant, so I propose to spend a few days upon your moors, and to occupy my mind as best I may. Whether I have the shelter of your roof or of the village inn is, of course, for you to decide."

I could see that the unfortunate doctor was in the last stage of indecision, from which he was rescued by the deep, sonorous voice of the red-bearded Duke, which boomed out like a dinner-gong.

"I agree with Mr. Wilder, Dr. Huxtable, that you would have done wisely to consult me. But since Mr. Holmes has already been taken into your confidence, it would indeed be absurd that we should not avail ourselves of his services. Far from going to the inn, Mr. Holmes, I should be pleased if you would come and stay with me at Holdernesse Hall."

"I thank your Grace. For the purposes of my investigation, I think that it would be wiser for me to remain at the scene of the mystery."

"Just as you like, Mr. Holmes. Any information which Mr. Wilder or I can give you is, of course, at your disposal."

"It will probably be necessary for me to see you at the Hall," said Holmes. "I would only ask you now, sir, whether you have formed any explanation in your own mind as to the mysterious disappearance of your son?"

"No, sir, I have not."

"Excuse me if I allude to that which is painful to you, but I have no alternative. Do you think that the Duchess had anything to do with the matter?"

The great minister showed perceptible hesitation.

"I do not think so," he said, at last.

"The other most obvious explanation is that the child has been kidnapped for the purpose of levying ransom. You have not had any demand of the sort?"

"No, sir."

"One more question, your Grace. I understand that you wrote to your son upon the day when this incident occurred."

"No, I wrote upon the day before."

"Exactly. But he received it on that day?"

"Yes."

"Was there anything in your letter which might have unbalanced him or induced him to take such a step?"

"No, sir, certainly not."

"Did you post that letter yourself?"

The nobleman's reply was interrupted by his secretary, who broke in with some heat.

"His Grace is not in the habit of posting letters himself," said he. "This letter was laid with others upon the study table, and I myself put them in the post-bag."

"You are sure this one was among them?"

"Yes, I observed it."

"How many letters did your Grace write that day?"

"Twenty or thirty. I have a large correspondence. But surely this is somewhat irrelevant?"

"Not entirely," said Holmes.

"For my own part," the Duke continued, "I have advised the police to turn their attention to the south of France. I have already said that I do not believe that the Duchess would encourage so monstrous an action, but the lad had the most wrong-headed opinions, and it is possible that he may have fled to her, aided and abetted by this German. I think, Dr. Huxtable, that we will now return to the Hall."

I could see that there were other questions which Holmes would have wished to put, but the nobleman's abrupt manner showed that the interview was at an end. It was evident that to his intensely aristocratic nature this discussion of his intimate family affairs with a stranger was most abhorrent, and that he feared lest every fresh question would throw a fiercer light into the discreetly shadowed corners of his ducal history.

When the nobleman and his secretary had left, my friend flung himself at once with characteristic eagerness into the investigation.

The boy's chamber was carefully examined, and yielded nothing save the absolute conviction that it was only through the window that he could have escaped. The German master's room and effects gave no further clue. In his case a trailer of ivy had given way under his weight, and we saw by the light of a lantern the mark on the lawn where his heels had come down. That one dint in the short, green grass was the only material witness left of this inexplicable nocturnal flight.

Sherlock Holmes left the house alone, and only returned after eleven. He had obtained a large ordnance map of the neighbourhood, and this he brought into my room, where he laid it out on the bed, and, having balanced the lamp in the middle of it, he began to smoke over it, and occasionally to point out objects of interest with the reeking amber of his pipe.

"This case grows upon me, Watson," said he. "There are decidedly some points of interest in connection with it. In this early stage, I want you to realize those geographical features which may have a good deal to do with our investigation.

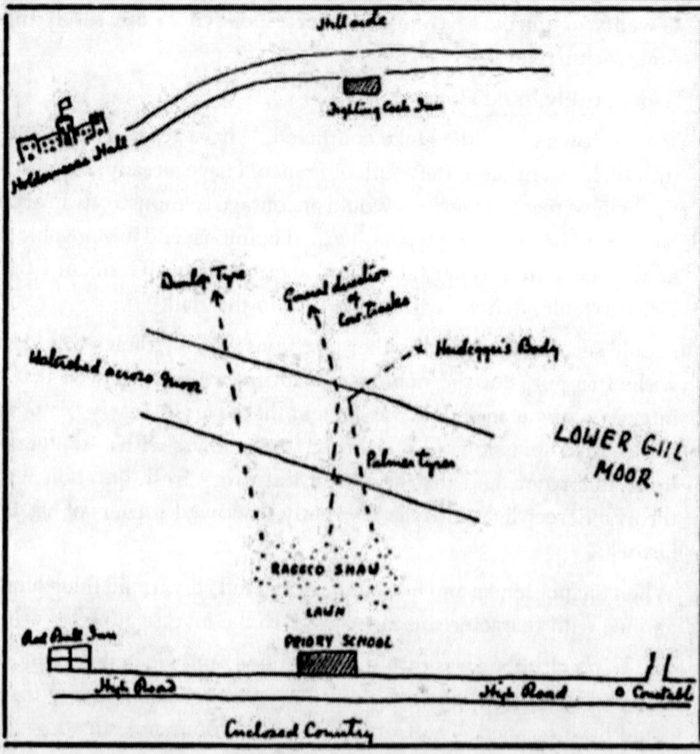

HOLMES' MAP OF THE NEIGHBOURHOOD OF THE SCHOOL.

"Look at this map. This dark square is the Priory School. I'll put a pin in it. Now, this line is the main road. You see that it runs east and west past the school, and you see also that there is no side road for a mile either way. If these two-folk passed away by road, it was *this* road."

"Exactly."

"By a singular and happy chance, we are able to some extent to check what passed along this road during the night in question. At this point, where my pipe is now resting, a county constable was on duty from twelve to six. It is, as you perceive, the first cross-road on the east side. This man declares that he was not absent from his post for an instant, and he is positive that neither boy nor man could have gone that way unseen. I have spoken with this policeman tonight and he appears to me to be a perfectly reliable person. That blocks this end. We have now to deal with the other. There is an inn here, the Red Bull, the landlady of which was ill. She had sent to Mackleton for a doctor, but he did not arrive until morning, being absent at another case. The people at the inn were alert all night, awaiting his coming, and one or other of them seems to have continually had an eye upon the road. They declare that no one passed. If their evidence is good, then we are fortunate enough to be able to block the west, and also to be able to say that the fugitives did *not* use the road at all."

"But the bicycle?" I objected.

"Quite so. We will come to the bicycle presently. To continue our reasoning: if these people did not go by the road, they must have traversed the country to the north of the house or to the south of the house. That is certain. Let us weigh the one against the other. On the south of the house is, as you perceive, a large district of arable land, cut up into small fields, with stone walls between them. There, I admit that a bicycle is impossible. We can dismiss the idea. We turn to the country on the north. Here there lies a grove of trees, marked as the 'Ragged Shaw,' and on the farther side stretches a great rolling moor, Lower Gill Moor, extending for ten miles and sloping gradually upward. Here, at one side of this wilderness, is Holdernesse Hall, ten miles by road, but only six across the moor. It is a peculiarly desolate plain. A few moor farmers have small holdings, where they rear sheep and cattle. Except these, the plover and the curlew are the only inhabitants until you come to the Chesterfield high road. There is a church there, you see, a few cottages, and an inn. Beyond that the hills become precipitous. Surely it is here to the north that our quest must lie."

"But the bicycle?" I persisted.

"Well, well!" said Holmes, impatiently. "A good cyclist does not need a high road. The moor is intersected with paths, and the moon was at the full. Halloa! what is this?"

There was an agitated knock at the door, and an instant afterwards Dr. Huxtable was in the room. In his hand he held a blue cricket-cap with a white chevron on the peak.

"At last, we have a clue!" he cried. "Thank heaven! at last we are on the dear boy's track! It is his cap."

"Where was it found?"

"In the van of the gipsies who camped on the moor. They left on Tuesday. Today the police traced them down and examined their caravan. This was found."

"How do they account for it?"

"They shuffled and lied—said that they found it on the moor on Tuesday morning. They know where he is, the rascals! Thank goodness, they are all safe under lock and key. Either the fear of the law or the Duke's purse will certainly get out of them all that they know."

"So far, so good," said Holmes, when the doctor had at last left the room. "It at least bears out the theory that it is on the side of the Lower Gill Moor that we must hope for results. The police have really done nothing locally, save the arrest of these gipsies. Look here, Watson! There is a watercourse across the moor. You see it marked here in the map. In some parts it widens into a morass. This is particularly so in the region between Holdernesse Hall and the school. It is vain to look elsewhere for tracks in this dry weather, but at *that* point there is certainly a chance of some record being left. I will call you early tomorrow morning, and you and I will try if we can throw some little light upon the mystery."

The day was just breaking when I woke to find the long, thin form of Holmes by my bedside. He was fully dressed and had apparently already been out.

"I have done the lawn, and the bicycle shed," said he. "I have also had a rumble through the Ragged Shaw. Now, Watson, there is cocoa ready in the next room. I must beg you to hurry, for we have a great day before us."

His eyes shone, and his cheek was flushed with the exhilaration of the master workman who sees his work lie ready before him. A very different Holmes, this active, alert man, from the introspective and pallid dreamer of Baker Street. I felt, as I looked upon that supple figure, alive with nervous energy, that it was indeed a strenuous day that awaited us.

And yet it opened in the blackest disappointment. With high hopes we struck across the peaty, russet moor, intersected with a thousand sheep paths, until we came to the broad, light-green belt which marked the morass between us and Holdernesse. Certainly, if the lad had gone homeward, he must have passed this, and he could not pass it without leaving his traces. But no sign of him or the German could be seen. With a darkening face my friend strode along the margin, eagerly observant of every muddy stain upon the mossy surface. Sheep-marks there were in profusion, and at one place, some miles down, cows had left their tracks. Nothing more.

"Check number one," said Holmes, looking gloomily over the rolling expanse of the moor. "There is another morass down yonder, and a narrow neck between. Halloa! halloa! halloa! what have we here?"

We had come on a small black ribbon of pathway. In the middle of it, clearly marked on the sodden soil, was the track of a bicycle.

"Hurrah!" I cried. "We have it."

But Holmes was shaking his head, and his face was puzzled and expectant rather than joyous.

"A bicycle, certainly, but not *the* bicycle," said he. "I am familiar with forty-two different impressions left by tires. This, as you perceive, is a Dunlop, with a patch upon the outer cover. Heidegger's tires were Palmer's, leaving longitudinal stripes. Aveling, the mathematical master, was sure upon the point. Therefore, it is not Heidegger's track."

"The boy's, then?"

"Possibly, if we could prove a bicycle to have been in his possession. But this we have utterly failed to do. This track, as you perceive, was made by a rider who was going from the direction of the school."

"Or towards it?"

"No, no, my dear Watson. The more deeply sunk impression is, of course, the hind wheel, upon which the weight rests. You perceive several places where it has passed across and obliterated the more shallow mark of the front one. It was undoubtedly heading away from the school. It may or may not be connected with our inquiry, but we will follow it backwards before we go any farther."

We did so, and at the end of a few hundred yards lost the tracks as we emerged from the boggy portion of the moor. Following the path backwards, we picked out another spot, where a spring trickled across it. Here, once again, was the mark of the bicycle, though nearly obliterated by the hoofs of cows. After that there was no sign, but the path ran right on into Ragged Shaw, the wood which backed on to the school. From this wood the cycle must have emerged. Holmes sat down on a boulder and rested his chin in his hands. I had smoked two cigarettes before he moved.

"Well, well," said he, at last. "It is, of course, possible that a cunning man might change the tires of his bicycle in order to leave unfamiliar tracks. A criminal who was capable of such a thought is a man whom I should be proud to do business with. We will leave this question undecided and hark back to our morass again, for we have left a good deal unexplored."

We continued our systematic survey of the edge of the sodden portion of the moor, and soon our perseverance was gloriously rewarded. Right across the lower part of the bog lay a miry path. Holmes gave a cry of delight as he approached it. An impression like a fine bundle of telegraph wires ran down the Centre of it. It was the Palmer tires.

"Here is Herr Heidegger, sure enough!" cried Holmes, exultantly. "My reasoning seems to have been pretty sound, Watson."

"I congratulate you."

"But we have a long way still to go. Kindly walk clear of the path. Now let us follow the trail. I fear that it will not lead very far."

We found, however, as we advanced that this portion of the moor is intersected with soft patches, and, though we frequently lost sight of the track, we always succeeded in picking it up once more.

"Do you observe," said Holmes, "that the rider is now undoubtedly forcing the pace? There can be no doubt of it. Look at this impression, where you get both tires clear. The one is as deep as the other. That can only mean that the rider is throwing his weight on to the handle-bar, as a man does when he is sprinting. By Jove! he has had a fall."

There was a broad, irregular smudge covering some yards of the track. Then there were a few footmarks, and the tire reappeared once more.

"A side-slip," I suggested.

Holmes held up a crumpled branch of flowering gorse. To my horror I perceived that the yellow blossoms were all dabbled with crimson. On the path, too, and among the heather were dark stains of clotted blood.

"Bad!" said Holmes. "Bad! Stand clear, Watson! Not an unnecessary footstep! What do I read here? He fell wounded—he stood up—he remounted—he proceeded. But there is no other track. Cattle on this side path. He was surely not gored by a bull? Impossible! But I see no traces of anyone else. We must push on, Watson. Surely, with stains as well as the track to guide us, he cannot escape us now."

Our search was not a very long one. The tracks of the tire began to curve fantastically upon the wet and shining path. Suddenly, as I looked ahead, the gleam of metal caught my eye from amid the thick gorse-bushes. Out of them we dragged a bicycle, Palmer-tired, one pedal bent, and the whole front of it horribly smeared and slobbered with blood. On the other side of the bushes a shoe was projecting. We ran round, and there lay the unfortunate rider. He was a tall man, full-bearded, with spectacles, one glass of which had been knocked out. The cause of his death was a frightful blow upon the head, which had crushed in part of his skull. That he could have gone on after receiving such an injury said much for the vitality and courage of the man. He wore shoes, but no socks, and his open coat disclosed a nightshirt beneath it. It was undoubtedly the German master.

Holmes turned the body over reverently and examined it with great attention. He then sat in deep thought for a time, and I could see by his ruffled brow that this grim discovery had not, in his opinion, advanced us much in our inquiry.

"It is a little difficult to know what to do, Watson," said he, at last. "My own inclinations are to push this inquiry on, for we have already lost so much time that we cannot afford to waste another hour. On the other hand, we are bound to inform the police of the discovery, and to see that this poor fellow's body is looked after."

"I could take a note back."

"But I need your company and assistance. Wait a bit! There is a fellow cutting peat up yonder. Bring him over here, and he will guide the police."

I brought the peasant across, and Holmes dispatched the frightened man with a note to Dr. Huxtable.

"Now, Watson," said he, "we have picked up two clues this morning. One is the bicycle with the Palmer tire, and we see what that has led to. The other is the bicycle with the patched Dunlop. Before we start to investigate that, let us try to realize what we *do* know, so as to make the most of it, and to separate the essential from the accidental."

"First of all, I wish to impress upon you that the boy certainly left of his own free-will. He got down from his window and he went off, either alone or with someone. That is sure."

I assented.

"Well, now, let us turn to this unfortunate German master. The boy was fully dressed when he fled. Therefore, he foresaw what he would do. But the German went without his socks. He certainly acted on very short notice."

"Undoubtedly."

"Why did he go? Because, from his bedroom window, he saw the flight of the boy, because he wished to overtake him and bring him back. He seized his bicycle, pursued the lad, and in pursuing him met his death."

"So, it would seem."

"Now I come to the critical part of my argument. The natural action of a man in pursuing a little boy would be to run after him. He would know that he could overtake him. But the German does not do so. He turns to his bicycle. I am told that he was an excellent cyclist. He would not do this, if he did not see that the boy had some swift means of escape."

"The other bicycle."

"Let us continue our reconstruction. He meets his death five miles from the school—not by a bullet, mark you, which even a lad might conceivably discharge, but by a savage blow dealt by a vigorous arm.

The lad, then, *had* a companion in his flight. And the flight was a swift one, since it took five miles before an expert cyclist could overtake them. Yet we survey the ground round the scene of the tragedy. What do we find? A few cattle-tracks, nothing more. I took a wide sweep round, and there is no path within fifty yards. Another cyclist could have had nothing to do with the actual murder, nor were there any human foot-marks."

"Holmes," I cried, "this is impossible."

"Admirable!" he said. "A most illuminating remark. It *is* impossible as I state it, and therefore I must in some respect have stated it wrong. Yet you saw for yourself. Can you suggest any fallacy?"

"He could not have fractured his skull in a fall?"

"In a morass, Watson?"

"I am at my wits' end."

"Tut, tut, we have solved some worse problems. At least we have plenty of material, if we can only use it. Come, then, and, having exhausted the Palmer, let us see what the Dunlop with the patched cover has to offer us."

We picked up the track and followed it onward for some distance, but soon the moor rose into a long, heather-tufted curve, and we left the watercourse behind us. No further help from tracks could be hoped for. At the spot where we saw the last of the Dunlop tire it might equally have led to Holdernesse Hall, the stately towers of which rose some miles to our left, or to a low, grey village which lay in front of us and marked the position of the Chesterfield high road.

As we approached the forbidding and squalid inn, with the sign of a game-cock above the door, Holmes gave a sudden groan and clutched me by the shoulder to save himself from falling. He had had one of those violent strains of the ankle which leave a man helpless. With difficulty he limped up to the door, where a squat, dark, elderly man was smoking a black clay pipe.

"How are you, Mr. Reuben Hayes?" said Holmes.

"Who are you, and how do you get my name so pat?" the countryman answered, with a suspicious flash of a pair of cunning eyes.

"Well, it's printed on the board above your head. It's easy to see a man who is master of his own house. I suppose you haven't such a thing as a carriage in your stables?"

"No, I have not."

"I can hardly put my foot to the ground."

"Don't put it to the ground."

"But I can't walk."

"Well, then hop."

Mr. Reuben Hayes's manner was far from gracious, but Holmes took it with admirable good-humour.

"Look here, my man," said he. "This is really rather an awkward fix for me. I don't mind how I get on."

"Neither do I," said the morose landlord.

"The matter is very important. I would offer you a sovereign for the use of a bicycle."

The landlord pricked up his ears.

"Where do you want to go?"

"To Holdernesse Hall."

"Pals of the Dook, I suppose?" said the landlord, surveying our mud-stained garments with ironical eyes.

Holmes laughed good-naturedly.

"He'll be glad to see us, anyhow."

"Why?"

"Because we bring him news of his lost son."

The landlord gave a very visible start.

"What, you're on his track?"

"He has been heard of in Liverpool. They expect to get him every hour."

Again, a swift change passed over the heavy, unshaven face. His manner was suddenly genial.

"I've less reason to wish the Dook well than most men," said he, "for I was head coachman once, and cruel bad he treated me. It was him that sacked me without a character on the word of a lying corn-chandler. But I'm glad to hear that the young lord was heard of in Liverpool, and I'll help you to take the news to the Hall."

"Thank you," said Holmes. "We'll have some food first. Then you can bring round the bicycle."

"I haven't got a bicycle."

Holmes held up a sovereign.

"I tell you, man, that I haven't got one. I'll let you have two horses as far as the Hall."

"Well, well," said Holmes, "we'll talk about it when we've had something to eat."

When we were left alone in the stone-flagged kitchen, it was astonishing how rapidly that sprained ankle recovered. It was nearly nightfall, and we had eaten nothing since early morning, so that we spent some time over our meal. Holmes was lost in thought, and once or twice he walked over to the window and stared earnestly out. It opened on to a squalid courtyard. In the far corner was a smithy, where a grimy lad was at work. On the other side were the stables. Holmes had sat down again after one of these excursions, when he suddenly sprang out of his chair with a loud exclamation.

"By heaven, Watson, I believe that I've got it!" he cried. "Yes, yes, it must be so. Watson, do you remember seeing any cow-tracks Today?"

"Yes, several."

"Where?"

"Well, everywhere. They were at the morass, and again on the path, and again near where poor Heidegger met his death."

"Exactly. Well, now, Watson, how many cows did you see on the moor?"

"I don't remember seeing any."

"Strange, Watson, that we should see tracks all along our line, but never a cow on the whole moor. Very strange, Watson, eh?"

"Yes, it is strange."

"Now, Watson, make an effort, throw your mind back. Can you see those tracks upon the path?"

"Yes, I can."

"Can you recall that the tracks were sometimes like that, Watson,"—he arranged a number of breadcrumbs in this fashion—: : : : :—"and sometimes like this"—: . : . : . : .—"and occasionally like this"—. ▪ . ▪ . ▪ . "Can you remember that?"

"No, I cannot."

"But I can. I could swear to it. However, we will go back at our leisure and verify it. What a blind beetle I have been, not to draw my conclusion."

"And what is your conclusion?"

"Only that it is a remarkable cow which walks, canters, and gallops. By George! Watson, it was no brain of a country publican that thought out such a blind as that. The coast seems to be clear, save for that lad in the smithy. Let us slip out and see what we can see."

There were two rough-haired, unkempt horses in the tumble-down stable. Holmes raised the hind leg of one of them and laughed aloud.

"Old shoes, but newly shod—old shoes, but new nails. This case deserves to be a classic. Let us go across to the smithy."

The lad continued his work without regarding us. I saw Holmes's eye darting to right and left among the litter of iron and wood which was scattered about the floor. Suddenly, however, we heard a step behind us, and there was the landlord, his heavy eyebrows drawn over his savage eyes, his swarthy features convulsed with passion. He held a short, metal-headed stick in his hand, and he advanced in so menacing a fashion that I was right glad to feel the revolver in my pocket.

"You infernal spies!" the man cried. "What are you doing there?"

"Why, Mr. Reuben Hayes," said Holmes, coolly, "one might think that you were afraid of our finding something out."

The man mastered himself with a violent effort, and his grim mouth loosened into a false laugh, which was more menacing than his frown.

"You're welcome to all you can find out in my smithy," said he. "But look here, mister, I don't care for folk poking about my place without my leave, so the sooner you pay your score and get out of this the better I shall be pleased."

"All right, Mr. Hayes, no harm meant," said Holmes. "We have been having a look at your horses, but I think I'll walk, after all. It's not far, I believe."

"Not more than two miles to the Hall gates. That's the road to the left." He watched us with sullen eyes until we had left his premises.

We did not go very far along the road, for Holmes stopped the instant that the curve hid us from the landlord's view.

"We were warm, as the children say, at that inn," said he. "I seem to grow colder every step that I take away from it. No, no, I can't possibly leave it."

"I am convinced," said I, "that this Reuben Hayes knows all about it. A more self-evident villain I never saw."

"Oh! he impressed you in that way, did he? There are the horses, there is the smithy. Yes, it is an interesting place, this Fighting Cock. I think we shall have another look at it in an unobtrusive way."

A long, sloping hillside, dotted with grey limestone boulders, stretched behind us. We had turned off the road, and were making our way up the hill, when, looking in the direction of Holdernesse Hall, I saw a cyclist coming swiftly along.

"Get down, Watson!" cried Holmes, with a heavy hand upon my shoulder. We had hardly sunk from view when the man flew past us on the road. Amid a rolling cloud of dust, I caught a glimpse of a pale, agitated face—a face with horror in every lineament, the mouth open, the eyes staring wildly in front. It was like some strange caricature of the dapper James Wilder whom we had seen the night before.

"The Duke's secretary!" cried Holmes. "Come, Watson, let us see what he does."

We scrambled from rock to rock, until in a few moments we had made our way to a point from which we could see the front door of the inn. Wilder's bicycle was leaning against the wall beside it. No one was moving about the house, nor could we catch a glimpse of any faces at the windows. Slowly the twilight crept down as the sun sank behind the high towers of Holdernesse Hall. Then, in the gloom, we saw the two side-lamps of a trap light up in the stable-yard of the inn, and shortly afterwards heard the rattle of hoofs, as it wheeled out into the road and tore off at a furious pace in the direction of Chesterfield.

"What do you make of that, Watson?" Holmes whispered.

"It looks like a flight."

"A single man in a dog-cart, so far as I could see. Well, it certainly was not Mr. James Wilder, for there he is at the door."

A red square of light had sprung out of the darkness. In the middle of it was the black figure of the secretary, his head advanced, peering out into the night. It was evident that he was expecting someone. Then at last there were steps in the road, a second figure was visible for an instant against the light, the door shut, and all was black once more. Five minutes later a lamp was lit in a room upon the first floor.

"It seems to be a curious class of custom that is done by the Fighting Cock," said Holmes.

"The bar is on the other side."

"Quite so. These are what one may call the private guests. Now, what in the world is Mr. James Wilder doing in that den at this hour of night, and who is the companion who comes to meet him there? Come, Watson, we must really take a risk and try to investigate this a little more closely."

Together we stole down to the road and crept across to the door of the inn. The bicycle still leaned against the wall. Holmes struck a match and held it to the back wheel, and I heard him chuckle as the light fell upon a patched Dunlop tire. Up above us was the lighted window.

"I must have a peep through that, Watson. If you bend your back and support yourself upon the wall, I think that I can manage."

An instant later, his feet were on my shoulders, but he was hardly up before he was down again.

"Come, my friend," said he, "our day's work has been quite long enough. I think that we have gathered all that we can. It's a long walk to the school, and the sooner we get started the better."

He hardly opened his lips during that weary trudge across the moor, nor would he enter the school when he reached it, but went on to Mackleton Station, whence he could send some telegrams. Late at night I heard him consoling Dr. Huxtable, prostrated by the tragedy of his master's death, and later still he entered my room as alert and vigorous as he had been when he started in the morning. "All goes well, my friend," said he. "I promise that before tomorrow evening we shall have reached the solution of the mystery."

At eleven o'clock next morning my friend and I were walking up the famous yew avenue of Holdernesse Hall. We were ushered through the magnificent Elizabethan doorway and into his Grace's study. There we found Mr. James Wilder, demure and courtly, but with some trace of that wild terror of the night before still lurking in his furtive eyes and in his twitching features.

"You have come to see his Grace? I am sorry, but the fact is that the Duke is far from well. He has been very much upset by the tragic news. We received a telegram from Dr. Huxtable yesterday afternoon, which told us of your discovery."

"I must see the Duke, Mr. Wilder."

"But he is in his room."

"Then I must go to his room."

"I believe he is in his bed."

"I will see him there."

Holmes's cold and inexorable manner showed the secretary that it was useless to argue with him.

"Very good, Mr. Holmes, I will tell him that you are here."

After an hour's delay, the great nobleman appeared. His face was more cadaverous than ever, his shoulders had rounded, and he seemed to me to be an altogether older man than he had been the morning before. He greeted us with a stately courtesy and seated himself at his desk, his red beard streaming down on the table.

"Well, Mr. Holmes?" said he.

But my friend's eyes were fixed upon the secretary, who stood by his master's chair.

"I think, your Grace, that I could speak more freely in Mr. Wilder's absence."

The man turned a shade paler and cast a malignant glance at Holmes.

"If your Grace wishes——"

"Yes, yes, you had better go. Now, Mr. Holmes, what have you to say?"

My friend waited until the door had closed behind the retreating secretary.

"The fact is, your Grace," said he, "that my colleague, Dr. Watson, and myself had an assurance from Dr. Huxtable that a reward had been offered in this case. I should like to have this confirmed from your own lips."

"Certainly, Mr. Holmes."

"It amounted, if I am correctly informed, to five thousand pounds to anyone who will tell you where your son is?"

"Exactly."

"And another thousand to the man who will name the person or persons who keep him in custody?"

"Exactly."

"Under the latter heading is included, no doubt, not only those who may have taken him away, but also those who conspire to keep him in his present position?"

"Yes, yes," cried the Duke, impatiently. "If you do your work well, Mr. Sherlock Holmes, you will have no reason to complain of niggardly treatment."

My friend rubbed his thin hands together with an appearance of avidity which was a surprise to me, who knew his frugal tastes.

"I fancy that I see your Grace's check-book upon the table," said he. "I should be glad if you would make me out a check for six thousand pounds. It would be as well, perhaps, for you to cross it. The Capital and Counties Bank, Oxford Street branch are my agents."

His Grace sat very stern and upright in his chair and looked stonily at my friend.

"Is this a joke, Mr. Holmes? It is hardly a subject for pleasantry."

"Not at all, your Grace. I was never more earnest in my life."

"What do you mean, then?"

"I mean that I have earned the reward. I know where your son is, and I know some, at least, of those who are holding him."

The Duke's beard had turned more aggressively red than ever against his ghastly white face.

"Where is he?" he gasped.

"He is, or was last night, at the Fighting Cock Inn, about two miles from your park gate."

The Duke fell back in his chair.

"And whom do you accuse?"

Sherlock Holmes's answer was an astounding one. He stepped swiftly forward and touched the Duke upon the shoulder.

"I accuse *you*," said he. "And now, your Grace, I'll trouble you for that check."

Never shall I forget the Duke's appearance as he sprang up and clawed with his hands, like one who is sinking into an abyss. Then, with an extraordinary effort of aristocratic self-command, he sat down and sank his face in his hands. It was some minutes before he spoke.

"How much do you know?" he asked at last, without raising his head.

"I saw you together last night."

"Does anyone else besides your friend know?"

"I have spoken to no one."

The Duke took a pen in his quivering fingers and opened his check-book.

"I shall be as good as my word, Mr. Holmes. I am about to write your check, however unwelcome the information which you have gained may be to me. When the offer was first made, I little thought the turn which events might take. But you and your friend are men of discretion, Mr. Holmes?"

"I hardly understand your Grace."

"I must put it plainly, Mr. Holmes. If only you two know of this incident, there is no reason why it should go any farther. I think twelve thousand pounds is the sum that I owe you, is it not?"

But Holmes smiled and shook his head.

"I fear, your Grace, that matters can hardly be arranged so easily. There is the death of this schoolmaster to be accounted for."

"But James knew nothing of that. You cannot hold him responsible for that. It was the work of this brutal ruffian whom he had the misfortune to employ."

"I must take the view, your Grace, that when a man embarks upon a crime, he is morally guilty of any other crime which may spring from it."

"Morally, Mr. Holmes. No doubt you are right. But surely not in the eyes of the law. A man cannot be condemned for a murder at which he was not present, and which he loathes and abhors as much as you do. The instant that he heard of it he made a complete confession to me, so filled was he with horror and remorse. He lost not an hour in breaking entirely with the murderer. Oh, Mr. Holmes, you must save him—you must save him! I tell you that you must save him!" The Duke had dropped the last attempt at self-command and was pacing the room with a convulsed face and with his clenched hands raving in the air. At last, he mastered himself and sat down once more at his desk. "I appreciate your conduct in coming here before you spoke to anyone else," said he. "At least, we may take counsel how far we can minimize this hideous scandal."

"Exactly," said Holmes. "I think, your Grace, that this can only be done by absolute frankness between us. I am disposed to help your Grace to the best of my ability, but, in order to do so, I must understand to the last detail how the matter stands. I realize that your words applied to Mr. James Wilder, and that he is not the murderer."

"No, the murderer has escaped."

Sherlock Holmes smiled demurely.

"Your Grace can hardly have heard of any small reputation which I possess, or you would not imagine that it is so easy to escape me. Mr. Reuben Hayes was arrested at Chesterfield, on my information, at eleven o'clock last night. I had a telegram from the head of the local police before I left the school this morning."

The Duke leaned back in his chair and stared with amazement at my friend.

"You seem to have powers that are hardly human," said he. "So Reuben Hayes is taken? I am right glad to hear it, if it will not react upon the fate of James."

"Your secretary?"

"No, sir, my son."

It was Holmes's turn to look astonished.

"I confess that this is entirely new to me, your Grace. I must beg you to be more explicit."

"I will conceal nothing from you. I agree with you that complete frankness, however painful it may be to me, is the best policy in this desperate situation to which James's folly and jealousy have reduced us. When I was a very young man, Mr. Holmes, I loved with such a love as comes only once in a lifetime. I offered the lady marriage, but she refused it on the grounds that such a match might mar my career. Had she lived, I would certainly never have married anyone else. She died, and left this one child, whom for her sake I have cherished and cared for. I could not acknowledge the paternity to the world, but I gave him the best of educations, and since he came to manhood I have kept him near my person. He surmised my secret and has presumed ever since upon the claim which he has upon me, and upon his power of provoking a scandal which would be abhorrent to me. His presence had something to do with the unhappy issue of my marriage. Above all, he hated my young legitimate heir from the first with a persistent hatred. You may well ask me why, under these circumstances, I still kept James under my roof. I answer that it was because I could see his mother's face in his, and that for her dear sake there was no end to my long-suffering. All her pretty ways too—there was not one of them which he could not suggest and bring back to my memory. I *could* not send him away. But I feared so much lest he should do Arthur—that is, Lord Saltire—a mischief, that I dispatched him for safety to Dr. Huxtable's school.

"James came into contact with this fellow Hayes, because the man was a tenant of mine, and James acted as agent. The fellow was a rascal from the beginning, but, in some extraordinary way, James became intimate with him. He had always a taste for low company. When James determined to kidnap Lord Saltire, it was of this man's service that he availed himself. You remember that I wrote to Arthur upon that last day. Well, James opened the letter and inserted a note asking Arthur to meet him in a little wood called the Ragged Shaw, which is near to the school. He used the Duchess's name, and in that way got the boy to come. That evening James bicycled over—I am telling you what he has himself confessed to me—and he told Arthur, whom he met in the wood, that his mother longed to see him, that she was awaiting him on the moor, and that if he would come back into the wood at midnight he would find a man with a horse, who would take him to her. Poor Arthur fell into the trap. He came to the appointment and found this fellow Hayes with a led pony. Arthur mounted, and they set off together. It appears—though this James only heard yesterday—that they were pursued, that Hayes struck the pursuer with his stick, and that the man died of his injuries. Hayes brought Arthur to his public-house, the Fighting Cock, where he was confined in an upper room, under the care of Mrs. Hayes, who is a kindly woman, but entirely under the control of her brutal husband.

"Well, Mr. Holmes, that was the state of affairs when I first saw you two days ago. I had no more idea of the truth than you. You will ask me what James's motive was in doing such a deed. I answer that there was a great deal which was unreasoning and fanatical in the hatred which he bore my heir. In his view he should himself have been heir of all my estates, and he deeply resented those social laws which made it impossible. At the same time, he had a definite motive also. He was eager that I should break the entail, and he was of opinion that it lay in my power to do so. He intended to make a bargain with me—to restore Arthur if I would break the entail, and so make it possible for the estate to be left to him by will. He knew well that I should never willingly invoke the aid of the police against him. I say that he would have proposed such a bargain to me, but he did not actually do so, for events moved too quickly for him, and he had not time to put his plans into practice.

"What brought all his wicked scheme to wreck was your discovery of this man Heidegger's dead body. James was seized with horror at the news. It came to us yesterday, as we sat together in this study. Dr. Huxtable had sent a telegram. James was so overwhelmed with grief and agitation that my suspicions, which had never been entirely absent, rose instantly to a certainty, and I taxed him with the deed. He made a complete voluntary confession. Then he implored me to keep his secret for three days longer, so as to give his wretched accomplice a chance of saving his guilty life. I yielded—as I have always yielded—to his prayers, and instantly James hurried off to the Fighting Cock to warn Hayes and give him the means of flight. I could not go there by daylight without provoking comment, but as soon as night fell I hurried off to see my dear Arthur. I found him safe and well but horrified beyond expression by the dreadful deed he had witnessed. In deference to my promise, and much against my will, I consented to leave him there for three days, under the charge of Mrs. Hayes, since it was evident that it was impossible to inform the police where he was without telling them also who the murderer was, and I could not see how that murderer could be punished without ruin to my unfortunate James. You asked for frankness, Mr. Holmes, and I have taken you at your word, for I have now told you everything without an attempt at circumlocution or concealment. Do you in turn be as frank with me."

"I will," said Holmes. "In the first place, your Grace, I am bound to tell you that you have placed yourself in a most serious position in the eyes of the law. You have condoned a felony, and you have aided the escape of a murderer, for I cannot doubt that any money which was taken by James Wilder to aid his accomplice in his flight came from your Grace's purse."

The Duke bowed his assent.

"This is, indeed, a most serious matter. Even more culpable in my opinion, your Grace, is your attitude towards your younger son. You leave him in this den for three days."

"Under solemn promises——"

"What are promises to such people as these? You have no guarantee that he will not be spirited away again. To humour your guilty elder son, you have exposed your innocent younger son to imminent and unnecessary danger. It was a most unjustifiable action."

The proud lord of Holdernesse was not accustomed to be so rated in his own ducal hall. The blood flushed into his high forehead, but his conscience held him dumb.

"I will help you, but on one condition only. It is that you ring for the footman and let me give such orders as I like."

Without a word, the Duke pressed the electric bell. A servant entered.

"You will be glad to hear," said Holmes, "that your young master is found. It is the Duke's desire that the carriage shall go at once to the Fighting Cock Inn to bring Lord Saltire home.

"Now," said Holmes, when the rejoicing lackey had disappeared, "having secured the future, we can afford to be more lenient with the past. I am not in an official position, and there is no reason, so long as the ends of justice are served, why I should disclose all that I know. As to Hayes, I say nothing. The gallows awaits him, and I would do nothing to save him from it. What he will divulge I cannot tell, but I have no doubt that your Grace could make him understand that it is to his interest to be silent. From the police point of view, he will have kidnapped the boy for the purpose of ransom. If they do not themselves find it out, I see no reason why I should prompt them to take a broader point of view. I would warn your Grace, however, that the continued presence of Mr. James Wilder in your household can only lead to misfortune."

"I understand that Mr. Holmes, and it is already settled that he shall leave me forever and go to seek his fortune in Australia."

"In that case, your Grace, since you have yourself stated that any unhappiness in your married life was caused by his presence, I would suggest that you make such amends as you can to the Duchess, and that you try to resume those relations which have been so unhappily interrupted."

"That also I have arranged, Mr. Holmes. I wrote to the Duchess this morning."

"In that case," said Holmes, rising, "I think that my friend and I can congratulate ourselves upon several most happy results from our little visit to the North. There is one other small point upon which I desire some light. This fellow Hayes had shod his horses with shoes which counterfeited the tracks of cows. Was it from Mr. Wilder that he learned so extraordinary a device?"

The Duke stood in thought for a moment, with a look of intense surprise on his face. Then he opened a door and showed us into a large room furnished as a museum. He led the way to a glass case in a corner and pointed to the inscription.

"These shoes," it ran, "were dug up in the moat of Holdernesse Hall. They are for the use of horses, but they are shaped below with a cloven foot of iron, so as to throw pursuers off the track. They are supposed to have belonged to some of the marauding Barons of Holdernesse in the Middle Ages."

Holmes opened the case, and moistening his finger he passed it along the shoe. A thin film of recent mud was left upon his skin.

"Thank you," said he, as he replaced the glass. "It is the second most interesting object that I have seen in the North."

"And the first?"

Holmes folded up his check and placed it carefully in his notebook. "I am a poor man," said he, as he patted it affectionately, and thrust it into the depths of his inner pocket.

THE FINAL PROBLEM

It is with a heavy heart that I take up my pen to write these the last words in which I shall ever record the singular gifts by which my friend Mr. Sherlock Holmes was distinguished. In an incoherent and, as I deeply feel, an entirely inadequate fashion, I have endeavoured to give some account of my strange experiences in his company from the chance which first brought us together at the period of the "Study in Scarlet," up to the time of his interference in the matter of the "Naval Treaty"—an interference which had the unquestionable effect of preventing a serious international complication. It was my intention to have stopped there, and to have said nothing of that event which has created a void in my life which the lapse of two years has done little to fill. My hand has been forced, however, by the recent letters in which Colonel James Moriarty defends the memory of his brother, and I have no choice but to lay the facts before the public exactly as they occurred. I alone know the absolute truth of the matter, and I am satisfied that the time has come when no good purpose is to be served by its suppression. As far as I know, there have been only three accounts in the public press: that in the *Journal de Genève* on May 6th, 1891, the Reuter's despatch in the English papers on May 7th, and finally the recent letter to which I have alluded. Of these the first and second were extremely condensed, while the last is, as I shall now show, an absolute perversion of the facts. It lies with me to tell for the first time what really took place between Professor Moriarty and Mr. Sherlock Holmes.

It may be remembered that after my marriage, and my subsequent start in private practice, the very intimate relations which had existed between Holmes and myself became to some extent modified. He still came to me from time to time when he desired a companion in his investigation, but these occasions grew more and more seldom, until I find that in the year 1890 there were only three cases of which I retain any record. During the winter of that year and the early spring of 1891, I saw in the papers that he had been engaged by the French government upon a matter of supreme importance, and I received two notes from Holmes, dated from Narbonne and from Nimes, from which I gathered that his stay in France was likely to be a long one. It was with some surprise, therefore, that I saw him walk into my consulting-room upon the evening of the 24th of April. It struck me that he was looking even paler and thinner than usual.

"Yes, I have been using myself up rather too freely," he remarked, in answer to my look rather than to my words; "I have been a little pressed of late. Have you any objection to my closing your shutters?"

The only light in the room came from the lamp upon the table at which I had been reading. Holmes edged his way round the wall and flinging the shutters together, he bolted them securely.

"You are afraid of something?" I asked.

"Well, I am."

"Of what?"

"Of air-guns."

"My dear Holmes, what do you mean?"

"I think that you know me well enough, Watson, to understand that I am by no means a nervous man. At the same time, it is stupidity rather than courage to refuse to recognise danger when it is close upon you. Might I trouble you for a match?" He drew in the smoke of his cigarette as if the soothing influence was grateful to him.

"I must apologise for calling so late," said he, "and I must further beg you to be so unconventional as to allow me to leave your house presently by scrambling over your back garden wall."

"But what does it all mean?" I asked.

He held out his hand, and I saw in the light of the lamp that two of his knuckles were burst and bleeding.

"It is not an airy nothing, you see," said he, smiling. "On the contrary, it is solid enough for a man to break his hand over. Is Mrs. Watson in?"

"She is away upon a visit."

"Indeed! You are alone?"

"Quite."

"Then it makes it the easier for me to propose that you should come away with me for a week to the Continent."

"Where?"

"Oh, anywhere. It's all the same to me."

There was something very strange in all this. It was not Holmes's nature to take an aimless holiday, and something about his pale, worn face told me that his nerves were at their highest tension. He saw the question in my eyes, and, putting his finger-tips together and his elbows upon his knees, he explained the situation.

"You have probably never heard of Professor Moriarty?" said he.

"Never."

"Aye, there's the genius and the wonder of the thing!" he cried. "The man pervades London, and no one has heard of him. That's what puts him on a pinnacle in the records of crime. I tell you, Watson, in all seriousness, that if I could beat that man, if I could free society of him, I should feel that my own career had reached its summit, and I should be prepared to turn to some more placid line in life. Between ourselves, the recent cases in which I have been of assistance to the royal family of Scandinavia, and to the French republic, have left me in such a position that I could continue to live in the quiet fashion, which is most congenial to me, and to concentrate my attention upon my chemical researches. But I could not rest, Watson, I could not sit quiet in my chair, if I thought that such a man as Professor Moriarty were walking the streets of London unchallenged."

"What has he done, then?"

"His career has been an extraordinary one. He is a man of good birth and excellent education, endowed by nature with a phenomenal mathematical faculty. At the age of twenty-one he wrote a treatise upon the Binomial Theorem, which has had a European vogue. On the strength of it he won the Mathematical Chair at one of our smaller universities, and had, to all appearances, a most brilliant career before him. But the man had hereditary tendencies of the most diabolical kind. A criminal strain ran in his blood, which, instead of being modified, was increased and rendered infinitely more dangerous by his extraordinary mental powers. Dark rumours gathered round him in the university town, and eventually he was compelled to resign his chair and to come down to London, where he set up as an Army coach. So much is known to the world, but what I am telling you now is what I have myself discovered.

"As you are aware, Watson, there is no one who knows the higher criminal world of London so well as I do. For years past I have continually been conscious of some power behind the malefactor, some deep organizing power which forever stands in the way of the law and throws its shield over the wrong-doer. Again and again in cases of the most varying sorts—forgery cases, robberies, murders—I have felt the presence of this force, and I have deduced its action in many of those undiscovered crimes in which I have not been personally consulted. For years I have endeavoured to break through the veil which shrouded it, and at last the time came when I seized my thread and followed it, until it led me, after a thousand cunning windings, to ex-Professor Moriarty of mathematical celebrity.

"He is the Napoleon of crime, Watson. He is the organizer of half that is evil and of nearly all that is undetected in this great city. He is a genius, a philosopher, an abstract thinker. He has a brain of the first order. He sits motionless, like a spider in the Centre of its web, but that web has a thousand radiations, and he knows well every quiver of each of them. He does little himself. He only plans. But his agents are numerous and splendidly organized. Is there a crime to be done, a paper to be abstracted, we will say, a house to be rifled, a man to be removed—the word is passed to the Professor, the matter is organized and carried out. The agent may be caught. In that case money is found for his bail or his defence. But the central power which uses the agent is never caught—never so much as suspected. This was the organization which I deduced, Watson, and which I devoted my whole energy to exposing and breaking up.

"But the Professor was fenced round with safeguards so cunningly devised that, do what I would, it seemed impossible to get evidence which would convict in a court of law. You know my powers, my dear Watson, and yet at the end of three months I was forced to confess that I had at last met an antagonist who was my intellectual equal. My horror at his crimes was lost in my admiration at his skill. But at last, he made a trip—only a little, little trip—but it was more than he could afford when I was so close upon him. I had my chance, and, starting from that point, I have woven my net round him until now it is all ready to close. In three days—that is to say, on Monday next—matters will be ripe, and the Professor, with all the principal members of his gang, will be in the hands of the police. Then will come the greatest criminal trial of the century, the clearing up of over forty mysteries, and the rope for all of them; but if we move at all prematurely, you understand, they may slip out of our hands even at the last moment.

"Now, if I could have done this without the knowledge of Professor Moriarty, all would have been well. But he was too wily for that. He saw every step which I took to draw my toils round him. Again and again, he strove to break away, but I as often headed him off. I tell you, my friend, that if a detailed account of that silent contest could be written, it would take its place as the most brilliant bit of thrust-and-parry work in the history of detection. Never have I risen to such a height and never have I been so hard pressed by an opponent. He cut deep, and yet I just undercut him. This morning the last steps were taken, and three days only were wanted to complete the business. I was sitting in my room thinking the matter over, when the door opened, and Professor Moriarty stood before me.

"My nerves are fairly proof, Watson, but I must confess to a start when I saw the very man who had been so much in my thoughts standing there on my threshhold. His appearance was quite familiar to me. He is extremely tall and thin, his forehead domes out in a white curve, and his two eyes are deeply sunken in his head. He is clean-shaven, pale, and ascetic-looking, retaining something of the professor in his features. His shoulders are rounded from much study, and his face protrudes forward, and is forever slowly oscillating from side to side in a curiously reptilian fashion. He peered at me with great curiosity in his puckered eyes.

"'You have less frontal development than I should have expected,' said he, at last. 'It is a dangerous habit to finger loaded firearms in the pocket of one's dressing-gown.'

"The fact is that upon his entrance I had instantly recognised the extreme personal danger in which I lay. The only conceivable escape for him lay in silencing my tongue. In an instant I had slipped the revolver from the drawer into my pocket and was covering him through the cloth. At his remark I drew the weapon out and laid it cocked upon the table. He still smiled and blinked, but there was something about his eyes which made me feel very glad that I had it there.

"'You evidently don't know me,' said he.

"'On the contrary,' I answered, 'I think it is fairly evident that I do. Pray take a chair. I can spare you five minutes if you have anything to say.'

"'All that I have to say has already crossed your mind,' said he.

"'Then possibly my answer has crossed yours,' I replied.

"'You stand fast?'

"'Absolutely.'

"He clapped his hand into his pocket, and I raised the pistol from the table. But he merely drew out a memorandum-book in which he had scribbled some dates.

"'You crossed my path on the 4th of January,' said he. 'On the 23rd you incommoded me; by the middle of February, I was seriously inconvenienced by you; at the end of March I was absolutely hampered in my plans; and now, at the close of April, I find myself placed in such a position through your continual persecution that I am in positive danger of losing my liberty. The situation is becoming an impossible one.'

"'Have you any suggestion to make?' I asked.

"'You must drop it, Mr. Holmes,' said he, swaying his face about. 'You really must, you know.'

"'After Monday,' said I.

"'Tut, tut,' said he. 'I am quite sure that a man of your intelligence will see that there can be but one outcome to this affair. It is necessary that you should withdraw. You have worked things in such a fashion that we have only one resource left. It has been an intellectual treat to me to see the way in which you have grappled with this affair, and I say, unaffectedly, that it would be a grief to me to be forced to take any extreme measure. You smile, sir, but I assure you that it really would.'

"'Danger is part of my trade,' I remarked.

"'That is not danger,' said he. 'It is inevitable destruction. You stand in the way not merely of an individual, but of a mighty organization, the full extent of which you, with all your cleverness, have been unable to realize. You must stand clear, Mr. Holmes, or be trodden under foot.'

"'I am afraid,' said I, rising, 'that in the pleasure of this conversation I am neglecting business of importance which awaits me elsewhere.'

"He rose also and looked at me in silence, shaking his head sadly.

"'Well, well,' said he, at last. 'It seems a pity, but I have done what I could. I know every move of your game. You can do nothing before Monday. It has been a duel between you and me, Mr. Holmes. You hope to place me in the dock. I tell you that I will never stand in the dock. You hope to beat me. I tell you that you will never beat me. If you are clever enough to bring destruction upon me, rest assured that I shall do as much to you.'

"'You have paid me several compliments, Mr. Moriarty,' said I. 'Let me pay you one in return when I say that if I were assured of the former eventuality I would, in the interests of the public, cheerfully accept the latter.'

"'I can promise you the one, but not the other,' he snarled, and so turned his rounded back upon me, and went peering and blinking out of the room.

"That was my singular interview with Professor Moriarty. I confess that it left an unpleasant effect upon my mind. His soft, precise fashion of speech leaves a conviction of sincerity which a mere bully could not produce. Of course, you will say: 'Why not take police precautions against him?' The reason is that I am well convinced that it is from his agents the blow will fall. I have the best proofs that it would be so."

"You have already been assaulted?"

"My dear Watson, Professor Moriarty is not a man who lets the grass grow under his feet. I went out about midday to transact some business in Oxford Street. As I passed the corner which leads from Bentinck Street on to the Welbeck Street crossing a two-horse van furiously driven whizzed round and was on me like a flash. I sprang for the foot-path and saved myself by the fraction of a second. The van dashed round by Marylebone Lane and was gone in an instant. I kept to the pavement after that, Watson, but as I walked down Vere Street a brick came down from the roof of one of the houses, and was shattered to fragments at my feet. I called the police and had the place examined. There were slates and bricks piled up on the roof preparatory to some repairs, and they would have me believe that the wind had toppled over one of these. Of course, I knew better but I could prove nothing. I took a cab after that and reached my brother's rooms in Pall Mall, where I spent the day. Now I have come round to you, and on my way I was attacked by a rough with a bludgeon. I knocked him down, and the police have him in custody; but I can tell you with the most absolute confidence that no possible connection will ever be traced between the gentleman upon whose front teeth I have barked my knuckles and the retiring mathematical coach, who is, I daresay, working out problems upon a blackboard ten miles away. You will not wonder, Watson, that my first act on entering your rooms was to close your shutters, and that I have been compelled to ask your permission to leave the house by some less conspicuous exit than the front door."

I had often admired my friend's courage, but never more than now, as he sat quietly checking off a series of incidents which must have combined to make up a day of horror.

"You will spend the night here?" I said.

"No, my friend, you might find me a dangerous guest. I have my plans laid, and all will be well. Matters have gone so far now that they can move without my help as far as the arrest goes, though my presence is necessary for a conviction. It is obvious, therefore, that I cannot do better than get away for the few days which remain before the police are at liberty to act. It would be a great pleasure to me, therefore, if you could come on to the Continent with me."

"The practice is quiet," said I, "and I have an accommodating neighbour. I should be glad to come."

"And to start tomorrow morning?"

"If necessary."

"Oh yes, it is most necessary. Then these are your instructions, and I beg, my dear Watson, that you will obey them to the letter, for you are now playing a double-handed game with me against the cleverest rogue and the most powerful syndicate of criminals in Europe. Now listen! You will dispatch whatever luggage you intend to take by a trusty messenger unaddressed to Victoria tonight. In the morning you will send for a hansom, desiring your man to take neither the first nor the second which may present itself. Into this hansom you will jump, and you will drive to the Strand end of the Lowther Arcade, handing the address to the cabman upon a slip of paper, with a request that he will not throw it away. Have your fare ready, and the instant that your cab stops, dash through the Arcade, timing yourself to reach the other side at a quarter-past nine. You will find a small brougham waiting close to the curb, driven by a fellow with a heavy black cloak tipped at the collar with red. Into this you will step, and you will reach Victoria in time for the Continental express."

"Where shall I meet you?"

"At the station. The second first-class carriage from the front will be reserved for us."

"The carriage is our rendezvous, then?"

"Yes."

It was in vain that I asked Holmes to remain for the evening. It was evident to me that he thought he might bring trouble to the roof he was under, and that that was the motive which impelled him to go. With a few hurried words as to our plans for the morrow he rose and came out with me into the garden, clambering over the wall which leads into Mortimer Street, and immediately whistling for a hansom, in which I heard him drive away.

In the morning, I obeyed Holmes's injunctions to the letter. A hansom was procured with such precaution as would prevent its being one which was placed ready for us, and I drove immediately after breakfast to the Lowther Arcade, through which I hurried at the top of my speed. A brougham was waiting with a very massive driver wrapped in a dark cloak, who, the instant that I had stepped in, whipped up the horse and rattled off to Victoria Station. On my alighting there he turned the carriage and dashed away again without so much as a look in my direction.

So far all had gone admirably. My luggage was waiting for me, and I had no difficulty in finding the carriage which Holmes had indicated, the less so as it was the only one in the train which was marked "Engaged." My only source of anxiety now was the non-appearance of Holmes. The station clock marked only seven minutes from the time when we were due to start. In vain I searched among the groups of travellers and leave-takers for the lithe figure of my friend. There was no sign of him. I spent a few minutes in assisting a venerable Italian priest, who was endeavouring to make a porter understand, in his broken English, that his luggage was to be booked through to Paris. Then, having taken another look round, I returned to my carriage, where I found that the porter, in spite of the ticket, had given me my decrepit Italian friend as a traveling companion. It was useless for me to explain to him that his presence was an intrusion, for my Italian was even more limited than his English, so I shrugged my shoulders resignedly, and continued to look out anxiously for my friend. A chill of fear had come over me, as I thought that his absence might mean that some blow had fallen during the night. Already the doors had all been shut and the whistle blown, when—

"My dear Watson," said a voice, "you have not even condescended to say good-morning."

I turned in uncontrollable astonishment. The aged ecclesiastic had turned his face towards me. For an instant the wrinkles were smoothed away, the nose drew away from the chin, the lower lip ceased to protrude and the mouth to mumble, the dull eyes regained their fire, the drooping figure expanded. The next the whole frame collapsed again, and Holmes had gone as quickly as he had come.

"Good heavens!" I cried. "How you startled me!"

"Every precaution is still necessary," he whispered. "I have reason to think that they are hot upon our trail. Ah, there is Moriarty himself."

The train had already begun to move as Holmes spoke. Glancing back, I saw a tall man pushing his way furiously through the crowd, and waving his hand as if he desired to have the train stopped. It was too late, however, for we were rapidly gathering momentum, and an instant later had shot clear of the station.

"With all our precautions, you see that we have cut it rather fine," said Holmes, laughing. He rose, and throwing off the black cassock and hat which had formed his disguise, he packed them away in a hand-bag.

"Have you seen the morning paper, Watson?"

"No."

"You haven't seen about Baker Street, then?"

"Baker Street?"

"They set fire to our rooms last night. No great harm was done."

"Good heavens, Holmes! This is intolerable."

"They must have lost my track completely after their bludgeon-man was arrested. Otherwise, they could not have imagined that I had returned to my rooms. They have evidently taken the precaution of watching you, however, and that is what has brought Moriarty to Victoria. You could not have made any slip in coming?"

"I did exactly what you advised."

"Did you find your brougham?"

"Yes, it was waiting."

"Did you recognise your coachman?"

"No."

"It was my brother Mycroft. It is an advantage to get about in such a case without taking a mercenary into your confidence. But we must plan what we are to do about Moriarty now."

"As this is an express, and as the boat runs in connection with it, I should think we have shaken him off very effectively."

"My dear Watson, you evidently did not realize my meaning when I said that this man may be taken as being quite on the same intellectual plane as myself. You do not imagine that if I were the pursuer I should allow myself to be baffled by so slight an obstacle. Why, then, should you think so meanly of him?"

"What will he do?"

"What should I do?"

"What would you do, then?"

"Engage a special."

"But it must be late."

"By no means. This train stops at Canterbury; and there is always at least a quarter of an hour's delay at the boat. He will catch us there."

"One would think that we were the criminals. Let us have him arrested on his arrival."

"It would be to ruin the work of three months. We should get the big fish, but the smaller would dart right and left out of the net. On Monday we should have them all. No, an arrest is inadmissible."

"What then?"

"We shall get out at Canterbury."

"And then?"

"Well, then we must make a cross-country journey to Newhaven, and so over to Dieppe. Moriarty will again do what I should do. He will get on to Paris, mark down our luggage, and wait for two days at the depôt. In the meantime, we shall treat ourselves to a couple of carpet-bags, encourage the manufactures of the countries through which we travel, and make our way at our leisure into Switzerland, via Luxembourg and Basle."

At Canterbury, therefore, we alighted, only to find that we should have to wait an hour before we could get a train to Newhaven.

I was still looking rather ruefully after the rapidly disappearing luggage-van which contained my wardrobe, when Holmes pulled my sleeve and pointed up the line.

"Already, you see," said he.

Far away, from among the Kentish woods there rose a thin spray of smoke. A minute later a carriage and engine could be seen flying along the open curve which leads to the station. We had hardly time to take our place behind a pile of luggage when it passed with a rattle and a roar, beating a blast of hot air into our faces.

"There he goes," said Holmes, as we watched the carriage swing and rock over the points. "There are limits, you see, to our friend's intelligence. It would have been a *coup-de-maître* had he deduced what I would deduce and acted accordingly."

"And what would he have done had he overtaken us?"

"There cannot be the least doubt that he would have made a murderous attack upon me. It is, however, a game at which two may play. The question now is whether we should take a premature lunch here or run our chance of starving before we reach the buffet at Newhaven."

We made our way to Brussels that night and spent two days there, moving on upon the third day as far as Strasburg. On the Monday morning Holmes had telegraphed to the London police, and in the evening we found a reply waiting for us at our hotel. Holmes tore it open, and then with a bitter curse hurled it into the grate.

"I might have known it!" he groaned. "He has escaped!"

"Moriarty?"

"They have secured the whole gang with the exception of him. He has given them the slip. Of course, when I had left the country there was no one to cope with him. But I did think that I had put the game in their hands. I think that you had better return to England, Watson."

"Why?"

"Because you will find me a dangerous companion now. This man's occupation is gone. He is lost if he returns to London. If I read his character right he will devote his whole energies to revenging himself upon me. He said as much in our short interview, and I fancy that he meant it. I should certainly recommend you to return to your practice."

It was hardly an appeal to be successful with one who was an old campaigner as well as an old friend. We sat in the Strasburg *salle-à-*

manger arguing the question for half an hour, but the same night we had resumed our journey and were well on our way to Geneva.

For a charming week we wandered up the Valley of the Rhone, and then, branching off at Leuk, we made our way over the Gemmi Pass, still deep in snow, and so, by way of Interlaken, to Meiringen. It was a lovely trip, the dainty green of the spring below, the virgin white of the winter above; but it was clear to me that never for one instant did Holmes forget the shadow which lay across him. In the homely Alpine villages or in the lonely mountain passes, I could tell by his quick glancing eyes and his sharp scrutiny of every face that passed us, that he was well convinced that, walk where we would, we could not walk ourselves clear of the danger which was dogging our footsteps.

Once, I remember, as we passed over the Gemmi, and walked along the border of the melancholy Daubensee, a large rock which had been dislodged from the ridge upon our right clattered down and roared into the lake behind us. In an instant Holmes had raced up on to the ridge and standing upon a lofty pinnacle, craned his neck in every direction. It was in vain that our guide assured him that a fall of stones was a common chance in the spring-time at that spot. He said nothing, but he smiled at me with the air of a man who sees the fulfillment of that which he had expected.

And yet for all his watchfulness he was never depressed. On the contrary, I can never recollect having seen him in such exuberant spirits. Again and again, he recurred to the fact that if he could be assured that society was freed from Professor Moriarty he would cheerfully bring his own career to a conclusion.

"I think that I may go so far as to say, Watson, that I have not lived wholly in vain," he remarked. "If my record were closed tonight I could still survey it with equanimity. The air of London is the sweeter for my presence. In over a thousand cases I am not aware that I have ever used my powers upon the wrong side. Of late I have been tempted to look into the problems furnished by nature rather than those more superficial ones for which our artificial state of society is responsible. Your memoirs will draw to an end, Watson, upon the day that I crown my career by the capture or extinction of the most dangerous and capable criminal in Europe."

I shall be brief, and yet exact, in the little which remains for me to tell. It is not a subject on which I would willingly dwell, and yet I am conscious that a duty devolves upon me to omit no detail.

It was on the 3rd of May that we reached the little village of Meiringen, where we put up at the Englischer Hof, then kept by Peter Steiler the elder. Our landlord was an intelligent man, and spoke excellent English, having served for three years as waiter at the Grosvenor Hotel in London. At his advice, on the afternoon of the 4th we set off together, with the intention of crossing the hills and spending the night at the hamlet of Rosenlaui. We had strict injunctions, however, on no account to pass the falls of Reichenbach, which are about half-way up the hill, without making a small détour to see them.

It is indeed, a fearful place. The torrent, swollen by the melting snow, plunges into a tremendous abyss, from which the spray rolls up like the smoke from a burning house. The shaft into which the river hurls itself is an immense chasm, lined by glistening coal-black rock, and narrowing into a creaming, boiling pit of incalculable depth, which brims over and shoots the stream onward over its jagged lip. The long sweep of green water roaring forever down, and the thick flickering curtain of spray hissing forever upward, turn a man giddy with their constant whirl and clamour. We stood near the edge peering down at the gleam of the breaking water far below us against the black rocks and listening to the half-human shout which came booming up with the spray out of the abyss.

The path has been cut half-way round the fall to afford a complete view, but it ends abruptly, and the traveler has to return as he came. We had turned to do so, when we saw a Swiss lad come running along it with a letter in his hand. It bore the mark of the hotel which we had just left and was addressed to me by the landlord. It appeared that within a very few minutes of our leaving, an English lady had arrived who was in the last stage of consumption. She had wintered at Davos Platz and was journeying now to join her friends at Lucerne, when a sudden hemorrhage had overtaken her. It was thought that she could hardly live a few hours, but it would be a great consolation to her to see an English doctor, and, if I would only return, etc. The good Steiler assured me in a postscript that he would himself look upon my compliance as a very great favour, since the lady absolutely refused to see a Swiss physician, and he could not but feel that he was incurring a great responsibility.

The appeal was one which could not be ignored. It was impossible to refuse the request of a fellow-countrywoman dying in a strange land. Yet I had my scruples about leaving Holmes. It was finally agreed, however, that he should retain the young Swiss messenger with him as guide and companion while I returned to Meiringen. My friend would stay some little time at the fall, he said, and would then walk slowly over the hill to Rosenlaui, where I was to rejoin him in the evening. As I turned away I saw Holmes, with his back against a rock and his arms folded, gazing down at the rush of the waters. It was the last that I was ever destined to see of him in this world.

When I was near the bottom of the descent I looked back. It was impossible, from that position, to see the fall, but I could see the curving path which winds over the shoulder of the hill and leads to it. Along this a man was, I remember, walking very rapidly.

I could see his black figure clearly outlined against the green behind him. I noted him, and the energy with which he walked but he passed from my mind again as I hurried on upon my errand.

It may have been a little over an hour before I reached Meiringen. Old Steiler was standing at the porch of his hotel.

"Well," said I, as I came hurrying up, "I trust that she is no worse?"

A look of surprise passed over his face, and at the first quiver of his eyebrows my heart turned to lead in my breast.

"You did not write this?" I said, pulling the letter from my pocket. "There is no sick Englishwoman in the hotel?"

"Certainly not!" he cried. "But it has the hotel mark upon it! Ha, it must have been written by that tall Englishman who came in after you had gone. He said—"

But I waited for none of the landlord's explanations. In a tingle of fear, I was already running down the village street, and making for the path which I had so lately descended. It had taken me an hour to come down. For all my efforts two more had passed before I found myself at the fall of Reichenbach once more. There was Holmes's Alpine-stock still leaning against the rock by which I had left him. But there was no sign of him, and it was in vain that I shouted. My only answer was my own voice reverberating in a rolling echo from the cliffs around me.

It was the sight of that Alpine-stock which turned me cold and sick. He had not gone to Rosenlaui, then. He had remained on that three-foot path, with sheer wall on one side and sheer drop on the other, until his enemy had overtaken him. The young Swiss had gone too. He had probably been in the pay of Moriarty and had left the two men together. And then what had happened? Who was to tell us what had happened then?

I stood for a minute or two to collect myself, for I was dazed with the horror of the thing. Then I began to think of Holmes's own methods and to try to practise them in reading this tragedy. It was, alas, only too easy to do. During our conversation we had not gone to the end of the path, and the Alpine-stock marked the place where we had stood. The blackish soil is kept forever soft by the incessant drift of spray, and a bird would leave its tread upon it. Two lines of footmarks were clearly marked along the farther end of the path, both leading away from me. There were none returning. A few yards from the end the soil was all ploughed up into a patch of mud, and the branches and ferns which fringed the chasm were torn and bedraggled. I lay upon my face and peered over with the spray spouting up all around me. It had darkened since I left, and now I could only see here and there the glistening of moisture upon the black walls, and far away down at the end of the shaft the gleam of the broken water. I shouted; but only the same half-human cry of the fall was borne back to my ears.

But it was destined that I should after all have a last word of greeting from my friend and comrade. I have said that his Alpine-stock had been left leaning against a rock which jutted on to the path. From the top of this boulder the gleam of something bright caught my eye, and, raising my hand, I found that it came from the silver cigarette-case which he used to carry. As I took it up a small square of paper upon which it had lain fluttered down on to the ground. Unfolding it, I found that it consisted of three pages torn from his note-book and addressed to me. It was characteristic of the man that the direction was a precise, and the writing as firm and clear, as though it had been written in his study.

"My dear Watson," he said, "I write these few lines through the courtesy of Mr. Moriarty, who awaits my convenience for the final discussion of those questions which lie between us. He has been giving me a sketch of the methods by which he avoided the English police and kept himself informed of our movements. They certainly confirm the very high opinion which I had formed of his abilities. I am pleased to think that I shall be able to free society from any further effects of his presence, though I fear that it is at a cost which will give pain to my friends, and especially, my dear Watson, to you. I have already explained to you, however, that my career had in any case reached its crisis, and that no possible conclusion to it could be more congenial to me than this. Indeed, if I may make a full confession to you, I was quite convinced that the letter from Meiringen was a hoax, and I allowed you to depart on that errand under the persuasion that some development of this sort would follow. Tell Inspector Patterson that the papers which he needs to convict the gang are in pigeonhole M., done up in a blue envelope and inscribed 'Moriarty.' I made every disposition of my property before leaving England and handed it to my brother Mycroft. Pray give my greetings to Mrs. Watson, and believe me to be, my dear fellow,

"Very sincerely yours,
"Sherlock Holmes."

A few words may suffice to tell the little that remains. An examination by experts leaves little doubt that a personal contest between the two men ended, as it could hardly fail to end in such a situation, in their reeling over, locked in each other's arms. Any attempt at recovering the bodies was absolutely hopeless, and there, deep down in that dreadful caldron of swirling water and seething foam, will lie for all time the most dangerous criminal and the foremost champion of the law of their generation. The Swiss youth was never found again, and there can be no doubt that he was one of the numerous agents whom Moriarty kept in his employ. As to the gang, it will be within the memory of the public how completely the evidence which Holmes had accumulated exposed their organization, and how heavily the hand of the dead man weighed upon them. Of their terrible chief few details came out during the proceedings, and if I have now been compelled to make a clear statement of his career it is due to those injudicious champions who have endeavoured to clear his memory by attacks upon him whom I shall ever regard as the best and the wisest man whom I have ever known.

THE MUSGRAVE RITUAL

An anomaly which often struck me in the character of my friend Sherlock Holmes was that, although in his methods of thought he was the neatest and most methodical of mankind, and although also he affected a certain quiet primness of dress, he was none the less in his personal habits one of the most untidy men that ever drove a fellow-lodger to distraction. Not that I am in the least conventional in that respect myself. The rough-and-tumble work in Afghanistan, coming on the top of a natural Bohemianism of disposition, has made me rather more lax than befits a medical man. But with me there is a limit, and when I find a man who keeps his cigars in the coal-scuttle, his tobacco in the toe end of a Persian slipper, and his unanswered correspondence transfixed by a jack-knife into the very centre of his wooden mantelpiece, then I begin to give myself virtuous airs. I have always held, too, that pistol practice should be distinctly an open-air pastime; and when Holmes, in one of his queer humours, would sit in an armchair with his hair-trigger and a hundred Boxer cartridges, and proceed to adorn the opposite wall with a patriotic V. R. done in bullet-pocks, I felt strongly that neither the atmosphere nor the appearance of our room was improved by it.

Our chambers were always full of chemicals and of criminal relics which had a way of wandering into unlikely positions, and of turning up in the butter-dish or in even less desirable places. But his papers were my great crux. He had a horror of destroying documents, especially those which were connected with his past cases, and yet it was only once in every year or two that he would muster energy to docket and arrange them; for, as I have mentioned somewhere in these incoherent memoirs, the outbursts of passionate energy when he performed the remarkable feats with which his name is associated were followed by reactions of lethargy during which he would lie about with his violin and his books, hardly moving save from the sofa to the table. Thus, month after month his papers accumulated, until every corner of the room was stacked with bundles of manuscript which were on no account to be burned, and which could not be put away save by their owner. One winter's night, as we sat together by the fire, I ventured to suggest to him that, as he had finished pasting extracts into his common-place book, he might employ the next two hours in making our room a little more habitable. He could not deny the justice of my request, so with a rather rueful face he went off to his bedroom, from which he returned presently pulling a large tin box behind him. This he placed in the middle of the floor and, squatting down upon a stool in front of it, he threw back the lid. I could see that it was already a third full of bundles of paper tied up with red tape into separate packages.

"There are cases enough here, Watson," said he, looking at me with mischievous eyes. "I think that if you knew all that I had in this box you would ask me to pull some out instead of putting others in."

"These are the records of your early work, then?" I asked. "I have often wished that I had notes of those cases."

"Yes, my boy, these were all done prematurely before my biographer had come to glorify me." He lifted bundle after bundle in a tender, caressing sort of way. "They are not all successes, Watson," said he. "But there are some pretty little problems among them. Here's the record of the Tarleton murders, and the case of Vamberry, the wine merchant, and the adventure of the old Russian woman, and the singular affair of the aluminium crutch, as well as a full account of Ricoletti of the club-foot, and his abominable wife. And here—ah, now, this really is something a little *recherché*."

He dived his arm down to the bottom of the chest, and brought up a small wooden box with a sliding lid, such as children's toys are kept in. From within he produced a crumpled piece of paper, an old-fashioned brass key, a peg of wood with a ball of string attached to it, and three rusty old disks of metal.

"Well, my boy, what do you make of this lot?" he asked, smiling at my expression.

"It is a curious collection."

"Very curious, and the story that hangs round it will strike you as being more curious still."

"These relics have a history then?"

"So much so that they *are* history."

"What do you mean by that?"

Sherlock Holmes picked them up one by one and laid them along the edge of the table. Then he reseated himself in his chair and looked them over with a gleam of satisfaction in his eyes.

"These," said he, "are all that I have left to remind me of the adventure of the Musgrave Ritual."

I had heard him mention the case more than once, though I had never been able to gather the details.

"I should be so glad," said I, "if you would give me an account of it."

"And leave the litter as it is?" he cried, mischievously. "Your tidiness won't bear much strain after all, Watson. But I should be glad that you should add this case to your annals, for there are points in it which make it quite unique in the criminal records of this or, I believe, of any other country. A collection of my trifling achievements would certainly be incomplete which contained no account of this very singular business.

"You may remember how the affair of the *Gloria Scott*, and my conversation with the unhappy man whose fate I told you of, first turned my attention in the direction of the profession which has become my life's work. You see me now when my name has become known far and wide, and when I am generally recognised both by the public and by the official force as being a final court of appeal in doubtful cases. Even when you knew me first, at the time of the affair which you have commemorated in 'A Study in Scarlet,' I had already established a considerable, though not a very lucrative, connection. You can hardly realize, then, how difficult I found it at first, and how long I had to wait before I succeeded in making any headway.

"When I first came up to London I had rooms in Montague Street, just round the corner from the British Museum, and there I waited, filling in my too abundant leisure time by studying all those branches of science which might make me more efficient. Now and again cases came in my way, principally through the introduction of old fellow-students, for during my last years at the University there was a good deal of talk there about myself and my methods. The third of these cases was that of the Musgrave Ritual, and it is to the interest which was aroused by that singular chain of events, and the large issues which proved to be at stake, that I trace my first stride towards the position which I now hold.

"Reginald Musgrave had been in the same college as myself, and I had some slight acquaintance with him. He was not generally popular among the undergraduates, though it always seemed to me that what was set down as pride was really an attempt to cover extreme natural diffidence. In appearance he was a man of exceedingly aristocratic type, thin, high-nosed, and large-eyed, with languid and yet courtly manners. He was indeed a scion of one of the very oldest families in the kingdom, though his branch was a cadet one which had separated from the northern Musgraves sometime in the sixteenth century, and had established itself in western Sussex, where the Manor House of Hurlstone is perhaps the oldest inhabited building in the county. Something of his birthplace seemed to cling to the man, and I never looked at his pale, keen face or the poise of his head without associating him with grey archways and mullioned windows and all the venerable wreckage of a feudal keep. Once or twice, we drifted into talk, and I can remember that more than once he expressed a keen interest in my methods of observation and inference.

"For four years I had seen nothing of him until one morning he walked into my room in Montague Street. He had changed little, was dressed like a young man of fashion—he was always a bit of a dandy—and preserved the same quiet, suave manner which had formerly distinguished him.

"'How has all gone with you Musgrave?' I asked, after we had cordially shaken hands.

"'You probably heard of my poor father's death,' said he; 'he was carried off about two years ago. Since then, I have of course had the Hurlstone estates to manage, and as I am member for my district as well, my life has been a busy one. But I understand, Holmes, that you are turning to practical ends those powers with which you used to amaze us?'

"'Yes,' said I, 'I have taken to living by my wits.'

"'I am delighted to hear it, for your advice at present would be exceedingly valuable to me. We have had some very strange doings at Hurlstone, and the police have been able to throw no light upon the matter. It is really the most extraordinary and inexplicable business.'

"You can imagine with what eagerness I listened to him, Watson, for the very chance for which I had been panting during all those months of inaction seemed to have come within my reach. In my inmost heart I believed that I could succeed where others failed, and now I had the opportunity to test myself.

"'Pray, let me have the details,' I cried.

"Reginald Musgrave sat down opposite to me and lit the cigarette which I had pushed towards him.

"'You must know,' said he, 'that though I am a bachelor, I have to keep up a considerable staff of servants at Hurlstone, for it is a rambling old place, and takes a good deal of looking after. I preserve, too, and in the pheasant months I usually have a house-party, so that it would not do to be short-handed. Altogether there are eight maids, the cook, the butler, two footmen, and a boy. The garden and the stables of course have a separate staff.

"'Of these servants the one who had been longest in our service was Brunton the butler. He was a young schoolmaster out of place when he was first taken up by my father, but he was a man of great energy and character, and he soon became quite invaluable in the household. He was a well-grown, handsome man, with a splendid forehead, and though he has been with us for twenty years he cannot be more than forty now. With his personal advantages and his extraordinary gifts—for he can speak several languages and play nearly every musical instrument—it is wonderful that he should have been satisfied so long in such a position, but I suppose that he was comfortable and lacked energy to make any change. The butler of Hurlstone is always a thing that is remembered by all who visit us.

"'But this paragon has one fault. He is a bit of a Don Juan, and you can imagine that for a man like him it is not a very difficult part to play in a quiet country district. When he was married it was all right, but since he has been a widower we have had no end of trouble with him. A few months ago, we were in hopes that he was about to settle down again for he became engaged to Rachel Howells, our second housemaid; but he has thrown her over since then and taken up with Janet Tregellis, the daughter of the head gamekeeper. Rachel—who is a very good girl, but of an excitable Welsh temperament—had a sharp touch of brain-fever and goes about the house now—or did until yesterday—like a black-eyed shadow of her former self. That was our first drama at Hurlstone; but a second one came to drive it from our minds, and it was prefaced by the disgrace and dismissal of butler Brunton.

"'This was how it came about. I have said that the man was intelligent, and this very intelligence has caused his ruin, for it seems to have led to an insatiable curiosity about things which did not in the least concern him. I had no idea of the lengths to which this would carry him, until the merest accident opened my eyes to it.

"'I have said that the house is a rambling one. One day last week—on Thursday night, to be more exact—I found that I could not sleep, having foolishly taken a cup of strong *café noir* after my dinner. After struggling against it until two in the morning, I felt that it was quite hopeless, so I rose and lit the candle with the intention of continuing a novel which I was reading. The book, however, had been left in the billiard-room, so I pulled on my dressing-gown and started off to get it.

"'In order to reach the billiard-room I had to descend a flight of stairs and then to cross the head of a passage which led to the library and the gun-room. You can imagine my surprise when, as I looked down this corridor, I saw a glimmer of light coming from the open door of the library. I had myself extinguished the lamp and closed the door before coming to bed. Naturally my first thought was of burglars. The corridors at Hurlstone have their walls largely decorated with trophies of old weapons. From one of these I picked a battle-axe, and then, leaving my candle behind me, I crept on tiptoe down the passage and peeped in at the open door.

"'Brunton, the butler, was in the library. He was sitting, fully dressed, in an easy-chair, with a slip of paper which looked like a map upon his knee, and his forehead sunk forward upon his hand in deep thought. I stood dumb with astonishment, watching him from the darkness. A small taper on the edge of the table shed a feeble light which sufficed to show me that he was fully dressed. Suddenly, as I looked, he rose from his chair, and walking over to a bureau at the side, he unlocked it and drew out one of the drawers. From this he took a paper, and returning to his seat he flattened it out beside the taper on the edge of the table and began to study it with minute attention. My indignation at this calm examination of our family documents overcame me so far that I took a step forward, and Brunton, looking up, saw me standing in the doorway. He sprang to his feet, his face turned livid with fear, and he thrust into his breast the chart-like paper which he had been originally studying.

"'"So!" said I. "This is how you repay the trust which we have reposed in you. You will leave my service tomorrow."

"'He bowed with the look of a man who is utterly crushed and slunk past me without a word. The taper was still on the table, and by its light I glanced to see what the paper was which Brunton had taken from the bureau. To my surprise it was nothing of any importance at all, but simply a copy of the questions and answers in the singular old observance called the Musgrave Ritual. It is a sort of ceremony peculiar to our family, which each Musgrave for centuries past has gone through on his coming of age—a thing of private interest, and perhaps of some little importance to the archaeologist, like our own blazoning's and charges, but of no practical use whatever.'

"'We had better come back to the paper afterwards,' said I.

"'If you think it really necessary,' he answered, with some hesitation. 'To continue my statement, however: I relocked the bureau, using the key which Brunton had left, and I had turned to go when I was surprised to find that the butler had returned, and was standing before me.

"'"Mr. Musgrave, sir," he cried, in a voice which was hoarse with emotion, "I can't bear disgrace, sir. I've always been proud above my station in life, and disgrace would kill me. My blood will be on your head, sir—it will, indeed—if you drive me to despair. If you cannot keep me after what has passed, then for God's sake let me give you notice and leave in a month, as if of my own free will. I could stand that, Mr. Musgrave, but not to be cast out before all the folk that I know so well."

"'"You don't deserve much consideration, Brunton," I answered. "Your conduct has been most infamous. However, as you have been a long time in the family, I have no wish to bring public disgrace upon you. A month, however, is too long. Take yourself away in a week and give what reason you like for going."

"'"Only a week, sir?" he cried, in a despairing voice. "A fortnight—say at least a fortnight!"

"'"A week," I repeated, "and you may consider yourself to have been very leniently dealt with."

"'He crept away, his face sunk upon his breast, like a broken man, while I put out the light and returned to my room.

"'For two days after this Brunton was most assiduous in his attention to his duties. I made no allusion to what had passed, and waited with some curiosity to see how he would cover his disgrace. On the third morning, however he did not appear, as was his custom, after breakfast to receive my instructions for the day. As I left the dining-room I happened to meet Rachel Howells, the maid. I have told you that she had only recently recovered from an illness and was looking so wretchedly pale and wan that I remonstrated with her for being at work.

"'"You should be in bed," I said. "Come back to your duties when you are stronger."

"'She looked at me with so strange an expression that I began to suspect that her brain was affected.

"'"I am strong enough, Mr. Musgrave," said she.

"'"We will see what the doctor says," I answered. "You must stop work now, and when you go downstairs just say that I wish to see Brunton."

"'"The butler is gone," said she.

"'"Gone! Gone where?"

"'"He is gone. No one has seen him. He is not in his room. Oh, yes, he is gone, he is gone!" She fell back against the wall with shriek after shriek of laughter, while I, horrified at this sudden hysterical attack, rushed to the bell to summon help. The girl was taken to her room, still screaming and sobbing, while I made inquiries about Brunton. There was no doubt about it that he had disappeared. His bed had not been slept in, he had been seen by no one since he had retired to his room the night before, and yet it was difficult to see how he could have left the house, as both windows and doors were found to be fastened in the morning. His clothes, his watch, and even his money were in his room, but the black suit which he usually wore was missing. His slippers, too, were gone, but his boots were left behind. Where then could butler Brunton have gone in the night, and what could have become of him now?

"'Of course we searched the house from cellar to garret, but there was no trace of him. It is, as I have said, a labyrinth of an old house, especially the original wing, which is now practically uninhabited; but we ransacked every room and cellar without discovering the least sign of the missing man. It was incredible to me that he could have gone away leaving all his property behind him, and yet where could he be? I called in the local police, but without success. Rain had fallen on the night before and we examined the lawn and the paths all-round the house, but in vain. Matters were in this state, when a new development quite drew our attention away from the original mystery.

"'For two days Rachel Howells had been so ill, sometimes delirious, sometimes hysterical, that a nurse had been employed to sit up with her at night. On the third night after Brunton's disappearance, the nurse, finding her patient sleeping nicely, had dropped into a nap in the armchair, when she woke in the early morning to find the bed empty, the window open, and no signs of the invalid. I was instantly aroused, and, with the two footmen, started off at once in search of the missing girl. It was not difficult to tell the direction which she had taken, for, starting from under her window, we could follow her footmarks easily across the lawn to the edge of the mere, where they vanished close to the gravel path which leads out of the grounds. The lake there is eight feet deep, and you can imagine our feelings when we saw that the trail of the poor demented girl came to an end at the edge of it.

"'Of course, we had the drags at once, and set to work to recover the remains, but no trace of the body could we find. On the other hand, we brought to the surface an object of a most unexpected kind. It was a linen bag which contained within it a mass of old rusted and discoloured metal and several dull-coloured pieces of pebble or glass. This strange find was all that we could get from the mere, and, although we made every possible search and inquiry yesterday, we know nothing of the fate either of Rachel Howells or of Richard Brunton. The county police are at their wits' end, and I have come up to you as a last resource.'

"You can imagine, Watson, with what eagerness I listened to this extraordinary sequence of events, and endeavoured to piece them together, and to devise some common thread upon which they might all hang. The butler was gone. The maid was gone. The maid had loved the butler, but had afterwards cause to hate him. She was of Welsh blood, fiery and passionate. She had been terribly excited immediately after his disappearance. She had flung into the lake a bag containing some curious contents. These were all factors which had to be taken into consideration, and yet none of them got quite to the heart of the matter. What was the starting-point of this chain of events? There lay the end of this tangled line.

"'I must see that paper, Musgrave,' said I, 'which this butler of yours thought it worth his while to consult, even at the risk of the loss of his place.'

"'It is rather an absurd business, this ritual of ours,' he answered. 'But it has at least the saving grace of antiquity to excuse it. I have a copy of the questions and answers here if you care to run your eye over them.'

"He handed me the very paper which I have here, Watson, and this is the strange catechism to which each Musgrave had to submit when he came to man's estate. I will read you the questions and answers as they stand.

"'Whose was it?'

"'His who is gone.'

"'Who shall have it?'

"'He who will come.'

"'Where was the sun?'

"'Over the oak.'

"'Where was the shadow?'

"'Under the elm.'

"How was it stepped?'

"'North by ten and by ten, east by five and by five, south by two and by two, west by one and by one, and so under.'

"'What shall we give for it?'

"'All that is ours.'

"'Why should we give it?'

"'For the sake of the trust.'

"'The original has no date but is in the spelling of the middle of the seventeenth century,' remarked Musgrave. 'I am afraid, however, that it can be of little help to you in solving this mystery.'

"'At least,' said I, 'it gives us another mystery, and one which is even more interesting than the first. It may be that the solution of the one may prove to be the solution of the other. You will excuse me, Musgrave, if I say that your butler appears to me to have been a very clever man, and to have had a clearer insight than ten generations of his masters.'

"'I hardly follow you,' said Musgrave. 'The paper seems to me to be of no practical importance.'

"'But to me it seems immensely practical, and I fancy that Brunton took the same view. He had probably seen it before that night on which you caught him.'

"'It is very possible. We took no pains to hide it.'

"'He simply wished, I should imagine, to refresh his memory upon that last occasion. He had, as I understand, some sort of map or chart which he was comparing with the manuscript, and which he thrust into his pocket when you appeared.'

"'That is true. But what could he have to do with this old family custom of ours, and what does this rigmarole mean?'

"'I don't think that we should have much difficulty in determining that,' said I; 'with your permission we will take the first train down to Sussex and go a little more deeply into the matter upon the spot.'

"The same afternoon saw us both at Hurlstone. Possibly you have seen pictures and read descriptions of the famous old building, so I will confine my account of it to saying that it is built in the shape of an **L**, the long arm being the more modern portion, and the shorter the ancient nucleus, from which the other had developed. Over the low, heavily-lintelled door, in the centre of this old part, is chiseled the date, 1607, but experts are agreed that the beams and stonework are really much older than this. The enormously thick walls and tiny windows of this part had in the last century driven the family into building the new wing, and the old one was used now as a storehouse and a cellar, when it was used at all. A splendid park with fine old timber surrounds the house, and the lake, to which my client had referred, lay close to the avenue, about two hundred yards from the building.

"I was already firmly convinced, Watson, that there were not three separate mysteries here, but one only, and that if I could read the Musgrave Ritual aright I should hold in my hand the clue which would lead me to the truth concerning both the butler Brunton and the maid Howells. To that then I turned all my energies. Why should this servant be so anxious to master this old formula? Evidently because he saw something in it which had escaped all those generations of country squires, and from which he expected some personal advantage. What was it then, and how had it affected his fate?

"It was perfectly obvious to me, on reading the Ritual, that the measurements must refer to some spot to which the rest of the document alluded, and that if we could find that spot, we should be in a fair way towards finding what the secret was which the old Musgraves had thought it necessary to embalm in so curious a fashion. There were two guides given us to start with, an oak and an elm. As to the oak there could be no question at all. Right in front of the house, upon the left-hand side of the drive, there stood a patriarch among oaks, one of the most magnificent trees that I have ever seen.

"'That was there when your Ritual was drawn up,' said I, as we drove past it.

"'It was there at the Norman Conquest in all probability,' he answered. 'It has a girth of twenty-three feet.'

"'Have you any old elms?' I asked.

"'There used to be a very old one over yonder, but it was struck by lightning ten years ago, and we cut down the stump.'

"'You can see where it used to be?'

"'Oh, yes.'

"'There are no other elms?'

"'No old ones, but plenty of beeches.'

"'I should like to see where it grew.'

"We had driven up in a dog-cart, and my client led me away at once, without our entering the house, to the scar on the lawn where the elm had stood. It was nearly midway between the oak and the house. My investigation seemed to be progressing.

"'I suppose it is impossible to find out how high the elm was?' I asked.

"'I can give you it at once. It was sixty-four feet.'

"'How do you come to know it?' I asked, in surprise.

"'When my old tutor used to give me an exercise in trigonometry, it always took the shape of measuring heights. When I was a lad I worked out every tree and building in the estate.'

"This was an unexpected piece of luck. My data were coming more quickly than I could have reasonably hoped.

"'Tell me,' I asked, 'did your butler ever ask you such a question?'

"Reginald Musgrave looked at me in astonishment. 'Now that you call it to my mind,' he answered, 'Brunton did ask me about the height of the tree some months ago, in connection with some little argument with the groom.'

"This was excellent news, Watson, for it showed me that I was on the right road. I looked up at the sun. It was low in the heavens, and I calculated that in less than an hour it would lie just above the topmost branches of the old oak. One condition mentioned in the Ritual would then be fulfilled. And the shadow of the elm must mean the farther end of the shadow, otherwise the trunk would have been chosen as the guide. I had, then, to find where the far end of the shadow would fall when the sun was just clear of the oak."

"That must have been difficult, Holmes, when the elm was no longer there."

"Well, at least I knew that if Brunton could do it, I could also. Besides, there was no real difficulty. I went with Musgrave to his study and whittled myself this peg, to which I tied this long string with a knot at each yard. Then I took two lengths of a fishing-rod, which came to just six feet, and I went back with my client to where the elm had been. The sun was just grazing the top of the oak. I fastened the rod on end, marked out the direction of the shadow, and measured it. It was nine feet in length.

"Of course, the calculation now was a simple one. If a rod of six feet threw a shadow of nine, a tree of sixty-four feet would throw one of ninety-six, and the line of the one would of course be the line of the other. I measured out the distance, which brought me almost to the wall of the house, and I thrust a peg into the spot. You can imagine my exultation, Watson, when within two inches of my peg I saw a conical depression in the ground. I knew that it was the mark made by Brunton in his measurements, and that I was still upon his trail.

"From this starting-point I proceeded to step, having first taken the cardinal points by my pocket-compass. Ten steps with each foot took me along parallel with the wall of the house, and again I marked my spot with a peg. Then I carefully paced off five to the east and two to the south. It brought me to the very threshold of the old door. Two steps to the west meant now that I was to go two paces down the stone-flagged passage, and this was the place indicated by the Ritual.

"Never have I felt such a cold chill of disappointment, Watson. For a moment it seemed to me that there must be some radical mistake in my calculations. The setting sun shone full upon the passage floor, and I could see that the old, foot-worn grey stones with which it was paved were firmly cemented together and had certainly not been moved for many a long year. Brunton had not been at work here. I tapped upon the floor, but it sounded the same all over, and there was no sign of any crack or crevice. But, fortunately, Musgrave, who had begun to appreciate the meaning of my proceedings, and who was now as excited as myself, took out his manuscript to check my calculation.

"'And under,' he cried. 'You have omitted the "and under."'

"I had thought that it meant that we were to dig, but now, of course, I saw at once that I was wrong. 'There is a cellar under this then?' I cried.

"'Yes, and as old as the house. Down here, through this door.'

"We went down a winding stone stair, and my companion, striking a match, lit a large lantern which stood on a barrel in the corner. In an instant it was obvious that we had at last come upon the true place, and that we had not been the only people to visit the spot recently.

"It had been used for the storage of wood, but the billets, which had evidently been littered over the floor, were now piled at the sides, so as to leave a clear space in the middle. In this space lay a large and heavy flagstone with a rusted iron ring in the centre to which a thick shepherd's-check muffler was attached.

"'By Jove!' cried my client. 'That's Brunton's muffler. I have seen it on him and could swear to it. What has the villain been doing here?'

"At my suggestion a couple of the county police were summoned to be present, and I then endeavoured to raise the stone by pulling on the cravat. I could only move it slightly, and it was with the aid of one of the constables that I succeeded at last in carrying it to one side. A black hole yawned beneath into which we all peered, while Musgrave, kneeling at the side, pushed down the lantern.

"A small chamber about seven feet deep and four feet square lay open to us. At one side of this was a squat, brass-bound wooden box, the lid of which was hinged upwards, with this curious old-fashioned key projecting from the lock. It was furred outside by a thick layer of dust, and damp and worms had eaten through the wood, so that a crop of livid fungi was growing on the inside of it. Several discs of metal, old coins apparently, such as I hold here, were scattered over the bottom of the box, but it contained nothing else.

"At the moment, however, we had no thought for the old chest, for our eyes were riveted upon that which crouched beside it. It was the figure of a man, clad in a suit of black, who squatted down upon his hams with his forehead sunk upon the edge of the box and his two arms thrown out on each side of it. The attitude had drawn all the stagnant blood to the face, and no man could have recognised that distorted liver-coloured countenance; but his height, his dress, and his hair were all sufficient to show my client, when we had drawn the body up, that it was indeed his missing butler. He had been dead some days, but there was no wound or bruise upon his person to show how he had met his dreadful end. When his body had been carried from the cellar we found ourselves still confronted with a problem which was almost as formidable as that with which we had started.

"I confess that so far, Watson, I had been disappointed in my investigation. I had reckoned upon solving the matter when once I had found the place referred to in the Ritual; but now I was there and was apparently as far as ever from knowing what it was which the family had concealed with such elaborate precautions. It is true that I had thrown a light upon the fate of Brunton, but now I had to ascertain how that fate had come upon him, and what part had been played in the matter by the woman who had disappeared. I sat down upon a keg in the corner and thought the whole matter carefully over.

"You know my methods in such cases, Watson. I put myself in the man's place and, having first gauged his intelligence, I try to imagine how I should myself have proceeded under the same circumstances. In this case the matter was simplified by Brunton's intelligence being quite first-rate, so that it was unnecessary to make any allowance for the personal equation, as the astronomers have dubbed it. He knew that something valuable was concealed. He had spotted the place. He found that the stone which covered it was just too heavy for a man to move unaided. What would he do next? He could not get help from outside, even if he had someone whom he could trust, without the unbarring of doors and considerable risk of detection. It was better, if he could, to have his helpmate inside the house. But whom could he ask? This girl had been devoted to him. A man always finds it hard to realize that he may have finally lost a woman's love, however badly he may have treated her. He would try by a few attentions to make his peace with the girl Howells, and then would engage her as his accomplice. Together they would come at night to the cellar, and their united force would suffice to raise the stone. So far I could follow their actions as if I had actually seen them.

"But for two of them, and one a woman, it must have been heavy work the raising of that stone. A burly Sussex policeman and I had found it no light job. What would they do to assist them? Probably what I should have done myself. I rose and examined carefully the different billets of wood which were scattered round the floor. Almost at once I came upon what I expected. One piece, about three feet in length, had a very marked indentation at one end, while several were flattened at the sides as if they had been compressed by some considerable weight. Evidently, as they had dragged the stone up they had thrust the chunks of wood into the chink, until at last, when the opening was large enough to crawl through, they would hold it open by a billet placed lengthwise, which might very well become indented at the lower end, since the whole weight of the stone would press it down on to the edge of this other slab. So far I was still on safe ground.

"And now how was I to proceed to reconstruct this midnight drama? Clearly, only one could fit into the hole, and that one was Brunton. The girl must have waited above. Brunton then unlocked the box, handed up the contents presumably—since they were not to be found—and then—and then what happened?

"What smouldering fire of vengeance had suddenly sprung into flame in this passionate Celtic woman's soul when she saw the man who had wronged her—wronged her, perhaps, far more than we suspected—in her power? Was it a chance that the wood had slipped, and that the stone had shut Brunton into what had become his sepulchre? Had she only been guilty of silence as to his fate? Or had some sudden blow from her hand dashed the support away and sent the slab crashing down into its place? Be that as it might, I seemed to see that woman's figure still clutching at her treasure trove and flying wildly up the winding stair, with her ears ringing perhaps with the muffled screams from behind her and with the drumming of frenzied hands against the slab of stone which was choking her faithless lover's life out.

"Here was the secret of her blanched face, her shaken nerves, her peals of hysterical laughter on the next morning. But what had been in the box? What had she done with that? Of course, it must have been the old metal and pebbles which my client had dragged from the mere. She had thrown them in there at the first opportunity to remove the last trace of her crime.

"For twenty minutes I had sat motionless, thinking the matter out. Musgrave still stood with a very pale face, swinging his lantern and peering down into the hole.

"'These are coins of Charles the First,' said he, holding out the few which had been in the box; 'you see we were right in fixing our date for the Ritual.'

"'We may find something else of Charles the First,' I cried, as the probable meaning of the first two questions of the Ritual broke suddenly upon me. 'Let me see the contents of the bag which you fished from the mere.'

"We ascended to his study, and he laid the *débris* before me. I could understand his regarding it as of small importance when I looked at it, for the metal was almost black and the stones lustreless and dull. I rubbed one of them on my sleeve, however, and it glowed afterwards like a spark in the dark hollow of my hand. The metal work was in the form of a double ring, but it had been bent and twisted out of its original shape.

"'You must bear in mind,' said I, 'that the Royal party made head in England even after the death of the King, and that when they at last fled they probably left many of their most precious possessions buried behind them, with the intention of returning for them in more peaceful times.'

"'My ancestor, Sir Ralph Musgrave, was a prominent Cavalier and the right-hand man of Charles the Second in his wanderings,' said my friend.

"'Ah, indeed!' I answered. 'Well now, I think that really should give us the last link that we wanted. I must congratulate you on coming into the possession, though in rather a tragic manner of a relic which is of great intrinsic value, but of even greater importance as an historical curiosity.'

"'What is it, then?' he gasped in astonishment.

"'It is nothing less than the ancient crown of the Kings of England.'

"'The crown!'

"'Precisely. Consider what the Ritual says: How does it run? "Whose was it?" "His who is gone." That was after the execution of Charles. Then, "Who shall have it?" "He who will come." That was Charles the Second, whose advent was already foreseen. There can, I think, be no doubt that this battered and shapeless diadem once encircled the brows of the royal Stuarts.'

"'And how came it in the pond?'

"'Ah, that is a question that will take some time to answer.' And with that I sketched out to him the whole long chain of surmise and of proof which I had constructed. The twilight had closed in and the moon was shining brightly in the sky before my narrative was finished.

"'And how was it then that Charles did not get his crown when he returned?' asked Musgrave, pushing back the relic into its linen bag.

"'Ah, there you lay your finger upon the one point which we shall probably never be able to clear up. It is likely that the Musgrave who held the secret died in the interval, and by some oversight left this guide to his descendant without explaining the meaning of it. From that day to this it has been handed down from father to son, until at last it came within reach of a man who tore its secret out of it and lost his life in the venture.'

"And that's the story of the Musgrave Ritual, Watson. They have the crown down at Hurlstone—though they had some legal bother and a considerable sum to pay before they were allowed to retain it. I am sure that if you mentioned my name they would be happy to show it to you. Of the woman nothing was ever heard, and the probability is that she got away out of England and carried herself and the memory of her crime to some land beyond the seas."

THE REIGATE SQUIRES

It was some time before the health of my friend Mr. Sherlock Holmes recovered from the strain caused by his immense exertions in the spring of '87. The whole question of the Netherland-Sumatra Company and of the colossal schemes of Baron Maupertuis are too recent in the minds of the public and are too intimately concerned with politics and finance to be fitting subjects for this series of sketches. They led, however, in an indirect fashion to a singular and complex problem which gave my friend an opportunity of demonstrating the value of a fresh weapon among the many with which he waged his life-long battle against crime.

On referring to my notes I see that it was upon the 14th of April that I received a telegram from Lyons which informed me that Holmes was lying ill in the Hotel Dulong. Within twenty-four hours I was in his sick-room and was relieved to find that there was nothing formidable in his symptoms. Even his iron constitution, however, had broken down under the strain of an investigation which had extended over two months, during which period he had never worked less than fifteen hours a day, and had more than once, as he assured me, kept to his task for five days at a stretch. Even the triumphant issue of his labours could not save him from reaction after so terrible an exertion, and at a time when Europe was ringing with his name and when his room was literally ankle-deep with congratulatory telegrams I found him a prey to the blackest depression. Even the knowledge that he had succeeded where the police of three countries had failed, and that he had outmanœuvred at every point the most accomplished swindler in Europe, was insufficient to rouse him from his nervous prostration.

Three days later we were back in Baker Street together; but it was evident that my friend would be much the better for a change, and the thought of a week of springtime in the country was full of attractions to me also. My old friend, Colonel Hayter, who had come under my professional care in Afghanistan, had now taken a house near Reigate in Surrey, and had frequently asked me to come down to him upon a visit. On the last occasion he had remarked that if my friend would only come with me he would be glad to extend his hospitality to him also. A little diplomacy was needed, but when Holmes understood that the establishment was a bachelor one, and that he would be allowed the fullest freedom, he fell in with my plans and a week after our return from Lyons we were under the Colonel's roof. Hayter was a fine old soldier who had seen much of the world, and he soon found, as I had expected, that Holmes and he had much in common.

On the evening of our arrival, we were sitting in the Colonel's gun-room after dinner, Holmes stretched upon the sofa, while Hayter and I looked over his little armoury of fire-arms.

"By the way," said he suddenly, "I think I'll take one of these pistols upstairs with me in case we have an alarm."

"An alarm!" said I.

"Yes, we've had a scare in this part lately. Old Acton, who is one of our county magnates, had his house broken into last Monday. No great damage done, but the fellows are still at large."

"No clue?" asked Holmes, cocking his eye at the Colonel.

"None as yet. But the affair is a petty one, one of our little country crimes, which must seem too small for your attention, Mr. Holmes, after this great international affair."

Holmes waved away the compliment, though his smile showed that it had pleased him.

"Was there any feature of interest?"

"I fancy not. The thieves ransacked the library and got very little for their pains. The whole place was turned upside down, drawers burst open, and presses ransacked, with the result that an odd volume of Pope's 'Homer,' two plated candlesticks, an ivory letter-weight, a small oak barometer, and a ball of twine are all that have vanished."

"What an extraordinary assortment!" I exclaimed.

"Oh, the fellows evidently grabbed hold of everything they could get."

Holmes grunted from the sofa.

"The county police ought to make something of that," said he; "why, it is surely obvious that—"

But I held up a warning finger.

"You are here for a rest, my dear fellow. For Heaven's sake don't get started on a new problem when your nerves are all in shreds."

Holmes shrugged his shoulders with a glance of comic resignation towards the Colonel, and the talk drifted away into less dangerous channels.

It was destined, however, that all my professional caution should be wasted, for next morning the problem obtruded itself upon us in such a way that it was impossible to ignore it, and our country visit took a turn which neither of us could have anticipated. We were at breakfast when the Colonel's butler rushed in with all his propriety shaken out of him.

"Have you heard the news, sir?" he gasped. "At the Cunningham's sir!"

"Burglary!" cried the Colonel, with his coffee-cup in mid-air.

"Murder!"

The Colonel whistled. "By Jove!" said he. "Who's killed, then? The J.P. or his son?"

"Neither sir. It was William the coachman. Shot through the heart, sir, and never spoke again."

"Who shot him, then?"

"The burglar, sir. He was off like a shot and got clean away. He'd just broke in at the pantry window when William came on him and met his end in saving his master's property."

"What time?"

"It was last night, sir, somewhere about twelve."

"Ah, then, we'll step over afterwards," said the Colonel, coolly settling down to his breakfast again. "It's a baddish business," he added when the butler had gone; "he's our leading man about here, is old Cunningham, and a very decent fellow too. He'll be cut up over this, for the man has been in his service for years and was a good servant. It's evidently the same villains who broke into Acton's."

"And stole that very singular collection," said Holmes, thoughtfully.

"Precisely."

"Hum! It may prove the simplest matter in the world, but all the same at first glance this is just a little curious, is it not? A gang of burglars acting in the country might be expected to vary the scene of their operations, and not to crack two cribs in the same district within a few days. When you spoke last night of taking precautions I remember that it passed through my mind that this was probably the last parish in England to which the thief or thieves would be likely to turn their attention—which shows that I have still much to learn."

"I fancy it's some local practitioner," said the Colonel. "In that case, of course, Acton's and Cunningham's are just the places he would go for, since they are far the largest about here."

"And richest?"

"Well, they ought to be, but they've had a lawsuit for some years which has sucked the blood out of both of them, I fancy. Old Acton has some claim on half Cunningham's estate, and the lawyers have been at it with both hands."

"If it's a local villain there should not be much difficulty in running him down," said Holmes with a yawn. "All right, Watson, I don't intend to meddle."

"Inspector Forrester, sir," said the butler, throwing open the door.

The official, a smart, keen-faced young fellow, stepped into the room. "Good-morning, Colonel," said he; "I hope I don't intrude, but we hear that Mr. Holmes of Baker Street is here."

The Colonel waved his hand towards my friend, and the Inspector bowed.

"We thought that perhaps you would care to step across, Mr. Holmes."

"The fates are against you, Watson," said he, laughing. "We were chatting about the matter when you came in, Inspector. Perhaps you can let us have a few details." As he leaned back in his chair in the familiar attitude I knew that the case was hopeless.

"We had no clue in the Acton affair. But here we have plenty to go on, and there's no doubt it is the same party in each case. The man was seen."

"Ah!"

"Yes, sir. But he was off like a deer after the shot that killed poor William Kirwan was fired. Mr. Cunningham saw him from the bedroom window, and Mr. Alec Cunningham saw him from the back passage. It was quarter to twelve when the alarm broke out. Mr. Cunningham had just got into bed, and Mr. Alec was smoking a pipe in his dressing-gown. They both heard William the coachman calling for help, and Mr. Alec ran down to see what the matter was. The back door was open, and as he came to the foot of the stairs he saw two men wrestling together outside. One of them fired a shot, the other dropped, and the murderer rushed across the garden and over the hedge. Mr. Cunningham, looking out of his bedroom, saw the fellow as he gained the road, but lost sight of him at once. Mr. Alec stopped to see if he could help the dying man, and so the villain got clean away. Beyond the fact that he was a middle-sized man and dressed in some dark stuff, we have no personal clue; but we are making energetic inquiries, and if he is a stranger we shall soon find him out."

"What was this William doing there? Did he say anything before he died?"

"Not a word. He lives at the lodge with his mother, and as he was a very faithful fellow we imagine that he walked up to the house with the intention of seeing that all was right there. Of course, this Acton business has put everyone on their guard. The robber must have just burst open the door—the lock has been forced—when William came upon him."

"Did William say anything to his mother before going out?"

"She is very old and deaf, and we can get no information from her. The shock has made her half-witted, but I understand that she was never very bright. There is one very important circumstance, however. Look at this!"

He took a small piece of torn paper from a note-book and spread it out upon his knee.

"This was found between the finger and thumb of the dead man. It appears to be a fragment torn from a larger sheet. You will observe that the hour mentioned upon it is the very time at which the poor fellow met his fate. You see that his murderer might have torn the rest of the sheet from him, or he might have taken this fragment from the murderer. It reads almost as though it were an appointment."

Holmes took up the scrap of paper, a facsimile of which is here reproduced.

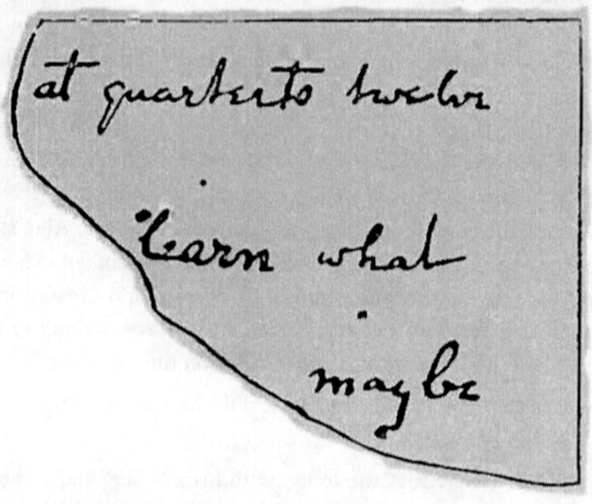

"Presuming that it is an appointment," continued the Inspector, "it is of course a conceivable theory that this William Kirwan—though he had the reputation of being an honest man, may have been in league with the thief. He may have met him there, may even have helped him to break in the door, and then they may have fallen out between themselves."

"This writing is of extraordinary interest," said Holmes, who had been examining it with intense concentration. "These are much deeper waters than I had thought." He sank his head upon his hands, while the

Inspector smiled at the effect which his case had had upon the famous London specialist.

"Your last remark," said Holmes, presently, "as to the possibility of there being an understanding between the burglar and the servant, and this being a note of appointment from one to the other, is an ingenious and not entirely impossible supposition. But this writing opens up—" He sank his head into his hands again and remained for some minutes in the deepest thought. When he raised his face again, I was surprised to see that his cheek was tinged with colour, and his eyes as bright as before his illness. He sprang to his feet with all his old energy.

"I'll tell you what," said he, "I should like to have a quiet little glance into the details of this case. There is something in it which fascinates me extremely. If you will permit me, Colonel, I will leave my friend Watson and you, and I will step round with the Inspector to test the truth of one or two little fancies of mine. I will be with you again in half an hour."

An hour and half had elapsed before the Inspector returned alone.

"Mr. Holmes is walking up and down in the field outside," said he. "He wants us all four to go up to the house together."

"To Mr. Cunningham's?"

"Yes, sir."

"What for?"

The Inspector shrugged his shoulders. "I don't quite know, sir. Between ourselves, I think Mr. Holmes had not quite got over his illness yet. He's been behaving very queerly, and he is very much excited."

"I don't think you need alarm yourself," said I. "I have usually found that there was method in his madness."

"Some folks might say there was madness in his method," muttered the Inspector. "But he's all on fire to start, Colonel, so we had best go out if you are ready."

We found Holmes pacing up and down in the field, his chin sunk upon his breast, and his hands thrust into his trousers pockets.

"The matter grows in interest," said he. "Watson, your country-trip has been a distinct success. I have had a charming morning."

"You have been up to the scene of the crime, I understand," said the Colonel.

"Yes; the Inspector and I have made quite a little reconnaissance together."

"Any success?"

"Well, we have seen some very interesting things. I'll tell you what we did as we walk. First of all, we saw the body of this unfortunate man. He certainly died from a revolver wound as reported."

"Had you doubted it, then?"

"Oh, it is as well to test everything. Our inspection was not wasted. We then had an interview with Mr. Cunningham and his son, who were able to point out the exact spot where the murderer had broken through the garden-hedge in his flight. That was of great interest."

"Naturally."

"Then we had a look at this poor fellow's mother. We could get no information from her, however, as she is very old and feeble."

"And what is the result of your investigations?"

"The conviction that the crime is a very peculiar one. Perhaps our visit now may do something to make it less obscure. I think that we are both agreed, Inspector that the fragment of paper in the dead man's hand, bearing, as it does, the very hour of his death written upon it, is of extreme importance."

"It should give a clue, Mr. Holmes."

"It *does* give a clue. Whoever wrote that note was the man who brought William Kirwan out of his bed at that hour. But where is the rest of that sheet of paper?"

"I examined the ground carefully in the hope of finding it," said the Inspector.

"It was torn out of the dead man's hand. Why was someone so anxious to get possession of it? Because it incriminated him. And what would he do with it? Thrust it into his pocket, most likely, never noticing that a corner of it had been left in the grip of the corpse. If we could get the rest of that sheet it is obvious that we should have gone a long way towards solving the mystery."

"Yes, but how can we get at the criminal's pocket before we catch the criminal?"

"Well, well, it was worth thinking over. Then there is another obvious point. The note was sent to William. The man who wrote it could not have taken it; otherwise, of course, he might have delivered his own message by word of mouth. Who brought the note, then? Or did it come through the post?"

"I have made inquiries," said the Inspector. "William received a letter by the afternoon post yesterday. The envelope was destroyed by him."

"Excellent!" cried Holmes, clapping the Inspector on the back. "You've seen the postman. It is a pleasure to work with you. Well, here is the lodge, and if you will come up, Colonel, I will show you the scene of the crime."

We passed the pretty cottage where the murdered man had lived and walked up an oak-lined avenue to the fine old Queen Anne house, which bears the date of Malplaquet upon the lintel of the door. Holmes and the Inspector led us round it until we came to the side gate, which is separated by a stretch of garden from the hedge which lines the road. A constable was standing at the kitchen door.

"Throw the door open, officer," said Holmes. "Now, it was on those stairs that young Mr. Cunningham stood and saw the two men struggling just where we are. Old Mr. Cunningham was at that window—the second on the left—and he saw the fellow get away just to the left of that bush. Then Mr. Alec ran out and knelt beside the wounded man. The ground is very hard, you see, and there are no marks to guide us." As he spoke two men came down the garden path, from round the angle of the house. The one was an elderly man, with a strong, deep-lined, heavy-eyed face; the other a dashing young fellow, whose bright, smiling expression and showy dress were in strange contrast with the business which had brought us there.

"Still at it, then?" said he to Holmes. "I thought you Londoners were never at fault. You don't seem to be so very quick, after all."

"Ah, you must give us a little time," said Holmes good-humoredly.

"You'll want it," said young Alec Cunningham. "Why, I don't see that we have any clue at all."

"There's only one," answered the Inspector. "We thought that if we could only find—Good heavens, Mr. Holmes! What is the matter?"

My poor friend's face had suddenly assumed the most dreadful expression. His eyes rolled upwards, his features writhed in agony, and with a suppressed groan he dropped on his face upon the ground. Horrified at the suddenness and severity of the attack, we carried him into the kitchen, where he lay back in a large chair, and breathed heavily for some minutes. Finally, with a shamefaced apology for his weakness, he rose once more.

"Watson would tell you that I have only just recovered from a severe illness," he explained. "I am liable to these sudden nervous attacks."

"Shall I send you home in my trap?" asked old Cunningham.

"Well, since I am here, there is one point on which I should like to feel sure. We can very easily verify it."

"What was it?"

"Well, it seems to me that it is just possible that the arrival of this poor fellow William was not before, but after, the entrance of the burglar into the house. You appear to take it for granted that, although the door was forced, the robber never got in."

"I fancy that is quite obvious," said Mr. Cunningham, gravely. "Why, my son Alec had not yet gone to bed, and he would certainly have heard anyone moving about."

"Where was he sitting?"

"I was smoking in my dressing-room."

"Which window is that?"

"The last on the left next my father's."

"Both of your lamps were lit, of course?"

"Undoubtedly."

"There are some very singular points here," said Holmes, smiling. "Is it not extraordinary that a burglar—and a burglar who had had some previous experience—should deliberately break into a house at a time when he could see from the lights that two of the family were still afoot?"

"He must have been a cool hand."

"Well, of course, if the case were not an odd one we should not have been driven to ask you for an explanation," said young Mr. Alec. "But as to your ideas that the man had robbed the house before William tackled him, I think it a most absurd notion. Wouldn't we have found the place disarranged, and missed the things which he had taken?"

"It depends on what the things were," said Holmes. "You must remember that we are dealing with a burglar who is a very peculiar fellow, and who appears to work on lines of his own. Look, for example, at the queer lot of things which he took from Acton's—what was it?—a ball of string, a letter-weight, and I don't know what other odds and ends."

"Well, we are quite in your hands, Mr. Holmes," said old Cunningham. "Anything which you or the Inspector may suggest will most certainly be done."

"In the first place," said Holmes, "I should like you to offer a reward—coming from yourself, for the officials may take a little time before they would agree upon the sum, and these things cannot be done too promptly. I have jotted down the form here, if you would not mind signing it. Fifty pounds was quite enough, I thought."

"I would willingly give five hundred," said the J.P., taking the slip of paper and the pencil which Holmes handed to him. "This is not quite correct, however," he added, glancing over the document.

"I wrote it rather hurriedly."

"You see you begin, 'Whereas, at about a quarter to one on Tuesday morning an attempt was made,' and so on. It was at a quarter to twelve, as a matter of fact."

I was pained at the mistake, for I knew how keenly Holmes would feel any slip of the kind. It was his specialty to be accurate as to fact, but his recent illness had shaken him, and this one little incident was enough to show me that he was still far from being himself. He was obviously embarrassed for an instant, while the Inspector raised his eyebrows, and Alec Cunningham burst into a laugh. The old gentleman corrected the mistake, however, and handed the paper back to Holmes.

"Get it printed as soon as possible," he said; "I think your idea is an excellent one."

Holmes put the slip of paper carefully away into his pocket-book.

"And now," said he, "it really would be a good thing that we should all go over the house together and make certain that this rather erratic burglar did not, after all, carry anything away with him."

Before entering, Holmes made an examination of the door which had been forced. It was evident that a chisel or strong knife had been thrust in, and the lock forced back with it. We could see the marks in the wood where it had been pushed in.

"You don't use bars, then?" he asked.

"We have never found it necessary."

"You don't keep a dog?"

"Yes, but he is chained on the other side of the house."

"When do the servants go to bed?"

"About ten."

"I understand that William was usually in bed also at that hour."

"Yes."

"It is singular that on this particular night he should have been up. Now, I should be very glad if you would have the kindness to show us over the house, Mr. Cunningham."

A stone-flagged passage, with the kitchens branching away from it, led by a wooden staircase directly to the first floor of the house. It came out upon the landing opposite to a second more ornamental stair which came up from the front hall. Out of this landing opened the drawing-room and several bedrooms, including those of Mr. Cunningham and his son. Holmes walked slowly, taking keen note of the architecture of the house. I could tell from his expression that he was on a hot scent, and yet I could not in the least imagine in what direction his inferences were leading him.

"My good sir," said Mr. Cunningham with some impatience, "this is surely very unnecessary. That is my room at the end of the stairs, and my son's is the one beyond it. I leave it to your judgment whether it was possible for the thief to have come up here without disturbing us."

"You must try round and get on a fresh scent, I fancy," said the son with a rather malicious smile.

"Still, I must ask you to humour me a little further. I should like, for example, to see how far the windows of the bedrooms command the front. This, I understand is your son's room"—he pushed open the door—"and that, I presume, is the dressing-room in which he sat smoking when the alarm was given. Where does the window of that look out to?" He stepped across the bedroom, pushed open the door, and glanced round the other chamber.

"I hope that you are satisfied now?" said Mr. Cunningham, tartly.

"Thank you, I think I have seen all that I wished."

"Then if it is really necessary we can go into my room."

"If it is not too much trouble."

The J.P. shrugged his shoulders, and led the way into his own chamber, which was a plainly furnished and commonplace room. As we moved across it in the direction of the window, Holmes fell back until he and I were the last of the group. Near the foot of the bed stood a dish of oranges and a carafe of water. As we passed it Holmes, to my unutterable astonishment, leaned over in front of me and deliberately knocked the whole thing over. The glass smashed into a thousand pieces and the fruit rolled about into every corner of the room.

"You've done it now, Watson," said he, coolly. "A pretty mess you've made of the carpet."

I stooped in some confusion and began to pick up the fruit, understanding for some reason my companion desired me to take the blame upon myself. The others did the same and set the table on its legs again.

"Halloa!" cried the Inspector, "where's he got to?"

Holmes had disappeared.

"Wait here an instant," said young Alec Cunningham. "The fellow is off his head, in my opinion. Come with me, father, and see where he has got to!"

They rushed out of the room, leaving the Inspector, the Colonel, and me staring at each other.

"'Pon my word, I am inclined to agree with Master Alec," said the official. "It may be the effect of this illness, but it seems to me that—"

His words were cut short by a sudden scream of "Help! Help! Murder!" With a thrill I recognised the voice of that of my friend. I rushed madly from the room on to the landing. The cries, which had sunk down into a hoarse, inarticulate shouting, came from the room which we had first visited. I dashed in, and on into the dressing-room beyond. The two Cunninghams were bending over the prostrate figure of Sherlock Holmes, the younger clutching his throat with both hands, while the elder seemed to be twisting one of his wrists. In an instant the three of us had torn them away from him, and Holmes staggered to his feet, very pale and evidently greatly exhausted.

"Arrest these men, Inspector!" he gasped.

"On what charge?"

"That of murdering their coachman, William Kirwan!"

The Inspector stared about him in bewilderment. "Oh, come now, Mr. Holmes," said he at last, "I'm sure you don't really mean to—"

"Tut, man, look at their faces!" cried Holmes, curtly.

Never, certainly, have I seen a plainer confession of guilt upon human countenances. The older man seemed numbed and dazed with a heavy, sullen expression upon his strongly-marked face. The son, on the other hand, had dropped all that jaunty, dashing style which had characterized him, and the ferocity of a dangerous wild beast gleamed in his dark eyes and distorted his handsome features. The Inspector said nothing, but, stepping to the door, he blew his whistle. Two of his constables came at the call.

"I have no alternative, Mr. Cunningham," said he. "I trust that this may all prove to be an absurd mistake, but you can see that—Ah, would you? Drop it!" He struck out with his hand, and a revolver which the younger man was in the act of cocking clattered down upon the floor.

"Keep that," said Holmes, quietly putting his foot upon it; "you will find it useful at the trial. But this is what we really wanted." He held up a little crumpled piece of paper.

"The remainder of the sheet!" cried the Inspector.

"Precisely."

"And where was it?"

"Where I was sure it must be. I'll make the whole matter clear to you presently. I think, Colonel, that you and Watson might return now, and I will be with you again in an hour at the furthest. The Inspector and I must have a word with the prisoners, but you will certainly see me back at luncheon time."

Sherlock Holmes was as good as his word, for about one o'clock he rejoined us in the Colonel's smoking-room. He was accompanied by a little elderly gentleman, who was introduced to me as the Mr. Acton whose house had been the scene of the original burglary.

"I wished Mr. Acton to be present while I demonstrated this small matter to you," said Holmes, "for it is natural that he should take a keen interest in the details. I am afraid, my dear Colonel, that you must regret the hour that you took in such a stormy petrel as I am."

"On the contrary," answered the Colonel, warmly, "I consider it the greatest privilege to have been permitted to study your methods of working. I confess that they quite surpass my expectations, and that I am utterly unable to account for your result. I have not yet seen the vestige of a clue."

"I am afraid that my explanation may disillusionize you, but it has always been my habit to hide none of my methods, either from my friend Watson or from anyone who might take an intelligent interest in them. But, first, as I am rather shaken by the knocking about which I had in the dressing-room, I think that I shall help myself to a dash of your brandy, Colonel. My strength has been rather tried of late."

"I trust that you had no more of those nervous attacks."

Sherlock Holmes laughed heartily. "We will come to that in its turn," said he. "I will lay an account of the case before you in its due order, showing you the various points which guided me in my decision. Pray interrupt me if there is any inference which is not perfectly clear to you.

"It is of the highest importance in the art of detection to be able to recognise, out of a number of facts, which are incidental and which vital. Otherwise, your energy and attention must be dissipated instead of being concentrated. Now, in this case there was not the slightest doubt in my mind from the first that the key of the whole matter must be looked for in the scrap of paper in the dead man's hand.

"Before going into this, I would draw your attention to the fact that, if Alec Cunningham's narrative was correct, and if the assailant, after shooting William Kirwan, had *instantly* fled, then it obviously could not be he who tore the paper from the dead man's hand. But if it was not he, it must have been Alec Cunningham himself, for by the time that the old man had descended several servants were upon the scene. The point is a simple one, but the Inspector had overlooked it because he had started with the supposition that these county magnates had had nothing to do with the matter. Now, I make a point of never having any prejudices, and of following docilely wherever fact may lead me, and so, in the very first stage of the investigation, I found myself looking a little askance at the part which had been played by Mr. Alec Cunningham.

"And now I made a very careful examination of the corner of paper which the Inspector had submitted to us. It was at once clear to me that it formed part of a very remarkable document. Here it is. Do you not now observe something very suggestive about it?"

"It has a very irregular look," said the Colonel.

"My dear sir," cried Holmes, "there cannot be the least doubt in the world that it has been written by two persons doing alternate words. When I draw your attention to the strong t's of 'at' and 'to', and ask you to compare them with the weak ones of 'quarter' and 'twelve,' you will instantly recognise the fact. A very brief analysis of these four words would enable you to say with the utmost confidence that the 'learn' and the 'maybe' are written in the stronger hand, and the 'what' in the weaker."

"By Jove, it's as clear as day!" cried the Colonel. "Why on earth should two men write a letter in such a fashion?"

"Obviously the business was a bad one, and one of the men who distrusted the other was determined that, whatever was done, each should have an equal hand in it. Now, of the two men, it is clear that the one who wrote the 'at' and 'to' was the ringleader."

"How do you get at that?"

"We might deduce it from the mere character of the one hand as compared with the other. But we have more assured reasons than that for supposing it. If you examine this scrap with attention you will come to the conclusion that the man with the stronger hand wrote all his words first, leaving blanks for the other to fill up. These blanks were not always sufficient, and you can see that the second man had a squeeze to fit his 'quarter' in between the 'at' and the 'to,' showing that the latter were already written. The man who wrote all his words first is undoubtedly the man who planned the affair."

"Excellent!" cried Mr. Acton.

"But very superficial," said Holmes. "We come now, however, to a point which is of importance. You may not be aware that the deduction of a man's age from his writing is one which has been brought to considerable accuracy by experts. In normal cases one can place a man in his true decade with tolerable confidence. I say normal cases, because ill-health and physical weakness reproduce the signs of old age, even when the invalid is a youth. In this case, looking at the bold, strong hand of the one, and the rather broken-backed appearance of the other, which still retains its legibility although the t's have begun to lose their crossing, we can say that the one was a young man and the other was advanced in years without being positively decrepit."

"Excellent!" cried Mr. Acton again.

"There is a further point, however, which is subtler and of greater interest. There is something in common between these hands. They belong to men who are blood-relatives. It may be most obvious to you in the Greek e's, but to me there are many small points which indicate the same thing. I have no doubt at all that a family mannerism can be traced in these two specimens of writing. I am only, of course, giving you the leading results now of my examination of the paper. There were twenty-three other deductions which would be of more interest to experts than to you. They all tend to deepen the impression upon my mind that the Cunninghams, father and son, had written this letter.

"Having got so far, my next step was, of course, to examine into the details of the crime, and to see how far they would help us. I went up to the house with the Inspector and saw all that was to be seen. The wound upon the dead man was, as I was able to determine with absolute confidence, fired from a revolver at the distance of something over four yards. There was no powder-blackening on the clothes. Evidently, therefore, Alec Cunningham had lied when he said that the two men were struggling when the shot was fired. Again, both father and son agreed as to the place where the man escaped into the road. At that point, however, as it happens, there is a broadish ditch, moist at the bottom. As there were no indications of bootmarks about this ditch, I was absolutely sure not only that the Cunninghams had again lied, but that there had never been any unknown man upon the scene at all.

"And now I have to consider the motive of this singular crime. To get at this, I endeavoured first of all to solve the reason of the original burglary at Mr. Acton's. I understood, from something which the Colonel told us, that a lawsuit had been going on between you, Mr. Acton, and the Cunninghams. Of course, it instantly occurred to me that they had broken into your library with the intention of getting at some document which might be of importance in the case."

"Precisely so," said Mr. Acton. "There can be no possible doubt as to their intentions. I have the clearest claim upon half of their present estate, and if they could have found a single paper—which, fortunately, was in the strong-box of my solicitors—they would undoubtedly have crippled our case."

"There you are," said Holmes, smiling. "It was a dangerous, reckless attempt, in which I seem to trace the influence of young Alec. Having found nothing they tried to divert suspicion by making it appear to be an ordinary burglary, to which end they carried off whatever they could lay their hands upon. That is all clear enough, but there was much that was still obscure. What I wanted above all was to get the missing part of that note. I was certain that Alec had torn it out of the dead man's hand, and almost certain that he must have thrust it into the pocket of his dressing-gown. Where else could he have put it? The only question was whether it was still there. It was worth an effort to find out, and for that object we all went up to the house.

"The Cunninghams joined us, as you doubtless remember, outside the kitchen door. It was, of course, of the very first importance that they should not be reminded of the existence of this paper, otherwise they would naturally destroy it without delay. The Inspector was about to tell them the importance which we attached to it when, by the luckiest chance in the world, I tumbled down in a sort of fit and so changed the conversation.

"Good heavens!" cried the Colonel, laughing, "do you mean to say all our sympathy was wasted and your fit an imposture?"

"Speaking professionally, it was admirably done," cried I, looking in amazement at this man who was forever confounding me with some new phase of his astuteness.

"It is an art which is often useful," said he. "When I recovered I managed, by a device which had perhaps some little merit of ingenuity, to get old Cunningham to write the word 'twelve,' so that I might compare it with the 'twelve' upon the paper."

"Oh, what an ass I have been!" I exclaimed.

"I could see that you were commiserating me over my weakness," said Holmes, laughing. "I was sorry to cause you the sympathetic pain which I know that you felt. We then went upstairs together, and having entered the room and seen the dressing-gown hanging up behind the door, I contrived, by upsetting a table, to engage their attention for the moment, and slipped back to examine the pockets. I had hardly got the paper, however—which was, as I had expected, in one of them—when the two Cunninghams were on me, and would, I verily believe, have murdered me then and there but for your prompt and friendly aid. As it is, I feel that young man's grip on my throat now, and the father has twisted my wrist round in the effort to get the paper out of my hand. They saw that I must know all about it, you see, and the sudden change from absolute security to complete despair made them perfectly desperate.

"I had a little talk with old Cunningham afterwards as to the motive of the crime. He was tractable enough, though his son was a perfect demon, ready to blow out his own or anybody else's brains if he could have got to his revolver. When Cunningham saw that the case against him was so strong he lost all heart and made a clean breast of everything. It seems that William had secretly followed his two master's on the night when they made their raid upon Mr. Acton's, and having thus got them into his power, proceeded, under threats of exposure, to levy blackmail upon them. Mr. Alec, however, was a dangerous man to play games of that sort with. It was a stroke of positive genius on his part to see in the burglary scare which was convulsing the countryside an opportunity of plausibly getting rid of the man whom he feared. William was decoyed up and shot, and had they only got the whole of the note and paid a little more attention to detail in the accessories, it is very possible that suspicion might never have been aroused."

"And the note?" I asked.

Sherlock Holmes placed the subjoined paper before us.

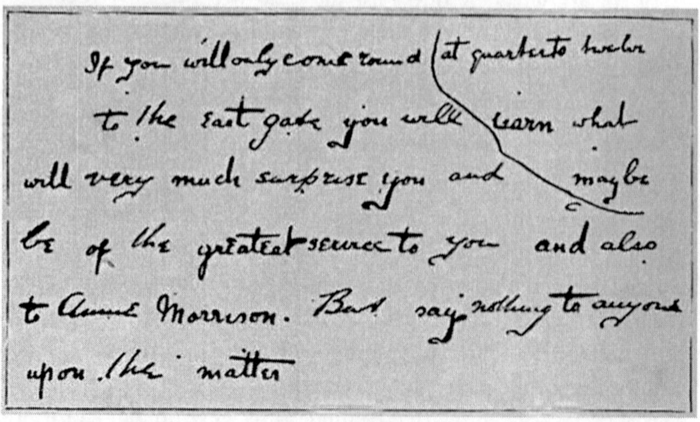
If you will only come round at quarter to twelve
to the east gate you will learn what
will very much surprise you and maybe
be of the greatest service to you and also
to Annie Morrison. But say nothing to anyone
upon the matter

If you will only come round at quarter to twelve
to the east gate you will learn what

will very much surprise you and maybe
be of the greatest service to you and also
to Annie Morrison. But say nothing to anyone
upon the matter

"It is very much the sort of thing that I expected," said he. "Of course, we do not yet know what the relations may have been between Alec Cunningham, William Kirwan, and Annie Morrison. The results shows that the trap was skillfully baited. I am sure that you cannot fail to be delighted with the traces of heredity shown in the p's and in the tails of the g's. The absence of the i-dots in the old man's writing is also most characteristic. Watson, I think our quiet rest in the country has been a distinct success, and I shall certainly return much invigorated to Baker Street tomorrow."

THE ADVENTURE OF THE SECOND STAIN

I had intended "The Adventure of the Abbey Grange" to be the last of those exploits of my friend, Mr. Sherlock Holmes, which I should ever communicate to the public. This resolution of mine was not due to any lack of material, since I have notes of many hundreds of cases to which I have never alluded, nor was it caused by any waning interest on the part of my readers in the singular personality and unique methods of this remarkable man. The real reason lay in the reluctance which Mr. Holmes has shown to the continued publication of his experiences. So long as he was in actual professional practice the records of his successes were of some practical value to him, but since he has definitely retired from London and be taken himself to study and bee-farming on the Sussex Downs, notoriety has become hateful to him, and he has peremptorily requested that his wishes in this matter should be strictly observed. It was only upon my representing to him that I had given a promise that "The Adventure of the Second Stain" should be published when the times were ripe, and pointing out to him that it is only appropriate that this long series of episodes should culminate in the most important international case which he has ever been called upon to handle, that I at last succeeded in obtaining his consent that a carefully guarded account of the incident should at last be laid before the public. If in telling the story I seem to be somewhat vague in certain details, the public will readily understand that there is an excellent reason for my reticence.

It was, then, in a year, and even in a decade, that shall be nameless, that upon one Tuesday morning in autumn we found two visitors of European fame within the walls of our humble room in Baker Street.

The one, austere, high-nosed, eagle-eyed, and dominant, was none other than the illustrious Lord Bellinger, twice Premier of Britain. The other, dark, clear-cut, and elegant, hardly yet of middle age, and endowed with every beauty of body and of mind, was the Right Honourable Trelawney Hope, Secretary for European Affairs, and the most rising statesman in the country. They sat side by side upon our paper-littered settee, and it was easy to see from their worn and anxious faces that it was business of the most pressing importance which had brought them. The Premier's thin, blue-veined hands were clasped tightly over the ivory head of his umbrella, and his gaunt, ascetic face looked gloomily from Holmes to me. The European Secretary pulled nervously at his moustache and fidgeted with the seals of his watch-chain.

"When I discovered my loss, Mr. Holmes, which was at eight o'clock this morning, I at once informed the Prime Minister. It was at his suggestion that we have both come to you."

"Have you informed the police?"

"No, sir," said the Prime Minister, with the quick, decisive manner for which he was famous. "We have not done so, nor is it possible that we should do so. To inform the police must, in the long run, mean to inform the public. This is what we particularly desire to avoid."

"And why, sir?"

"Because the document in question is of such immense importance that its publication might very easily—I might almost say probably—lead to European complications of the utmost moment. It is not too much to say that peace or war may hang upon the issue. Unless its recovery can be attended with the utmost secrecy, then it may as well not be recovered at all, for all that is aimed at by those who have taken it is that its contents should be generally known."

"I understand. Now, Mr. Trelawney Hope, I should be much obliged if you would tell me exactly the circumstances under which this document disappeared."

"That can be done in a very few words, Mr. Holmes. The letter—for it was a letter from a foreign potentate—was received six days ago. It was of such importance that I have never left it in my safe but have taken it across each evening to my house in Whitehall Terrace and kept it in my bedroom in a locked despatch-box. It was there last night. Of that I am certain. I actually opened the box while I was dressing for dinner and saw the document inside. This morning it was gone. The despatch-box had stood beside the glass upon my dressing-table all night. I am a light sleeper, and so is my wife. We are both prepared to swear that no one could have entered the room during the night. And yet I repeat that the paper is gone."

"What time did you dine?"

"Half-past seven."

"How long was it before you went to bed?"

"My wife had gone to the theatre. I waited up for her. It was half-past eleven before we went to our room."

"Then for four hours the despatch-box had lain unguarded?"

"No one is ever permitted to enter that room save the house-maid in the morning and my valet, or my wife's maid, during the rest of the day. They are both trusty servants who have been with us for some time. Besides, neither of them could possibly have known that there was anything more valuable than the ordinary departmental papers in my despatch-box."

"Who did know of the existence of that letter?"

"No one in the house."

"Surely your wife knew?"

"No, sir. I had said nothing to my wife until I missed the paper this morning."

The Premier nodded approvingly.

"I have long known, sir, how high is your sense of public duty," said he. "I am convinced that in the case of a secret of this importance it would rise superior to the most intimate domestic ties."

The European Secretary bowed.

"You do me no more than justice, sir. Until this morning, I have never breathed one word to my wife upon this matter."

"Could she have guessed?"

"No, Mr. Holmes, she could not have guessed—nor could anyone have guessed."

"Have you lost any documents before?"

"No, sir."

"Who is there in England who did know of the existence of this letter?"

"Each member of the Cabinet was informed of it yesterday, but the pledge of secrecy which attends every Cabinet meeting was increased by the solemn warning which was given by the Prime Minister. Good heavens, to think that within a few hours I should myself have lost it!" His handsome face was distorted with a spasm of despair, and his hands tore at his hair. For a moment we caught a glimpse of the natural man, impulsive, ardent, keenly sensitive. The next the aristocratic mask was replaced, and the gentle voice had returned. "Besides the members of the Cabinet there are two, or possibly three, departmental officials who know of the letter. No one else in England, Mr. Holmes, I assure you."

"But abroad?"

"I believe that no one abroad has seen it save the man who wrote it. I am well convinced that his Ministers—that the usual official channels have not been employed."

Holmes considered for some little time.

"Now, sir, I must ask you more particularly what this document is, and why its disappearance should have such momentous consequences?"

The two statesmen exchanged a quick glance and the Premier's shaggy eyebrows gathered in a frown.

"Mr. Holmes, the envelope is a long, thin one of pale blue colour. There is a seal of red wax stamped with a crouching lion. It is addressed in large, bold handwriting to——"

"I fear, sir," said Holmes, "that, interesting and indeed essential as these details are, my inquiries must go more to the root of things. What *was* the letter?"

"That is a State secret of the utmost importance, and I fear that I cannot tell you, nor do I see that it is necessary. If by the aid of the powers which you are said to possess you can find such an envelope as I describe with its enclosure, you will have deserved well of your country and earned any reward which it lies in our power to bestow."

Sherlock Holmes rose with a smile.

"You are two of the most busy men in the country," said he, "and in my own small way I have also a good many calls upon me. I regret exceedingly that I cannot help you in this matter, and any continuation of this interview would be a waste of time."

The Premier sprang to his feet with that quick, fierce gleam of his deep-set eyes before which a Cabinet has cowered. "I am not accustomed, sir," he began, but mastered his anger and resumed his seat. For a minute or more we all sat in silence. Then the old statesman shrugged his shoulders.

"We must accept your terms, Mr. Holmes. No doubt you are right, and it is unreasonable for us to expect you to act unless we give you our entire confidence."

"I agree with you," said the younger statesman.

"Then I will tell you, relying entirely upon your honour and that of your colleague, Dr. Watson. I may appeal to your patriotism also, for I could not imagine a greater misfortune for the country than that this affair should come out."

"You may safely trust us."

"The letter, then, is from a certain foreign potentate who has been ruffled by some recent Colonial developments of this country. It has been written hurriedly and upon his own responsibility entirely. Inquiries have shown that his Ministers know nothing of the matter. At the same time, it is couched in so unfortunate a manner, and certain phrases in it are of so provocative a character, that its publication would undoubtedly lead to a most dangerous state of feeling in this country. There would be such a ferment, sir, that I do not hesitate to say that within a week of the publication of that letter this country would be involved in a great war."

Holmes wrote a name upon a slip of paper and handed it to the Premier.

"Exactly. It was he. And it is this letter—this letter which may well mean the expenditure of a thousand millions and the lives of a hundred thousand men—which has become lost in this unaccountable fashion."

"Have you informed the sender?"

"Yes, sir, a cipher telegram has been despatched."

"Perhaps he desires the publication of the letter."

"No, sir, we have strong reason to believe that he already understands that he has acted in an indiscreet and hot-headed manner. It would be a greater blow to him and to his country than to us if this letter were to come out."

"If this is so, whose interest is it that the letter should come out? Why should anyone desire to steal it or to publish it?"

"There, Mr. Holmes, you take me into regions of high international politics. But if you consider the European situation you will have no difficulty in perceiving the motive. The whole of Europe is an armed camp. There is a double league which makes a fair balance of military power. Great Britain holds the scales. If Britain were driven into war with one confederacy, it would assure the supremacy of the other confederacy, whether they joined in the war or not. Do you follow?"

"Very clearly. It is then the interest of the enemies of this potentate to secure and publish this letter, so as to make a breach between his country and ours?"

"Yes, sir."

"And to whom would this document be sent if it fell into the hands of an enemy?"

"To any of the great Chancelleries of Europe. It is probably speeding on its way thither at the present instant as fast as steam can take it."

Mr. Trelawney Hope dropped his head on his chest and groaned aloud. The Premier placed his hand kindly upon his shoulder.

"It is your misfortune, my dear fellow. No one can blame you. There is no precaution which you have neglected. Now, Mr. Holmes, you are in full possession of the facts. What course do you recommend?"

Holmes shook his head mournfully.

"You think, sir, that unless this document is recovered there will be war?"

"I think it is very probable."

"Then, sir, prepare for war."

"That is a hard saying, Mr. Holmes."

"Consider the facts, sir. It is inconceivable that it was taken after eleven-thirty at night, since I understand that Mr. Hope and his wife were both in the room from that hour until the loss was found out. It was taken, then, yesterday evening between seven-thirty and eleven-thirty, probably near the earlier hour, since whoever took it evidently knew that it was there and would naturally secure it as early as possible. Now, sir, if a document of this importance were taken at that hour, where can it be now? No one has any reason to retain it. It has been passed rapidly on to those who need it. What chance have we now to overtake or even to trace it? It is beyond our reach."

The Prime Minister rose from the settee.

"What you say is perfectly logical, Mr. Holmes. I feel that the matter is indeed out of our hands."

"Let us presume, for argument's sake, that the document was taken by the maid or by the valet——"

"They are both old and tried servants."

"I understand you to say that your room is on the second floor, that there is no entrance from without, and that from within no one could go up unobserved. It must, then, be somebody in the house who has taken it. To whom would the thief take it? To one of several international spies and secret agents, whose names are tolerably familiar to me. There are three who may be said to be the heads of their profession. I will begin my research by going round and finding if each of them is at his post. If one is missing—especially if he has disappeared since last night—we will have some indication as to where the document has gone."

"Why should he be missing?" asked the European Secretary. "He would take the letter to an Embassy in London, as likely as not."

"I fancy not. These agents work independently, and their relations with the Embassies are often strained."

The Prime Minister nodded his acquiescence.

"I believe you are right, Mr. Holmes. He would take so valuable a prize to headquarters with his own hands. I think that your course of action is an excellent one. Meanwhile, Hope, we cannot neglect all our other duties on account of this one misfortune. Should there be any fresh developments during the day we shall communicate with you, and you will no doubt let us know the results of your own inquiries."

The two statesmen bowed and walked gravely from the room.

When our illustrious visitors had departed Holmes lit his pipe in silence and sat for some time lost in the deepest thought. I had opened the morning paper and was immersed in a sensational crime which had occurred in London the night before, when my friend gave an exclamation, sprang to his feet, and laid his pipe down upon the mantelpiece.

"Yes," said he, "there is no better way of approaching it. The situation is desperate, but not hopeless. Even now, if we could be sure which of them has taken it, it is just possible that it has not yet passed out of his hands. After all, it is a question of money with these fellows, and I have the British treasury behind me. If it's on the market I'll buy it—if it means another penny on the income-tax. It is conceivable that the fellow might hold it back to see what bids come from this side before he tries his luck on the other. There are only those three capable of playing so bold a game—there are Oberstein, La Rothiere, and Eduardo Lucas. I will see each of them."

I glanced at my morning paper.

"Is that Eduardo Lucas of Godolphin Street?"

"Yes."

"You will not see him."

"Why not?"

"He was murdered in his house last night."

My friend has so often astonished me in the course of our adventures that it was with a sense of exultation that I realized how completely I had astonished him. He stared in amazement, and then snatched the paper from my hands. This was the paragraph which I had been engaged in reading when he rose from his chair:

MURDER IN WESTMINSTER

A crime of mysterious character was committed last night at 16, Godolphin Street, one of the old-fashioned and secluded rows of eighteenth-century houses which lie between the river and the Abbey, almost in the shadow of the great Tower of the Houses of Parliament. This small but select mansion has been inhabited for some years by Mr. Eduardo Lucas, well-known in society circles both on account of his charming personality and because he has the well-deserved reputation of being one of the best amateur tenors in the country. Mr. Lucas is an unmarried man, thirty-four years of age, and his establishment consists of Mrs. Pringle, an elderly housekeeper, and of Mitton, his valet. The former retires early and sleeps at the top of the house. The valet was out for the evening, visiting a friend at Hammersmith. From ten o'clock onward Mr. Lucas had the house to himself. What occurred during that time has not yet transpired, but at a quarter to twelve Police-constable Barrett, passing along Godolphin Street observed that the door of No. 16 was ajar. He knocked but received no answer. Perceiving a light in the front room, he advanced into the passage and again knocked, but without reply. He then pushed open the door and entered. The room was in a state of wild disorder, the furniture being all swept to one side, and one chair lying on its back in the centre. Beside this chair, and still grasping one of its legs, lay the unfortunate tenant of the house. He had been stabbed to the heart and must have died instantly. The knife with which the crime had been committed was a curved Indian dagger, plucked down from a trophy of Oriental arms which adorned one of the walls. Robbery does not appear to have been the motive of the crime, for there had been no attempt to remove the valuable contents of the room. Mr. Eduardo Lucas was so well-known and popular that his violent and mysterious fate will arouse painful interest and intense sympathy in a widespread circle of friends.

"Well, Watson, what do you make of this?" asked Holmes, after a long pause.

"It is an amazing coincidence."

"A coincidence! Here is one of the three men whom we had named as possible actors in this drama, and he meets a violent death during the very hours when we know that that drama was being enacted. The odds are enormous against its being coincidence. No figures could express them. No, my dear Watson, the two events are connected—*must* be connected. It is for us to find the connection."

"But now the official police must know all."

"Not at all. They know all they see at Godolphin Street. They know—and shall know—nothing of Whitehall Terrace. Only we know of both events and can trace the relation between them. There is one obvious point which would, in any case, have turned my suspicions against Lucas. Godolphin Street, Westminster, is only a few minutes' walk from Whitehall Terrace. The other secret agents whom I have named live in the extreme West End. It was easier, therefore, for Lucas than for the others to establish a connection or receive a message from the European Secretary's household—a small thing, and yet where events are compressed into a few hours it may prove essential. Halloa! what have we here?"

Mrs. Hudson had appeared with a lady's card upon her salver. Holmes glanced at it, raised his eyebrows, and handed it over to me.

"Ask Lady Hilda Trelawney Hope if she will be kind enough to step up," said he.

A moment later our modest apartment, already so distinguished that morning, was further honoured by the entrance of the most lovely woman in London. I had often heard of the beauty of the youngest daughter of the Duke of Belminster but no description of it, and no contemplation of colourless photographs, had prepared me for the subtle, delicate charm and the beautiful colouring of that exquisite head. And yet as we saw it that autumn morning, it was not its beauty which would be the first thing to impress the observer. The cheek was lovely, but it was paled with emotion, the eyes were bright, but it was the brightness of fever, the sensitive mouth was tight and drawn in an effort after self-command. Terror—not beauty—was what sprang first to the eye as our fair visitor stood framed for an instant in the open door.

"Has my husband been here, Mr. Holmes?"

"Yes, madam, he has been here."

"Mr. Holmes. I implore you not to tell him that I came here." Holmes bowed coldly and motioned the lady to a chair.

"Your ladyship places me in a very delicate position. I beg that you will sit down and tell me what you desire, but I fear that I cannot make any unconditional promise."

She swept across the room and seated herself with her back to the window. It was a queenly presence—tall, graceful, and intensely womanly. "Mr. Holmes," she said—and her white-gloved hands clasped and unclasped as she spoke—"I will speak frankly to you in the hopes that it may induce you to speak frankly in return. There is complete confidence between my husband and me on all matters save one. That one is politics. On this his lips are sealed. He tells me nothing. Now, I am aware that there was a most deplorable occurrence in our house last night. I know that a paper has disappeared. But because the matter is political my husband refuses to take me into his complete confidence. Now it is essential—essential, I say—that I should thoroughly understand it. You are the only other person, save only these politicians, who knows the true facts. I beg you then, Mr. Holmes, to tell me exactly what has happened and what it will lead to. Tell me all, Mr. Holmes. Let no regard for your client's interests keep you silent, for I assure you that his interests, if he would only see it, would be best served by taking me into his complete confidence. What was this paper which was stolen?"

"Madam, what you ask me is really impossible."

She groaned and sank her face in her hands.

"You must see that this is so, madam. If your husband thinks fit to keep you in the dark over this matter, is it for me, who has only learned the true facts under the pledge of professional secrecy, to tell what he has withheld? It is not fair to ask it. It is him whom you must ask."

"I have asked him. I come to you as a last resource. But without your telling me anything definite, Mr. Holmes, you may do a great service if you would enlighten me on one point."

"What is it, madam?"

"Is my husband's political career likely to suffer through this incident?"

"Well, madam, unless it is set right it may certainly have a very unfortunate effect."

"Ah!" She drew in her breath sharply as one whose doubts are resolved.

"One more question, Mr. Holmes. From an expression which my husband dropped in the first shock of this disaster I understood that terrible public consequences might arise from the loss of this document."

"If he said so, I certainly cannot deny it."

"Of what nature are they?"

"Nay, madam, there again you ask me more than I can possibly answer."

"Then I will take up no more of your time. I cannot blame you, Mr. Holmes, for having refused to speak more freely, and you on your side will not, I am sure, think the worse of me because I desire, even against his will, to share my husband's anxieties. Once more I beg that you will say nothing of my visit."

She looked back at us from the door, and I had a last impression of that beautiful, haunted face, the startled eyes and the drawn mouth. Then she was gone.

"Now, Watson, the fair sex is your department," said Holmes, with a smile, when the dwindling *frou-frou* of skirts had ended in the slam of the front door. "What was the fair lady's game? What did she really want?"

"Surely her own statement is clear and her anxiety very natural."

"Hum! Think of her appearance, Watson—her manner, her suppressed excitement, her restlessness, her tenacity in asking questions. Remember that she comes of a caste who do not lightly show emotion."

"She was certainly much moved."

"Remember also the curious earnestness with which she assured us that it was best for her husband that she should know all. What did she mean by that? And you must have observed, Watson, how she manœuvred to have the light at her back. She did not wish us to read her expression."

"Yes, she chose the one chair in the room."

"And yet the motives of women are so inscrutable. You remember the woman at Margate whom I suspected for the same reason. No powder on her nose—that proved to be the correct solution. How can you build on such a quicksand? Their most trivial action may mean volumes, or their most extraordinary conduct may depend upon a hairpin or a curling tongs. Good-morning, Watson."

"You are off?"

"Yes, I will while away the morning at Godolphin Street with our friends of the regular establishment. With Eduardo Lucas lies the solution of our problem, though I must admit that I have not an inkling as to what form it may take. It is a capital mistake to theorize in advance of the facts. Do you stay on guard, my good Watson, and receive any fresh visitors. I'll join you at lunch if I am able."

All that day and the next and the next Holmes was in a mood which his friends would call taciturn, and others morose. He ran out and ran in, smoked incessantly, played snatches on his violin, sank into reveries, devoured sandwiches at irregular hours, and hardly answered the casual questions which I put to him. It was evident to me that things were not going well with him or his quest. He would say nothing of the case, and it was from the papers that I learned the particulars of the inquest, and the arrest with the subsequent release of John Mitton, the valet of the deceased. The coroner's jury brought in the obvious Willful Murder, but the parties remained as unknown as ever. No motive was suggested. The room was full of articles of value, but none had been taken. The dead man's papers had not been tampered with. They were carefully examined and showed that he was a keen student of international politics, an indefatigable gossip, a remarkable linguist, and an untiring letter writer. He had been on intimate terms with the leading politicians of several countries. But nothing sensational was discovered among the documents which filled his drawers. As to his relations with women, they appeared to have been promiscuous but superficial. He had many acquaintances among them, but few friends, and no one whom he loved. His habits were regular, his conduct inoffensive. His death was an absolute mystery and likely to remain so.

As to the arrest of John Mitton, the valet, it was a council of despair as an alternative to absolute inaction. But no case could be sustained against him. He had visited friends in Hammersmith that night. The *alibi* was complete. It is true that he started home at an hour which should have brought him to Westminster before the time when the crime was discovered, but his own explanation that he had walked part of the way seemed probable enough in view of the fineness of the night. He had actually arrived at twelve o'clock and appeared to be overwhelmed by the unexpected tragedy. He had always been on good terms with his master. Several of the dead man's possessions—notably a small case of razors—had been found in the valet's boxes, but he explained that they had been presents from the deceased, and the housekeeper was able to corroborate the story. Mitton had been in Lucas's employment for three years. It was noticeable that Lucas did not take Mitton on the Continent with him. Sometimes he visited Paris for three months on end, but Mitton was left in charge of the Godolphin Street house. As to the housekeeper, she had heard nothing on the night of the crime. If her master had a visitor he had himself admitted him.

So for three mornings the mystery remained, so far as I could follow it in the papers. If Holmes knew more, he kept his own counsel, but, as he told me that Inspector Lestrade had taken him into his confidence in the case, I knew that he was in close touch with every development. Upon the fourth day there appeared a long telegram from Paris which seemed to solve the whole question.

A discovery has just been made by the Parisian police (said the *Daily Telegraph*) which raises the veil which hung round the tragic fate of Mr. Eduardo Lucas, who met his death by violence last Monday night at Godolphin Street, Westminster. Our readers will remember that the deceased gentleman was found stabbed in his room, and that some suspicion attached to his valet, but that the case broke down on an *alibi*. Yesterday a lady, who has been known as Mme. Henri Fournaye, occupying a small villa in the Rue Austerlitz, was reported to the authorities by her servants as being insane. An examination showed she had indeed developed mania of a dangerous and permanent form. On inquiry, the police have discovered that Mme. Henri Fournaye only returned from a journey to London on Tuesday last, and there is evidence to connect her with the crime at Westminster. A comparison of photographs has proved conclusively that M. Henri Fournaye and Eduardo Lucas were really one and the same person, and that the deceased had for some reason lived a double life in London and Paris. Mme. Fournaye, who is of Creole origin, is of an extremely excitable nature, and has suffered in the past from attacks of jealousy which have amounted to frenzy. It is conjectured that it was in one of these that she committed the terrible crime which has caused such a sensation in London. Her movements upon the Monday night have not yet been traced, but it is undoubted that a woman answering to her description attracted much attention at Charing Cross Station on Tuesday morning by the wildness of her appearance and the violence of her gestures. It is probable, therefore, that the crime was either committed when insane, or that its immediate effect was to drive the unhappy woman out of her mind. At present she is unable to give any coherent account of the past, and the doctors hold out no hopes of the reestablishment of her reason. There is evidence that a woman, who might have been Mme. Fournaye, was seen for some hours upon Monday night watching the house in Godolphin Street.

"What do you think of that, Holmes?" I had read the account aloud to him, while he finished his breakfast.

"My dear Watson," said he, as he rose from the table and paced up and down the room, "You are most long-suffering, but if I have told you nothing in the last three days, it is because there is nothing to tell. Even now this report from Paris does not help us much."

"Surely it is final as regards the man's death."

"The man's death is a mere incident—a trivial episode—in comparison with our real task, which is to trace this document and save a European catastrophe. Only one important thing has happened in the last three days, and that is that nothing has happened. I get reports almost hourly from the government, and it is certain that nowhere in Europe is there any sign of trouble. Now, if this letter were loose—no, it *can't* be loose—but if it isn't loose, where can it be? Who has it? Why is it held back? That's the question that beats in my brain like a hammer. Was it, indeed, a coincidence that Lucas should meet his death on the night when the letter disappeared? Did the letter ever reach him? If so, why is it not among his papers? Did this mad wife of his carry it off with her? If so, is it in her house in Paris? How could I search for it without the French police having their suspicions aroused? It is a case, my dear Watson, where the law is as dangerous to us as the criminals are. Every man's hand is against us, and yet the interests at stake are colossal. Should I bring it to a successful conclusion, it will certainly represent the crowning glory of my career. Ah, here is my latest from the front!" He glanced hurriedly at the note which had been handed in. "Halloa! Lestrade seems to have observed something of interest. Put on your hat, Watson, and we will stroll down together to Westminster."

It was my first visit to the scene of the crime—a high, dingy, narrow-chested house, prim, formal, and solid, like the century which gave it birth. Lestrade's bulldog features gazed out at us from the front window, and he greeted us warmly when a big constable had opened the door and let us in. The room into which we were shown was that in which the crime had been committed, but no trace of it now remained save an ugly, irregular stain upon the carpet. This carpet was a small square drugget in the centre of the room, surrounded by a broad expanse of beautiful, old-fashioned wood-flooring in square blocks, highly polished. Over the fireplace was a magnificent trophy of weapons, one of which had been used on that tragic night. In the window was a sumptuous writing-desk, and every detail of the apartment, the pictures, the rugs, and the hangings, all pointed to a taste which was luxurious to the verge of effeminacy.

"Seen the Paris news?" asked Lestrade.

Holmes nodded.

"Our French friends seem to have touched the spot this time. No doubt it's just as they say. She knocked at the door—surprise visit, I guess, for he kept his life in water-tight compartments—he let her in, couldn't keep her in the street. She told him how she had traced him, reproached him. One thing led to another, and then with that dagger so handy the end soon came. It wasn't all done in an instant, though, for these chairs were all swept over yonder, and he had one in his hand as if he had tried to hold her off with it. We've got it all clear as if we had seen it."

Holmes raised his eyebrows.

"And yet you have sent for me?"

"Ah, yes, that's another matter—a mere trifle, but the sort of thing you take an interest in—queer, you know, and what you might call freakish. It has nothing to do with the main fact—can't have on the face of it."

"What is it, then?"

"Well, you know, after a crime of this sort we are very careful to keep things in their position. Nothing has been moved. Officer in charge here day and night. This morning, as the man was buried and the investigation over—so far as this room is concerned—we thought we could tidy up a bit. This carpet. You see, it is not fastened down, only just laid there. We had occasion to raise it. We found——"

"Yes? You found——"

Holmes's face grew tense with anxiety.

"Well, I'm sure you would never guess in a hundred years what we did find. You see that stain on the carpet? Well, a great deal must have soaked through, must it not?"

"Undoubtedly it must."

"Well, you will be surprised to hear that there is no stain on the white woodwork to correspond."

"No stain! But there must——"

"Yes, so you would say. But the fact remains that there isn't."

He took the corner of the carpet in his hand and, turning it over, he showed that it was indeed as he said.

"But the underside is as stained as the upper. It must have left a mark."

Lestrade chuckled with delight at having puzzled the famous expert.

"Now, I'll show you the explanation. There *is* a second stain, but it does not correspond with the other. See for yourself." As he spoke he turned over another portion of the carpet, and there, sure enough, was a great crimson spill upon the square white facing of the old-fashioned floor. "What do you make of that, Mr. Holmes?"

"Why, it is simple enough. The two stains did correspond, but the carpet has been turned round. As it was square and unfastened it was easily done."

"The official police don't need you, Mr. Holmes, to tell them that the carpet must have been turned round. That's clear enough, for the stains lie above each other—if you lay it over this way. But what I want to know is, who shifted the carpet, and why?"

I could see from Holmes's rigid face that he was vibrating with inward excitement.

"Look here, Lestrade," said he, "has that constable in the passage been in charge of the place all the time?"

"Yes, he has."

"Well, take my advice. Examine him carefully. Don't do it before us. We'll wait here. You take him into the back room. You'll be more likely to get a confession out of him alone. Ask him how he dared to admit people and leave them alone in this room. Don't ask him if he has done it. Take it for granted. Tell him you *know* someone has been here. Press him. Tell him that a full confession is his only chance of forgiveness. Do exactly what I tell you!"

"By George, if he knows I'll have it out of him!" cried Lestrade. He darted into the hall, and a few moments later his bullying voice sounded from the back room.

"Now, Watson, now!" cried Holmes with frenzied eagerness. All the demoniacal force of the man masked behind that listless manner burst out in a paroxysm of energy. He tore the drugget from the floor, and in an instant was down on his hands and knees clawing at each of the squares of wood beneath it. One turned sideways as he dug his nails into the edge of it. It hinged back like the lid of a box. A small black cavity opened beneath it. Holmes plunged his eager hand into it and drew it out with a bitter snarl of anger and disappointment. It was empty.

"Quick, Watson, quick! Get it back again!" The wooden lid was replaced, and the drugget had only just been drawn straight when Lestrade's voice was heard in the passage. He found Holmes leaning languidly against the mantelpiece, resigned and patient, endeavouring to conceal his irrepressible yawns.

"Sorry to keep you waiting, Mr. Holmes, I can see that you are bored to death with the whole affair. Well, he has confessed, all right. Come in here, MacPherson. Let these gentlemen hear of your most inexcusable conduct."

The big constable, very hot and penitent, sidled into the room.

"I meant no harm, sir, I'm sure. The young woman came to the door last evening—mistook the house, she did. And then we got talking. It's lonesome, when you're on duty here all day."

"Well, what happened then?"

"She wanted to see where the crime was done—had read about it in the papers, she said. She was a very respectable, well-spoken young woman, sir, and I saw no harm in letting her have a peep. When she saw that mark on the carpet, down she dropped on the floor, and lay as if she were dead. I ran to the back and got some water, but I could not bring her to. Then I went round the corner to the Ivy Plant for some brandy, and by the time I had brought it back the young woman had recovered and was off—ashamed of herself, I daresay, and dared not face me."

"How about moving that drugget?"

"Well, sir, it was a bit rumpled, certainly, when I came back. You see, she fell on it, and it lies on a polished floor with nothing to keep it in place. I straightened it out afterwards."

"It's a lesson to you that you can't deceive me, Constable MacPherson," said Lestrade, with dignity. "No doubt you thought that your breach of duty could never be discovered, and yet a mere glance at that drugget was enough to convince me that someone had been admitted to the room. It's lucky for you, my man, that nothing is missing, or you would find yourself in Queer Street. I'm sorry to have called you down over such a petty business, Mr. Holmes, but I thought the point of the second stain not corresponding with the first would interest you."

"Certainly, it was most interesting. Has this woman only been here once, constable?"

"Yes, sir, only once."

"Who was she?"

"Don't know the name, sir. Was answering an advertisement about typewriting and came to the wrong number—very pleasant, genteel young woman, sir."

"Tall? Handsome?"

"Yes, sir, she was a well-grown young woman. I suppose you might say she was handsome. Perhaps some would say she was very handsome. 'Oh, officer, do let me have a peep!' says she. She had pretty, coaxing ways, as you might say, and I thought there was no harm in letting her just put her head through the door."

"How was she dressed?"

"Quiet, sir—a long mantle down to her feet."

"What time was it?"

"It was just growing dusk at the time. They were lighting the lamps as I came back with the brandy."

"Very good," said Holmes. "Come, Watson, I think that we have more important work elsewhere."

As we left the house Lestrade remained in the front room, while the repentant constable opened the door to let us out. Holmes turned on the step and held up something in his hand. The constable stared intently.

"Good Lord, sir!" he cried, with amazement on his face. Holmes put his finger on his lips, replaced his hand in his breast pocket, and burst out laughing as we turned down the street. "Excellent!" said he. "Come, friend Watson, the curtain rings up for the last act. You will be relieved to hear that there will be no war, that the Right Honourable Trelawney Hope will suffer no setback in his brilliant career, that the indiscreet Sovereign will receive no punishment for his indiscretion, that the Prime Minister will have no European complication to deal with, and that with a little tact and management upon our part nobody will be a penny the worse for what might have been a very ugly incident."

My mind filled with admiration for this extraordinary man.

"You have solved it!" I cried.

"Hardly that, Watson. There are some points which are as dark as ever. But we have so much that it will be our own fault if we cannot get the rest. We will go straight to Whitehall Terrace and bring the matter to a head."

When we arrived at the residence of the European Secretary it was for Lady Hilda Trelawney Hope that Sherlock Holmes inquired. We were shown into the morning-room.

"Mr. Holmes!" said the lady, and her face was pink with her indignation. "This is surely most unfair and ungenerous upon your part. I desired, as I have explained, to keep my visit to you a secret, lest my husband should think that I was intruding into his affairs. And yet you compromise me by coming here and so showing that there are business relations between us."

"Unfortunately, madam, I had no possible alternative. I have been commissioned to recover this immensely important paper. I must therefore ask you, madam, to be kind enough to place it in my hands."

The lady sprang to her feet, with the colour all dashed in an instant from her beautiful face. Her eyes glazed—she tottered—I thought that she would faint. Then with a grand effort she rallied from the shock, and a supreme astonishment and indignation chased every other expression from her features.

"You—you insult me, Mr. Holmes."

"Come, come, madam, it is useless. Give up the letter."

She darted to the bell.

"The butler shall show you out."

"Do not ring, Lady Hilda. If you do, then all my earnest efforts to avoid a scandal will be frustrated. Give up the letter and all will be set right. If you will work with me I can arrange everything. If you work against me I must expose you."

She stood grandly defiant, a queenly figure, her eyes fixed upon his as if she would read his very soul. Her hand was on the bell, but she had forborne to ring it.

"You are trying to frighten me. It is not a very manly thing, Mr. Holmes, to come here and browbeat a woman. You say that you know something. What is it that you know?"

"Pray sit down, madam. You will hurt yourself there if you fall. I will not speak until you sit down. Thank you."

"I give you five minutes, Mr. Holmes."

"One is enough, Lady Hilda. I know of your visit to Eduardo Lucas, of your giving him this document, of your ingenious return to the room last night, and of the manner in which you took the letter from the hiding-place under the carpet."

She stared at him with an ashen face and gulped twice before she could speak.

"You are mad, Mr. Holmes—you are mad!" she cried, at last.

He drew a small piece of cardboard from his pocket. It was the face of a woman cut out of a portrait.

"I have carried this because I thought it might be useful," said he. "The policeman has recognized it."

She gave a gasp, and her head dropped back in the chair.

"Come, Lady Hilda. You have the letter. The matter may still be adjusted. I have no desire to bring trouble to you. My duty ends when I have returned the lost letter to your husband. Take my advice and be frank with me. It is your only chance."

Her courage was admirable. Even now she would not own defeat.

"I tell you again, Mr. Holmes, that you are under some absurd illusion."

Holmes rose from his chair.

"I am sorry for you, Lady Hilda. I have done my best for you. I can see that it is all in vain."

He rang the bell. The butler entered.

"Is Mr. Trelawney Hope at home?"

"He will be home, sir, at a quarter to one."

Holmes glanced at his watch.

"Still a quarter of an hour," said he. "Very good, I shall wait."

The butler had hardly closed the door behind him when Lady Hilda was down on her knees at Holmes's feet, her hands outstretched, her beautiful face upturned and wet with her tears.

"Oh, spare me, Mr. Holmes! Spare me!" she pleaded, in a frenzy of supplication. "For heaven's sake, don't tell him! I love him so! I would not bring one shadow on his life, and this I know would break his noble heart."

Holmes raised the lady. "I am thankful, madam, that you have come to your senses even at this last moment! There is not an instant to lose. Where is the letter?"

She darted across to a writing-desk, unlocked it, and drew out a long blue envelope.

"Here it is, Mr. Holmes. Would to heaven I had never seen it!"

"How can we return it?" Holmes muttered. "Quick, quick, we must think of some way! Where is the despatch-box?"

"Still in his bedroom."

"What a stroke of luck! Quick, madam, bring it here!" A moment later she had appeared with a red flat box in her hand.

"How did you open it before? You have a duplicate key? Yes, of course you have. Open it!"

From out of her bosom Lady Hilda had drawn a small key. The box flew open. It was stuffed with papers. Holmes thrust the blue envelope deep down into the heart of them, between the leaves of some other document. The box was shut, locked, and returned to the bedroom.

"Now we are ready for him," said Holmes. "We have still ten minutes. I am going far to screen you, Lady Hilda. In return you will spend the time in telling me frankly the real meaning of this extraordinary affair."

"Mr. Holmes, I will tell you everything," cried the lady. "Oh, Mr. Holmes, I would cut off my right hand before I gave him a moment of sorrow! There is no woman in all London who loves her husband as I do, and yet if he knew how I have acted—how I have been compelled to act—he would never forgive me. For his own honour stands so high that he could not forget or pardon a lapse in another. Help me, Mr. Holmes! My happiness, his happiness, our very lives are at stake!"

"Quick, madam, the time grows short!"

"It was a letter of mine, Mr. Holmes, an indiscreet letter written before my marriage—a foolish letter, a letter of an impulsive, loving girl. I meant no harm, and yet he would have thought it criminal. Had he read that letter his confidence would have been forever destroyed. It is years since I wrote it. I had thought that the whole matter was forgotten. Then at last I heard from this man, Lucas, that it had passed into his hands, and that he would lay it before my husband. I implored his mercy. He said that he would return my letter if I would bring him a certain document which he described in my husband's despatch-box. He had some spy in the office who had told him of its existence. He assured me that no harm could come to my husband. Put yourself in my position, Mr. Holmes! What was I to do?"

"Take your husband into your confidence."

"I could not, Mr. Holmes, I could not! On the one side seemed certain ruin, on the other, terrible as it seemed to take my husband's paper, still in a matter of politics I could not understand the consequences, while in a matter of love and trust they were only too clear to me. I did it, Mr. Holmes! I took an impression of his key. This man, Lucas, furnished a duplicate. I opened his despatch-box, took the paper, and conveyed it to Godolphin Street."

"What happened there, madam?"

"I tapped at the door as agreed. Lucas opened it. I followed him into his room, leaving the hall door ajar behind me, for I feared to be alone with the man. I remember that there was a woman outside as I entered. Our business was soon done. He had my letter on his desk, I handed him the document. He gave me the letter. At this instant there was a sound at the door. There were steps in the passage. Lucas quickly turned back the drugget, thrust the document into some hiding-place there, and covered it over.

"What happened after that is like some fearful dream. I have a vision of a dark, frantic face, of a woman's voice, which screamed in French, 'My waiting is not in vain. At last, at last I have found you with her!' There was a savage struggle. I saw him with a chair in his hand, a knife gleamed in hers. I rushed from the horrible scene, ran from the house, and only next morning in the paper did I learn the dreadful result. That night I was happy, for I had my letter, and I had not seen yet what the future would bring.

"It was the next morning that I realized that I had only exchanged one trouble for another. My husband's anguish at the loss of his paper went to my heart. I could hardly prevent myself from there and then kneeling down at his feet and telling him what I had done. But that again would mean a confession of the past. I came to you that morning in order to understand the full enormity of my offence. From the instant that I grasped it my whole mind was turned to the one thought of getting back my husband's paper. It must still be where Lucas had placed it, for it was concealed before this dreadful woman entered the room. If it had not been for her coming, I should not have known where his hiding-place was. How was I to get into the room? For two days I watched the place, but the door was never left open. Last night I made a last attempt. What I did and how I succeeded, you have already learned. I brought the paper back with me, and thought of destroying it, since I could see no way of returning it without confessing my guilt to my husband. Heavens, I hear his step upon the stair!"

The European Secretary burst excitedly into the room. "Any news, Mr. Holmes, any news?" he cried.

"I have some hopes."

"Ah, thank heaven!" His face became radiant. "The Prime Minister is lunching with me. May he share your hopes? He has nerves of steel, and yet I know that he has hardly slept since this terrible event. Jacobs, will you ask the Prime Minister to come up? As to you, dear, I fear that this is a matter of politics. We will join you in a few minutes in the dining-room."

The Prime Minister's manner was subdued, but I could see by the gleam of his eyes and the twitching's of his bony hands that he shared the excitement of his young colleague.

"I understand that you have something to report, Mr. Holmes?"

"Purely negative as yet," my friend answered. "I have inquired at every point where it might be, and I am sure that there is no danger to be apprehended."

"But that is not enough, Mr. Holmes. We cannot live forever on such a volcano. We must have something definite."

"I am in hopes of getting it. That is why I am here. The more I think of the matter the more convinced I am that the letter has never left this house."

"Mr. Holmes!"

"If it had it would certainly have been public by now."

"But why should anyone take it in order to keep it in his house?"

"I am not convinced that anyone did take it."

"Then how could it leave the despatch-box?"

"I am not convinced that it ever did leave the despatch-box."

"Mr. Holmes, this joking is very ill-timed. You have my assurance that it left the box."

"Have you examined the box since Tuesday morning?"

"No. It was not necessary."

"You may conceivably have overlooked it."

"Impossible, I say."

"But I am not convinced of it. I have known such things to happen. I presume there are other papers there. Well, it may have got mixed with them."

"It was on the top."

"Someone may have shaken the box and displaced it."

"No, no, I had everything out."

"Surely it is easily decided, Hope," said the Premier. "Let us have the despatch-box brought in."

The Secretary rang the bell.

"Jacobs, bring down my despatch-box. This is a farcical waste of time, but still, if nothing else will satisfy you, it shall be done. Thank you, Jacobs, put it here. I have always had the key on my watch-chain. Here are the papers, you see. Letter from Lord Merrow, report from Sir Charles Hardy, memorandum from Belgrade, note on the Russo-German grain taxes, letter from Madrid, note from Lord Flowers——Good heavens! what is this? Lord Bellinger! Lord Bellinger!"

The Premier snatched the blue envelope from his hand.

"Yes, it is it—and the letter is intact. Hope, I congratulate you."

"Thank you! Thank you! What a weight from my heart. But this is inconceivable—impossible. Mr. Holmes, you are a wizard, a sorcerer! How did you know it was there?"

"Because I knew it was nowhere else."

"I cannot believe my eyes!" He ran wildly to the door. "Where is my wife? I must tell her that all is well. Hilda! Hilda!" we heard his voice on the stairs.

The Premier looked at Holmes with twinkling eyes.

"Come, sir," said he. "There is more in this than meets the eye. How came the letter back in the box?"

Holmes turned away smiling from the keen scrutiny of those wonderful eyes.

"We also have our diplomatic secrets," said he and, picking up his hat, he turned to the door.

THE ADVENTURE OF THE DEVIL'S FOOT

In recording from time to time some of the curious experiences and interesting recollections which I associate with my long and intimate friendship with Mr. Sherlock Holmes, I have continually been faced by difficulties caused by his own aversion to publicity. To his sombre and cynical spirit all popular applause was always abhorrent, and nothing amused him more at the end of a successful case than to hand over the actual exposure to some orthodox official, and to listen with a mocking smile to the general chorus of misplaced congratulation. It was indeed this attitude upon the part of my friend and certainly not any lack of interesting material which has caused me of late years to lay very few of my records before the public. My participation in some of his adventures was always a privilege which entailed discretion and reticence upon me.

It was, then, with considerable surprise that I received a telegram from Holmes last Tuesday--he has never been known to write where a telegram would serve--in the following terms:

Why not tell them of the Cornish horror--strangest case I have handled.

I have no idea what backward sweep of memory had brought the matter fresh to his mind, or what freak had caused him to desire that I should recount it; but I hasten, before another cancelling telegram may arrive, to hunt out the notes which give me the exact details of the case and to lay the narrative before my readers.

It was, then, in the spring of the year 1897 that Holmes's iron constitution showed some symptoms of giving way in the face of constant hard work of a most exacting kind, aggravated, perhaps, by occasional indiscretions of his own. In March of that year Dr. Moore Agar, of Harley Street, whose dramatic introduction to Holmes I may someday recount, gave positive injunctions that the famous private agent lay aside all his cases and surrender himself to complete rest if he wished to avert an absolute breakdown. The state of his health was not a matter in which he himself took the faintest interest, for his mental detachment was absolute, but he was induced at last, on the threat of being permanently disqualified from work, to give himself a complete change of scene and air. Thus, it was that in the early spring of that year we found ourselves together in a small cottage near Poldhu Bay, at the further extremity of the Cornish peninsula.

It was a singular spot, and one peculiarly well suited to the grim humour of my patient. From the windows of our little whitewashed house, which stood high upon a grassy headland, we looked down upon the whole sinister semicircle of Mounts Bay, that old death trap of sailing vessels, with its fringe of black cliffs and surge-swept reefs on which innumerable seamen have met their end. With a northerly breeze it lies placid and sheltered, inviting the storm-tossed craft to tack into it for rest and protection.

Then come the sudden swirl round of the wind, the blistering gale from the south-west, the dragging anchor, the lee shore, and the last battle in the creaming breakers. The wise mariner stands far out from that evil place.

On the land side our surroundings were as sombre as on the sea. It was a country of rolling moors, lonely and dun-colored, with an occasional church tower to mark the site of some old-world village. In every direction upon these moors there were traces of some vanished race which had passed utterly away and left as its sole record strange monuments of stone, irregular mounds which contained the burned ashes of the dead, and curious earthworks which hinted at prehistoric strife. The glamour and mystery of the place, with its sinister atmosphere of forgotten nations, appealed to the imagination of my friend, and he spent much of his time in long walks and solitary meditations upon the moor. The ancient Cornish language had also arrested his attention, and he had, I remember, conceived the idea that it was akin to the Chaldean, and had been largely derived from the Phoenician traders in tin. He had received a consignment of books upon philology and was settling down to develop this thesis when suddenly, to my sorrow and to his unfeigned delight, we found ourselves, even in that land of dreams, plunged into a problem at our very doors which was more intense, more engrossing, and infinitely more mysterious than any of those which had driven us from London. Our simple life and peaceful, healthy routine were violently interrupted, and we were precipitated into the midst of a series of events which caused the utmost excitement not only in Cornwall but throughout the whole west of England. Many of my readers may retain some recollection of what was called at the time "The Cornish Horror," though a most imperfect account of the matter reached the London press. Now, after thirteen years, I will give the true details of this inconceivable affair to the public.

I have said that scattered towers marked the villages which dotted this part of Cornwall. The nearest of these was the hamlet of Tredannick Wollas, where the cottages of a couple of hundred inhabitants clustered round an ancient, moss-grown church. The vicar of the parish, Mr. Roundhay, was something of an archaeologist, and as such Holmes had made his acquaintance. He was a middle-aged man, portly and affable, with a considerable fund of local lore. At his invitation we had taken tea at the vicarage and had come to know, also, Mr. Mortimer Tregennis, an independent gentleman, who increased the clergyman's scanty resources by taking rooms in his large, straggling house. The vicar, being a bachelor, was glad to come to such an arrangement, though he had little in common with his lodger, who was a thin, dark, spectacled man, with a stoop which gave the impression of actual, physical deformity. I remember that during our short visit we found the vicar garrulous, but his lodger strangely reticent, a sad-faced, introspective man, sitting with averted eyes, brooding apparently upon his own affairs.

These were the two men who entered abruptly into our little sitting-room on Tuesday, March the 16th, shortly after our breakfast hour, as we were smoking together, preparatory to our daily excursion upon the moors.

"Mr. Holmes," said the vicar in an agitated voice, "the most extraordinary and tragic affair has occurred during the night. It is the most unheard-of business. We can only regard it as a special Providence that you should chance to be here at the time, for in all England you are the one man we need."

I glared at the intrusive vicar with no very friendly eyes; but Holmes took his pipe from his lips and sat up in his chair like an old hound who hears the view-halloa. He waved his hand to the sofa, and our palpitating visitor with his agitated companion sat side by side upon it. Mr. Mortimer Tregennis was more self-contained than the clergyman, but the twitching of his thin hands and the brightness of his dark eyes showed that they shared a common emotion.

"Shall I speak or you?" he asked of the vicar.

"Well, as you seem to have made the discovery, whatever it may be, and the vicar to have had it second-hand, perhaps you had better do the speaking," said Holmes.

I glanced at the hastily clad clergyman, with the formally dressed lodger seated beside him, and was amused at the surprise which Holmes's simple deduction had brought to their faces.

"Perhaps I had best say a few words first," said the vicar, "and then you can judge if you will listen to the details from Mr. Tregennis, or whether we should not hasten at once to the scene of this mysterious affair. I may explain, then, that our friend here spent last evening in the company of his two brothers, Owen and George, and of his sister Brenda, at their house of Tredannick Wartha, which is near the old stone cross upon the moor. He left them shortly after ten o'clock, playing cards round the dining-room table, in excellent health and spirits. This morning, being an early riser, he walked in that direction before breakfast and was overtaken by the carriage of Dr. Richards, who explained that he had just been sent for on a most urgent call to Tredannick Wartha. Mr. Mortimer Tregennis naturally went with him. When he arrived at Tredannick Wartha he found an extraordinary state of things. His two brothers and his sister were seated round the table exactly as he had left them, the cards still spread in front of them and the candles burned down to their sockets. The sister lay back stone-dead in her chair, while the two brothers sat on each side of her laughing, shouting, and singing, the senses stricken clean out of them. All three of them, the dead woman and the two demented men, retained upon their faces an expression of the utmost horror--a convulsion of terror which was dreadful to look upon. There was no sign of the presence of anyone in the house, except Mrs. Porter, the old cook and housekeeper, who declared that she had slept deeply and heard no sound during the night. Nothing had been stolen or disarranged, and there is absolutely no explanation of what the horror can be which has frightened a woman to death and two strong men out of their senses. There is the situation, Mr. Holmes, in a nutshell, and if you can help us to clear it up you will have done a great work."

I had hoped that in some way I could coax my companion back into the quiet which had been the object of our journey; but one glance at his intense face and contracted eyebrows told me how vain the expectation was now. He sat for some little time in silence, absorbed in the strange drama which had broken in upon our peace.

"I will look into this matter," he said at last. "On the face of it, it would appear to be a case of a very exceptional nature. Have you been there yourself, Mr. Roundhay?"

"No, Mr. Holmes. Mr. Tregennis brought back the account to the vicarage, and I at once hurried over with him to consult you."

"How far is it to the house where this singular tragedy occurred?"

"About a mile inland."

"Then we shall walk over together. But before we start I must ask you a few questions, Mr. Mortimer Tregennis."

The other had been silent all this time, but I had observed that his more controlled excitement was even greater than the obtrusive emotion of the clergyman. He sat with a pale, drawn face, his anxious gaze fixed upon Holmes, and his thin hands clasped convulsively together. His pale lips quivered as he listened to the dreadful experience which had befallen his family, and his dark eyes seemed to reflect something of the horror of the scene.

"Ask what you like, Mr. Holmes," said he eagerly. "It is a bad thing to speak of, but I will answer you the truth."

"Tell me about last night."

"Well, Mr. Holmes, I supped there, as the vicar has said, and my elder brother George proposed a game of whist afterwards. We sat down about nine o'clock. It was a quarter-past ten when I moved to go. I left them all round the table, as merry as could be."

"Who let you out?"

"Mrs. Porter had gone to bed, so I let myself out. I shut the hall door behind me. The window of the room in which they sat was closed, but the blind was not drawn down. There was no change in door or window this morning, or any reason to think that any stranger had been to the house. Yet there they sat, driven clean mad with terror, and Brenda lying dead of fright, with her head hanging over the arm of the chair. I'll never get the sight of that room out of my mind so long as I live."

"The facts, as you state them, are certainly most remarkable," said Holmes. "I take it that you have no theory yourself which can in any way account for them?"

"It's devilish, Mr. Holmes, devilish!" cried Mortimer Tregennis. "It is not of this world. Something has come into that room which has dashed the light of reason from their minds. What human contrivance could do that?"

"I fear," said Holmes, "that if the matter is beyond humanity it is certainly beyond me. Yet we must exhaust all natural explanations before we fall back upon such a theory as this. As to yourself, Mr. Tregennis, I take it you were divided in some way from your family, since they lived together, and you had rooms apart?"

"That is so, Mr. Holmes, though the matter is past and done with. We were a family of tin-miners at Redruth, but we sold our venture to a company, and so retired with enough to keep us. I won't deny that there was some feeling about the division of the money, and it stood between us for a time, but it was all forgiven and forgotten, and we were the best of friends together."

"Looking back at the evening which you spent together, does anything stand out in your memory as throwing any possible light upon the tragedy? Think carefully, Mr. Tregennis, for any clue which can help me."

"There is nothing at all, sir."

"Your people were in their usual spirits?"

"Never better."

"Were they nervous people? Did they ever show any apprehension of coming danger?"

"Nothing of the kind."

"You have nothing to add then, which could assist me?"

Mortimer Tregennis considered earnestly for a moment.

"There is one thing occurs to me," said he at last. "As we sat at the table my back was to the window, and my brother George, he being my partner at cards, was facing it. I saw him once look hard over my shoulder, so I turned round and looked also. The blind was up, and the window shut, but I could just make out the bushes on the lawn, and it seemed to me for a moment that I saw something moving among them. I couldn't even say if it was man or animal, but I just thought there was something there. When I asked him what he was looking at, he told me that he had the same feeling. That is all that I can say."

"Did you not investigate?"

"No; the matter passed as unimportant."

"You left them, then, without any premonition of evil?"

"None at all."

"I am not clear how you came to hear the news so early this morning."

"I am an early riser and generally take a walk before breakfast. This morning, I had hardly started when the doctor in his carriage overtook me. He told me that old Mrs. Porter had sent a boy down with an urgent message. I sprang in beside him and we drove on. When we got there we looked into that dreadful room. The candles and the fire must have burned out hours before, and they had been sitting there in the dark until dawn had broken. The doctor said Brenda must have been dead at least six hours. There were no signs of violence. She just lay across the arm of the chair with that look on her face. George and Owen were singing snatches of songs and gibbering like two great apes. Oh, it was awful to see! I couldn't stand it, and the doctor was as white as a sheet. Indeed, he fell into a chair in a sort of faint, and we nearly had him on our hands as well."

"Remarkable--most remarkable!" said Holmes, rising and taking his hat. "I think, perhaps, we had better go down to Tredannick Wartha without further delay. I confess that I have seldom known a case which at first sight presented a more singular problem."

Our proceedings of that first morning did little to advance the investigation. It was marked, however, at the outset by an incident which left the most sinister impression upon my mind. The approach to the spot at which the tragedy occurred is down a narrow, winding, country lane. While we made our way along it we heard the rattle of a carriage coming towards us and stood aside to let it pass. As it drove by us I caught a glimpse through the closed window of a horribly contorted, grinning face glaring out at us. Those staring eyes and gnashing teeth flashed past us like a dreadful vision.

"My brothers!" cried Mortimer Tregennis, white to his lips. "They are taking them to Helston."

We looked with horror after the black carriage, lumbering upon its way. Then we turned our steps towards this ill-omened house in which they had met their strange fate.

It was a large and bright dwelling, rather a villa than a cottage, with a considerable garden which was already, in that Cornish air, well filled with spring flowers. Towards this garden the window of the sitting-room fronted, and from it, according to Mortimer Tregennis, must have come that thing of evil which had by sheer horror in a single instant blasted their minds. Holmes walked slowly and thoughtfully among the flower-plots and along the path before we entered the porch. So absorbed was he in his thoughts, I remember, that he stumbled over the watering-pot, upset its contents, and deluged both our feet and the garden path. Inside the house we were met by the elderly Cornish housekeeper, Mrs. Porter, who, with the aid of a young girl, looked after the wants of the family. She readily answered all Holmes's questions. She had heard nothing in the night. Her employers had all been in excellent spirits lately, and she had never known them more cheerful and prosperous. She had fainted with horror upon entering the room in the morning and seeing that dreadful company round the table. She had, when she recovered, thrown open the window to let the morning air in, and had run down to the lane, whence she sent a farm-lad for the doctor. The lady was on her bed upstairs if we cared to see her. It took four strong men to get the brothers into the asylum carriage. She would not herself stay in the house another day and was starting that very afternoon to rejoin her family at St. Ives.

We ascended the stairs and viewed the body. Miss Brenda Tregennis had been a very beautiful girl, though now verging upon middle age. Her dark, clear-cut face was handsome, even in death, but there still lingered upon it something of that convulsion of horror which had been her last human emotion. From her bedroom we descended to the sitting-room, where this strange tragedy had actually occurred. The charred ashes of the overnight fire lay in the grate. On the table were the four guttered and burned-out candles, with the cards scattered over its surface. The chairs had been moved back against the walls, but all else was as it had been the night before. Holmes paced with light, swift steps about the room; he sat in the various chairs, drawing them up and reconstructing their positions. He tested how much of the garden was visible; he examined the floor, the ceiling, and the fireplace; but never once did I see that sudden brightening of his eyes and tightening of his lips which would have told me that he saw some gleam of light in this utter darkness.

"Why a fire?" he asked once. "Had they always a fire in this small room on a spring evening?"

Mortimer Tregennis explained that the night was cold and damp. For that reason, after his arrival, the fire was lit. "What are you going to do now, Mr. Holmes?" he asked.

My friend smiled and laid his hand upon my arm. "I think, Watson, that I shall resume that course of tobacco-poisoning which you have so often and so justly condemned," said he. "With your permission, gentlemen, we will now return to our cottage, for I am not aware that any new factor is likely to come to our notice here. I will turn the facts over in my mind, Mr. Tregennis, and should anything occur to me I will certainly communicate with you and the vicar. In the meantime, I wish you both good-morning."

It was not until long after we were back in Poldhu Cottage that Holmes broke his complete and absorbed silence. He sat coiled in his armchair, his haggard and ascetic face hardly visible amid the blue swirl of his tobacco smoke, his black brows drawn down, his forehead contracted, his eyes vacant and far away. Finally, he laid down his pipe and sprang to his feet.

"It won't do, Watson!" said he with a laugh. "Let us walk along the cliffs together and search for flint arrows. We are more likely to find them than clues to this problem. To let the brain work without sufficient material is like racing an engine. It racks itself to pieces. The sea air, sunshine, and patience, Watson--all else will come.

"Now, let us calmly define our position, Watson," he continued as we skirted the cliffs together. "Let us get a firm grip of the very little which we DO know, so that when fresh facts arise we may be ready to fit them into their places. I take it, in the first place, that neither of us is prepared to admit diabolical intrusions into the affairs of men. Let us begin by ruling that entirely out of our minds. Very good. There remain three persons who have been grievously stricken by some conscious or unconscious human agency. That is firm ground. Now, when did this occur? Evidently, assuming his narrative to be true, it was immediately after Mr. Mortimer Tregennis had left the room. That is a very important point. The presumption is that it was within a few minutes afterwards. The cards still lay upon the table. It was already past their usual hour for bed. Yet they had not changed their position or pushed back their chairs. I repeat, then, that the occurrence was immediately after his departure, and not later than eleven o'clock last night.

"Our next obvious step is to check, so far as we can, the movements of Mortimer Tregennis after he left the room. In this there is no difficulty, and they seem to be above suspicion. Knowing my methods as you do, you were, of course, conscious of the somewhat clumsy water-pot expedient by which I obtained a clearer impress of his foot than might otherwise have been possible. The wet, sandy path took it admirably. Last night was also wet, you will remember, and it was not difficult--having obtained a sample print--to pick out his track among others and to follow his movements. He appears to have walked away swiftly in the direction of the vicarage.

"If then, Mortimer Tregennis disappeared from the scene, and yet some outside person affected the card-players, how can we reconstruct that person, and how was such an impression of horror conveyed? Mrs. Porter may be eliminated. She is evidently harmless. Is there any evidence that someone crept up to the garden window and in some manner produced so terrific an effect that he drove those who saw it out of their senses? The only suggestion in this direction comes from Mortimer Tregennis himself, who says that his brother spoke about some movement in the garden. That is certainly remarkable, as the night was rainy, cloudy, and dark. Anyone who had the design to alarm these people would be compelled to place his very face against the glass before he could be seen. There is a three-foot flower-border outside this window, but no indication of a footmark. It is difficult to imagine, then, how an outsider could have made so terrible an impression upon the company, nor have we found any possible motive for so strange and elaborate an attempt. You perceive our difficulties, Watson?"

"They are only too clear," I answered with conviction.

"And yet, with a little more material, we may prove that they are not insurmountable," said Holmes. "I fancy that among your extensive archives, Watson, you may find some which were nearly as obscure. Meanwhile, we shall put the case aside until more accurate data are available and devote the rest of our morning to the pursuit of neolithic man."

I may have commented upon my friend's power of mental detachment, but never have I wondered at it more than upon that spring morning in Cornwall when for two hours he discoursed upon celts, arrowheads, and shards, as lightly as if no sinister mystery were waiting for his solution. It was not until we had returned in the afternoon to our cottage that we found a visitor awaiting us, who soon brought our minds back to the matter in hand. Neither of us needed to be told who that visitor was. The huge body, the craggy and deeply seamed face with the fierce eyes and hawk-like nose, the grizzled hair which nearly brushed our cottage ceiling, the beard--golden at the fringes and white near the lips, save for the nicotine stain from his perpetual cigar--all these were as well known in London as in Africa, and could only be associated with the tremendous personality of Dr. Leon Sterndale, the great lion-hunter and explorer.

We had heard of his presence in the district and had once or twice caught sight of his tall figure upon the moorland paths. He made no advances to us, however, nor would we have dreamed of doing so to him, as it was well known that it was his love of seclusion which caused him to spend the greater part of the intervals between his journeys in a small bungalow buried in the lonely wood of Beauchamp Arriance. Here, amid his books and his maps, he lived an absolutely lonely life, attending to his own simple wants and paying little apparent heed to the affairs of his neighbours. It was a surprise to me, therefore, to hear him asking Holmes in an eager voice whether he had made any advance in his reconstruction of this mysterious episode. "The county police are utterly at fault," said he, "but perhaps your wider experience has suggested some conceivable explanation. My only claim to being taken into your confidence is that during my many residences here I have come to know this family of Tregennis very well--indeed, upon my Cornish mother's side I could call them cousins--and their strange fate has naturally been a great shock to me. I may tell you that I had got as far as Plymouth upon my way to Africa, but the news reached me this morning, and I came straight back again to help in the inquiry."

Holmes raised his eyebrows.

"Did you lose your boat through it?"

"I will take the next."

"Dear me! that is friendship indeed."

"I tell you they were relatives."

"Quite so--cousins of your mother. Was your baggage aboard the ship?"

"Some of it, but the main part at the hotel."

"I see. But surely this event could not have found its way into the Plymouth morning papers."

"No, sir; I had a telegram."

"Might I ask from whom?"

A shadow passed over the gaunt face of the explorer.

"You are very inquisitive, Mr. Holmes."

"It is my business."

With an effort Dr. Sterndale recovered his ruffled composure.

"I have no objection to telling you," he said. "It was Mr. Roundhay, the vicar, who sent me the telegram which recalled me."

"Thank you," said Holmes. "I may say in answer to your original question that I have not cleared my mind entirely on the subject of this case, but that I have every hope of reaching some conclusion. It would be premature to say more."

"Perhaps you would not mind telling me if your suspicions point in any particular direction?"

"No, I can hardly answer that."

"Then I have wasted my time and need not prolong my visit." The famous doctor strode out of our cottage in considerable ill-humour, and within five minutes Holmes had followed him. I saw him no more until the evening, when he returned with a slow step and haggard face which assured me that he had made no great progress with his investigation. He glanced at a telegram which awaited him and threw it into the grate.

"From the Plymouth hotel, Watson," he said. "I learned the name of it from the vicar, and I wired to make certain that Dr. Leon Sterndale's account was true. It appears that he did indeed spend last night there, and that he has actually allowed some of his baggage to go on to Africa, while he returned to be present at this investigation. What do you make of that, Watson?"

"He is deeply interested."

"Deeply interested--yes. There is a thread here which we had not yet grasped, and which might lead us through the tangle. Cheer up, Watson, for I am very sure that our material has not yet all come to hand. When it does we may soon leave our difficulties behind us."

Little did I think how soon the words of Holmes would be realized, or how strange and sinister would be that new development which opened up an entirely fresh line of investigation. I was shaving at my window in the morning when I heard the rattle of hoofs and, looking up, saw a dog-cart coming at a gallop down the road. It pulled up at our door, and our friend, the vicar, sprang from it and rushed up our garden path. Holmes was already dressed, and we hastened down to meet him.

Our visitor was so excited that he could hardly articulate, but at last in gasps and bursts his tragic story came out of him.

"We are devil-ridden, Mr. Holmes! My poor parish is devil-ridden!" he cried. "Satan himself is loose in it! We are given over into his hands!" He danced about in his agitation, a ludicrous object if it were not for his ashy face and startled eyes. Finally, he shot out his terrible news.

"Mr. Mortimer Tregennis died during the night, and with exactly the same symptoms as the rest of his family."

Holmes sprang to his feet, all energy in an instant.

"Can you fit us both into your dog-cart?"

"Yes, I can."

"Then, Watson, we will postpone our breakfast. Mr. Roundhay, we are entirely at your disposal. Hurry--hurry, before things get disarranged."

The lodger occupied two rooms at the vicarage, which were in an angle by themselves, the one above the other. Below was a large sitting-room; above, his bedroom. They looked out upon a croquet lawn which came up to the windows. We had arrived before the doctor or the police, so that everything was absolutely undisturbed. Let me describe exactly the scene as we saw it upon that misty March morning. It has left an impression which can never be effaced from my mind.

The atmosphere of the room was of a horrible and depressing stuffiness. The servant who had first entered had thrown up the window, or it would have been even more intolerable. This might partly be due to the fact that a lamp stood flaring and smoking on the centre table. Beside it sat the dead man, leaning back in his chair, his thin beard projecting, his spectacles pushed up on to his forehead, and his lean dark face turned towards the window and twisted into the same distortion of terror which had marked the features of his dead sister. His limbs were convulsed, and his fingers contorted as though he had died in a very paroxysm of fear. He was fully clothed, though there were signs that his dressing had been done in a hurry. We had already learned that his bed had been slept in, and that the tragic end had come to him in the early morning.

One realized the red-hot energy which underlay Holmes's phlegmatic exterior when one saw the sudden change which came over him from the moment that he entered the fatal apartment. In an instant he was tense and alert, his eyes shining, his face set, his limbs quivering with eager activity. He was out on the lawn, in through the window, round the room, and up into the bedroom, for all the world like a dashing foxhound drawing a cover. In the bedroom he made a rapid cast around and ended by throwing open the window, which appeared to give him some fresh cause for excitement, for he leaned out of it with loud ejaculations of interest and delight. Then he rushed down the stair, out through the open window, threw himself upon his face on the lawn, sprang up and into the room once more, all with the energy of the hunter who is at the very heels of his quarry. The lamp, which was an ordinary standard, he examined with minute care, making certain measurements upon its bowl. He carefully scrutinized with his lens the talc shield which covered the top of the chimney and scraped off some ashes which adhered to its upper surface, putting some of them into an envelope, which he placed in his pocketbook. Finally, just as the doctor and the official police put in an appearance, he beckoned to the vicar and we all three went out upon the lawn.

"I am glad to say that my investigation has not been entirely barren," he remarked. "I cannot remain to discuss the matter with the police, but I should be exceedingly obliged, Mr. Roundhay, if you would give the inspector my compliments and direct his attention to the bedroom window and to the sitting-room lamp. Each is suggestive, and together they are almost conclusive. If the police would desire further information I shall be happy to see any of them at the cottage. And now, Watson, I think that, perhaps, we shall be better employed elsewhere."

It may be that the police resented the intrusion of an amateur, or that they imagined themselves to be upon some hopeful line of investigation; but it is certain that we heard nothing from them for the next two days. During this time Holmes spent some of his time smoking and dreaming in the cottage; but a greater portion in country walks which he undertook alone, returning after many hours without remark as to where he had been. One experiment served to show me the line of his investigation. He had bought a lamp which was the duplicate of the one which had burned in the room of Mortimer Tregennis on the morning of the tragedy. This he filled with the same oil as that used at the vicarage, and he carefully timed the period which it would take to be exhausted. Another experiment which he made was of a more unpleasant nature, and one which I am not likely ever to forget.

"You will remember, Watson," he remarked one afternoon, "that there is a single common point of resemblance in the varying reports which have reached us. This concerns the effect of the atmosphere of the room in each case upon those who had first entered it. You will recollect that Mortimer Tregennis, in describing the episode of his last visit to his brother's house, remarked that the doctor on entering the room fell into a chair? You had forgotten? Well, I can answer for it that it was so. Now, you will remember also that Mrs. Porter, the housekeeper, told us that she herself fainted upon entering the room and had afterwards opened the window. In the second case--that of Mortimer Tregennis himself--you cannot have forgotten the horrible stuffiness of the room when we arrived, though the servant had thrown open the window. That servant, I found upon inquiry, was so ill that she had gone to her bed. You will admit, Watson, that these facts are very suggestive. In each case there is evidence of a poisonous atmosphere. In each case, also, there is combustion going on in the room--in the one case a fire, in the other a lamp. The fire was needed, but the lamp was lit--as a comparison of the oil consumed will show--long after it was broad daylight. Why? Surely because there is some connection between three things--the burning, the stuffy atmosphere, and, finally, the madness or death of those unfortunate people. That is clear, is it not?"

"It would appear so."

"At least we may accept it as a working hypothesis. We will suppose, then, that something was burned in each case which produced an atmosphere causing strange toxic effects. Very good. In the first instance--that of the Tregennis family--this substance was placed in the fire. Now the window was shut, but the fire would naturally carry fumes to some extent up the chimney. Hence one would expect the effects of the poison to be less than in the second case, where there was less escape for the vapour. The result seems to indicate that it was so, since in the first case only the woman, who had presumably the more sensitive organism, was killed, the others exhibiting that temporary or permanent lunacy which is evidently the first effect of the drug. In the second case the result was complete. The facts, therefore, seem to bear out the theory of a poison which worked by combustion.

"With this train of reasoning in my head I naturally looked about in Mortimer Tregennis's room to find some remains of this substance. The obvious place to look was the talc shelf or smoke-guard of the lamp. There, sure enough, I perceived a number of flaky ashes, and round the edges a fringe of brownish powder, which had not yet been consumed. Half of this I took, as you saw, and I placed it in an envelope."

"Why half, Holmes?"

"It is not for me, my dear Watson, to stand in the way of the official police force. I leave them all the evidence which I found. The poison still remained upon the talc had they the wit to find it. Now, Watson, we will light our lamp; we will, however, take the precaution to open our window to avoid the premature decease of two deserving members of society, and you will seat yourself near that open window in an armchair unless, like a sensible man, you determine to have nothing to do with the affair. Oh, you will see it out, will you? I thought I knew my Watson. This chair I will place opposite yours, so that we may be the same distance from the poison and face to face. The door we will leave ajar. Each is now in a position to watch the other and to bring the experiment to an end should the symptoms seem alarming. Is that all clear? Well, then, I take our powder--or what remains of it--from the envelope, and I lay it above the burning lamp. So! Now, Watson, let us sit down and await developments."

They were not long in coming. I had hardly settled in my chair before I was conscious of a thick, musky odour, subtle and nauseous. At the very first whiff of it my brain and my imagination were beyond all control. A thick, black cloud swirled before my eyes, and my mind told me that in this cloud, unseen as yet, but about to spring out upon my appalled senses, lurked all that was vaguely horrible, all that was monstrous and inconceivably wicked in the universe. Vague shapes swirled and swam amid the dark cloud-bank, each a menace and a warning of something coming, the advent of some unspeakable dweller upon the threshold, whose very shadow would blast my soul. A freezing horror took possession of me. I felt that my hair was rising, that my eyes were protruding, that my mouth was opened, and my tongue like leather. The turmoil within my brain was such that something must surely snap. I tried to scream and was vaguely aware of some hoarse croak which was my own voice, but distant and detached from myself. At the same moment, in some effort of escape, I broke through that cloud of despair and had a glimpse of Holmes's face, white, rigid, and drawn with horror--the very look which I had seen upon the features of the dead. It was that vision which gave me an instant of sanity and of strength. I dashed from my chair, threw my arms round Holmes, and together we lurched through the door, and an instant afterwards had thrown ourselves down upon the grass plot and were lying side by side, conscious only of the glorious sunshine which was bursting its way through the hellish cloud of terror which had girt us in. Slowly it rose from our souls like the mists from a landscape until peace and reason had returned, and we were sitting upon the grass, wiping our clammy foreheads, and looking with apprehension at each other to mark the last traces of that terrific experience which we had undergone.

"Upon my word, Watson!" said Holmes at last with an unsteady voice, "I owe you both my thanks and an apology. It was an unjustifiable experiment even for one's self, and doubly so for a friend. I am really very sorry."

"You know," I answered with some emotion, for I have never seen so much of Holmes's heart before, "that it is my greatest joy and privilege to help you."

He relapsed at once into the half-humorous, half-cynical vein which was his habitual attitude to those about him. "It would be superfluous to drive us mad, my dear Watson," said he. "A candid observer would certainly declare that we were so already before we embarked upon so wild an experiment. I confess that I never imagined that the effect could be so sudden and so severe." He dashed into the cottage, and, reappearing with the burning lamp held at full arm's length, he threw it among a bank of brambles. "We must give the room a little time to clear. I take it, Watson, that you have no longer a shadow of a doubt as to how these tragedies were produced?"

"None whatever."

"But the cause remains as obscure as before. Come into the arbour here and let us discuss it together. That villainous stuff seems still to linger round my throat. I think we must admit that all the evidence points to this man, Mortimer Tregennis, having been the criminal in the first tragedy, though he was the victim in the second one. We must remember, in the first place, that there is some story of a family quarrel, followed by a reconciliation. How bitter that quarrel may have been, or how hollow the reconciliation we cannot tell. When I think of Mortimer Tregennis, with the foxy face and the small shrewd, beady eyes behind the spectacles, he is not a man whom I should judge to be of a particularly forgiving disposition. Well, in the next place, you will remember that this idea of someone moving in the garden, which took our attention for a moment from the real cause of the tragedy, emanated from him. He had a motive in misleading us. Finally, if he did not throw the substance into the fire at the moment of leaving the room, who did do so? The affair happened immediately after his departure. Had anyone else come in, the family would certainly have risen from the table. Besides, in peaceful Cornwall, visitors did not arrive after ten o'clock at night. We may take it, then, that all the evidence points to Mortimer Tregennis as the culprit."

"Then his own death was suicide!"

"Well, Watson, it is on the face of it a not impossible supposition. The man who had the guilt upon his soul of having brought such a fate upon his own family might well be driven by remorse to inflict it upon himself. There are, however, some cogent reasons against it. Fortunately, there is one man in England who knows all about it, and I have made arrangements by which we shall hear the facts this afternoon from his own lips. Ah! he is a little before his time. Perhaps you would kindly step this way, Dr. Leon Sterndale. We have been conducting a chemical experiment indoors which has left our little room hardly fit for the reception of so distinguished a visitor."

I had heard the click of the garden gate, and now the majestic figure of the great African explorer appeared upon the path. He turned in some surprise towards the rustic arbour in which we sat.

"You sent for me, Mr. Holmes. I had your note about an hour ago, and I have come, though I really do not know why I should obey your summons."

"Perhaps we can clear the point up before we separate," said Holmes. "Meanwhile, I am much obliged to you for your courteous acquiescence. You will excuse this informal reception in the open air, but my friend Watson and I have nearly furnished an additional chapter to what the papers call the Cornish Horror, and we prefer a clear atmosphere for the present. Perhaps, since the matters which we have to discuss will affect you personally in a very intimate fashion, it is as well that we should talk where there can be no eavesdropping."

The explorer took his cigar from his lips and gazed sternly at my companion.

"I am at a loss to know, sir," he said, "what you can have to speak about which affects me personally in a very intimate fashion."

"The killing of Mortimer Tregennis," said Holmes.

For a moment I wished that I were armed. Sterndale's fierce face turned to a dusky red, his eyes glared, and the knotted, passionate veins started out in his forehead, while he sprang forward with clenched hands towards my companion. Then he stopped, and with a violent effort he resumed a cold, rigid calmness, which was, perhaps, more suggestive of danger than his hot-headed outburst.

"I have lived so long among savages and beyond the law," said he, "that I have got into the way of being a law to myself. You would do well, Mr. Holmes, not to forget it, for I have no desire to do you an injury."

"Nor have I any desire to do you an injury, Dr. Sterndale. Surely the clearest proof of it is that, knowing what I know, I have sent for you and not for the police."

Sterndale sat down with a gasp, overawed for, perhaps, the first time in his adventurous life. There was a calm assurance of power in Holmes's manner which could not be withstood. Our visitor stammered for a moment, his great hands opening and shutting in his agitation.

"What do you mean?" he asked at last. "If this is bluff upon your part, Mr. Holmes, you have chosen a bad man for your experiment. Let us have no more beating about the bush. What DO you mean?"

"I will tell you," said Holmes, "and the reason why I tell you is that I hope frankness may beget frankness. What my next step may be will depend entirely upon the nature of your own defence."

"My defence?"

"Yes, sir."

"My defence against what?"

"Against the charge of killing Mortimer Tregennis."

Sterndale mopped his forehead with his handkerchief. "Upon my word, you are getting on," said he. "Do all your successes depend upon this prodigious power of bluff?"

"The bluff," said Holmes sternly, "is upon your side, Dr. Leon Sterndale, and not upon mine. As a proof I will tell you some of the facts upon which my conclusions are based. Of your return from Plymouth, allowing much of your property to go on to Africa, I will say nothing save that it first informed me that you were one of the factors which had to be taken into account in reconstructing this drama--"

"I came back--"

"I have heard your reasons and regard them as unconvincing and inadequate. We will pass that. You came down here to ask me whom

I suspected. I refused to answer you. You then went to the vicarage, waited outside it for some time, and finally returned to your cottage."

"How do you know that?"

"I followed you."

"I saw no one."

"That is what you may expect to see when I follow you. You spent a restless night at your cottage, and you formed certain plans, which in the early morning you proceeded to put into execution. Leaving your door just as day was breaking, you filled your pocket with some reddish gravel that was lying heaped beside your gate."

Sterndale gave a violent start and looked at Holmes in amazement.

"You then walked swiftly for the mile which separated you from the vicarage. You were wearing, I may remark, the same pair of ribbed tennis shoes which are at the present moment upon your feet. At the vicarage you passed through the orchard and the side hedge, coming out under the window of the lodger Tregennis. It was now daylight, but the household was not yet stirring. You drew some of the gravel from your pocket, and you threw it up at the window above you."

Sterndale sprang to his feet.

"I believe that you are the devil himself!" he cried.

Holmes smiled at the compliment. "It took two, or possibly three, handfuls before the lodger came to the window. You beckoned him to come down. He dressed hurriedly and descended to his sitting-room. You entered by the window. There was an interview--a short one--during which you walked up and down the room. Then you passed out and closed the window, standing on the lawn outside smoking a cigar and watching what occurred. Finally, after the death of Tregennis, you withdrew as you had come. Now, Dr. Sterndale, how do you justify such conduct, and what were the motives for your actions? If you prevaricate or trifle with me, I give you my assurance that the matter will pass out of my hands forever."

Our visitor's face had turned ashen gray as he listened to the words of his accuser. Now he sat for some time in thought with his face sunk in his hands. Then with a sudden impulsive gesture he plucked a photograph from his breast-pocket and threw it on the rustic table before us.

"That is why I have done it," said he.

It showed the bust and face of a very beautiful woman. Holmes stooped over it.

"Brenda Tregennis," said he.

"Yes, Brenda Tregennis," repeated our visitor. "For years I have loved her. For years she has loved me. There is the secret of that Cornish seclusion which people have marvelled at. It has brought me close to the one thing on earth that was dear to me. I could not marry her, for I have a wife who has left me for years and yet whom, by the deplorable laws of England, I could not divorce. For years Brenda waited. For years I waited. And this is what we have waited for." A terrible sob shook his great frame, and he clutched his throat under his brindled beard. Then with an effort he mastered himself and spoke on:

"The vicar knew. He was in our confidence. He would tell you that she was an angel upon earth. That was why he telegraphed to me, and I returned. What was my baggage or Africa to me when I learned that such a fate had come upon my darling? There you have the missing clue to my action, Mr. Holmes."

"Proceed," said my friend.

Dr. Sterndale drew from his pocket a paper packet and laid it upon the table. On the outside was written "Radix pedis diaboli" with a red poison label beneath it. He pushed it towards me. "I understand that you are a doctor, sir. Have you ever heard of this preparation?"

"Devil's-foot root! No, I have never heard of it."

"It is no reflection upon your professional knowledge," said he, "for I believe that, save for one sample in a laboratory at Buda, there is no other specimen in Europe. It has not yet found its way either into the pharmacopoeia or into the literature of toxicology. The root is shaped like a foot, half human, half goatlike; hence the fanciful name given by a botanical missionary. It is used as an ordeal poison by the medicine-men in certain districts of West Africa and is kept as a secret among them. This particular specimen I obtained under very extraordinary circumstances in the Ubangi country." He opened the paper as he spoke and disclosed a heap of reddish-brown, snuff-like powder.

"Well, sir?" asked Holmes sternly.

"I am about to tell you, Mr. Holmes, all that actually occurred, for you already know so much that it is clearly to my interest that you should know all. I have already explained the relationship in which I stood to the Tregennis family. For the sake of the sister, I was friendly with the brothers. There was a family quarrel about money which estranged this man Mortimer, but it was supposed to be made up, and I afterwards met him as I did the others. He was a sly, subtle, scheming man, and several things arose which gave me a suspicion of him, but I had no cause for any positive quarrel.

"One day, only a couple of weeks ago, he came down to my cottage and I showed him some of my African curiosities. Among other things I exhibited this powder, and I told him of its strange properties, how it stimulates those brain centres which control the emotion of fear, and how either madness or death is the fate of the unhappy native who is subjected to the ordeal by the priest of his tribe. I told him also how powerless European science would be to detect it. How he took it I cannot say, for I never left the room, but there is no doubt that it was then, while I was opening cabinets and stooping to boxes, that he managed to abstract some of the devil's-foot root. I well remember how he plied me with questions as to the amount and the time that was needed for its effect, but I little dreamed that he could have a personal reason for asking.

"I thought no more of the matter until the vicar's telegram reached me at Plymouth. This villain had thought that I would be at sea before the news could reach me, and that I should be lost for years in Africa. But I returned at once. Of course, I could not listen to the details without feeling assured that my poison had been used. I came round to see you on the chance that some other explanation had suggested itself to you. But there could be none. I was convinced that Mortimer Tregennis was the murderer; that for the sake of money, and with the idea, perhaps, that if the other members of his family were all insane he would be the sole guardian of their joint property, he had used the devil's-foot powder upon them, driven two of them out of their senses, and killed his sister Brenda, the one human being whom I have ever loved or who has ever loved me. There was his crime; what was to be his punishment?

"Should I appeal to the law? Where were my proofs? I knew that the facts were true, but could I help to make a jury of countrymen believe so fantastic a story? I might or I might not. But I could not afford to fail. My soul cried out for revenge. I have said to you once before, Mr. Holmes, that I have spent much of my life outside the law, and that I have come at last to be a law to myself. So, it was even now. I determined that the fate which he had given to others should be shared by himself. Either that or I would do justice upon him with my own hand. In all England there can be no man who sets less value upon his own life than I do at the present moment.

"Now I have told you all. You have yourself supplied the rest. I did, as you say, after a restless night, set off early from my cottage. I foresaw the difficulty of arousing him, so I gathered some gravel from the pile which you have mentioned, and I used it to throw up to his window. He came down and admitted me through the window of the sitting-room. I laid his offence before him. I told him that I had come both as judge and executioner. The wretch sank into a chair, paralyzed at the sight of my revolver. I lit the lamp, put the powder above it, and stood outside the window, ready to carry out my threat to shoot him should he try to leave the room. In five minutes, he died. My God! how he died! But my heart was flint, for he endured nothing which my innocent darling had not felt before him. There is my story, Mr. Holmes. Perhaps, if you loved a woman, you would have done as much yourself. At any rate, I am in your hands. You can take what steps you like. As I have already said, there is no man living who can fear death less than I do."

Holmes sat for some little time in silence.

"What were your plans?" he asked at last.

"I had intended to bury myself in central Africa. My work there is but half finished."

"Go and do the other half," said Holmes. "I, at least, am not prepared to prevent you."

Dr. Sterndale raised his giant figure, bowed gravely, and walked from the arbour. Holmes lit his pipe and handed me his pouch.

"Some fumes which are not poisonous would be a welcome change," said he. "I think you must agree, Watson, that it is not a case in which we are called upon to interfere. Our investigation has been independent, and our action shall be so also. You would not denounce the man?"

"Certainly not," I answered.

"I have never loved, Watson, but if I did and if the woman I loved had met such an end, I might act even as our lawless lion-hunter has done. Who knows? Well, Watson, I will not offend your intelligence by explaining what is obvious. The gravel upon the window-sill was, of course, the starting-point of my research. It was unlike anything in the vicarage garden. Only when my attention had been drawn to Dr. Sterndale and his cottage did I find its counterpart. The lamp shining in broad daylight and the remains of powder upon the shield were successive links in a fairly obvious chain. And now, my dear Watson, I think we may dismiss the matter from our mind and go back with a clear conscience to the study of those Chaldean roots which are surely to be traced in the Cornish branch of the great Celtic speech."

END